BITCHES GIVE STITCHES

Bart Baker

Big Muddy Books

PICKING UP SLIGHTLY BEFORE WHERE WE LEFT OFF...

Trapped with the nightmare they had just witnessed, the four women spoke little as Curtis drove each of them back to their homes. Everything in Deanna's limited but horribly unlucky life experience informed her that accepting Martin Collique's offer, as they apparently just had, as if they were given a choice, would be just as deadly as stepping on the plastic sheeting rolled out in front of them less than an hour before. It would simply be a longer, deeper last breath. 'He's a sociopath. Or a psychopath. Or probably both of those -paths,' Deanna ruminated. 'And a germaphobe', she then thought, considering she watched him have a man killed right in front of her, on plastic sheeting no less, so it would expedite the cleaning of the mess and the disposing of the body. Bloody murder without getting your hands dirty.

But Martin Collique made it clear. He had no compunction eliminating someone he considered problematic. Worse, he was a killer who made promises to the women that, in Deanna's estimation, couldn't possibly happen as readily as his easy smile and relaxed yet snooty demeanor led any of them to believe. More than anyone in this car, she believed there would be hell to pay. Because in Deanna's life, there always was. And this situation was far nastier, far more complex, and far more dangerous, than anything she had survived up to this point.

How could the four of them earn the kind of profit Deanna assumed Collique would expect them to make? Money that would change their lives, buy them new homes, money that would keep them alive. Money for new cars. Money to put Deanna and Ava's kids through college. Especially if Collique took the lion's share of the profits? Deanna couldn't figure out how that would leave them enough to keep afloat from their small-time counterfeiting operation. It barely gave them 'scrape-by' money now without Collique's hand in the till. So far it had run with only minor hiccups, buying designer blouses and dresses at retail, duping the garment, returning the copy to the store and then selling the real item at a gathering of wealthy women at a discount, leaving a modest but sweet payday for the four of them. Deanna's cut was enough to pay rent, put food on the table and gas in the car. The downside being Deanna was working herself night and day to finish the copies because none of the other women could sew worth a damn. 'Even if I could teach the others to sew as good as they would need to be to copy the pieces, the four of us couldn't do much more than we're doing now', Deanna mused. And now advancing them a few steps further, what was going to happen when they wanted out of whatever this arrangement was they now found themselves in with Martin? Would he kill them like he did Santos? Would he kill their families? Digging her fingernails into the soft upholstery on the side of the car seat, Deanna had to stop torturing herself with 'what-ifs' or she feared she would start sobbing and never stop.

Holding her sister's hand as she sat between Deanna and Ava in the backseat, Izzy tried to rationalize and then compartmentalize what she had just done in that airplane hangar. Stick the barrel of a gun against a man's head. Squeeze the trigger. There were thousands of times in her life when she felt the vague, unrequited, desire to kill somebody. A million times she threatened it, usually joking, sometimes not as much as the target of her vitriol believed, but not in a billion years did she think she would be capable of ending someone's life. Until now.

Impulsive. Stupid. Reckless. She fired a bullet into the head of a man who was a boil on the ass of life. But regardless of the mea culpas, it was murder. And Izzy knew that the bullet she fired into his skull would lodge into her soul forever. And no watered-down justification could erase the fact that she had taken someone's life in a thoughtless moment of fury. She could run the list of excuses on a continuous mental loop, repeating to herself that he deserved it, but Izzy wasn't heartless enough for lip-service to ever become her truth. While she often got in over her head, and her irresponsibility habitually put her into precarious positions, like having sex with a high school student, taking someone's life was not something she thought she'd ever do. But now, Izzy found herself so deep in life's ugly mire that she suspected she might never be able to surface for air again.

Ava stared out the side window, the mid-century houses on the street blurred in slow-motion. Santos was dead. Right in front of her. The man she was sleeping with. The man she was falling for. The man who beat her up. The man she chained up in her basement. The image of the blood seeping out from his lifeless body as it lay on the plastic sheet, the dark puddle growing like a spreading virus, was seared into her mind as if someone had imprinted it with a cattle brand. As much as she hated him, as violent and out of control as things had gotten, Ava had a connection with this man she hadn't experienced with any man since her husband. If the women hadn't discovered he was the murderer, would he still be alive? Would they be shacked up by now? She physically shook her head hoping to rattle away the brutal thoughts, which were replaced by a single question that Ava had. 'What the fuck is the matter with me?' Ava tried to remember the last time she dated a decent guy who wasn't a thief, a cheater, or in Santos' case, a murderer involved in human trafficking and running a sweatshop. She wondered what it was about her that caused guys who had their shit together to be repelled like she was a gentleman's Kryptonite? How many more times could she pick badly before she just gave the hell up? Which right now sounded just fine and dandy to Ava.

Contemplating how she could make things right with Curtis, Candy knew how much the handsome man next to her, driving the car, craved her. He wouldn't have taken the chances he had to save her and her friends. She anticipated the hours in bed with him, making sure he knew how much she loved him and wanted to be his. How grateful she was that he would put his own life on the line for her and her 'sewing circle.'

But there was one thing Candy resented. Always had. Being blindsided. Candy established herself the lynchpin in her relationships, the glue that held everyone and every-thing together. Her relationship with Deanna, Ava, and Izzy, being the primary example. As much as it came with a lot of handholding and listening patiently often when she wanted to explode, being the person things revolved around made Candy feel necessary. And her being neces-sary made her feel safe. And if this insane white guy with the weird foreign accent wanted them to learn to make de-signer outfits for him on the promise that he would change their lives, Candy would instill herself into the center of that operation as well, learning to sew, cook meals, babysit kids, fire a gun, cheer on her friends, reminding them that out of every tragedy comes a nugget of hope. Even when she didn't believe it herself.

"Tomorrow, meet here at my place at eleven," Deanna told the other women as she stepped out of Curtis's car. "Anybody got a problem with that?"

No one said a word.

"Good. We have a lot to chew on tonight," Deanna answered their non-answer.

Curtis and Candy both gave a wave as they drove away. Deanna's eyes turned towards her apartment building. One thing she promised herself she would do is start looking for a new place to live. The day she moved out of this shithole would be marked on the calendar as a yearly celebration. She couldn't wait until she kissed good-bye the rickety-ass stairs, the rusty banister, the dimly lit walkway that led to her crappy second-floor apartment. She had already decided if they had to do this, and it was not like they were given an option; she would find another apartment or maybe rent a small house. 'And I'm not taking a stick of furniture from this dump. Even if I go more into debt. Not a chair, not a mattress, not a table,' Deanna told herself. If she had to live a rotten life, she intended to do it without all the rotting crap surrounding her. Whatever she got next didn't have to be high end, she would settle for it simply being new. Not found on a curb, not pulled out of a dumpster, not bought at a second-hand store. Regardless of what was to come, that shit was over. If her soul had a price and she was going to die in debt, she and her family were going to live a little better.

None of the women slept worth a damn that night, tossing and turning, a lot of staring at ceiling fans. Candy was the only one of them that had a delicious reason for not sleeping. She and Curtis made love until three in the morning. She relished having sex with him, because Curtis had mad skills and even better, he relished displaying his prowess. He desired Candy, the tightness of her body, the compact strength of her thighs, the curve of her small breasts which turned up at the nipple. There wasn't a part of her he didn't want to kiss or lick or tease. And after having been married to an older, heavy-set man for over twenty years, having a ripped, endowed man move her around a bed like a chess piece, a man who savored sex, enjoyed controlling her, pleasing her, was something she had never experienced, and Candy gave herself over to completely.

****

Tracee wondered why her mother didn't get up the next morning. Her mother always got up to pop into a toaster or pour into a bowl some sort of breakfast for Ford and make sure he got off to school. But not this morning, which meant Tracee had to cover for her, whipping up his usual breakfast of toast and cereal. When Tracee cracked open the door to check on her mother, Deanna was curled up tightly, almost in a fetal position under the blanket, the old fan whirring loudly overhead.

"Make sure Ford gets something in his belly?" Deanna asked, groggily, having not slept well, if at all, through the night.

"Took care of it, Mom," Tracee responded. "Are you okay?"

Deanna looked up at her daughter and forced a weak smile. "I'll be fine. Have a good day at school."

Tracee didn't know if having a good day was possible. Not after the kiss from Vince. As wrong as it was, Tracee wanted it to happen again. And while the thought terrified her, it thrilled her twice as much, tingling her body, head to toe. She thought about taking a longer route through the hallways to avoid walking past Vince's classroom. It was simply too tempting. She didn't know if what had happened between them was something she should encourage, and figured he was probably embarrassed, if not scared. Besides, how could a man like Vince really want a girl like her? Tracee was sure he viewed her as some sort of fan, thrilled to get a scintilla of attention from a gorgeous baseball coach, the kind of man women fantasize over while reading romance novels. Yet, this morning, she slipped on her best blouse, the one that gave a hint of her deep cleavage and wore her bra that held her ample breasts high, which was an attribute she was sick and tired of being ashamed of. And instead of sweats or jeans, Tracee slid on a skirt, something she seldom wore, but she was over being embarrassed of her thick legs as well. Some men liked that.

Especially in a skirt this short. All together the ensemble made her feel more like a woman and less like a girl.

Until she got to school, then being in a short skirt and blouse that outlined the size of her breasts just felt self-conscious and obvious. There were so many beautiful girls at school. Tall, athletic, straight hair, big smiles. She was short, top-heavy and her hair often had a plan all its own. Vince was idolized. Not just by his ball players, Tracee heard the girls gossip. And when they talked about Vince, it was usually fantastical and carnal. Girls would guestimate how big his penis was, what he liked to do in bed, what he would do to them to make them cum, and what they would do to reciprocate. There was always some buzz about girls in the school that he had taken advantage of, though to this day not one had stepped up and admitted it publicly. Some girls suggested Vince was so handsome and muscular, vainly so, that he had to be gay. But this Tracee knew was petty bullshit. 'It's not like Vince doesn't know that girls gossip about him,' Tracee thought. His body, his hair, his smile, the sun-kissed color of his face. Vince was not oblivious to how good-looking he was and its effect on females. Her smile faded as her insecurities mushroomed. 'Why would he want me?' she couldn't help but wonder, suddenly feeling pitiful and ridiculous simultaneously.

As she shuffled down the hallway towards the library, Tracee craned her neck to glance into Vince's classroom. It was empty. Her shoulders, which she realized were unconsciously pushed back to enhance her posture and lift her bosom, slumped. And so did her head until she was focused on her feet as she walked.

"I thought you'd drop by sometime today to say hi," she heard him say, immediately finding Vince standing in front of her, wearing a school baseball jersey which clung tightly to his chest, and coaching shorts, a thick stack of papers gripped in his large hands.

"Oh, hi," Tracee giggled. "You look like you're ready for practice."

"Have a few of the players' parents coming by today to talk about college and the potential for offers," Vince responded. "I dress like a coach on those days. Do you know which college your brother is leaning towards? There's a real handful of interest in him."

Tracee shrugged, making a face, which made Vince smile.

"You don't have to know. Or care," Vince added, his eyes locking in on her cleavage and then drifting down to her legs. He nodded, approving, his breathing noticeably heavier. "Walk me back to my classroom. I want to put these handouts on my desk," he said, more as a command than a request.

Turning, Tracee kept stride with Vince as he slipped into his classroom and around the wall where he dropped the stack of paper on his messy desk. He then spun around and, without a pause, dipped a finger into the top of her blouse and pulled it away from her breasts, so he could get a better view. Eyeballing her ample breasts, Vince let out a needy breath and smiled. Tracee wanted to pull away, shocked by his brazenness, but she was frozen with fear and want. Her eyes locked on his desirous smile.

"You are so fucking sexy," he spoke in a hush. "I can't get you out of my head."

Tracee let out an audible sigh of her own. Taking that as consent, Vince leaned down and let his lips touch hers softly. He didn't kiss her exactly, instead teasing her by brushing his lips against hers, and then sliding them down to her neck. His hand slipped from her shoulder, cupping her breast over her blouse before sliding down to the hem of her skirt. He lifted the skirt with one finger until he reached her panties. His finger glided along the edge of the material, under the elastic, across her bush, and up inside her.

Gasping, Tracee shivered. Vince chortled softly, his lips grazing hers without kissing her. "You like that…" he whispered, his lips almost touching hers.

Tracee didn't answer as Vince tantalized her more, slipping further inside her, moving his finger until it found her clit. Tracee's eyes closed as she fought her ecstasy, equally turned on and terrified as he played with her, working her to a climax.

"I want to be inside you so bad," Vince whispered, his free hand taking Tracee's hand and placing it on his shorts so she could feel his rock-hard penis. "That's what you do to me."

As Tracee shuddered with pleasure, coming, Vince smiled as he slithered his finger out of her and stepped back.

"I want to do things to you I can't. Not here," he growled. "Sorry. Sorry. I'm really sorry," he pleaded with an edge of yearning, "but you do things to me."

His words made Tracee smile. "It's okay," Tracee replied, smoothing out her skirt awkwardly.

He leaned in and kissed her. Hard.

"You should get to class," Vince stated as he pulled away.

As Tracee nodded, turning to go, he added, "And stop looking so fucking hot."

Beaming, Tracee almost skipped back around the wall like a little girl. Vince's smile dropped from his face once she was gone, replaced by a mix of satisfaction and calculation. As if he wasn't sure how he should be feeling about what he did, while planning on doing it again.

In the hallway, Tracee passed Kevin rough-housing with some of his knuckleheaded teammates. Knowing he spotted her, her cheeks flushed. Kevin continued messing with his friends, but his eyes followed his sister. Keenly aware of what a woman looked like when she recently got laid, Kevin could swear that his sister had just gotten laid. Though he thought his mind was playing tricks on him, that's exactly how Tracee appeared to him. "What the fuck did she do...there's no way," he muttered under his breath, knowing there had to be some other explanation for the rosiness in her cheeks and on her forehead, and the slightly sweaty dampness at her hairline. There's no way she got laid. Not here. Not on the school grounds. Only he could get away with that insanity. And certainly not his sister. As she continued down the hallway in the opposite direction, Kevin turned around, walking backwards, watching her. Something in her step made him think he wasn't wrong...she did something. With someone. Kevin just couldn't wrap his mind around it being true.

****

"There's no way he can turn us into some big-time operation, without using the women he's trafficking," Deanna stated with assurance as she poured everyone a morning cup of coffee. Including Curtis, who she still wasn't convinced should be there, despite everything he'd done for them.

"We can't make that our problem," Ava answered sharply, wanting to end this conversation. "This shit haunted me all night. We can't control whatever what's-his-name does. We have to worry about staying in one piece and keeping our kids alive. We all saw what he did to Santos, for Christ's sake. That could be us next."

"The way we make sure that doesn't happen is to make sure he keeps needing each of us," Curtis added.

Izzy whipped her head towards him, a scowl on her face. "Who's this 'us'? Seems only person you looked out for is you."

Curtis's body tensed. He wanted to pounce and rip her a new asshole but knew that would be an error. The women, at least the two sisters, still didn't trust him, even after everything he had done to take care of them, including keeping them alive. But Curtis accepted that he had to meet them where they were. Diplomatically. Curtis cracked his neck and pulled his lips tight, calming himself. "I looked out for Candy. And that's not going to change.

And even though you seem not to get it, I took care of each one of you, or you'd be wrapped up in plastic, buried in the dirt next to wherever Santos is right now," Curtis growled, letting Izzy know he was pissed but not irate. "I'm in as deep as you are. They kill you, they kill me. I don't get a pass. Martin Collique is a very suave, very demented, motherfucker with a five-hundred-dollar haircut and a two-thousand-dollar suit. Google him. It won't give you the complete story, but it'll give you enough of his past that when you couple it with what you already know and what you've already seen, you'll realize he's not someone you're going to outsmart or outplay."

"You think he'll give us the things we asked for?" Candy piped up.

Curtis shrugged, his head shaking, unsure. "We ask, we see what he delivers. Just know that if he doesn't deliver on certain things, it's not because he can't, it's because he doesn't want to," Curtis stated, taking Candy's hand and squeezing it. "I think first, we have to find out what he expects from you, what this "job" is exactly. And how fast you can deliver whatever it is he wants. That's all got to match up. But as a rule, don't believe anything he tells you. It's pretty obvious that he is not a man of his word, no matter how many times he claims he is."

"When do you think he'll call? Or do we call him?" Ava then asked.

Curtis nodded. "I'll get hold of him."

"Why only you?" Izzy snapped. "How can we trust you? Feels like you knew what was coming down when we were all taken and almost died, then you swept in for the rescue to impress your girlfriend."

"We'd all be dead if it weren't for Curtis!" Candy protested. "Most especially you Izzy! You killing that guy could have gotten us all killed."

"Izzy, you want Martin's phone number, I'll be happy to give it to you. Call him, I'm sure he'd like to have a conversation with you. But stop giving me shit about trying to take care of you. Because that could end," Curtis fired back.

Deanna stood, her arms going up between Izzy and Curtis like she was calling a bad play on a football field. "Okay, enough! Stop!" she snapped. "We have to rely on each other. We got nobody else. Together, we might stay alive, apart, I am sure we will all be dead. And the number one rule is to stay alive. Let's see what Mr. Collique wants us to do. If we can do it, good...if not, we have to stall, but either way, we need a Plan B or something. We got to be prepared.

"Well, what's our choice? Cut and run and hope he doesn't find us, or stay and fight, and hope he doesn't kill us," remarked Izzy, standing and pushing past Deanna, marching towards the kitchen to get herself more coffee. "We are fucked either way."

"We were fucked before this started," Ava yelled after her sister. "We were just starting to get unfucked. I want to see if we can keep that going. Let's see what he's talking about."

Taking in her friends, Deanna shook her head in defeat. "We really don't have another option at the moment."

The silence in the room only deepened. They all accepted that that was the hard truth.

"But," Deanna continued her voice more optimistic than it should have been, "Whatever we decide, we agree to it together. If we don't stand together, we all know we'll be standing on plastic. I'll admit I was scared when we started duping the stuff from the stores, 'fraid we'd get caught and go to jail. But I'm way more scared now. So, we all gotta agree. We're in this insanity together and no matter if we each like it or not, like each other or not, we do whatever we do together."

Each of them held their gaze on Deanna. She searched their faces for agreement. Candy nodded. Ava nodded. Izzy, who leaned against the wall near the kitchen, took a moment, then raised her steaming coffee mug. "What the fuck..." she said, almost as if to convince herself.

"I'm with all of you," Curtis stated. "Deanna's right. This guy will kill us. We have---"

A knock on Deanna's front door sent a horrifying chill through the room. Looks bounced back and forth between all of them. Deanna giggled trying to break the raw tension surging through her body. "Why are we acting like it's going to be someone with a gun?"

Everyone chuckled softly along with her, the tension deflating but certainly not disappearing as Deanna moved to the door and opened it.

A black woman, about their age, haggard, but with brittle determination locked in her gaze, stood in front of Deanna. Ava vaguely recognized the woman but she couldn't place where she knew her from.

"You Deanna?" the woman asked.

Deanna's eyes glanced back as Curtis stood up behind her.

Suddenly, the woman pulled a .45 from behind her and pointed it at Curtis.

"Sit your ass down, nigger. You don't want to be a hero," Clara barked, shoving past Deanna into the apartment, shutting the door behind her. "Which one of you bitches killed my husband?!" she squawked, wagging the gun at each of them.

"Who's your husband?" Ava questioned, afraid, but not as fearful as she would have been if this was someone sent by Martin.

"Marcus Silas. You all know him! One of you killed him!"

Realizing she was talking about Santos' friend, the cop that attacked her, Deanna stepped back. "Your husband attacked me," Deanna stated before realizing keeping her mouth shut would have been a better idea. She gulped down her fear and added, "He nearly killed me."

The barrel of the gun swung into Deanna's face. Clara smiled.

"He almost killed me a bunch of times. Thank you for getting rid of that dirty piece of shit."

"If you're so happy about it, why you pointing a gun at us?" Ava asked.

A mean smile curled onto Clara's lips. She swung the gun person-to-person in the room. "Because you all got money. I know it. You are doing something illegal or Marcus wouldn't have been involved. I want his cut. His cut is my cut now."

No one spoke as they sized-up Clara, all hundred and ten pounds of anger and resentment. Feeling the pressure of their stares, Clara waved the gun around again, "Don't you all look at me that way. You're cutting me in or you're going to die in this shithole apartment."

The gun shifted again into Deanna's face. Sadness, rage, and expectation crash together in Clara's eyes as she narrowed them at Deanna. "You owe me, sister," Clara barked, her lips upturning at the ends as if she was having a hard time believing she was holding a winning lottery ticket, "and I'm here to collect from you bitches."

FALL APART TOGETHER

The barrel of the gun in her face, Deanna stared past it, right into Clara's eyes. Marcus had to outweigh her by over a hundred and fifty pounds. Deanna knew that if Clara was still standing after being beaten by that man, she had to be both mean as hell and tough as steel. Weirdly, Deanna felt a connection to Clara. The rage. The pain. The defeat. The need to climb out of all the shit she had survived being married to a monstrous bully so filled with poison and ferocity that he didn't care about anything but his most feral needs. Deanna didn't want to battle Clara as much as comfort her, instinctively grasping what her life had been.

"So, what were you doing that Marcus was in on?" Clara barked again.

"We weren't doing anything he was in on. He was the friend of Ava's boyfriend," Deanna stated, wishing she hadn't uttered Ava's name. "He was into some bad things and thought we knew about them."

Spinning towards the other three women with the gun, Clara snapped, "Who's Ava? Who was your boyfriend?"

As soon as Clara gave Deanna her back, Curtis's eyes signaled Deanna that she had to move before this woman lost it. Deanna grabbed Clara and lifted her off her feet. At the same time, Deanna's fingers wrapped tightly around Clara's arm to keep the gun from aiming at anyone. Curtis leaped over the sofa and ducked low, coming up under Clara, wresting the gun from her. Clara screamed with frenzied ire as she battled back against Deanna and Curtis, kicking and clawing. Once Curtis had the gun, he backed away, as Deanna wrapped her arms around Clara, instinctively cooing, "I got you, honey, I got you..."

Izzy raced at Clara, cocking back her fist to punch her as hard as she could, but seeing Deanna reacting maternally to the woman, Izzy stopped in her tracks. Like candle wax dripping down, the fight went out of Clara's body as Deanna refused to release her. Clara crumpled towards the floor, sobbing hard. Deanna turned Clara so they were face to face, wrapping her arms around her even tighter as they slid to the floor together. Deanna wouldn't let go, allowing Clara to cry it out.

****

"Who'd you fuck?" Kevin barked at his sister as he backed her into a corner outside the gymnasium, near a row of trashcans.

Screwing up her face, Tracee shook her head. "What are you talking about?"

"I saw you," Kevin simmered, wanting to smile but trying to remain the stern older brother. "I know what someone looks like when they've had sex."

"You're completely mental," Tracee snarked back. "And if I did, why would it be your business? Not that it happened. But why would you care? You've never cared about anything I've done before. Why would me having sex interest you so much, Kevin? And apparently you don't know what people look like when they've had sex or you wouldn't be talking to me."

"Be smart. Make sure you're using protection. Mom got you on the pill?"

Tracee sneered again and made gagging noises.

"Who was it?" Kevin continued, "They didn't force themselves on you."

"Oh, my God! Shut up! Please, just shut up!!" screamed Tracee. "You're creepy!" Tracee declared, her arms waving in front of Kevin as if she were signaling a rescue plane that would never come. "Please, never speak to me again about sex! Ever!!" Pushing around her brother, Tracee dashed down the hallway, away from him. She couldn't help but smile as she continued away, wishing she could reveal the truth, wanting to tell Vince what had just happened and have him demand Kevin back the hell off. 'Kevin would shit his baseball pants,' Tracee thought, an image that utterly delighted her.

****

"My husband is the worst person I've ever known. Men like him...they're just rotten souls, born that way. God knows why I married him. Now I can't imagine what I was thinking. That I could change him. That he would protect me. I came from a bad family," Clara rambled, wiping the snot from under her nose as she sat between Ava and Deanna on the sofa.

Ava's eyes moved from Clara to Deanna, knowing Deanna's history with her husband, Henry wasn't abusive, but was dreadful in every other aspect of marriage. Ava's choices in men could best be described as pathetic. Ava felt that Clara's words squeezed the blood out of both of their hearts, causing Ava to reach over and touch Clara's hand. "You're not alone, honey. We all pick shitty..." Ava said. Just then Candy caught Ava's eye. "Some of us," Ava clarified. "You got yourself a good one. Twice. Which just pisses me off."

The tension broke for a moment, the women sharing a soft laugh.

"I should have killed Marcus myself. There were so many times I should have crawled out of bed, taken his gun and shot him in that big, ugly motherfucking face of his. When they told me his sorry ass was dead, I have never felt that kind of freedom. I wanted to dance and sing and go get real drunk! But that big motherfucker left me broke," Clara sniffed. "I gotta get some money. I got kids."

"I'm not sure you want to get involved in what we're doing," Deanna offered. "We're...in over our heads and your husband's death...he's not the only one dead."

"And we might be next," Candy inserted into the conversation.

Clara sat up, eyeing them. She smiled. "You must think I care about dying. Marcus put me in the hospital three times during our marriage. When I say I got nothing, I mean I got nothing. I want in. I don't care what it is. I want to be cut in. I'll carry my weight, I'll do what needs to be done, I'll do more, but if there's money, any money at all, you gotta let me in."

"We'll let you know," Izzy stated with a cold finality that surprised even her sister. "We don't know what the fuck we're doing yet but if we continue with this bullshit. Maybe there will be a place for you."

"Maybe..." Curtis reiterated vaguely, unsure why Izzy was saying this to Clara. What possible asset she could be to what was going on? They didn't even know this woman other than she was married to the cop they killed.

Clara stood. "I need my gun back."

Reluctantly, Curtis handed it back to her.

"What's your phone number?" Clara asked Deanna.

Before she could weigh whether or not this was a good idea, Deanna recited her number. Clara punched it into her phone, and Deanna's phone rang. "Now you got mine. Call me," Clara said. "Or I'll be calling you," she added with more than a patina of threat before she made it to the front door and disappeared, the evening sky almost magenta as a storm was approaching.

****

"What are you going to say to him?" Candy asked Curtis as they drove back to his place, the wipers melodiously brushing away the raindrops that were falling.

Curtis stared straight ahead, the rain pelting harder on the windshield. He still hadn't formulated what his response would be to Martin Collique. He knew the man was impatient, and worse, expected obedience. As far as Curtis was concerned, they were now under the employ of a psychopath. And it was not a question of 'if' any longer, just 'when' and 'how' and 'what' he wanted them to do exactly. "I'm going to call, see when he's available to meet. I want to talk face-to-face. Have all of you there if possible. If not all of you, then at least a representative, since Izzy thinks I have only *your* best interests at heart," Curtis responded to Candy's question.

"She can be a bitch. Always been something a little off about Izzy, a little crazy," Candy said insightfully.

"She killed a man yesterday. I'd say that's more than a little off," countered Curtis. "You need to get her under control. Because Collique is not the kind of guy who plays games. She gets crazy with him, he will kill her. He will kill all of you."

Candy sat silently, listening to the rhythm of the windshield wipers as Curtis drove. She knew it was true. Ava was the only person who might be able to pull Izzy back from saying or doing something really stupid. Something that could get them killed. Closing her eyes, Candy wanted her head cleared, wanted to have a moment that wasn't about 'this'. Candy wished that she could take all of it back. From the moment this craziness started when they climbed through that hole in the wall and saw all those sewing machines, she should have put a stop to it instead of encouraging it. They should have never touched those machines. They should have patched the wall and left it at that. Karma, that's what this was. Not just biting them in the ass but now gnawing its way through their sanity.

But if she had stopped her friends, she'd still be broke, living in a home without electricity, wondering where her next meal was coming from. And she would never have met Curtis. Candy recognized that nothing was ever completely good or completely bad. It was always a hilly, uneven mix. And whatever side you're on, it always seemed like you were edging along a slippery cliff, ready to fall into something worse at any moment. Candy knew she needed to take solace in what she had. Her hand drifted over to Curtis' and she let him wrap his fingers around it. Whatever was to come, the best thing, maybe the only thing that Candy relied on was that she felt safe with Curtis. And for now, that had to be enough.

****

Barry Wimmer walked into Commander Racine's office, realizing he'd tied his tie too long and it was fluttering as he walked, which annoyed him. Barry prided himself on his look. Crisp. From hair to clothing to the shine on his shoes. He was a handsome man, his eyes sparkling blue, his jaw chiseled like a TV actor. A poster boy for the Feds. Everything about him bore a tidiness that bordered on compulsion. But while he always looked sharp and in control, it was also too thoughtful, and his image felt ham-handedly dated. The haircut to the pleat in his slacks gave the appearance of someone who could have been handing out Gerald Ford bumper stickers decades ago.

Flashing his FBI credentials at Racine, who only slumped into his chair more as he eyed the ID, Barry explained he was there because he was part of the Bureau's Human Trafficking Task Force, and recent events in St. Louis, the murder of Officer Silas and the murder at the Goliath Printing Warehouse are connected through their database to Santos Rivera, who is a person of interest in a trafficking situation last year but the Bureau couldn't pin anything on him.

"Officer Silas and the man who died at the warehouses were both associates of Mr. Rivera," Barry continued. "We'd like to see if you could bring him in on a charge. We'd like to talk to him without tipping off what we really want to speak to him about."

While he felt the stripes on his uniform gave him a sense of confidence and looked great in photos, Racine secretly deplored his promotion to Commander. It had been nothing but a headache. And his daughter, Theresa, was already providing him with a lifetime of those, almost on a daily basis. Racine actually enjoyed his time at work more than his time at home with his wife and daughter. "Give me whatever information you have and I'll see what we can do," Racine grumbled, reaching out towards Agent Wimmer.

Wimmer smiled. "I've given you his name. I expect you to do your job. If I wanted to bring him in, I would myself. I'm asking you for a professional favor. No paper trail leading to me or the Bureau."

Sighing, Racine scribbled down Santos' name on a pad of paper that sat on his desk, before his eyes trailed up to Wimmer. "How do I get hold of you? Or is that a secret too?" he asked.

Agent Wimmer slipped a card from his jacket. Cards were another sign that Barry preferred things old school. He set the card on Racine's desk and tapped it with his finger twice, showing off a manicured fingernail, as he smiled.

"A card. Wow. Something from my generation," Racine chided.

Wimmer smiled and without another word, was gone from Racine's office. Picking up his phone, Racine made a call.

"Jenny, run a Santos Rivera. Local guy, I think. I need his rap sheet," he said, listening as she responded. "Can't imagine there would be more than one of Santos Rivera in St. Louis, but hell, who knows anymore. I see more and more Latino people here. Crazy. Why do they want to live here? Other than it is not an expensive city, and they can open a restaurant or a cleaning business. But what the—sorry, sorry, I'm thinking out loud, just find me a rap sheet on Santos Rivera, and get me a paper copy, I don't want this on my computer," Racine added before dropping the phone back into the cradle.

Racine knew everyone in the department hated him for not emailing his requests. The auditors liked an electronic footprint of every correspondence. But like Barry Wimmer, who was easily a decade younger, so he was just weird as far as Racine was concerned, the Commander vaunted himself on running his office old-school, the way he was most comfortable. Which meant unwritten, unrecorded, untraceable. If he could do something in person, he would. The phone was second best. Paper copies over electronic emails were preferred. Racine knew that getting on the computer left him susceptible to a trail of electronic blunders which could come back to haunt him. Shit ended up in the cloud, and Racine didn't even know what the hell "the cloud" was. But he heard the tech-officers use that term enough to hate it. Even more, Racine didn't want to know. He was so completely disinterested that he knew he wouldn't understand even if they explained it to him like he was a grade-schooler. This was all too new. This was all over his head. And he just didn't fucking care.

Like his drinking buddy Det. John Morrey, Racine was aiming at running out the clock to his retirement. Twenty-one months and counting. He needed to get there. His daughter would be in college. He could sell the house. Buy an RV. Travel. Hopefully, before the department investigated him and discovered all the side-dealings he had initiated and/or been involved in as a St. Louis cop for just shy of forty years. Every time he looked out of his office at the officers who worked under him, there wasn't one he considered a friend. Yeah, he drank with a few of them, like John, but all his real friends had all retired or died. And a select few were doing time, because they were stupid enough to get recorded during their "side-hustles." Some knew Racine's secrets. How he afforded that bass boat. Buying the bigger house in Afton. The Hawaiian vacations. Even his daughter's college fund. Which meant Racine was always looking over his shoulder. At least for another couple years. He just had to make it so he could collect that fat pension which was waiting.

****

Kevin pressed Izzy into the wall as he slid inside her from behind. Demanding that he pound her harder, wanting to feel the ruthless thrusts of him inside her, Izzy groaned each time his hips slapped against her ass. She needed this. The intensity allowed her to forget what she had done in the days before, and all the dark memories swirling around in her head. She always loved the raw physicality of rough sex. Focusing on the pleasure and the pain allowed her to shove away the mania that Izzy felt had swallowed her. Sex with Kevin, who was almost fearless when it came to the give and take of intercourse, gave her the escape she needed, even if it was only for a few hours.

Whatever was gnawing at Izzy, and Kevin knew there was something, he loved it as it allowed him to prey on her need. Seldom did she allow him to be the aggressor. Izzy was always dominant. He was there to please, unlike when he had sex with Cassie or the other high school girls, who were there to please him. 'I hope whatever it is, it lasts a while,' he thought as he continued to drive his hips into her, gritting his teeth, almost punishing her with his body. This was new. And great. When he went away to college, Kevin knew this was what he would miss the most about St. Louis. Forget friends. Forget family. Forget the city. Sex with Izzy would be the thing that would make him the most homesick.

Lying back after they finished, Izzy lit a cigarette and took a drag. By her estimation, if she was going to become a hardened cliché, why not?

"That was intense," Kevin offered, as he rolled over to watch her smoke.

Izzy didn't respond, reality smashing through the dam that sex allowed her to build. Kevin knew her mind was elsewhere, on something big. And what they had was just sex. But Kevin wasn't used to being ignored. Especially after sex. As far as he was concerned, if anyone was going to do the ignoring, it was going to be him. Opening his hand, he allowed the palm of his hand to glide over her nipples. Back and forth, until they were hard. He smiled. Izzy side-eyed him, scowling at his Cheshire Cat grin.

"This fun for you?" she asked Kevin.

His smile widened. "Yeah. I like the way your body responds, you know?"

"Like when I grab your dick," Izzy snapped, her hand plunging under the sheet, grabbing him, causing Kevin to bark out in surprise and pain. "Stop, goddamn it!!!" he called out, trying to squirm away.

But Izzy didn't. She continued to manhandle his penis. Weirded out and pissed, Kevin wrested her hand off his penis, knocking the cigarette out of her hand as he pinned her down on the bed, mounting her, his legs holding hers down to the mattress. "I don't know what the fuck you're going through, but it's got you more fucking crazy than usual," Kevin snarled, staring down at Izzy.

She laughed. "You're just figuring that out," Izzy answered.

Leaning over, Kevin kissed Izzy passionately.

"What did you do?" he questioned, his lips going to hers again.

"Killed a guy," Izzy stated, her eyes locking with his.

Kevin froze. His eyes searched hers for a hint of sarcasm or deflection. There was none. But the longer he stared into her dark eyes, the more he felt she was bullshitting. He smiled, then laughed. "Cool!" he clucked, letting go of her wrists, his head burrowing between her breasts as he caught his second wind. "That got me hard again!!" he crowed, his hand moving down to slip himself inside her for another round. Izzy allowed it, her body numbed from her admission, surprised she said it, but relieved that Kevin didn't believe her as he shifted her body completely under his before pressing his lips against hers.

****

Ava stared out the front window of her home. The events of the last week played repeatedly in her head, and she wanted any diversion to make it stop. But as she smiled, thinking to herself, 'Don't wish too hard...', a detailed Camry jerked to a stop in front of the house, startling Ava free from her memories. Seeing her daughter in the passenger seat leaning over and kissing the driver, a tall, black kid with dreads, Ava's back tightened all the way up to her shoulders. Ava stayed at the window as the kiss grew lasciviously. She watched as his large hands moved over her daughter's body, one dropping down and crawling up her skirt. Her usual instinct would have her marching out of the house and beating on the side window, interrupting the passion inside the Camry and then as the door opened, dragging Cassie out onto the front lawn, as Ava screamed threats at the kid driving. But Ava didn't move for the front door, something she would have done even a day before. When the young man lifted Cassie's shirt, his lips going to her breasts, Ava stepped back and allowed the curtains to drop, the movement causing Cassie to notice the curtains in the window sway. Cassie wrestled down her shirt and kissed the young man once more on the lips, before sliding out of the passenger seat, grabbing her backpack.

Pushing through the front door, Cassie almost ran into her mother as Cassie barreled towards the hallway to get to her bedroom. "Oh! Hey Mom!" Cassie said with a quick wave as she bustled past. "Enjoy the show?"

"Don't do that out in front of the house again. We live on a cul-de-sac, everyone can watch, even little Ford, and he doesn't need to be watching that bullshit," Ava said blithely, as if she really didn't care if it did or didn't.

Cassie spun around with surprise at her mother's ambivalence and sneered. "What?"

It was Ava's turn to sneer. "Who is the boy leaving with the smell of you on his fingers?"

"DeJames. Plays basketball. It's nothing really."

"If that was nothing, what do you do when you are actually interested? Bang him on the roof of the car in the school parking lot?" Ava responded, hating when her daughter lied so obviously.

"God, Mom! Seriously! How long were you watching?!"

Having snapped out of her funk thanks to this back-and-forth with her daughter, Ava opened her mouth to answer, wanting this to get really nasty between them to keep from falling back into her morbid thoughts, but her phone rang. Looking at it, it read POSSIBLY MC. There was only one MC in Ava's life: Martin Collique. Her body tensed noticeably.

"Who is it?" Cassie asked, seeing the dread on her mother's face.

Ava shook her head. "I got to take this," she said, moving off towards the kitchen before answering the phone.

****

Deanna stared at her phone as it rang. MC. Like Ava, Deanna knew who was calling immediately. She feared answering it. She feared not answering it.

"Mom, your phone is ringing," Ford called to his mother as he was heading out the front door to play.

"I know, honey," Deanna answered as Ford rushed out, pulling the door shut behind him.

Closing her eyes tightly, Deanna pressed ANSWER and said, "Hello..."

"Deanna. It's Martin Collique."

Deanna remained silent.

"Are you there?"

Deanna nodded nervously before she spoke. "I'm here."

"I'm returning to St. Louis the day after tomorrow."

"Okay," Deanna said as if she were giving him permission.

"I'd like to speak with you. Alone," Martin said.

"Alone? But...we're a team, and---"

"I know all of that," he cut her off. "Join me for an early dinner. Carnivore STL. I'm a meat-eater."

"I...I have kids."

"I'm absolutely sure they can rustle up their own dinner for one evening. If not, I can have something delivered," Martin stated with an amused lilt in his voice.

"No, no...they can make their own. So, when?" Deanna gulped.

"Day after tomorrow."

"Okay, yeah, fine..."

"Five p.m. I hope you like steak."

"I do. I don't eat it much but, yes. Okay. Five o'clock, Thursday. You said the name of the place is Carnivore STL?"

"Correct. I'll send a car."

Deanna blinked as if a stranger had walked up on the street and kissed her. "A car?" she quizzed, not getting it.

"I'll send a car for you. Be ready at four-forty. And one more thing..." Martin let his sentence tail off into a dramatic silence.

"Yes?"

"Do not tell your friends."

Deanna stared across her messy apartment, with the tables still set up with the sewing machines, pieces of cloth and remnants piled up. Putting her hand to her chest, she could feel her heart beating through her blouse. She resented being put in this position, keeping secrets from the people she was counting on to help keep her and her family alive. It terrified her. But it terrified her more to join Martin for dinner. What could he possibly want to talk about with her alone? And while he said not to tell the others about their dinner, he didn't say she couldn't tell them what they talked about.

Reluctance in her voice, Deanna muttered, "Okay..."

DINNER IS SERVED

Even after copying designer clothes, Deanna still only had one nice dress to wear. And she had sewn that herself as well. She also Googled the restaurant on her phone, peeked at the prices and gulped. She had never had a meal in a place anywhere near that expensive. 'Could the food actually be that good to ask for that much?' she wondered. Not that it would matter to Martin Collique. She figured that he probably ate like that daily. No PB&J, no Spam, no coupons, no day-old bread. Deanna assumed it was his normal as much as a box of $.99 pasta and a $1.79 jar of sauce were hers. Except he didn't have to feed a family, just himself.

All day, Deanna debated whether to call Ava and fill her in on what Collique had asked of her. She and Candy had spoken a few times over the last couple of days, but

Deanna remained tight-lipped about the dinner, honoring Martin's request. Deanna accepted that fear dictated much of that decision, but she also knew that wasn't the entire truth. She didn't tell them because she needed to ask the questions she wanted to ask, without all the other women's concerns rattling around in her head. And the first thing Deanna needed to know was why Collique didn't want the other women to know that he and her were meeting. What could he possibly have to say to her that he didn't want to say to the other women? Once she knew that, her second question would be about what he expected of them. And the third, if she had swallowed enough liquid bravery by that point, would be what would happen if they wanted out.

"He's sending a car for you?" Tracee quizzed as she helped her mother get dressed for her night out. "Who is this person?"

"And can he be our new daddy?" Kevin chimed in through the closed door, from across the hallway, clearly listening in.

"He's someone who wants to be in business with us..." Deanna responded, trying to quell any hint of fear in her voice, "...will be in business with us. He will be."

"Okay. Good...I guess. Whatever it is you're doing," Tracee answered, helping her mother pick out the best set of earrings with which to complement the dress that Deanna had created a few years ago, hoping to sell it, but kept for herself.

Looking at her reflection in the mirror, Deanna realized she could do with some sort of haircut or styling, or she would always be forced to do what she was doing this evening, which was curl it to give it some shape, and then pull it all back in a ponytail. She hadn't seen her face with make-up in a long time. While she wasn't very good at applying it, Deanna realized less was more or she would resemble a twenty-dollar hooker who gave blowjobs down at the Red Roof Inn a few blocks away. Henry always told her she was a natural beauty. But it was always because he wanted to get laid that night. Deanna heard it so often his words carried far less weight than if someone else paid her the compliment. And as her bills piled up, Deanna cared less about what she looked like and more about social services knocking on her door and taking the kids. Tonight, even though she didn't feel she held the beauty she once did, she felt she looked pretty good. And pretty good would have to be enough.

Kevin, Tracee, and Ford stood out on the second-floor walkway and watched their mother climb into the car that was sent for her. "Damn, that's not some crappy little

Uber, that's a town car," Kevin crowed. "With a driver. Momma is stylin' tonight."

Tracee looked over at her brother. "She's riding in that car and we're eating pasta and sauce from a jar. There's something wrong with all this."

"You two are living like this," Kevin answered as he walked back into the apartment. "I'm getting out of here and going to college," he laughed, heading back towards the bedrooms.

Ford touched Tracee's hand. "He's a wad."

Tracee nodded. "Yes, he is."

****

Stepping into the restaurant, Deanna toyed with her hair, glancing around, unsure if she'd even remember what Martin Collique looked like since she'd only seen him once and that entire day was a shock to the system, something she could only remember in fragments. She would recognize his voice, but she wasn't sure about his face. She was hoping if he was there, he would spot her as she walked in and stand. But no one did. No one even looked in her direction.

Then a hand touched her back. Deanna froze. "I'm sorry I'm tardy. I pride myself at being on time," Martin said as he brushed around Deanna and moved up to the hostess, giving his name.

Promptly, the hostess led them through the restaurant towards the back. As she walked behind Martin, Deanna assumed that meant something that they were heading to the back of the restaurant by how various diners glanced at them. She just didn't know what. But as she came around a pillar, Deanna sucked in a horrified breath. At a large table were Ava, Izzy, Candy, and Curtis. Not even one of them appeared happy. And seeing Deanna walking in with Martin didn't change that.

"Hello everyone," Martin greeted them all with a brash smile moving to the head of the table. Deanna slipped into a chair next to Izzy.

"What the hell?" Deanna said just to Izzy, as Deanna slipped into the seat next to her.

"We got played. All of us," Izzy whispered back.

"I appreciate you all being here. Please, look at the menu, select whatever you wish. I'm starting with a vodka. Feel free. We have much to discuss."

Estranged glances darted around the table, each woman realizing that Martin had asked each of them not to tell the others about the meal. And each held to their word, which now infuriated them. Anger, at each other, at themselves, and for the humiliation each was feeling for not divulging this dinner to the others, who just a few days before they each promised to have each other's backs. Now they sat at a circular table where they could view everyone else, feeling foolish and off their game. The trust they had built amongst themselves over the last few weeks oxidized before drinks were even served.

"I asked each of you not to tell the others that we were having dinner. And it seems each of you kept that promise. I appreciate that. I reward loyalty," Martin commented.

That didn't stop the self-conscious, irritated looks that crossed the table while everyone ordered a drink and Martin ordered appetizers for the table.

"It was shitty of you to try and divide us like this," Deanna spoke up first, not willing to hide her disdain. "It's not fair. And if you think it makes us trust you more or at all, you're wrong."

"You were the ones who chose not to tell each other. That's hardly my fault. Admittedly, this was a test to see if each of you could be trusted and where loyalty lies," Martin responded, "but it wasn't meant to be divisive. This was about the relationship each of you have with me, not each other."

"Our loyalty lies with each other," Deanna stated, her eyes burrowing in on Martin. "Just because we didn't tell each other we were having dinner with you, doesn't mean we wouldn't have afterwards. I'm sure, just like me, Candy, Izzy, and Ava wanted to know what you wanted. Then we'd all talk. We talk all the time. We're in business together. And I'm sure Curtis and Candy told each other."

Reacting, Candy glanced down. Curtis said nothing. The other women knew exactly what that meant.

Deanna stood. "I don't want to be here. I'm going to call my son and have him come get me."

"Sit. Please," Martin signaled her to sit. "Admittedly, this wasn't exactly a team-building exercise. But that's not why I asked you all to dinner. I understand you're all friends. Tonight is about other things. Now that you have had a couple of days to process things, I needed to sit with all of you. I want to lay out what I expect moving forward."

"Wait until the drinks come," Ava cracked. "I might be a little more willing to listen once I have a glass or two. And be sure, I'm ordering the most expensive thing on this fucking menu. I don't give a shit if I like it or I don't, I'm ordering it. And I might take something home for tomorrow too."

"Revenge eating," Martin replied with a smile, nodding. "Feel free."

"Let's cut to the chase, so we can enjoy the meal. What's this about, Mr. Collique? Why are we here, feeling shitty about ourselves for keeping this a secret?" Curtis asked, reaching over and taking Candy's hand.

"I have a plan to expand our business," Martin answered, his tone shifting to total business.

"*Our* business?" Izzy snapped, a bite in her voice. "Not yours?"

Not wanting this to get any more confrontational than it has, Candy's eyes locked with Izzy's as she softly, yet sharply, said "Izzy..."

"What? Is he going to shoot me here in the restaurant? Kill us all while I'm having a beer? Please," Izzy fired back. "This whole thing is bullshit. You've already made us feel like shit, made us realize that our relationship is constructed out of fucking paper mâché or something, so congratulations, you win. No steak is going to make me feel better. Just tell us what your big idea is in case I decide to leave early and do something more important, like shave my legs or masturbate to porn."

Deanna smirked, especially when she saw Martin blanch. Deanna could always count on Izzy to drop the mic and it was evident that Martin Collique was not accustomed to someone as blunt and direct as Izzy. There simply wasn't any deference as Izzy treated everyone with similar disdain.

Just then the drinks were served, the conversation immediately falling into necessary yet awkward silence. Once the waiter walked away, Martin laid out his plan. He expressed that he wanted the women to continue their operation. The only difference is they would no longer be trotting off to a high-end department store to buy togs and copy them, they would move up the ladder and be duping gowns. Gowns he sent. "Everything will be included, fabric, buttons, zippers, lining, beads, etcetera, etcetera, and the size I need the gown to fit. No more buying off the rack, making a copy and selling it. The gowns I'm sending you are extremely expensive, often one of a kind. I will expect the duplicates to look exactly like the originals," he said and then emphasized, "Exactly."

Knowing the brunt of this request would fall onto her shoulders, Deanna raised her hand, as if she had to be called on to speak. "This sounds incredibly work intensive. I've made dresses, I know how to do that, but gowns...? We're going to have to deconstruct them before we can construct them. Especially if they are all different sizes. There's going to be a learning curve. A big one. I'm gonna need time. And a lot of help."

"And other than Deanna, what the hell are the rest of us supposed to do?" Ava quizzed, her eyes narrowing, her voice giving away her worry about being cut out of this operation.

His eyes shifting from Deanna to the other women, Martin spoke softly but very direct. "I expect you to learn something from Deanna so you can be capable assistants, if not master some aspect of the business. You will all fill in, learn a piece of the work, learn skills you may not yet possess. And as this operation grows, there will be other aspects that need to be handled, problems that will arise that I will ask you to deal with," Martin offered. "Let me be clear, this entire business is yours. When I say ours, I consider myself the silent partner. The supplier. And the majority shareholder."

"Why can't we continue doing what we were doing? We were starting to get in the rhythm and making some money," Ava wanted to know as she took a long swing of her drink.

"Because sooner or later we'll get caught," Izzy chimed in, both knowing what Martin was going to say, and believing it herself.

"Thank you, Isabel," Martin smiled patronizingly. "And I don't get caught," he continued with flat authority.

That killed the conversation as they all looked up from their menus towards him.

"The gowns you will be copying will not be sold here. They are ordered from various buyers overseas. Women who want an original. But know the designer will not make it in their size, or they cannot come to terms. Which is where I come in," Martin continued. "I offer them a chance at something they could not get any other way."

Before anyone could respond, the waiter returned, asking if the table was ready to order or wanted another drink. Even though none of them were ready to order, they needed a respite from the conversation. Each eyed the menu and with expediency, ordering the first thing that appealed to them. Ava, true to her word, ordered the most expensive thing on the menu, and a pasta dish to go, just to see if she could get a rise out of Martin.

After the waiter left the table to put in the order, Martin's eyes returned to the women. "A partner of mine connects me with these clients," he stated. "They like to buy designer. And I'm not talking about what you can get off the rack in St. Louis with the label. But from the actual designer. After runway and before market. I want to manufacture these items. And if the copies are as good as the originals, our buyer pool will only expand."

"Wait," Candy snapped. "What about the designer? They can stop this if they want, right?"

"They often don't know. Certainly not until after the dress is worn. If there are photos they might find out. But what can they do then?" Martin responded.

"I don't know, sue?" Candy continued.

"Who?" Martin smiled.

The women shared a look.

"Long as it's not us," Ava answered.

"I can promise, this will never come back on you," Martin continued. "And some of the designers are compensated under the table. Professional courtesy for plausible denial," Martin chuckled, taking a drink.

"Where do these things get sold?" Deanna then questioned.

"We have buyers in Eastern Europe, Russia, the Middle East. As well as a handful here in America, but I can assure you, none in St. Louis."

"Where are we going to get these outfits to copy?" Deanna questioned. "You're talking designer gowns right off a runway, how do you get those?"

Martin smiled with condescending amusement. "I'll handle that," he quickly answered.

"I want to go back to what we were talking about before. Why can't we keep our side hustle?" Candy punched back into the conversation, everyone's attention spinning in her direction.

"No," was all Martin said with schoolmarm finality, which caused immediate silence at the table.

And it lasted. Curtis could see tears rimming in Candy's eyes, and Ava turning a heated shade of red like she was having a hot flash. To stave off any gasoline being poured over his girlfriend's emotions, he quickly asked, "Why not?"

Seeing the emotion of the faces of the women that his terseness caused, Martin raised a hand as if that was going to quell the fury, which maybe it did with other "employees" but not with the women at this table. Except for Izzy, who sat back, crossed her arms over her chest and glanced around the restaurant with flagrant disinterest.

"If you were to get caught, it would be the end of everything," he replied. "And as much as I enjoy your company, the feistiness of your conversation, your beauty, I can't trust that if you got caught, you would not bring my name into the conversation with the authorities. And that would be very bad for all of us."

Even if no one else at the table understood, Curtis instantly grasped the threat.

As the waiter set appetizers on the table, everyone ordered another drink. It was going to be that kind of night. Once the waiter was a few steps away, Martin took them all in as the plates of appetizers were passed around the table. "I will keep you all very busy. And together, we will make a lot of money," Martin again smiled with a pomposity that causes Deanna to bristle. She wished she had more of her son's moxie and could simply stand up and punch him in his face.

"How much can we make?" Ava jumped in, her eyes widening with her question, hoping to hear a large number. "Seriously. We make you a few, I dunno, gowns, dresses, whatever, and you sell them for, what, twenty grand, fifty grand, a hundred grand? I dunno what those kinds of things go for. I was excited when we were copying blouses for a few hundred bucks and splitting the money. The money you're talking about, the kind of operation or whatever, yeah, it changes our lives. How does it change yours?"

Remaining silent, Martin's eyes stayed on Ava, making her uncomfortable. "I'm not looking for my life to change," Martin finally countered, taking a drink of the costly glass of wine in front of him.

"Then what?" Ava continued. "What do you get out of us doing this for you?"

'Martin is big on smiles being his answer,' Curtis thought as Martin allowed a grin, a smirk, a leer, Curtis wasn't sure, but Martin brandished it on his lips. 'Does he think that gives him power? Makes him mysterious? Douche...' mused Curtis, hiding his own smile. Curtis didn't understand why Martin didn't just lay it all on the line and save the questions. There was nothing Curtis or the women could do, no matter what Martin spit out. This parsing out of information, like a cat playing with a dying mouse, was agitating the hell out of Curtis.

"I am always looking to expand my reach. Keep certain people happy. You women can help me do that. It's not just about the clothes. It's all about influence. Influence is priceless, and these gowns you will be copying will help me create new inroads that will ultimately lead to exactly that, influence," Martin answered. "Influence I intend to exploit."

"Wow," Izzy growled with a laugh. "What you're saying is we're giving you a lot. So, tell me again exactly what we are getting out of this?

"Lives," Martin stated directly without any self-congratulations or humor, "real, upwardly mobile, financially secure, lives. The kind you wished you had but had no real chance of ever achieving. I hope I answered your questions, because I would like to enjoy the evening with you, without a thousand more."

The energy at the table immediately iced over as the women traded furtive glances but said nothing. Even Curtis felt diminished, which pissed him off. As if on cue, they all picked up their drinks and brought the glass to their lips. None of them really wanted the drink, but they knew it would keep them quiet as Martin slowly drew his wine glass to his lips and allowed a swallow to swirl in his mouth and slide down his throat, savoring the flavor of the Chateau Lafite Rothschild 2000 Red.

****

As she stood out front of the restaurant, waiting for the town car to take her home, Deanna waved as Ava drove past in the town car sent for her. Ava waved back, signaling Deanna that she would call her as Martin walked up behind Deanna.

"I just texted. He went to fill up with gas. The driver should do that before. But..."

"It's okay. It's a nice night," smiled Deanna. "You can go. I'll be fine."

"No," Martin said. "I wouldn't think of letting a beautiful woman stand out here alone."

His flattery tickled Deanna. Even coming from someone who terrified her, it felt good. It'd been a long time since anyone referred to her as "beautiful". And dressing up, putting on make-up, it was the first time in ages since she actually felt like it. There would be no climbing into dumpsters to find food tonight.

Martin pulled out his phone and texted. He then smiled again, only this smile registered differently with Deanna. "Come on," Martin said, signaling her to follow. "My car is over here. I canceled your car. I'm taking you home."

Deanna shook her head, taking a step back. "You don't have to do that, Mr. Collique. I can call my son."

"You don't have to be frightened of me, Deanna," Martin stated, squaring off with her.

Deanna laughed at the absurdity of his words. "I don't, I'm not..." she stuttered but then stopped herself and looked directly at him. "The past few weeks tells me I do have to be scared of you."

"Fair. But I have no intention of hurting you. You have to believe that."

Deanna didn't move. He took a few steps towards his town car parked right up front. Martin spun towards her again. "Come on," he insisted in a tone that felt like a command to Deanna.

The moment she took the first step towards his car, Deanna hated herself. As he held the door open and Deanna nervously slipped past him with a "thank you," she wanted to kick herself. 'It's just a ride,' she insisted to herself. But as they drove, the silence in the car grew uncomfortable. What does one say to a man who threatened to murder you? A man who had blackmailed her into working for him? Whose henchman tried to kill her son? Martin glanced over at her with yet another oozing smile. "You know, you can say what you want to say to me. I know there's plenty you want to say when I'm not drinking my favorite wine...or when there's not someone pointing a gun at you," Martin smirked.

Deanna turned to look out the passenger window, wishing she were anywhere else. But hell, why not? Why not say what she felt like saying? "How do I know you don't have a gun?" she asked.

"You don't. But assume for the moment I'm unarmed," Martin replied. "The tension between us is undeniable, and since it's not sexual tension I'm giving you this moment, Deanna, say what you want to say. Get it off your chest."

"You tried to murder my son," she stated.

"And you as well," Martin added.

"And me. Yeah, and me!" she snapped. "And now, lickety-split, you want me to trust you? I don't. And these gowns you want us to make. What happens if we can't do it? Or can't do it fast enough or well enough or whatever enough? Then what? You kill us? You cut us loose with nothing? We had a profitable little thing going. I mean it was profitable enough to keep a roof over my head, and food on the table. And we weren't hurting anyone. Not really. But now, joining you. I believe a lot of people are going to get hurt. Or worse. This whole thing...we just wanted to pay our bills. Not be living on the bottom rung all the time. We found our way out and you're taking that from us."

"And giving you more. You'll see. You keep doing what you do best, for me, and you will never see the ugly side of me again," Martin said, in a voice so soothing that it actually scared Deanna more than she'd been frightened all night.

As they pulled up in front of her apartment building, Martin startled Deanna by reaching over and taking her hand. Her first reaction was to pull it back, but her better sense kicked in immediately and she stopped herself, turning to look at him. "First thing I need to do is get you out of this neighborhood. This is unacceptable," Martin commented.

"My kids and I are fine here," Deanna answered.

"No, your kids are not fine here. And this is not up for debate. Even if you're happy here, I do not want the expensive packages I'm sending to you delivered to this location. It's simply not acceptable. This is too dangerous. And there are too many neighbors," Martin stated. "I am making arrangements for you and your friends to live elsewhere," Martin announced. "I think it would be best if you were all closer together."

Deanna couldn't grasp what he was talking about. And while she'd love to never have to step foot in this apartment again, her fear of the unknown, having her life quarter-backed by a known killer, terrified her far more.

"I know it's silly to say after what has occurred between us, but I think if you'll trust me, you'll see that I will deliver what I promise," Martin reiterated.

"This is a promise?" asked Deanna.

"You're an asset. You may not know it, and you certainly don't treat yourself like one, but you are. I reward those who are an asset to me. Handsomely. But full disclosure, don't cross me." Again, he smiled. "I'll prove I'm a man of my word. As long as you and your friends prove you are women of yours, I vow this relationship will be mutually beneficial."

Still, Deanna couldn't muster a look of confidence. "Mutually beneficial..." she repeated. "I hope that's true. Thank you for the ride."

And with those words, she slid past him and out of the car. She stayed out front of her building, signaling the driver to go. As the town car pulled away, reflexively, she waved, as if she were saying good-bye to a friend. But Deanna recognized that Martin Collique was anything but a friend.

He was now her employer.

And her enemy.

****

"Can we trust him?" Candy asked Curtis, as they stepped out of the town car they shared for the ride back to Curtis' townhouse. They hadn't spoken the entire way home. Both were secretly stung from not telling the other that Martin had contacted them about a meeting. And while both Candy and Curtis understood intellectually why the others didn't mention it, the omission had dinged their faith in each other. Nothing irreparable, but it hurt.

"No," Curtis stated as they climbed the stairs to the front doors of the building. "We fucked up," he stated as they entered the building and moved to the elevator. "He now believes he can get us to turn on each other."

"What were we all thinking?" Candy asked, more to herself than Curtis.

As they entered Curtis' unit and shut the door, Curtis turned towards Candy. "I'm sorry," he announced.

Sliding her body against his, her arms wrapping around his waist. Curtis kissed Candy. She knew he was sorry, she could feel it. And she hoped he knew she was equally, if not more, apologetic about keeping this stupid secret. The first thing she should have done was tell him.

"No more keeping things. I don't care who or what it is, but especially when it comes to Martin," Candy said softly, her face looking up at his.

Curtis nodded. "Most especially when it comes to Martin Collique," he added before their lips met, his body pushing her back against the wall, his lips never leaving hers. Candy wrapped her legs around him, his hands going under her ass and lifting her up, holding her up against the wall for only a moment longer, before carrying her back to the bedroom.

****

Crawling into bed, Deanna's body finally collapsed. The day was bad enough, but piling this insane dinner on top of it really made it all feel like well-dressed indentured servitude. She had no choice in what was coming. No choice in what they would do. And she was the only one who could actually do it. It brought tears to her eyes, knowing all this was now squarely on her shoulders, and it took her a long time to fall asleep. And just as quickly, she began dreaming.

About Martin. More aptly, sex with Martin.

She had never seen him naked, but it didn't stop Deanna's subconscious from having him undress in front of her. Then suddenly, she was nude as well, Martin on top of her. Her hands clawed at his back as he drove into her powerfully. He instinctively knew how to play her body, his touch, his lips, his tongue, every part of him was to pleasure her. He was fearless in arousing Deanna. Her body reacted, her back arching as her mouth opened to free an ecstatic shriek.

Waking in the dark, the off-kilter ceiling fan clanging rhythmically overhead, Deanna gasped, sitting up. Sweat beaded her hairline. "What the hell...?" she muttered aloud to no one. This was not okay with Deanna. Of everything that happened that night, this scared the shit out of her the most.

BY DESIGN

"What do you think this means?" Deanna asked Ava, who she called to grab coffee when she couldn't get hold of Candy.

"Means you're horny," Ava reacted. "Horny enough to dream about fucking a psycho."

"How did it feel when Santos was killed? He did a lot of bad things, I get that. I mean, to you especially but to all of us. But...you had something with him," Deanna asked, wishing she hadn't put as much sweetener into her coffee.

Ava sipped from her cup, staring out the window at the traffic as it passed. 'Jesus, does everybody in South City drive a piece of shit car,' Ava thought, trying to decipher an answer that would satisfy Deanna, since Ava hadn't organized her feelings into anything logical that even she could understand.

"You know what it's like to watch someone die," Ava said, remembering that Deanna watched Marcus take his last breath in her living room. "There was a few days there

I actually thought he might be a guy I could get serious about. Like forever serious. I mean the sex was great and I haven't had a man pay that much attention to me in, hell, like since high school. I don't know if I'll ever have it again, Deanna. And I kinda want a guy. Like Candy's got."

"Yeah, she's got a good guy," Deanna agreed.

"Big dick too. She told me," Ava laughed.

"I figured," Deanna chortled as well, "you can just tell."

"It's not the only thing but feeling a man in your bed. The warmth. That body that you snuggle against. That big arm that lays across you. Pulling you close. Hot breath on the back of your neck," Ava lamented. "God, I want that, Deanna. I thought I had it. I had it for a minute. But..."

Deanna reached over and took Ava's coffee cup out of her hand. "Forget coffee this morning. Let's go get a drink."

Astonishment splattered across Ava's face faster than her smile. "Fuck girl, now you're speaking my language..." she responded, standing just as fast.

****

Finding Cassie walking side-by-side with her two closest girlfriends, who hated Kevin even more than Cassie, Kevin signaled to her that he wanted to talk. Cassie instantly shot up her middle finger in his direction, causing Kevin to mouth the words, "come on." Cassie stopped and turned to her friends, speaking closely with them. They turned and gave Kevin stink eye before flipping him off and walking on from Cassie, allowing Kevin to cross the hall to her.

"What?" Cassie sneered.

"This isn't about me. Or you. But I need something," Kevin rattled off quickly, knowing Cassie could walk away at any time.

"No," Cassie quickly answered, turning to go.

Grabbing her arm, Kevin stopped her. Her eyes went to his hand and he immediately released her. "Look," he sighed, "I just want to know if you know if my sister is seeing anyone."

"What? Why would you care? Why should I?"

"I think she's getting laid."

Cassie's eyes widened, then she chuckled. "Good for her. What's it your business?"

"I dunno," responded Kevin. "I just get the feeling that whoever it is isn't good for her. I'm just looking out for my sister."

"Did she ask you to?"

Kevin didn't respond, causing Cassie to nod with a smirk.

"Then she doesn't want you to know. Tracee is a big girl. She's smart. Smarter than you. She can handle herself. Stay out of her business."

"If you hear anything, tell me. Please. I just want to make sure it's not somebody bad for her."

"Like one of your friends?"

Kevin's jaw clenched. "Yeah. Like one of my friends."

Cassie laughed loudly, obviously, as she sauntered down the hallway, away from Kevin.

****

Arriving back at her home, a little buzzed but not tipsy, there was a FedEx van parked in front of Deanna's building, running. Often not a smart move in South St. Louis as it invited thievery. Deanna walked past it, her eyes connecting with the driver's as she did. Heading up the stairs and arriving at her door, she heard the van door open below and a voice yelled at her, "That your apartment?"

Turning, the driver was down by the van, looking up at her. Deanna's heart pounded.

"Yes," she responded reluctantly.

"I got a delivery for you," he said, turning the van off.

It took him three trips up and down the stairs with three bulky wardrobe boxes and two other large square boxes. Deanna only had a few dollars in her wallet to tip him for his trouble.

Ripping open one of the wardrobe boxes first, she found a gown bag inside. She unzipped it and laid out a spectacular gown, copper in color, the material something she had never felt before, an underlay of copper and gold thread. "He can't expect me to copy this...what the hell...where would I get any of this..." Deanna mumbled to herself as she grabbed her phone and called Ava first.

"Don't tell me you left something at the bar," Ava answered.

"Call the other girls and get over here. You gotta see this," Deanna said with enough drama in her voice for Ava to get goosebumps.

"Is it bad?"

"It's nuts. It's fucking nuts."

****

The women all arrived within twenty minutes. The other wardrobe boxes were open and two more incredible gowns were now lying over the back of the sofa. The larger, square boxes were also opened and inside were reams of the material that they would need to recreate the dresses.

"Is this a test?" Izzy asked. "To see if we can do it?"

Candy couldn't stop touching the dresses, awed by the beauty of the material. These were the most stunning gowns she had ever seen. World-class beautiful.

Ava held up a sheet of paper that she found in one of the larger boxes. Her head shook as she read it. "He wants us to make three copies of each. He's got the sizes he needs. Some sizes of the dresses are different, so that means he must have different buyers. He emphasized that we need to make sure nothing should happen to the originals. We have two weeks."

"Two weeks!" Deanna exclaimed. "There's no way! He is turning us into a sweatshop. Where did he get these dresses?"

"Who knows? If these are the originals, and I'm guessing they are on loan from the designers. Probably the originals. That's why the two weeks," Candy remarked, her hands unable to stay away from the gowns.

Deanna sat on the sofa, in the corner, away from the gowns. "How much are these things worth, Candy?"

"That would depend on which house they are from. Custom gowns, could be as little as thirty up, but look at the handwork in this gown...this could cost a hundred thousand. These are probably priceless by now. Vintage couture. I'm not sure who designed these gorgeous things, but they're probably museum quality," Candy answered.

Staring at the paper in her sister's hand, Izzy asked, "So, what do you think he'll make off these twelve gowns if we do them right?"

"If he sells them as original, upwards of a half a million," Candy shrugged.

"So, he has us do these every couple weeks, say we do multiples of forty-something copies a year, he makes a few million dollars. And we get what? A hundred grand a piece?" Ava questioned.

"A hundred grand is a shitload of money," Izzy reminded her sister.

"Everybody slow their horses. We don't even know if we can copy these. Especially in that time. Look at the beadwork on this one! I'm supposed to copy that exactly?! And to be doing it continually, day after day, week after week, for however long? That's crazy. What are we doing?" Deanna wanted to know. "What's he doing to us?"

"Right now," Ava said, breathing out dramatically, "figuring out what we're capable of."

"Or what?" Deanna posed. "We die?"

The women all trade glances, knowing Deanna's question was what they were all wondering but were afraid to vocalize.

****

Barry Wimmer simmered with frustration after he got the word that he would stay in St. Louis for an extended length of time after the police department connected Santos Rivera and Reilly Johans, whose body they found burned at the Goliath Warehouse, as well as Santos Rivera and Officer Marcus Silas. And they were all connected to a human trafficking ring that ran through the city as well as a counterfeiting ring that manufactured knock-off sportswear that's sold outside the stadiums and arenas.

And now Rivera was missing. If he could find that son-of-a-bitch, Wimmer had no doubt he could break Rivera during questioning. Known for being a cunning adversary during interviews, the Bureau often used Wimmer as the cleanup man on tough interviews. It didn't take him long to get up to speed, and he enjoyed the hunt. But Barry hated working out of town. Even though Chicago wasn't that far, he preferred being close to his wife and kids. Agents had needs, and Wimmer's appetite for women, while only hinted at the Bureau, was a sore spot within his household. His wife, Cyndi, hated when he was away, because she couldn't trust him. If there was a flaw in her husband, it was that women could not only turn his head, they could also easily flatter him into bed. Or a bathroom stall. Or a dark alley. So far, it hadn't interfered with his work, just wrecked his home life. He vowed to work on curbing his libido to save his marriage, but it was a promise he couldn't keep. Barry liked sex. He liked variety. He liked what he couldn't get at home. He loathed himself because of it, but even a wide swath of self-hate didn't stop him. When he banged a waitress in the back room of the Chili's attached to his hotel, Barry threated to have her arrested if she told anybody. Lucky for him, she was easily convinced and found sex with him nothing more than fast and breathy, not a conquest she could coyly brag about on social media.

****

Wasting as little time as possible, Deanna chose to start on the metallic dress first, assuming it would be the most difficult, especially since she couldn't deconstruct the original to see how they put it together. She demanded that Izzy and Candy stay with her until she was done. Besides being an expert on color, Izzy had shown an eye for cutting patterns, which would be indispensable to Deanna, saving her hours. Especially since each size demanded a different pattern be cut.

Candy would have to hold Deanna's hand. Deanna recognized that Candy knew these clothes better than any of them and wouldn't allow Deanna to miss a detail. Ava would be the swing, running errands, picking up things they might need, including food. Ava wasn't happy about it, but staying active with the group, hell, just staying active, not giving the past few weeks any more space in her head, is what she needed to do for her mental health.

As Deanna toiled, trying to get the outfits cut and stitched, Ava cooked meals for her kids. One evening, Cassie came over and ate with all of them because she was tired of the refrigerator at her house being empty. She glared at Kevin when she could and he rolled his eyes, but they didn't say a word to each other. Deanna didn't sleep, or more to the point, couldn't, but she would cat nap, which she was keenly aware made her more vulnerable to making a mistake, but she needed to get these copies made in the narrow time frame Martin had given.

"We need someone with her twenty-four-seven," Candy whispered to Ava, recognizing that Deanna would not make this deadline doing what she was doing.

"What we need is someone else who can sew at the level Deanna can. She doesn't have the time to teach any of us. We've learned some, but not enough to work on those gowns," Ava stated.

"Get that cop's wife. She wanted to help. Maybe we can help her," Deanna called from across the room, where she and Izzy were discussing a draped panel, trying to figure out the dimension that needed to be cut for a size twelve.

Ava and Candy came from the kitchen where they were talking, their eyes on Deanna.

"I'm exhausted. Not deaf," she said.

"Do you mean Marcus Silas's wife?" Ava asked.

"Why not?" Deanna questioned. "I've thought about her a few times since he busted in here waving that gun. Maybe we could help her."

"I'm not worried about helping her, I mean, come on, how do we trust her? We know nothing about her," Ava added.

"We know her husband was abusive. We've been there. We know she's broke. We've been there. We know she's got balls. We've been there," Deanna said as she nodded to Izzy, who took a deep, calming breath before putting shears to the material.

The women shared various shades of uneasy looks, Ava shaking her head. But they knew they needed to do something. Candy shrugged. "I'll have Curtis talk to her," Candy agreed while Ava continued to shake her head, now adding giving Candy the finger.

****

This was a first for Curtis. Going into the home of the man he killed to talk to his wife about joining them in an endeavor that might make them some money but also might get them all killed. He was there when she came to Deanna's waving a gun and then collapsing into a puddle of tears. He wondered who he would get today and if she was stable enough to join the women, who were treading water psychologically and physically as well.

Clara nodded at Curtis over and over but the first thing she asked was "Do I get paid?" as her eyes narrowed as if she were sizing him up to either sleep with him or kill him.

"Deferred," Curtis commented.

Clara's eyes narrowed further. "What does that mean?"

"Once we're done with the job. We turn it in; we get paid," Curtis offered.

"How much?"

"Don't know."

Clara shook her head. "You don't know? You don't know much, do you?"

"I don't," Curtis admitted without a bit of irony. "Like I don't know why the women want your help. I don't understand what value you'd bring to this operation. Do you even know how to use a sewing machine? Thread a goddamn needle?"

Finally, Clara let a sliver of a smile slip onto her lips. "You see the size of my husband?"

Off Curtis's nonresponse, Clara chuckled. "I carried that man. In every way. Gave him six kids. I'm sure he has other little bastards running around, but I gave him six. None of his clothes the police department gave him ever fit right. He was big. Everywhere. I tailored every shirt, every pair of pants. There was underwear I bought him I had to add size to. My six kids wore things I made. Even though he was a cop, he spent his money. What happens when you have other women and other families. What was left, I got. So yeah, I know how to thread a goddamn needle. I know how to run a goddamn sewing machine. If this job is sewing, shit, I'm gonna be good at it."

Curtis kept his mouth shut. He had to take her at her word. He stood up and stuck out his cell phone to her.

"Put your phone number in there. So, I can get hold of you without coming here," he said, wanting to go.

Clara did. But as he reached for his phone, Clara pulled it back.

"You fucking that little Asian doll?" she asked.

"Yeah," Curtis answered with unvarnished distain.

Clara sniffed the air like it was putrid. "You should be ashamed. All the beautiful black girls in the world. Looking for a solid black man. You wonder why we all end up with shitty men? Because our men go off and find themselves someone they ain't. Someone impressed with your blackness. Not that I think you're a good man or will take care of the little Asian doll. But I don't know if she much cares, she got your blackness. Exotic to her," Clara simmered, adding, "and we get the rest."

Curtis held his gaze on Clara for a moment, the lines in her face almost deepening before his eyes. He held out his hand again for his phone. Once she handed it to him, he called Clara's phone. "There. You got my phone. I'll call you. You already know where Deanna lives. That's where they are working. Make arrangements for your kids. The days are going to be long 'til we're done with this job. I don't want to be calling you or coming by here to find you. If I have to be after you, you're done. So as soon as you have things squared away, show up. You'll go to work," he said, before walking out.

****

As her phone rang, Candy almost answered it, believing it was Curtis. Luckily, she looked before she swiped. Ramona. Shit. She'd forgotten about her after they were kidnapped in front of Ramona's home and the plethora of madness that had happened since. Candy didn't want to speak to her. Not now, not in the middle of trying to keep Deanna awake, alert, and motivated to get these gowns done before the deadline. The first one Deanna finished with Izzy's assistance was breathtaking, and so close in design and finishes you wouldn't know it was a copy. But in Candy's estimation, just like Deanna had done with the blouses she copied, this gown was weirdly, intrinsically, better than the original. Candy couldn't solve just why, but when she compared the two gowns, Deanna's work was simply an upgrade.

Only there were two more duplicates of that gown and then two more gowns to duplicate in three different sizes still to be finished. And neither Candy nor Ava trusted themselves enough with scissors or a sewing machine to help. They had been sent enough material to create the three gowns with maybe enough for one extra gown...but maybe not. So Deanna knew that any mistake would cause her more sleepless nights. And it was obvious to the others that Deanna, who was not afraid of hard work, had never worked under this sort of brutal schedule before. Struggle and toil were not foreign to Deanna, but this was different. The concentration, the acumen, the eye, each skill had to be firing on all cylinders. And there weren't enough energy drinks at the Seven-Eleven to keep this on schedule.

When Curtis arrived and relayed what had happened with Clara, Ava and Candy made it clear: get her over here now. Curtis tried to speak up about his reservations, but Ava and Candy shouted him down. "If that bitch can sew, we need her. I'll hand her a hundred bucks when she gets here. But get her ass over here now. We have to do what we can to help Deanna, before she completely shuts down," Ava insisted.

Candy opted to go with Curtis to pick up Clara. On the way back, Candy sat in the back seat with Clara and explained what they were doing. That it was going to be a lot of work in a limited amount of time. But if she came through for them, Candy promised her a thousand dollars, a hundred when she arrived. Clara was in, and just as quickly got on the phone with her oldest daughter. "You got the kids until I'm done with this job. No bullshit. I don't want to hear about you sneaking out on them, and that son-of-a-bitch you call a boyfriend is not allowed in the house without me there."

Clara was so stern, she scared Candy.

When they got to Deanna's, Ava slapped a hundred dollars "good faith money" into Clara's open hand. Deanna explained what she needed from Clara and Clara jumped right in. Maybe not knowing the pressure they were under and how expensive the gowns were that they were copying helped, but Clara was cool under fire, her mood lightening extensively until Ava commented to Candy, "Fuck, she's actually nice to be around."

Twenty-eight hours before the deadline, all nine gowns were complete. And better, they looked and felt "better than exact," which is how Candy phrased it. As she boxed up each gown with Candy's help, Ava couldn't figure out how Deanna did what she did, and more, how the copies were so ridiculously similar to the originals yet even she could see that Deanna's were just a touch more beautiful. 'That's fucking art,' Ava thought as she taped the top of one of the boxes shut, 'Deanna is a fucking artist too fucking broke and broken to realize it.'

Once everything was ready to be shipped, Curtis called Martin to have the gowns picked up. But Martin instructed them to meet him at the hangar at Chesterfield Airport at four that afternoon. He would fly in and take possession of the gowns. While being back at the place where they thought they all might die didn't sit well with Ava, she needed to know exactly how much money Martin would hand them for the work they did, and what he expected next. But this time, she wasn't going without being armed. 'Fool me once...' Ava thought as she devised a way to strap her small gun to her ankle using a cut-up pair of pantyhose.

Deanna, Izzy, and Clara spread themselves across the floor of Deanna's apartment, eating chips, drinking light beers, drained, giggly, and relieved. Deanna kept muttering that she wasn't getting out of bed for a week. Curtis ran out and bought four bottles of champagne, popping the first as he came through the door upon his return. Deanna wanted to cry. She couldn't feel her fingertips. Nor could she remember ever working that diligently for that long. And as reluctant as Izzy was having a fifth woman in the group, she couldn't deny that Clara was a far greater asset than her sister, or Candy or herself. Clara busted her ass over the week and a half that she worked with them, even rallying the women when they were completely overwhelmed. "Listen bitches, I need that thousand dollars. We ain't stopping. So, pull your big girl panties out of your tight little twats and let's finish," Clara demanded just two days prior at a low moment, when Deanna had broken down into tears, fearing they would not finish on time.

Izzy put on music and the women pulled themselves up and danced. Clara remembered when she was young and out at the clubs. She'd work a full shift at the hospital, sometimes two, and then slip on her tightest dress and go dancing all night, until she entered a state that surpassed exhaustion, where everything was a heady high and stupidly funny. As the women emptied the four bottles of champagne, they howled with laughter, trying to out-dance each other to the hoots and catcalls from each other. Finally, Deanna collapsed in a heap on her saggy sofa. She wasn't getting up. Looking up at her friends, she muttered, "You all can let yourselves out," and she curled up with a pillow, closing her eyes.

"Let her sleep," Clara said to the others, giving Curtis a nod, silently asking for a ride home. The other women did as Deanna asked and followed them out. The silence enveloped Deanna, allowing her to fall deeply and entirely asleep for the first time in a week and a half.

Curtis dropped Clara off at her home, vowing to come by once they were paid and hand her the money she was promised. "You don't, I'll find you," vowed Clara. And Curtis knew she would.

The women arrived at the hangar in Curtis's car and Izzy's truck, the gowns bagged, boxed and stacked one on top of the other in the back seat of Izzy's truck. Martin's plane was already there. They stepped out, Curtis helping Izzy unload the gowns as Martin stepped from his private plane.

"Good to see you all," Martin announced with a smile. Two men waited behind him at the entrance to the small jet.

"I hope nothing happened to any of the originals," he said.

"They're just as they were when we got them," Ava answered.

Martin nodded at the two men, and they removed a rolling clothing rack from the jet, moved to the boxes, cutting them open. Ava couldn't help but reach down and pretend to scratch her leg, feeling the gun she had tied in pantyhose just above her ankle. One by one, the men removed the garment bags and unzipped them, taking out the gowns and placing them on the rack. The three separate designs were all placed together. Once they were all on the rack, Martin stepped over quickly, pulling on a pair of latex gloves and took his time inspecting each of them.

"This is exquisite work. Remarkable, actually. No wonder they did not catch you ladies," Martin stated. "The clients will be ecstatic."

Nodding to one of the men, he returned to the jet and came out with an attaché case as the other man re-bagged each of the gowns carefully. Setting the attaché on the floor of the hanger, almost exactly where Santos died, he popped the locks and opened it. Piled neatly inside were stacks of cash.

"Ten thousand dollars. Each," Martin announced. "Thank you, ladies, and gentleman. I'll be in touch."

As the men carried the gowns into the jet, Deanna, looking like she had just gotten up, which she had just before Curtis helped her down the stairs and into his car, took a step towards Martin. "There's a problem," she blurted out, causing Martin to turn.

"There's someone else. She's part of our team now," Deanna continued, tired enough to be completely direct. "We need to pay her, too."

"That wasn't our deal and I'm not pleased someone else knows about this," Martin snapped.

"She already knew," Deanna replied. "We killed her husband. The policeman. Santos's guy. She knew we were involved with something," Deanna explained.

"Well, if you need her, that's up to you. There are five of you. Figure it out," Martin responded, continuing towards the jet.

That was not the answer that Deanna wanted to hear. "Hold on!" she called to Martin. "This woman is going to be part of our team. We need her. We'll cover her this time. But from now on, she needs to get paid too."

Turning around fully to face Deanna, Martin's eyes stayed on her as if everyone else had disappeared. The longer he remained silent, the more Deanna and the others grew unnerved. Despite her discomfort, Deanna's exhaustion caused her to stand her ground, her gaze locked on him. He could afford another person. And she couldn't afford to lose Clara.

"You want to renegotiate our deal?" Martin asked

Deanna's bloodshot eyes glanced at the other women and Curtis. Ava's hand ready to drop down to her ankle.

"I didn't know we had a deal. We never discussed what that would be. This felt more like some kind of test. Which we wouldn't have finished without Clara. You want us to perform, to make you money, especially in the time you gave us, which, by the way, was ridiculous. We busted our asses. I'm so fucking tired I can't feel my arms. I have a family. A little boy. He needs me. They need me. They deserve better. We all do. You want us to do this? You need to understand that we're going to need help. And that those people are going to have to be taken care of too," Deanna stated, never pleading. Through her delirium, this seemed like common sense to her.

Martin smiled. "You're very, very lucky," he responded, turning again towards the jet.

Deanna's forehead furrowed as she pulled her hair off her face abruptly. "Lucky? What? What does that mean?"

Signaling the men to carry the rack into the jet ahead of him, Martin said over his shoulder, "That you're gifted at what you do."

Those were his last words before he climbed the steps into the jet and disappeared. Once the steps were pulled into the jet and it rolled out of the hangar, the women sighed collectively as Curtis laughed. "You got balls, Deanna," he stated, causing every one of them to laugh. Tensely.

Deanna shook her head. "I'm too tired and don't care. Now get me home and don't nobody knock on my door tomorrow."

****

On the ride back, they pitched in five hundred a piece for Clara, making her cut twenty-five hundred dollars. Stopping by her house together, the women presented her with the cash, which caused Clara to break down sobbing.

"The police are giving me a hard time 'bout collecting death benefits. Making it out that Marcus killed himself. Such bullshit," she sobbed. "You bitches...thank you."

"Won't be the end. They'll be more if you want to work with us," Ava stated.

Clara sobbed harder. "Thank you, Jesus! Fuck, yes. Fuck yes, fuck yes, fuck yes!" She crowed as she waved all of them to come to her, wrapping her arms around them tightly. This was the first time in a long time that Clara could see a way out. Marcus's death opened the door, but Clara believed this was God stepping in, and she was grateful for 'another door opening'.

****

As Curtis dropped Deanna at her apartment, Candy kissed her friend's cheek. "Sugar, you were a rock star. Get some sleep," she told her.

Watching to make sure Deanna made it through her apartment door, Curtis pulled the car out as Candy looked at her phone. There were eleven missed calls and four messages. All from Ramona. Pulling the phone to her ear, Candy listened. As she did, a disturbed expression remained locked on her face.

"What's going on?" Curtis questioned.

Candy pulled the phone from her ear and put it on speaker. "Damn it, Candy, how dare you ignore me! I thought I was clear about what I expected!" Ramona's voice cawed, the cadence of her words shrill and pointed. "I'm calling the police. Letting them know what you and your friend are doing. You are working for me, dear. I can move your otherwise worthless merchandise. Call me. By tomorrow. Or I will call the police!"

Candy's eyes locked with Curtis's. "That bitch," she muttered, furiously frightened.

Curtis remained silent for the rest of the ride back to his place. When he pulled into the driveway, he didn't turn off the car as Candy stepped out. Confused, she looked back in at him, unsure. "Curtis...?"

"Her address. Give it to me," is all he said.

GOING DOWN

Deanna's living room was still a complete mess of scrap fabric, smashed boxes, spools of thread, empty cans of energy drinks and fast-food containers. She would clean that later, but after putting her nine-ty-five-hundred dollars in the bank, she wanted to sit and relish the moment. This was the first time she'd ever had that kind of money in her checking account. She could pay back rent, pay back bills, and still have enough left over to survive until whatever came next. She had done it. She had gotten her family out of debt. She didn't want to cry but since she was too tired to celebrate, she did. She actually had money in the bank.

Right now, though, all Deanna wanted to do was hug her kids. Seeing that she still had tears in her eyes, Ford wrapped his arms around his mother tightly, knowing his mother had completed something difficult, but he was clueless as to how difficult and exhausting it was. Or how deadly it could have been. And he didn't know she had over a thousand dollars cash in her dresser drawer. The ten thousand was the most money Deanna could remember ever holding in her hand at one time, a hand that shook as Curtis piled the cash into it.

"Thanks for putting up with me these last two weeks," she said to her children, her voice cracking.

"You were psycho. You and the rest of your sewing circle," Kevin said as he threw a backpack over his shoulder and told his mother he was going to a friend's to get a report done, kissing her on the cheek.

"Mom," Tracee stated with concern, "you know you can't do that all the time. It'll kill you."

Deanna assured her it wouldn't be all the time before adding, "But I made some money, and tomorrow night we are going out to dinner. Everybody up for Golden Corral?"

Kevin stopped at the apartment door, spinning back towards his mother. "Serious?"

Deanna laughed, nodding.

"That's a lot of money for all of us to eat there. Kevin and I don't get the kids' price anymore," Tracee stated.

Waving away her concern, Deanna's smile widened. "Let me worry about that."

"Fuckin' A," Kevin barked, happy, "count me in! I hope it's prime rib night!"

He disappeared out the door, as happy about his home life as he could remember for quite a while. Even better, he was not heading over to a friend's place to work on a report. Kevin was dashing over to Izzy's. Having her in his house every day for the last few weeks, unable to sneak away even for a few minutes, made him completely horny. Even with Cassie there too often, giving him stink-eye. Kevin spent the last two weeks jerking off in his room to fantasies of climbing atop Izzy's naked body. He was rushing over to her place to do just that and now he was going to his favorite place to eat! 'Life's fucking awesome,' he thought, dashing down the block on a run.

****

"What are you going to do?" Candy demanded, not letting go of the car door.

Curtis refused to answer, staring straight ahead.

"Curtis!" Candy pleaded with him to speak.

"Take care of it," Curtis said, emphasizing each word. "It's that, or I call Mr. Collique and let him know."

"No!" Candy snapped, shaking her head as she leaned into the car. She didn't know what else to say to Curtis. There was no suitable solution to this problem. Ramona would continue to be a thorn in their side. Or worse. And if she followed through on her threat, hellfire could rain down on all of them. Ramona felt she was being edged out of this little enterprise, and she wasn't letting that happen. She felt they were obligated to honor the deal they made. But that deal was dead and gone. Usurped by Martin and grander expectations. With grander paydays. Candy slid back into the passenger seat and thumbed in Ramona's address on the GPS. She said nothing as she climbed back out of the car, shut the door, and watched Curtis pull away.

****

Pissed off that Izzy turned down her offer to go out and get drunk, and Candy went home with Curtis, Ava accepted she'd be drinking alone. She knew better than to ask Deanna. Deanna deserved to crawl into bed and not get up for days. It was the first time she'd been back in the bar where she got reacquainted with Santos. She thought of sliding into the back booth, like she did with Candy, but she was alone and didn't want to take up that space in case a couple came in and wanted some privacy, so she plopped into a seat at the bar.

As she quickly downed her first drink, she waved at the bartender. "Get me another, Matt," she called out, surprised she remembered his name. Vodka did that to her.

"Am I going to have to call you an Uber?" Matt asked, only half-joking.

"Probably," Ava answered.

As he set the screwdriver down on the bar, Matt smiled. "You were pretty serious with Santos Rivera, weren't you?"

Before she could stop herself, she reacted to Santos' name. She wished she hadn't but the question caught her off-guard. Opening her mouth to respond, Ava was still searching for the words. "We broke up," was all she was willing to reveal, relieved she didn't say more.

"You know where he's been? He's a regular. Hasn't been in, in at least a week, probably longer. Didn't say nothing about going on vacation or anything," Matt stated.

Ava tried to shut down the conversation with an indifferent shrug. "Probably shacked up with a new bitch."

"You know, they pulled his friend out of the fucking river. Remember the cop he hung out with?" Matt continued, not taking Ava's obvious apathy at face value. "Big black guy? Marcus? Scary guy."

"Yeah. I remember," was Ava's answer. "Never talked much."

"Can you believe he was a cop here in the city?" Matt chuckled, his elbows settling on the bar, his chin resting on his knuckles. "Jesus, I'd hate to have that big motherfucker come after me."

'Oh shit, this guy's hitting on me,' Ava thought, her mood brightening. She'd never really looked at Matt before. He had one of those amiable faces, neither good looking nor bad looking enough to remember. Pleasant enough, with literally not one memorable feature. Medium build. Brown hair. Brown eyes. 'Wow. He would make the perfect criminal,' Ava thought. 'He's completely average. Nobody'd remember him. Looks like a thousand other guys.'

But the liquor was hitting Ava, making her bolder and more desperate to change the conversation. "What makes you special, Matt?" Ava quizzed.

"Huh?" his face screwed up like she asked him to bend over and cough.

"What makes you different? From other guys. Every guy's got, like, I dunno, one superpower. Some reason for women to want to sleep with him. I'm trying to figure out what's yours since I'm trying to decide whether or not to have sex with you," Ava said before downing half the screwdriver.

Matt had to think about it. His head shook as he stood there in silence, nothing coming to him.

"Can't think of any reason a woman would want to sleep with me," Matt commented with a dispirited shrug of his shoulders. "But I guess my superpower is I'm gay, so I don't give a shit if women want to sleep with me or not. Guys aren't as discriminating. Even guys like me get fucked. A lot."

He laughed as he walked away from Ava. She had to join him, laughing even harder than he did.

****

Lying back in her bed, Izzy pulled the pillows under her head. After the last couple weeks, just being in her own bed felt amazing. Even better was having Kevin between her legs, going down on her. She knew it would piss him off if she fell asleep, so she kept her mind on the pleasure she was receiving. From his surprising eagerness servicing her, Izzy realized that fourteen days with no sex was harder on him than her. What she wanted was for Kevin to spend the night. It's rare she wanted any man to sleep in her bed. But tonight, Izzy craved the sensation of being held. Someone to nuzzle against. A warm, hard body to wrap their arms around her. But she knew Kevin not only wouldn't. He couldn't. Too many questions. Crawling up her body, Kevin's hands slid up her arms, pinning them over her head. He kissed her hungrily. Looking down at her, his eyes announced he wanted to ask her something.

"What?" she said, as he massaged his groin against hers.

"What you're doing with my mom—"

"After two weeks of no sex, you're going to bring up your mom?" Izzy huffed.

"It's illegal. Isn't it?" Kevin continued.

Izzy could feel her chastising Kevin didn't kill his hard-on. "Yeah," was all she said, his nose brushing against hers.

Kevin kissed her again, this time with even more passion. She slithered her tongue into his mouth as he reached down and slid himself into her. "That's hot," he groaned as he pounded on her, his hands going to the headboard behind her as she pulled her legs up around him and let him do the work until they both came.

As he dressed before he made his way back home, Izzy curled up with the pillows and looked at his body. He was beautiful. His body was long, muscled, tight. Spying her watching him, Kevin smiled. And he had a smile that could melt icebergs. Izzy mused that Kevin was too good looking to be born as poor as he was. And unless he went through the windshield of a car, his looks more than baseball, were going to carry him through life. 'This kid is going to spend his entire time in college getting laid,' Izzy thought. Not that high school was much different.

Izzy knew when Kevin left for college, she was going to miss him. She'd never tell him that. This was never supposed to be more than her hooking up with a younger stud and the great sex that came along with that. Izzy assured herself she didn't have feelings for Kevin, not in the traditional sense. But she wanted something good for him. She knew she could never be that thing, even if they were closer in age and weren't connected through Deanna. It wasn't her. Coaxing a young man into her bed was her. Anything more, Izzy didn't find appealing, even in fantasy. If her life could just be about sex, Kevin and she would be the perfect couple. In the real world, he was nothing more than a young, pretty, eager guy who was good in bed that she couldn't mention to anyone.

Kevin hustled home. Two weeks without him and Izzy hooking up had been unbearable. He got a blow job from Theresa McGee within the last week. She drove him home from practice and they pulled onto a side street about a block from his apartment. She wanted to. And Kevin was more than happy to oblige, even though he thought she wasn't very good at it. While she was trying to throat him, he kept his hand on the back of her head, while he wondered if every seventeen-year-old guy thought about sex as much as he did. Or if he was some sort of sex addict. Not that if he was, it would bother him. Kevin found being horny all the time exhilarating. The conquest of getting laid or blown fulfilled him on a level even baseball couldn't. And while baseball could get him into college, and maybe into the minors or if he had a few great seasons, the majors, Kevin knew that it was his secret hope that it would increase his sexual gravity.

"Maybe I am a sex addict," Kevin said out loud, laughing, as he started jogging back towards his home, getting a hard-on again as he thought about going down on Izzy.

****

After driving by the house and walking past it twice, Curtis parked his car three blocks away from Ramona's and slipped down the alley behind her home, cutting through a tall hedge to come up along the side of her house, hoping the people with the barking dog would think it was just a raccoon raiding garbage cans. Curtis still wasn't sure what he was going to do. He just knew he had to do something because if this woman screwed up what they had going on, Collique would murder them all.

'Rich, white, privileged women,' Curtis thought. He'd dealt with their harpy classism all his life. St. Louis possessed more than their fair share of upper-middle-class, suburban women either raised with an ugly sense of entitlement or married into it. These women expected things to be the way they saw them, and even worse, "the way they've always been." While working security at the bank, daily, Curtis heard these women through the walls. Complaining about having to stand in line. About how busy they were. How valuable their time was. About not feeling appreciated as a customer. That there were perks the bank should offer them. This was how they conducted their lives; constructing their worlds so that any bristled edges they could bump against that might toss them back to the reality everyone else lived in, had been chiseled to a soft, dull lip. They took pride in being the epicenter of the world they created for themselves. Or, as Curtis's ex-wife, Naomi, used to call them, "ignorant, selfish nothing bitches who suffer from GES, Generational Entitlement Syndrome."

Slipping on a pair of gloves, Curtis glanced through the kitchen door window. He couldn't see an alarm system hooked to the windows, but he had to believe Ramona had the house wired. From what Candy told him about this woman, she wasn't haphazard. And while her tony neighborhood wasn't dangerous, like many of the older, expensive neighborhoods in St. Louis, it wasn't far away from crime. A wealthy, older woman living in an enormous home alone, Ramona had to feel vulnerable to predators. Stepping up atop the recycle bin, Curtis muscled his way up to the roof over the kitchen. Padding softly to the back of the house, Curtis pulled himself up to the pitched roof of the two-story home, where the bedroom windows were located. He knew he'd find an unlocked window. Older homes settled, and even the most fastidious homeowner had a window that no longer locked. Three windows down, he found one ever-so-slight ajar. Shimmying open the window, he slid inside. The bedroom was now a craft room, tables loaded with fabric and whatnots for creating things her kids would toss in the trash once she died. Curtis pulled on a mask and took the gun from his waistband before stepping from the room.

The fireplace poker swung at his head. Able to get his forearm up quick enough to prevent the blow from hitting him in the face, the gun flew from his hand and clattered across the wood floor. Ramona yanked back the poker to swing again, but Curtis caught her by the wrist with his free hand as the poker grazed his shoulder. His hand then shot up to her throat, and he grasped her tightly, running her backward, her feet dragging as she couldn't get her heels down to stop him from almost carrying her by her neck.

"I know who you are," Ramona croaked as she smashed her fists against Curtis' arm, trying to get him to release his grip on her throat. "That black boyfriend of Candy's! She tell you to do this!? She tell you what trouble she's in with me?! I hope she enjoys visiting you in prison! You triggered the alarm. Police are on their way, you stupid nigger!"

"Greet them at the door," Curtis growled as he reached the top of the stairwell leading to the first floor and flung

Ramona down the steps. She flew down almost the entire flight before hitting the hardwood with a gruesome thud, her head slamming off the stairs as her body tumbled the rest of the way down until she landed in a broken heap on the tile floor at the entrance of the house.

Curtis stared down as blood pooled around Ramona's head. Catching his breath, horror and regret festered in Curtis' eyes. Step by step, he backed away from the top of the stairwell until he found his gun. Picking it up, he moved back into the craft room and out the window. Shimmying the window back down, Curtis jumped off the roof, rushing back through the hedges, past the barking dog, and down the alley, pulling off his hood before ripping off his gloves. He drove the speed limit all the way home, not taking a chance of a St. Louis cop pulling him over for 'driving while black'. Curtis knew that if the police pulled him over, his guilt might tsunami his better sense and he'd confess to a murder they didn't know yet had even happened.

THE KNOCKOUT PUNCH

Vince watched Tracee striding down the hallway towards him. She was by herself. She almost always was. And he was grateful for that fact. It meant that Tracee didn't have many close friends. Which meant there wouldn't be any late-night slumber party confessions. Vince liked the lonely girls. The girls with problems at home. They gravitated towards him and easily consumed his line of bullshit.

Seeing him, Tracee smiled, her pace quickening. Forget boys her age, Vince was so good-looking. Especially with stubble along his jawline. Even better, he was a man. The difference in their ages didn't bother Tracee. If she was going to have sex, she'd rather it be with a man, someone who knew how to take care of her, rather than some fumbling boy making her first time a tragedy rather than something memorable. She lowered the books in her arms, making sure they did not cover her breasts, as she stepped towards him. "Mr. Cunello, can I pick your brain a minute?" Tracee asked with a coy smile.

Vince waved her into his classroom and led her around the wall into his office area. As soon as they were out of sight, Tracee leaned up and kissed Vince. Her lips hitting his hard, surprising him. But he was never a man to resist stimulation. Vince's tongue immediately slithered into her mouth, his hands gliding over her breasts to her waist before he yanked her body against his abruptly, needing to press her breasts against him, pushing a thigh between her legs, letting her ride it.

"See what you do to me," he huffed out with a chuckle as his hands slid down along her breasts until he grabbed her hand and led it to the bulge in his sweatpants.

"No more," Vince whispered, pulling away from her to peek around the wall. He had to be sure no students had quietly walked into the classroom. "I can't teach class with a hard-on," he added, almost to himself, pushing his penis down as best he could to hide it along his leg, untucking his shirt to cover it.

Tracee smirked, feeling empowered by the fact that she could excite him so quickly.

"Tonight. Can you get out of your house? I want you alone. Not here." Vince requested, knowing she was willing and it was time to consummate his next conquest.

"My mom...she doesn't really let me go out."

"Tell her you're going over to a friend's house to study. I'll pick you up somewhere else," Vince suggested.

"I don't know if I can—"

"Are you serious about being with me or are you just a tease?" Vince asked, cutting her off. "If you want to be with me, let's do this. Tonight. Because I got to have you."

A deep breath trapped in Tracee's chest. She couldn't breathe in, she couldn't breathe out. She'd fantasized about this moment. This man wanting her as much as she wanted him. Tracee wasn't some stupid girl. She grasped how terribly wrong everything was that she said, did, or planned on doing, with this man. But the more taboo it became, the more she wished all of it to occur. She understood that Vince thought he was seducing her, but in Tracee's reality, which was closer to reality than Vince's, she felt in charge of everything that was happening between them. She knew he wasn't very intuitive. Like her brother. Generic jocks. Incapable of thinking past the end of a bat, or the end of their dicks, while Tracee thought long game. No one had ever made her feel like Vince did. She didn't want to call it love, she was smart enough to know it wasn't that, and even if it was, which she assured herself it wasn't, she didn't even know what that should feel like anyway. And she didn't care. Love, not love, it didn't matter. This made her feel electric. Like nothing ever had in her life. And that was enough for Tracee.

Vince smirked. "Give me your phone. I'll put my number in under a different name. You can text me."

Embarrassed, Tracee's face coiled up. "I don't have a phone," she lamented, grabbing a piece of paper off his desk. Tracee scribbled something on the paper and handed it to him. "I have a gmail account my mom doesn't know about it. Use that. I'll keep checking it. But I'm going to get out of my house tonight."

Using his phone, Vince emailed Tracee at her hidden account from his private e-mail. "Done. Now you have mine."

Tracee took a step towards Vince again, but the sound of students entering the classroom on the other side of the wall stopped her. She smiled, whispering, "I promise, I'll get out of my house tonight," before her smile disappeared and she audibly said for the students already in Vince's classroom, "Thank you, Mr. Cunello," before she rounded the wall and walked through towards the door, pushing through the students entering.

After a moment, Vince also rounded the wall and stepped into the class, greeting his entering students. But his mind stayed with Tracee. What he was doing, not just with her but with the litany of girls, fed his ego and his undernourished need for power, but there was a narrow shaving of his soul that felt some current of shame. He didn't know exactly how young Tracee was, but he suspected she was the youngest girl he intended to conquer. Watching as all the kids flooded through the door as the bell rang, Vince wondered if he'd ever again have an actual relationship with an adult woman. If that could ever satisfy him? Would he get married, have children? And even if he did would he still be trolling for some pliable young girl who thought he was something special? What sort of man did this? 'One day I'll go to prison for this,' he thought, 'and I deserve it.' But he knew he couldn't stop. Or more aptly, wouldn't.

"Excuse me a second," Vince announced to his class before stepping out. He jogged down the hallway to the bathroom, crashed into a stall, and threw up.

****

Hugging the side of the bed away from where Candy slept, Curtis barely closed his eyes. Candy didn't ask him what had happened, but she knew whatever it was, it was already haunting Curtis. She crawled out of bed and shuffled into the bathroom. 'He'll tell me when he's ready,' she thought, knowing he was already awake but still giving her his back. Turning on the water in the shower, a wave of guilt roiled over Candy. She felt she was to blame for pulling Curtis in this deep. He'd saved them from Marcus. And now he saved them from Ramona. As he heard the shower door close, Curtis pulled himself from the bed. He went to the door of the bathroom and watched her shower. There was something so insanely tantalizing about Candy's body, and with water streaming down from her jet black hair to the olive skin on her back, he craved her. With what he had done the night before, Curtis accepted that his only escape from his remorse was losing himself in her.

Opening the shower door, Curtis stepped in. Candy turned to face him, making him only want her more. Curtis' hand went to her face, their eyes locked. "Ramona is dead," Curtis admitted.

Candy hid her trepidation and slid her body against his, wrapping her arms around him. Her man needed to know that she understood that this was the only way to solve this problem. Ramona wasn't going to go away with a warning. She would make their life hell. She had already started. Candy rationalized that Ramona sealed her own fate. She thought she was in control. But Martin was. Again, Curtis kept the women alive. "Are you okay?" Candy asked.

Curtis's hands slipped under her ass and lifted her up, gently laying her back against the wall as she guided him into her.

"I don't want to talk about it. I don't want to talk about anything," he said, his lips going to hers. "Less you know, the better..."

They stayed in the shower until the water went cold.

****

Deanna walked through her home, piling small scraps of cloth, thread, empty energy drinks, and fast-food containers into a trash bag. She held a stale mug of coffee in her hand, too tired to make a fresh pot. Deanna slept long enough for the kids to all get off to school by themselves, but it wasn't a restful sleep. She had passed out rather than fallen asleep. But she needed to make the apartment feel like home again rather than a factory. For herself as well as her kids. But a knock at her door caused Deanna to freeze. She'd been through enough that when anyone she wasn't expecting knocked on her door, Deanna was spooked. Setting down the bag of trash, she silently tip-toed to the door and placed her foot against the back of it. Opening the door a crack, Deanna peeked out. Clara stood at the door with two Starbucks coffees, one in each hand. Pulling the door open wide, Deanna smiled. "What are you doing here?" she asked.

"Figured you could use one of these. Not a big fan of their coffee, but they were on the way," Clara joked.

Taking a coffee from Clara, Deanna stepped back to allow her in. "Better than my day-old brew," she said, setting the coffee mug down and taking a sip of the Starbucks. "Thank you so much."

"Shit is so hot," Clara said after taking a drink. "I think it's to hide the bitterness."

Laughing, the flavor of the coffee was a godsend to Deanna. She loved the bite of Starbucks coffee. And the hotter the better.

"I figured you'd need help getting your place in order. My way of saying thank you for what you all gave me. It got me out of a jam," Clara stated.

"I've been there," Deanna replied as they both picked up the mess in the living area and straightened up. "So, the police are hassling your husband's pension, or death benefits, or whatever it is?"

Taking a sip of the scalding coffee, Clara nodded. "They're holding them up. Sayin' Marcus might have committed suicide. Until the investigation is over, I can't collect," admitted Clara.

"Fuckers," Deanna responded, tired.

"Yes, they are. Motherfuckers, actually," Clara answered, causing Deanna to laugh as Clara picked up some of the metal thread they used on three of the gowns. "Those gowns were beautiful. You're good at this, I mean real good," remarked Clara.

Smiling once again, Deanna thanked Clara.

"You know," Clara said, rolling up some of the leftover material. "There's enough material here to make something."

"I thought that too. Don't throw it away. It's expensive stuff. We can do something with it," Deanna agreed.

"Make our own gowns. A prom dress. A formal," Clara added.

Believing she found a kindred spirit in Clara, Deanna reached out and touched her arm. Clara jumped back, startled. "I'm sorry," Deanna said, taking a step back. "I didn't mean..."

Clara forced a smile, embarrassed, waving away Deanna's regret. "It's good. I...I've been through a lot. It's not you. I'm kinda jumpy when people, you know...make contact. Contact for me usually means hurt, you know."

"I get it. For a while my ex- was pretty rough with me," Deanna said, compassion locked in her voice, seeing Clara much clearer now than ever before.

"I don't miss Marcus. Don't miss him at all. Hope he's rotting in hell."

Deanna smiled. She got it. "While we're sitting around waiting for whatever the hell comes next, let's make something out of this material," offered Deanna.

Clara smiled. "Yes, ma'am, let's sew," she said, adding, "Making something from scraps is medicine for the soul."

****

While coffee dripped into the pot, Candy turned on the television. She needed to know if there was anything on the local news about Ramona's death. The local news in the morning was pretty much only good for traffic and weather reports. Nothing came on about a suspicious death in Ramona's neighborhood, which Candy assumed meant that no one had discovered her body yet. She took a long breath in, believing the longer it went before anyone found Ramona, the better off it would be for them. Just then, Erika clambered into the kitchen, tossing her bookbag on the kitchen table. Candy relayed to her that her father wasn't feeling great so he was sleeping in, but that she was happy to make Erika some breakfast.

Looking Candy up and down as if it were the first time she had ever seen her, Erika curled up her face. "I'm fine," Erika said sharply, grabbing an apple from a bowl on the kitchen counter.

"Do you need a ride to school?" Candy asked.

"I'll walk," she answered as she disappeared out the back door.

Candy waited until Erika walked past the window, heading down the driveway before she uttered, "Fuck you. Done with your shit too…"

****

Clara and Deanna sat on chairs side by side, flipping through fashion magazines as they visualized what they would do with the remnants from the gowns that boarded a private jet with Martin.

"How many kids you got?" Deanna asked.

"Six."

Deanna stopped looking at the magazine and turned to Clara. "All Marcus'?"

Clara shrugged, indicating that yes, in fact, they were all Marcus'. And that she wasn't particularly proud of that. Her hate for him resonated even in a shrug. "Did you kill him?" Clara asked so matter-of-factly it scared Deanna a little bit.

Deanna wished she could answer that as directly as Clara asked it. She wanted to say, 'No, he tried to kill me and luckily didn't succeed.' But she didn't want to slap Clara across the face with that tidbit of horror. Nor did Deanna want to relive that night. But Clara's gaze stayed on Deanna, wanting an answer. "No," Deanna said, her eyes going back to the magazine in front of them. "If I could have…" she added, before continuing, "Your husband, Marcus, he broke in and attacked me. I don't think I'd ever been so scared. He would have killed me. And Candy."

"So, it was Curtis," Clara realized.

Deanna didn't respond so Clara took that as a yes. Deanna wasn't going to tell her it was Candy who jammed the heel of her shoe into Marcus' eye.

"Did he die slow?" Clara wanted to know, bitterness almost pouring out of her.

Deanna took her hand. "Not slow enough."

"My only regret," Clara responded, reaching out and squeezing Deanna's hand, "I wasn't the one who killed him."

****

Over the next few days, the women didn't interact much, except for Clara and Deanna, who were determined to create their own gown. And while each thought they were the captain of this ship, somehow this collaboration went smoother than either of them expected. They worked long into the night, which made it easy for Tracee to escape the house for three nights in a row.

She'd dash down the block where Vince would be waiting in his car. Their first night together, he taught her the joys of oral sex. Giving and receiving. She was a little rough on the giving, but Vince still loved watching her struggle to take as much as she could. The second night, he penetrated her, taking it slow, relishing teaching his new student how to "make love," as Vince cooed in Tracee's ear. Her young, ample body, her large round breasts were exactly as Vince had imagined, rocketing his desire. The third night, he took a half of a Viagra so he could continue for hours, making Tracee orgasm a half dozen times over the four hours they were together.

Laying across his flat stomach, feeling his chest rise and fall with each breath, Tracee was dizzy from everything that had happened in the last three days. She couldn't remember feeling more fulfilled. Different. She'd heard the girls in the bathroom yammering about their first time, how horrible it was, how happy they were it was over. But Tracee dreamed this would last forever. She didn't pick some high school tuba player to shove his penis into her. Tracee selected a man who knew what he was doing. Unlike so many other girls, at least from the conversations she overheard at school, Tracee didn't want her first time to be something she regretted.

As he stroked her hair, Tracee wouldn't allow herself to believe Vince loved her, though after having sex she wanted to. Not that she knew what love from a man should feel like. She'd never had it. Not even from her father. But Vince, no. There's no way he could love her. She knew he wasn't capable, and that she wasn't his first high school girl. Just the latest. The sister of his star baseball player. Tracee knew there would be an end to this. She just hoped it wouldn't be soon. Not until she was ready for it to be over. Tracee accepted that Vince would tire of her and be eyeing his next victim. And she would eventually learn everything she could from a sexy but immature and narcissistic, predatory man, and would ultimately have to find someone more grownup and less vain to teach her about love. She wouldn't cry. Or threaten Vince with exposure. She would just smile at him as she passed his classroom, remembering her first time. Everything they did would stay their secret. Not because he demanded it, but because she did.

Tracee believed that where Vince was in life was as far as he would ever get. Even at her young age, Tracee recognized Vince had already peaked. While her world was opening, Vince's was stuck forever coaching high school baseball. Or to use terminology Vince could relate to, he was never getting off second base. But right now, in this moment, she wanted to lie on this man's stomach and pretend he could love her and she could be in love with him. Relishing the thrill of what had happened over the last three nights. Tracee smiled, knowing that in ten years, she'd have great stories to tell.

****

Ava had been to a spa once in her life and didn't really find much pleasure in it. She didn't like strangers touching her. Especially women. But today, being able to pay for it made this a delight for Ava. A facial, manicure, pedicure, massage. She earned it. When her phone rang, she grabbed it, hoping it was one of the girls so she could crow about where she was.

The phone read: Martin.

Ava froze. She weirdly felt he could see her. That he knew where she was and what she was doing. He was calling to scold her about wasting her money on frivolous bullshit.

"Hello..." Ava reluctantly answered.

She listened. Her eyes shifted around the room, looking for anyone who might be spying on her. But there was no one.

"Okay. When?" she responded to whatever Martin was saying.

Nodding, Ava finished the call by saying, "I'll be there."

****

The gown, while piecemealed, was gorgeous. And all from the leftovers. Clara twirled as she held it against her body, laughing.

"We have a fucking talent!" Clara cried with glee.

Deanna howled, clapping as Clara strutted across the room, still holding the dress to her body. "Now, what are we going to do with this?" Clara asked.

"Sell it," Deanna answered as if she wondered why Clara would ask.

"To who? How?"

"I don't care. We'll put it on eBay or Craigslist if we have to. But we're going to sell this and pocket a little cash," Deanna insisted as her phone rang.

Seeing it was Martin, Deanna's demeanor changed. She told Clara she had to take the call and disappeared down the hallway into her bedroom, closing the door. Setting the gown on the back of the sofa, Clara instantly recognized that while she was on the 'ins' with Deanna, she wasn't on the 'ins' with whatever the operation was that they just finished. She was still the 'hired help.'

Deanna hung up with Martin. She quickly called Candy.

"Did you just get a call---" Deanna asked but was cut off by Candy.

"From Martin. Yes." Candy answered.

"Have you talked to---" again, Candy cut Deanna off before she finished her sentence.

"Ava. Yes. She'll be there. So will Izzy."

"Do you know what this is---"

"About?" Candy asked.

Smiling, Deanna asked, "You going to answer all my questions---"

"Before you finish asking them? Yes," Candy laughed. "We'll all be there. Together. But I have no idea why he's back in St. Louis and why he wants to see us at a different place. I don't like it."

Neither did Deanna. She needed to Google the location. Make sure it wasn't a landfill. Or some abandoned dead-end street in North City.

Making an excuse why she had to leave, Deanna promised Clara they would get together again soon. Clara didn't question it, keeping her disappointment hidden. Her place in this hierarchy was clear. But as she walked back to her car, Clara made a promise to herself. This was going to change. She had kids to feed too. Six of them. Kids that deserved a future as much as Deanna's kids. And with Marcus gone, all this mattered more to Clara than it did before they found him at the bottom of the Mississippi River. Clara had relied on her savvy and wits most of her life. She knew how to ingratiate herself into places where she wanted to be. She would make herself invaluable to Deanna and the others if necessary. Make sure the person pulling the strings knew she was more important to whatever this operation was than the others, even if it meant cutting out some of the other women.

****

Stepping from her truck, Izzy sidled up between Candy and Ava. Curtis stood back by Deanna. The address Martin gave them was a cul-de-sac where new-build homes had recently been erected. They all looked similar. Modern, especially in South City, where brick bungalows, shotgun row homes, and multifamily properties were the usual. They were large, larger than any house any of them had lived in, except Candy. Ava would refer to this type of house as a "McMansions", big, boxy, with wood exteriors, with tiny yards and limited space between the houses. There were still homes being finished down the block, and another street still to be built.

"He's not going to kill us here and bury us under the concrete?" Deanna quizzed Curtis in an effort to make him smile, recognizing he was wrestling with something even darker than they were.

Checking his watch, Curtis answered, "Crossed my mind, too. But I don't know why the hell we're here."

They all turned when they heard a car pull down the block. A town car, which for them had become synonymous with Martin Collique, stopped in the middle of the street, blocking them all in. Not waiting for the driver to open his door, Martin stepped from the back and smiled at the women and Curtis as he moved to them. "Like them?" he asked, opening his arms towards the large houses at the end of the cul-de-sac.

They all turned around, giving the houses another confused glare, before returning their gaze back to Martin.

"Welcome home. These four..." he said, pointing to each of the four houses at the end of the cul-de-sac, one by one, "...are yours."

Simultaneously, all of their jaws fell open as if they were living in a cartoon. Their eyes shifted back-and-forth among each other.

'Did he just say what he said? Ours? What's that mean?" Deanna's mind raced, disbelief in her voice.

"What the fuck...?" Izzy muttered so just her crew could hear it. "Is he serious?"

Again, nearly simultaneously, they all turned to Martin. He just smiled with Cheshire Cat satisfaction. "These are your new homes. Bought and paid for. You can move in anytime."

"Our new homes?" Ava remarked. "As in we own them?"

"As in I own them, but you live here, free and clear. No rent," he answered.

Ava and Deanna immediately had the same thought. This truly was a deal with the devil. Not only did he own each of the women, he intended to own where they lived as well. And there was no way to back out now.

"You're giving us free homes? As in rent-free?" Deanna said, needing to speak the words aloud.

Martin's smile remained, relishing their surprise even though he could see in their eyes there was a margin of suspicion as well.

"The three on the end of the block here. I know that's not ideal, there being four of you, but this home here," he said, pointing, "is a four-bedroom, for you Deanna, and the one next to it is four-bedrooms as well. Ava, Izzy, I hope you don't mind sharing. Along with your daughter, Ava, there would still be an extra bedroom, with master suites on both floors, so you don't have quite as large a primary space of your own. And Candy, you and Curtis will occupy this one here," he continued, pointing at another house. "It is a three-bedroom with a loft area. Very stylish. You and Curtis and your lovely daughter, Curtis, should have plenty of room. All of you should, as the basements are finished as well."

"We all have an extra bedroom?" Ava asked. "You staying with one of us while you're in town? If so, don't expect breakfast."

Martin chuckled, more obligatory than sincere. "No, no...these are yours. Furnish them as you see fit. But I think it would be best if you were all closer, and in a safer environment than you are now. I hope none of you feel I've overstepped," Martin said, checking his watch. "I have to get back to the airport."

He then handed each of the women keys to the homes. "Walk through, make sure everything is to your liking. There are still some design elements that can be changed," he added, before moving back to the town car and sliding into the backseat, the door shutting.

As he drove away, all the women and Curtis watched in silence, then turned back towards the three brand new homes.

"What the hell...?" Izzy stated. "What the fuck just happened? He moved us. Into these? I like my place."

"I like you in your place, rather than living with me," her sister responded.

"Certainly, a hell of a lot nicer than where I'm living now," mumbled Deanna, her head shaking. "So, we don't have to pay him rent, there is no mortgage, insurance or any of that, right?"

"I think these are a gift," Curtis said, turning towards the women. "A gift with strings attached. We may not have to pay him anything, but never forget, he owns them. Which means we can be on the street whenever he's done with us. But he wants us all close. Like end of a cul-de-sac close. A place he controls."

Still holding Candy's hand, Curtis took a few steps towards the house Martin gifted he and Candy. "This is a blessing and a curse," Curtis remarked, then turned to the women again. "But let's never forget that Martin is in control. We accept these homes, he owns us that much more."

"You're forgetting one thing, Curtis," Ava stated, everyone's eyes turning towards her. "He didn't give us a choice."

MOVING DAY

Kevin and Ford were ecstatic about moving into the house at the end of the cul-de-sac. For the first time in his life, Ford would have his own room. Kevin planted his flag in the basement bonus room, off what would be a TV room/den. The basement had a bathroom with a shower as well, which Kevin would make 'his kingdom', announcing to his mother, sister and brother that no one could go down there unless he granted them permission.

"Yeah, let's see how that works out for you, son," Deanna responded, signaling for Kevin to pick up one of the boxes jammed into the back of the car and carry it inside.

As he muscled the box into the house, he saw Izzy pull into the driveway next door. 'Bonus, Izzy will be right next door,' Kevin thought, not grasping how the proximity would make their hooking up more difficult. As blindly optimistic as he was, Kevin believed everything was easy. Until it wasn't.

For Tracee, this move was happening way too fast. She knew her mother had stayed insanely busy and overworked these last six weeks, sewing dresses or whatever, with Ava, Izzy, Candy and Clara. But how could her mother make enough to move the family into a brand-new house, a house three times the size of the apartment they were leaving, when just a few weeks before they were close to being put out on the streets? While her brothers didn't question this, she did. Unfortunately, Tracee didn't feel she was in any position to make waves. Her mother had barely said anything about her nearly nightly "joining friends to do homework." Nor had her mother noticed that Tracee had been having sex, which Tracee believed Deanna would pick up on immediately, sniffing it out like a foxhound on the trail of its furry prey. But so far, Deanna remained oblivious to what Tracee assumed was obvious, easily something her mother would catch if she wasn't so overwhelmed, allowing Tracee to avoid a huge drama.

Packing was a chore. Detesting it almost as much as she did working for Leo at the dry cleaners, Deanna grew more grateful with each piece of furniture she and Kevin hauled down the stairs and dumped down by the bin in the alley behind the apartment building. She told the kids they weren't taking their beds, dressers, or desks. Neither of the two sofas was going into the new house either. She debated about the kitchen table and chairs because they weren't that worn, but no, she wasn't taking any of it. Nothing more than their clothes, personal items, and the one television that worked was making the move. Having vowed that when she and the kids finally moved, she would furnish the next place with new things. Nothing pulled out of a dumpster. Nothing picked up on the street. Nothing from a garage sale. Nothing that had been sat on, laid on, eaten at, or used. This time it was all going to be new. Because Deanna knew there may never be a next time. This was it.

Ava didn't mind her little South City house. But she recognized she had little choice in the move onto the cul-de-sac, and the house was far nicer. But still, this was a business decision. And banking the money from the sale of her home would allow Ava to finally get out of debt to Brain T. Money she wouldn't mind shoving up his ass. But her profit from her home would give Ava a financial pad that she never had. And just in case Martin pulled the houses out from under them, she could slap some cash down on an apartment immediately. And the new place was beautiful. She had a large bedroom on the main floor, with Cassie upstairs, which meant they wouldn't have to share a bathroom any longer. Izzy would be downstairs with her own bathroom, and the finished den, which Ava conceded to Izzy, so Izzy could have a space completely her own. They would all coexist, but each on their own floors.

Cleaning out her house, Ava discovered bloodstains on the rug in her bedroom. She didn't know if it was Santos' or hers. Regardless, it was bad mojo. All the shit that went down with him, whatever vibes attached, would stay with the house. Ava was starting fresh. 'I'm not ever holding anyone hostage in the new place,' she thought to herself before accepting how insane and stupid that thought was, realizing that a mere two months ago that would have never entered her head.

The most relieved to exit her present home was Candy. Curtis was kind enough to hire a moving company to come in and haul everything from her present house, as well as his place – which he would rent out, and together they would move into "Martin's gift," as Candy referred to it. Curtis couldn't help but remind her a little too often that "Martin's gift" came with a cost and to always remember that they didn't own the house, it was on loan. Martin could yank her out at any time. "Be aware," Curtis warned, "I don't want to get blindsided."

The brevity of his statement shook Candy. But like Ava, she didn't see another option. And she wanted out of the house she had shared with Earl. The home morphed from a place she adored into an albatross which drained her shallow finances. She was sleeping over at Curtis's home more and more, not wanting to be in her home That house was her past. For better or worse, the new house was her future. A future she didn't own, but nonetheless, her future.

****

With Kevin behind the wheel of a U-Haul, Deanna sat next to him in the passenger seat. Packed into the U-Haul were four new mattresses, metal bed legs for four beds, a dining table, chairs, a kitchen table and chairs, a sofa and two side chairs, a coffee table and two matching end tables, four rugs, three desks and chairs to go with them. With the sale she found at Bob's Furniture, Deanna was able to furnish the new place for under five grand. Everyone came together to carry the furniture into the new house. Ava shot Deanna a smile as they moved the sofa into the position so it would face the wall where Deanna intended to mount a flatscreen TV.

"Congratulations," Ava said to her. "You've arrived."

Deanna almost cried as she looked at the new furniture. She wasn't leaving the store without it. This was her butterfly moment. For the first time in her life, she would sleep on a new mattress. And she was determined to find a TV and have it mounted this week. And for the first time, they would get cable. Maybe even Netflix.

"Are we doing the right thing?" Deanna asked Ava.

"May I," Ava asked, before she sat on the sofa.

"Let's christen this bitch," Deanna announced with excitement, jumping over the back of the sofa and onto the couch.

Ava joined her, both of them laughing.

"If this can handle my big ass, it's a good sofa. Comfy...I love the color," she said of the burnt orange sofa.

"Never had a choice of furniture before. I wanted something that felt like I was in a movie," Deanna answered, opening her arms to her other living room furniture, each piece a bright color. "And to have my own washer and dryer right in the kitchen...no more collecting quarters to do a load. Hauling all my stuff to the laundromat. I'm so happy. So happy. But still..."

Ava's mood shifted immediately with Deanna's unfinished sentence. What Deanna was feeling they were all feeling. "D, we don't have a choice," Ava stated. "And that's not just how I'm trying to spin this, it's a fact. What were we gonna do, say no? And then we wouldn't be living in these places, we'd be buried under them. Don't ever forget that Martin had Santos killed right in front of us to make a point."

"I remember," Deanna muttered.

"And don't forget he tried to murder your son," Ava continued. "As nice as Mr. Collique is acting, these homes, the dinners, don't for a minute think he won't kill us. He doesn't like us. Not really. We are only as valuable to him as the clothes we create for him. And I'm sure there's more shit he's going to have us doing. I'm sure of it. We're going to be doing all sorts of shit for him we're not gonna like."

Hearing Curtis and Kevin come into the house with the mattress going down into Kevin's lair, the women abruptly stopped speaking. They both smiled as they carried it down the stairs but got serious as soon as they were out of earshot. "Think of your last job. The shit you put up with there. I know the shit I put up with at mine. And other than the possibility of being murdered, this one is a shit-ton better," Ava avowed.

"Other than being murdered," Deanna paraphrased, laughing. "Oh, is that all..."

"Yeah. That's hanging over our head like a bucket full of shit," Ava sighed, recognizing her intense rationalization. "But again, what choice we got?"

After a moment of silence, Deanna turned to Ava. The look on Deanna's face was calculated determination, as she said, "Long game, Ava. Long game."

Ava shook her head, not understanding. But one thing she loved about Deanna was that Deanna was a planner. She first saw it when Deanna started copying the blouses. Deanna didn't just jump in, she measured everything first, kept notes, studying the construction of the blouse before she even began cutting anything. There was a method to her madness. Time wasn't wasted. Neither was material. When Martin shipped them the first set of gowns, Deanna plotted out the best way to construct the copies, making sure everything was clear to everyone before they got to work. As badly a hand as Deanna had been dealt in life, and as horribly as Deanna had played her cards, most especially with men where she led with her heart, Deanna was alive, she kept a roof over her kids' heads, and food in their bellies. Because she figured out how to do it, put the work in to make it happen, and while none of it was easy, it all got done.

"One day, Martin will turn on us," Deanna said softly as her hand bumped along the fresh fabric on the back of her new sofa. "We have to prepare for that now, Ava. We can't wait. I don't want to be caught unprepared when it happens."

Ava nodded in agreement as the guys came back up the stairs, heading towards the front door.

"My room is going to be awesome!" Kevin bragged. "A sex pit!"

"Not on my watch," Deanna said as the men headed back outside, Kevin laughing.

"Boys," Ava chuckled.

"Soft in the head," Deanna laughed.

"Don't we both know it," Ava answered.

****

Cassie watched from her bedroom window upstairs as Kevin and Curtis pulled off their sweaty shirts before climbing back into the back of the hot U-Haul to pull out more furniture. 'Kevin has a sweet body,' she thought, but equally admired Curtis's well-muscled frame. She was dating a basketball player now but part of her missed Kevin. Even though Kevin cheated on her whenever and wherever the chance arose, he was funny and still sort of boyish, which offset his aggressive sexual appetite. She knew her present beau was screwing around when he could, seemed all guys did, but there was no boyish sweetness in DeJames. Probably hadn't been in years. Shootings and death had already marred his life. DeJames was all business. Even when it came to sex. Women were props to DeJames. Cassie was just one of the high school's more popular props. And she knew it. She was with DeJames for the same reason. High school validity.

But as Kevin and Curtis carried another mattress out of the back of the U-Haul, Cassie wished she hadn't shit all over Kevin as badly as she had. Her only solace was if she hadn't, he might very well have been shot dead on the ballfield.

****

That night, they all got together at Candy and Curtis' and had a big dinner, promising that no one would bring up business. This night was a celebration. About food and wine. And laughs. As many as possible. They didn't want to talk about the bind they all found themselves in, rather, they wanted to celebrate their new homes. Far more beautiful than what they'd lived in, except for Candy, whose previous home had once been a showplace, and Curtis, whose townhome was high-end. Candy and Curtis' home would be beautiful, a melding of two tastes, and it already looked put-together in less than two days. Candy had an eye. For fashion. For home decoration. And she had Curtis. 'Three for three,' as far as Ava was concerned.

After an evening run to get acclimated to the new neighborhood, Kevin rested against the side of the family car in the driveway, staying in the shade. Seeing him from her window, Cassie gritted her teeth and walked outside, acting like she was surprised he was out as well. She tentatively moved towards him. "I've heard nothing about who your sister is hooking up with," Cassie confided. "Nobody seems to know anything about it."

"Thanks," Kevin said with more enthusiasm than Cassie expected, wiping the sweat from his face with his shirt.

"So, where are you looking at going to college?" Cassie asked. "You figured it out?"

"I'm already talking to Truman and Mizzou. But I'd like to go farther away. Got another year before any legit offers can come in. I mean, my mom will pick the place that gives me the most aid. I'm hoping somewhere in Florida or any place sunny and warm where we can practice outside all year long," he answered.

Cassie looked down a moment, knowing she wouldn't get the opportunity to go that far away. "Good for you," she said, turning to head back towards the house next door. But she stopped herself and spun towards him. "I want to apologize. I was really shitty to you. Not that you weren't really shitty to me, but I shouldn't have played you. Interfering with your baseball, I knew it was the one thing I could fuck with where you might get how I felt."

"It's over," Kevin responded evenly. "I was a really horrible boyfriend."

"Are there any guys who aren't?" Cassie asked with a sardonic, sad smile.

"DeJames not treating you well?"

"He fucks more side-pieces than you do. None of you know how to treat a woman," added Cassie, eyeing all the "adults" in Candy's new house, through the large front window. Candy stood next to Curtis, his arm around her as she leaned against him. Cassie winced, not from any-thing negative but from desire. "Candy's lucky. Her man's an actual man."

Hearing this as she walked past, Tracee smiled at Cassie, raising her hand. Cassie high-fived her. After his sister passed, continuing up the driveway, Kevin turned back to Cassie and cracked quietly, "See. Am I wrong? She got laid."

Cassie shrugged. "I mean, maybe you're right. She hates me and she just high fived me. About guys..."

Shaking his head, Kevin threw up his hands. "Some-body is working some magic on her because she's actually been kind of pleasant to be around."

Cassie turned and watched Tracee sashay into her new home. There was a sway of the ass and a lightness in her step. If there was somebody, maybe he wasn't from their school. Cassie would have heard. But Kevin was right, somebody had given Tracee a new lease on her teenage years. And it had to be a guy.

****

While everyone else was relaxing in the living room, watching a Cardinals game on the TV that Curtis mount-ed above the fireplace earlier in the day, Candy and Deanna finished loading the dishwasher. "I got something to show you," Deanna said to Candy, nodding towards the door leading to the deck off the kitchen.

As Candy followed Deanna to her new house, Candy softly announced, "Ramona is dead."

Deanna turned, eyes wide, holding on Candy. "She threatened to expose us," Candy continued, as Deanna unlocked her front door and led Candy into her place. "As far as I know, they haven't discovered her body."

"Martin?" Deanna quizzed.

Candy blinked a few times as she followed Deanna into the master bedroom. "Yes," she lied.

Deanna pulled out a garment bag from her closet and unzipped it. Inside was the gown she and Clara created from the remnants of the gowns they made for Mr. Collique. Candy stepped up and took the gown, feeling the weight, holding it up in front of her and checking herself out in the bathroom mirror.

"This is gorgeous!" Candy exclaimed. "You made this?"

"Clara and I. From what was left over from the gowns."

"Beautiful," Candy complimented.

"Think you could sell it?" Deanna asked.

Pausing, Candy quickly assessed the ramifications of selling a gown while they were working for Mr. Collique. If it could even be done. And if they got caught, what he would do?

"You think that's a good idea?" Candy asked.

"You said it was beautiful. You know these things. I want to sell my own things, not just copy other people's," Deanna answered.

"Get permission first," Candy offered firmly.

"But—"

"Ramona is dead so that we wouldn't have any hassles with Martin, and he wouldn't think about getting rid of us all! Get permission first!" Candy demanded, tossing the gown onto Deanna's new bed. "Number one thing is we stay alive."

"Do you think any of us are going to live through this?!" Deanna fought back. "That once Martin has all he needs from us, that he won't kill us? I mean, aren't we just fooling ourselves with these houses and the money? None of this is real. He IS going to kill us when he doesn't need us anymore."

Tears whispered into the corner of Candy's eyes as she fought her emotions. Deanna knew she could use a good breakdown too. It was as if they were all dolls in a playhouse and someone was moving them around, pretending they had some amazing new life.

"We're fucked, aren't we?" Candy huffed, losing her battle with her tears.

"I'm afraid that's true," Deanna answered, taking Candy in her arms.

"I'm sorry I ever got you involved in this," Candy whispered into Deanna's ear as they held each other. "This has gotten so crazy. We aren't these people."

"There's where we disagree," Deanna responded, pulling back so she could look into Candy's eyes. Deanna wiped Candy's tears as she said, "We are these women. We did this to fight back. We still got fight. The best time to fight back is when the other side thinks they've won. We prepare. We pick our time. Our place. How. Point is, we get ready."

Deanna held Candy until Candy could gain control over her emotions again. They walked back down the hallway and stepped out the front door just as a van pulled up in front. Instinctively, Deanna stepped in front of Candy as if to protect her. A man stepped from the van and nodded at them, moving to the back of the van. He pulled out three large boxes and three garment boxes as well, setting them on the curb.

"Oh shit, no..." Deanna said.

"More gowns."

"More gowns."

The delivery guy carried the first one onto the front porch, a clipboard on top. He handed Deanna the clipboard. "You want to sign for these?" he asked.

Deanna scribbled her signature onto the delivery slip as the man carried up the other boxes and took back his clipboard.

"Hope you're having a nice night," he said, jogging back to his truck and leaving.

"We were," Deanna muttered, her eyes going to Candy.

"I'll move that gown. I have an idea where I can sell it," Candy stated with a nod. "But for now, we go back to work."

"And prepare," Deanna flatly added.

Candy paused, weighing every side. Finally, she nodded. "And prepare."

BAD ASS, BADDER ASS

This new order from Martin was four different gowns, again, three apiece. There was a two-week deadline on this order. Even with Clara, Deanna didn't feel they had found a rhythm that would make her workload easier. But she wasn't about to kill herself like she did on the first batch of gowns. Deanna intended on finding better use for Ava. Rather than being a cheerleader, cooking meals for everyone, and helping Ford with his homework, she needed Ava in the mix, sewing and cutting. And with four of the team now living at the end of a cul-de-sac together, everybody wouldn't have to hang out at Deanna's for hours on end. They could go home.

Knowing Clara would feel slighted when she found out that all the women were now living in new homes, Deanna offered to pick her up. Clara's thrill at having another set of gowns to make, coupled with Candy working to sell the one she and Deanna created, was short-lived when Deanna pulled into the driveway of her new home.

"You're living here now?" Clara asked, surprise in her voice.

"Yeah. Moved. The other girls are living here, too. We all got places. This was in the works before you joined us," Deanna apologized.

"All okay. How many bedrooms?"

"Mine's four. And a basement. My oldest son took that as his," Deanna answered.

"Nice," Clara stated. "More room. Something for me to work towards."

Deanna gave Clara a confident smile, hoping Clara couldn't sense that Deanna was holding something back. She didn't want any more complications, and more to the point, she needed Clara. She could also sew better than anyone but Deanna, and even better, what she didn't know she learned quickly. That made her invaluable when they were working on the intense deadlines set by Martin, not daring to disappoint him. "If you want, we'll work on getting you here too," Deanna said.

"Oh honey, I want, I want," Clara laughed.

****

Stacy viewed the report first. It connected Santos to the two known dead men, Officer Marcus Silas and Reilly Johans, whose body they found in the burned pickup truck behind the old Goliath Printing Building. Stalking down the hallway and swinging open the door to Earl's office, Stacy dropped the report on his desk as he turned towards her. "Coincidence?" she asked, knowing he would comprehend what she was talking about.

Earl slowly picked up the report, thumbing through it before he responded. "Isn't this the Fed's case?" Earl asked, more than willing to punt the case.

"Technically, they took it over. But don't you find this more interesting now?" Stacy asked Earl.

"Stacy, stop with this. Let that Fed deal with it. All it can do to us is drag us down another rabbit hole. And I got better things to do. We have hundreds of unsolved cases that we could be working on if we want busy work," Earl fired back.

Stacy abhorred working with Earl and she knew he could feel it. It radiated off her. She accepted that he had his eye on the prize: his retirement. Earl wanted nothing to upset his ability to keep his head down and float down the lazy river towards that day. But Stacy was tired of running dead-end cases, playing Whack-A-Mole with the multitude of North City drug dealers. Once they arrested one, the dealer was back on the street within a few days or some-one else took over his business. It was an exercise in futility and Stacy resented making the arrests that meant nothing more than making numbers on a report in an effort to pretend there was progress, so the Police Commission, the Mayor, and the City Council, stayed off their ass.

"I want this, Earl. Fuck. Do something worth a shit before you retire to Lake of the Ozarks or wherever you old white people go."

"If I didn't know better, Stacy, I'd think you're a racist," Earl snarked.

"I'm just not lazy, Earl. Fuck it, I'll talk to Racine, see if I can work with the Fed. You can sit your ever-widening ass here at your desk and answer phones," she said rapidly, grabbing the report from in front of him and storming towards Racine's office.

Earl sighed and stood up. He wasn't going to rush into Racine's office. Racine hated that and besides, everything Stacy hammered on about when it came to him was true. No, he didn't want this case. Yes, he'd be perfectly happy clocking in and answering the phone, maybe spending an hour or so of his workday playing online games or fo-cused on the new betting app that the state approved, then punching out at five.

"I want to be the department liaison with the Fed who's working the case," Stacy announced as Earl shuffled sluggishly into Racine's office. Racine had the same look on his face that Earl had.

"Detective Lipton, we have so many open cases. We need to focus on bringing down our open case numbers. If that Fed, what's his name..."

"Agent Barry Wimmer," Stacy reminded Racine.

"Right. Wimmer. Whatever. If the F.B.I. is that interested in this case that they sent him, let him do his thing. He has more resources than we do. Let's focus on what we can accomplish. What helps us," Racine continued.

"All I'm asking is to let me be the contact to Agent Wimmer. If this is human trafficking, we need to have some sort of presence on the case, so when it breaks, you can put your face in front of a camera," Stacy chided Racine. "We need some skin in the game." Stacy wasn't giving this up without a fight. A fight she believed she could win if for no other reason, Racine wanted her to shut the fuck up and stay out of his office.

"How? Do you have a family member who got trafficked? Know someone? The woman that cleans your house?" Racine scolded more than asked.

Stacy glared. Saying nothing for a moment long enough to make things uncomfortable, she leaned towards Racine.

"Because I'm a woman."

****

It was just after eight o'clock when Candy got a call from Vi Miller, a frienemy of Ramona's, announcing that Ramona suffered an accident and was dead. According to Vi, Ramona fell down the stairs in her home and wasn't found for nearly two weeks because everyone thought she was out of town. "Her regular mailman was on vacation, so even the mail piling up didn't become a red flag until the regular mailman returned from Florida and realized Ramona hadn't collected her mail in a few weeks," Vi told Candy.

"I don't think it's much of a secret that Ramona didn't have any close friends," Vi then confided to Candy. "We all loved her, but you know Ramona, she was such a private woman. Not that she ever hesitated to bother someone when she needed something, but otherwise, she didn't like to be bothered, so no one bothered her."

Candy made a few calls, and a few of Ramona's other friends called her. They swapped information, trying to weave a tale of intrigue for the gossip mill. But Ramona's death appeared to be nothing more than a tragic accident.

Even the police, whom Ramona's friend, Betsy, spoke to because she was the sister of a city alderman, were calling the death accidental. Relaying all the information she had gathered to Curtis, they both allowed the news to scratch away some of the discomfort but neither mentioned that it did nothing to alleviate the guilt. Ramona's death had been ruled an accident. The police weren't viewing it as anything more. No one mentioned that Ramona's alarm system didn't connect to the upstairs windows, just the doors and windows downstairs. And she didn't have a camera system in the house even though she mentioned having an elaborate system to her friends, in an effort to impress. And maybe scare.

That Ramona's death could be so easily written off as an accident strangely annoyed Curtis. Maybe as penance, he felt there should be some sort of investigation. Clearly, Ramona's friends were searching to create some sort of dark secret that snuffed out Ramona's life. A secret lover. A night bandit. A begrudged nephew. But the police found nothing to cause them to dig further. Ramona fell, end of story. While Curtis spent a few nights sweating that he would be implicated once someone found Ramona's body, with each passing day, the stress of possible arrest waned into confusion. Confusion that no one found her. Once she was discovered, he again felt like he was holding his breath. But again, his dread amounted to nothing. And now the police closed the case. Having a conscience, Curtis couldn't help but feel there should be a greater punishment for his crime.

"You're a good man. And we had no choice," Candy said, brushing off his concern, hoping Curtis would believe her concerns were minimal, when her own guilt rivaled Curtis's own. "Ramona was not a good person. She was going to cause us hell. Or worse. Only way to look at all of this is karma."

Curtis accepted Candy's assessment. He had to, to live with himself. But he also believed karma turned sour easily. And he was now on karma's shit list.

****

"Fuck him," Cassie thought as she stared at the grade in her health class. D on her report on female reproductive diseases.

It was bullshit, as far as she was concerned. She knew that taking a class with Kevin's coach that their disastrous relationship would taint her. "That report was fucking great. Especially since he loads his class with his idiot baseball players and gives them A's and B's so they can stay eligible to play," she roared at her friends over the lunch table. She wanted to punch Vince in his smug, handsome face. "He thinks every girl in this school will drop her panties for him. Well, I'm going to show him just how fucking wrong he is," Cassie continued as she stood up and threw her book bag onto a shoulder, carrying her open Chromebook as she stomped out of the cafeteria. She was tired of this double standard. It was an open secret that Kevin had cheated his way through school. And Cassie was done with letting some dumbass man tell her the report she did on female diseases was D work.

His classroom was empty. 'Well fuck it,' Cassie thought, 'I'll find his sorry ass.' She turned to storm back out the door when a strange sound caught her ear. A sigh of pleasure. A male sigh. Knowing his reputation, which she had confirmed to be true, Cassie's eyes narrowed. Feeling caught, she started out of the room. But hearing another sigh, she spun on her heels. 'Fuck him,' she snarled to herself and stalked towards his office area behind the partition. As she came around the corner, Cassie could see a woman sitting on the edge of the desk, her face down at his crotch. Vince's pants and underwear were down past his ass, and the woman held him by both ass cheeks as she blew him. Cassie smiled, her mouth opening to speak before she thought to pull out her cell phone and record the moment.

"This what I have to do in this class for extra credit?" she snapped with a laugh.

Vince jumped back, his hands wrestling his underwear and pants back up over his ass, as he kept his back to Cassie, his neck craned to peer back over his shoulder. The woman sat frozen on the edge of the desk, her hands going to her face. But as Vince moved away, revealing who it was, Cassie's jaw slackened in a storm of anger and sadness.

Tracee.

"Are you fucking kidding me?" Cassie said in a voice that sounded like she'd gotten punched in the solar plexus. "How old are you? Fourteen? Fifteen?!"

Her teeth gritting, Cassie stepped towards Vince, who now had his pants up and was facing Cassie. "You piece of shit. You're fucking your star player's sister. Let me rephrase that, your star player's underage sister! Wow, you really are everything they say you are. And worse. Well, I hope you like sucking dick yourself, because a handsome guy like you, you're going to be taking a lot of Nazi or homeboy dick in prison!"

"Cassie, please. You don't understand! This is—" Vince tried to explain, his hands shaking.

"I know what a blowjob is, Coach!" Cassie fired back. "You're never going to work around kids again, you fucking freak!"

"No!" Tracee barked, stepping down off the desk. "You're going to shut up and mind your own business!"

"This motherfucker is taking advantage of you!" Cassie responded incredulously.

"Do you think I'm an idiot?! I'm one of the smartest girls in this school! I'm not being taken advantage of! I know what I'm doing. What I want. And you are going to keep your big mouth shut. You're not ruining Vince's career or life or even his day. Or mine! You think you're queen bee around here, you set all the rules, pick who is popular, who isn't, fuck you! You're nothing but some skanky dumb girl whose destiny is working the shipping line at Amazon and marrying some guy who will be fat in five years and pumping out a few kids for him until your body is as fat as his is. So, shut up and stay out of our business. You tell a single soul, I will make you look like the biggest liar in the school. You'll get knocked so far off that pedestal you think you're on, you'll be pulling gum off the bottom of my shoe."

As Vince opened his mouth to speak, Cassie puts her hand up into his face, her focus never leaving Tracee. "I'm telling your brother!" Cassie stated.

"Please do. Because who do you think he'll believe? His scuzzy ex-girlfriend who fucked him over or his coach and his sister? So, go ahead. You'll look like a complete lying, desperate nobody trying to get back with the baseball star, or some psycho-bitch using his coach and sister to get back at him. Kevin will run with that. There won't be a guy who will go near you. Especially the guy you're fucking now. I'll make sure they're all afraid of your psycho-lying-self," Tracee growled.

Cassie felt her chest tighten. She'd never been talked to quite like that, and certainly never seen sweet, unassuming Tracee like this, claws out, spitting out directions. Cassie realized that whatever voodoo Vince was working, Tracee was under his spell. And her threats terrified Cassie. They hit at the heart of who she was, what she had done, and what would be believed.

"Fuck it. I don't care what you do with this pervert," she said to Tracee before turning to Vince. "But know I know. And I want an A in this class."

"Earn it," Vince answered, though his gut was telling him he probably shouldn't have.

"I just did," Cassie snapped back with a tortured smile before her eyes shifted back to Tracee. "This is the best you can do? Some needy, washed-up baseball player who is too pathetic and immature to attract a woman his own age? Fuck...then have at him."

Striding back into the hallway quickly, Cassie stopped as students milled around her. Clueless on how to handle this, Cassie wasn't sure if she should tell Kevin, tell the school, tell her mother, tell Deanna. What was she supposed to do? The only thing she knew for sure was that Tracee was in a really nasty spot. And as much as she didn't like her, their mothers were working together, and she was Kevin's sister. And now she lived next door, so Tracee was in her life whether she liked it or not.

She had to help her.

And even more, she wanted Vince to bleed.

REVENGE FASHION

Four gowns. Three each. Deanna had all four gowns hanging on a rack so she could get a good look at them, taking each one in, the pieces that would be needed, the work each would entail, deciding which they should tackle first. Clara was inverting sleeves and hem lines to check the stitching. Twelve gowns meant she was in for an even bigger payday, and that was perfectly fine with her. Until the Policeman's Union came to her assistance and she could collect Marcus's death benefits, she would take as much work as Deanna handed her. And if her assistance could get her moved into one of these new houses on the block, that would really ease some of her worry.

"This one?" Deanna asked, holding up a gorgeous red gown, with a high hemline and a plunging neckline that would require tape, so even a woman with a C-cup wouldn't fall out.

"Certainly won't take much material," Clara responded, holding the gown on its hanger, flipping it back and forth, her hand caressing the material. "Where would you wear this?"

"I'm sure some women wear things like this to dinner. Or out on the town. Just no one we know," laughed Deanna.

"I don't gotta worry about it. My ass wouldn't fit in this thing and my tits would be hanging out like I was the neighborhood milkman," Clara answered, now both of them laughing.

As they measured the pieces they would need to construct copies in the sizes Martin provided, Candy knocked at the front door and barreled in quickly, her heels clattering on the wood floor as she made her way to the den of Deanna's home, which she had turned into her workspace.

"Sold it!" Candy declared, as Clara and Deanna spun in her direction. "I sold your gown!"

The news made Clara giddy. A quick infusion of money was more than welcome.

"How much?!" Clara asked with excitement.

Candy smirked proudly for a moment before responding. "Society gala. Her ex is bringing his new girlfriend. Wants to look better than, and I'm quoting, 'That bitch'."

Laughing, Clara asked again, "How much?"

Candy opened her bag and took out a small stack of hundreds. She counted out six grand. Even though she had seen more than that from her last payday, Deanna gasped. No matter how you dressed this up, six thousand dollars was a lot of money. A few weeks ago this amount of money would have been life-changing. Now it was padding. Much-needed but still padding.

"Holy shit," Clara muttered before clasping her hands and looking up. "Praise Jesus."

"Praise vanity," Candy chuckled. "You hit the right woman on the right day with the right need, and bam, you make a killing."

"I don't mean to bring all this back to earth, but we never talked about how to divide this," Deanna remarked uncomfortably. "If Clara is good with it, I think we should divide it equally, three ways. I mean, we created the dress but we wouldn't have made anything if we didn't sell it. Clara, you good with that?"

Clara nodded. While she would have loved three thousand dollars fluttering into her palm, two thousand still made her giddy. And fighting this would form a wave that could swamp her future payouts. And where else was she going to make two grand for a week's work without spreading her legs?

"Candy, you good?" Deanna asked.

Candy grabbed Deanna's hand, reaching out for Clara's. Clara gave it to her.

"I appreciate you making me a partner in this little side business. Only thing I ask is that we keep this between ourselves. I don't want to make anyone mad that we got this going on," Candy said in all seriousness before adding, "And you two need to make a label to put in what you make. I think it will help sell them."

Deanna nodded, knowing that if Ava and Izzy found out about this, they would feel pushed out of a piece of the profits. But truth was, Deanna didn't need them. Clara and she were working from the remnants and leftovers. And Candy knew the people who could pay top dollar for an amazing gown. Keeping this among the three of them was smart business.

Hearing a knock at the front door before the front door opened and closed, the three women quickly split the money and slid it into a pocket, a purse and a bra strap before Ava came into the den with a smile.

"Which of these gowns are we getting done first?" she asked.

****

Checking the clock, Izzy realized she was running exactly twelve minutes late. She hated being late. It seemed that since Deanna's was now yards away instead of a few miles, getting there on time had grown more difficult. It was now easier to lounge in bed until the very last minute. Or beyond.

Just as she was heading out the door, her phone rang. Pulling it out, the screen read: Martin Collique. Izzy froze. Did he know she was late for their workday? Why else would he be calling her? She had barely spoken to him except to confront him in the airplane hangar. Izzy thought about letting it go to voicemail, but on the last ring, she gritted her teeth and answered. "Hello," she said, swallowing her greeting nervously.

"Isabel, this is Martin Collique."

Izzy remained silent for a beat, hoping he would continue talking, but he didn't. "Right. Hi. What's going on?"

"I have been informed of a minor hiccup, which I'm hoping won't become a problem for us. I thought you might be the person to help me figure out what to do," Martin said, as Izzy put him on speaker.

"Yeah, sure. What is it?"

"There is an FBI agent in St. Louis. He's looking into the connection between Santos and the man killed at the warehouse, as well as Officer Marcus Silas. He's looking into the operation that Santos was running out of the warehouse."

"Trafficking the women?" Izzy quizzed flatly, cutting to the chase. She hated that Collique tip-toed around his crimes. Too elegant, too pussyfied.

"Yes," Martin answered. "And I would prefer this not wind its way back to what you girls are doing for me now."

Izzy leaned against the doorjamb, looking out at the street, wondering if he was in a car down the block, watching her. "What do you want me to do?"

"I'm going to send you a short dossier on Agent Wimmer. It would be so, so, helpful if you could ingratiate yourself to Agent Wimmer."

Izzy stood up straight. She had no idea what Collique meant by that and could only assume the worst. "Mind giving me that in English?"

"Read the dossier. He's been in a little trouble with the Bureau because of an extramarital affair that was discovered when he was on assignment a couple years ago. His wife almost left him. He has two children. The Bureau frowns on that, not because of the affair but the vulnerability of extortion an affair puts on an agent."

"Okay," Izzy uttered with a vagueness that told Martin she still didn't know what he was asking.

"Maybe you can find a way to get close to him."

"Close?" Izzy purred, finally he was talking about her being trafficked to trap an FBI agent. "That's a loaded fucking word. Okay. Why me?"

"His wife is the daughter of an Arizona State Representative. A Republican. Very conservative. And it seems that Agent Wimmer has a thing for, well, lack of a less crass term, bad girls."

This made Izzy smile. She knew the type. Clean-cut frat boys who came into the shop to get tattoos who thought they were going to fuck her as well. Successful businessmen who liked their dicks inked. Family men who had their wife's names tattooed on their shoulder, while their hand reached around for Izzy's ass.

"Don't you think he would have learned his lesson?" she asked Martin.

"Only one way to find out. I have emailed you his dossier. Take a read. I've had someone following him. You can figure out how to meet him." And with that, Martin hung up.

Izzy hovered in the doorway, opening the email with the information about Agent Wimmer. Including a photo. He was hot in that law-and-order, right-wing, nasty-on-the-downlow sort of way. If this got her out of chasing down buttons or snaps or whipping up mac and cheese for Deanna's youngest child because he liked "the way she did it best," Izzy was up for this challenge. Even though she was clueless about exactly what this challenge, and it would be a challenge, would entail. After dialing, Izzy put the phone up to her ear. "Hey, it's me. Yeah, yeah, I know I'm supposed to be there. Collique called me. Yeah, I'm serious. Fucker called me. Needs me to do some recon for him. I shit you not."

****

Ruminating on what she had witnessed, Cassie knew she couldn't keep this a secret. For lots of reasons. Fuck Tracee. She wasn't scared of her. And she now hated Coach Cunello. Felt he was part of the male toxicity at the high school. Having his dick inside Tracee only proved it. But she could no longer confide in Kevin. That would be a nonstarter. Especially when it came to his beloved baseball coach. Cassie knew Izzy would flip her shit if she found out about a fifteen-year-old girl being seduced by a thirty-something-year-old man. She'd take a metal pipe to him and then suggest they cut off his penis. That alone made her the best candidate of all of Deanna's cohorts to take this information to. Cassie didn't like the idea of being a rat, but fuck it, wrong was wrong. And blowing the whistle on Cunello had a good feel to it. 'Tracee is just fifteen,' Cassie mused, remembering she lost her virginity at fifteen, but it wasn't to a man almost twenty-years-older. 'This fucker needs to die,' Cassie steamed, as she walked onto her new street, seeing Izzy pulling down her driveway. Walking into the street toward Izzy's truck, Cassie waved. Izzy pulled up next to her, rolling down her window. Seeing her aunt dressed in a tight tank top and tight jeans, Cassie fired Izzy a questioning look.

"Don't ask," Izzy stated with exasperation. "What's going on?"

"I need to talk to you about something," Cassie answered.

"Your mother?"

"Surprisingly, no. Not this time."

Izzy grew concerned. "Are you okay?"

"Yeah, yeah," Cassie responded, touching Izzy's arm warmly. "It's not me. But... it's kinda involved, so when you got some time..."

Izzy nodded. "Let me get this bullshit I gotta do, done. Not like I don't know where you live now."

Smiling, Cassie nodded. She backed away from Izzy's pickup and let her drive on. As she turned back to her house, she saw Tracee on the front porch of her home, watching her. Cassie just shook her head. Tracee glowered in her direction before she entered the house and shut the door hard. "Fuck you, girl. I don't care what you want. That fucker is getting his legs broke. All three of them."

THE DEEP DIG

"What does he have her doing?" Candy asked Ava as they whipped up a quick meal after trying to convince Ford that 'Taco Wednesday' was a thing.

Ava shrugged as she dug her hand into a bag of grated Mexican cheese and settled it into a bowl, while Candy sliced tomatoes. "She wouldn't say. Just told me Martin called her and asked her for a favor."

"Not sure I'm good with this," Candy stated. "I mean, we are doing what he asked. Now he wants more? There should be a price tag on that. He wants anything more from us, that should come with a cost. Do you know where she is?"

Ava shook her head. She should have pressed Izzy harder for this information. Letting her sister pull some side job for Martin, who Ava knew didn't have their best inter-ests at heart and murdered people who crossed him, was short-sighted and stupid. It left them all vulnerable. But especially her sister. What if she didn't get the result he wanted? What then? This whole thing stank. And Ava had lived enough life to know that when it stank, it stank. And no number of perfumed promises can cover that.

"Text her. See if she answers you. We can always join her. Or at least keep tabs on her," Candy suggested.

Immediately, Ava was typing with her thumbs.

****

Having perused the information that Martin provided, Izzy knew Barry Wimmer had two drinks and dinner, usually beef or pork and a potato, nightly at 360, the restaurant in the Hilton down in Ballpark Village, which was a stone's throw from the Cardinals' baseball stadium. Izzy had never been to Ballpark Village. Not being much of a baseball fan, too much of nothing happening, and hating drunk crowds of white guys wearing Cardinal shirts or polos, with their west county shorts and Sperry Top-Siders. There were local bars a few miles away in South St. Louis where Izzy felt far more comfortable and could glance at the score ever so often, hoping for a winner, and still not lose sight of any hot guys that walked in or the conversation she was having with Ava or one of her friends. And if she was going to get drunk, Izzy wanted it to be around friends, not tourists, not suburbanites clad in red, nor drunk assholes she didn't want to fuck but wanted to fuck her. But the 360 being in a hotel meant she could avoid most of the yahoos. These were more monied out-of-towners, and high-end locals. And while still not her scene by a long stretch, it was heads-and-tails above the baseball bar across the street. Plus, the view of the Arch was exceptional.

Reading in the dossier that he was punctual, arriving at just after five p.m. consistently, Izzy had some time to kill. She could sit, relax and people-watch, if her sister would stop texting her. Which Ava wouldn't even after Izzy thumbed back, 'It's all good. Leave me the fuck alone,' after which Izzy again pulled up the photo of Barry on her phone which Martin had attached. While he was undoubtedly a handsome guy, he wasn't anything even remotely close to someone she would be interested in. She gravitated towards the bad boys and wild men. And Kevin. Who already had the makings of a bad boy and would probably end up a wild man but that would be a long day off, after they broke off their thing, which Izzy assumed would happen once Kevin went off to college. He'd be getting laid by a whole new breed of woman and wouldn't look back. Their affair would be remembered in smiles as they passed each other in the driveway while he was home for holidays or the summer. Izzy assumed she would start to look old to him, especially as he became an upperclassman, working on banging the hottest freshman. She'd move on too. An actual adult this time. Or at least someone closer to her own age. Izzy could never see herself married but she knew there'd come a time when a 'provider' would be more important than 'six-pack abs'.

Glancing down the bar as she nursed a warming Bud Lite, the hair on the back of Izzy's neck stood up. Martin. He smiled, slipping from the far end of the bar and gliding past the other patrons to the empty seat next to her. "What are you doing here?" Izzy demanded, pissed.

"Business brought me back," he replied, setting a small coin envelope on the counter and covering it with his hand. "So, I thought I would help you help me."

Sliding his hand over to hers, he lifted it from the bar and Izzy quickly placed hers on top of the small envelope.

"What is this?" Izzy questioned.

"Slip it in his drink. Get him up to his room."

"You're asking me to roofie him?" she whispered, her eyes wide.

"We need insurance. Photos. If you read what I sent you, you know he has had some problems with his scruples in the past. That's where he's vulnerable," Martin answered. "And I believe a woman like you is temptation. But I need to be sure." Martin smiled. Izzy wanted to knock the smirk off his face. Martin, himself, wasn't a bad-looking man. A little too angular and refined for her liking, even so, she had to admit, if he had walked up and wanted to buy her a drink, she would have let him. But then skipped out before he attempted to seal the deal and take her home.

"How's your new home?" Martin asked purposefully.

Nodding with her own dark smile, Izzy answered, "I feel a little trapped on a cul-de-sac with only one way in and one way out."

"Isn't that the American dream? A large home on a private street?"

"Mr. Collique, do I look like a woman who cares about the American dream? You've mistaken me for my sister."

Again, Martin smiled, this time with an easiness that surprised Izzy. "Isabel, of all the women working for me...you're my second favorite," he said before sliding off the seat as he signaled the bartender, saying, "Put her drinks on my tab."

"Fuck you," Izzy answered once Martin was far enough away from the bar to hear. "I already paid."

****

After running errands and cooking a meal at Deanna's, Candy dashed home when she saw Curtis pull into the driveway. He hadn't completely moved in. His daughter was battling to stay in their home. They opted not to make a big deal out of it, mainly because they didn't want Martin to know. He assumed Curtis would move in with Candy and his daughter would be in tow. While Erika was at school, Curtis was usually at Candy's or Deanna's. He also slipped out after Erika went to bed, just so he and Candy could have sex. Since the women started counterfeiting gowns, it left Curtis with little to do and a lot of free time. There were only so many hours he could spend at the gym. Sex helped burn off some of the boredom and Candy certainly wasn't complaining because Curtis had grown more inventive over the past couple of weeks, and while she loved the craziness of his passions, Candy didn't realize he was feeling underused and ineffective. Boredom was never good for a man.

Curtis was not cut out for a life of leisure. He needed a goal, a reason, a job. Being the conduit between the women and Martin, being their protector, juiced him but when things were running smoothly, it left him with little to handle. And while he understood business better than any of them, and how this operation should run, that wasn't his domain. Ava would resent him. Deanna would resent him. That left him the gym and sex. And as much as he liked both of those things, it wasn't enough.

****

Stacy Lipton stared into Barry Wimmer's blue eyes and couldn't remember another man she abhorred more. He wasn't arrogant, for a Fed. For a normal person, yes, he was what classmates in college referred to as a 'dwee', a dick with ears, but her being a black, lesbian police officer, he wasn't the first asshole she ever had to deal with that wore a badge. Actually, that described the lion's share of men in her department, and in law enforcement. She had dealt with other Federal Agents who were rudely arrogant and treated everyone on the local level like they were bumpkins. Agent Wimmer couldn't be bothered to be overly arrogant; he was simply dismissive. He came intending to run his own investigation and didn't feel he needed the SLPD's assistance. Most certainly Stacy's.

"You don't want our help, that's fine," Stacy sniffed. "But any information you find, any leads, I hope I don't have to call your boss to get them."

Barry's face didn't move. He shrugged. "I'll write a report. And make sure you're CC'd." Then without another word or even a glance in her direction, he walked out of the station, his heels hitting the tile in a steady rhythm as he exited.

"Fine, just know when I get information or a lead, it'll be in a report too. I'll make sure you're CC'd," she answered.

Barry simply nodded, ignoring her cynicism, his lips pursed as if he was already thinking about something more important. She watched, imagining Barry had a stick jammed up his ass, which she would have to remove to crawl up there and stay. Because she was not about to be cut out of this case. Certainly not by some uptight, straight, white, Fed with a nasty streak. Barry couldn't get away from Stacy fast enough. There was something about local cops that irked the shit out of him. They badly wanted to make a name for themselves. Wanted to move up the ladder. Wimmer wanted nothing more than to be a Fed. It's why he studied criminal justice in college. Also, why he never applied to be a police officer. Only wanted to work for the Bureau. Didn't need to run it, never wanted to be a boss, wanted to be boots on the ground, working cases. He moved over to human trafficking because it took him around the country, which made him feel more like a celebrity crime solver than just another wonk in D.C. Yet, he didn't work well with others, which is why he never worked huge cases. Too many other agents. Barry preferred the perception of the lone wolf, which he could do when he traveled.

And he quit working every day at the same time. His father, having worked a factory job, clocked out at the same minute almost every day. And while an agent's work was certainly not akin to an assembly line, Barry taught himself to turn it off. A glass of Old Forester, dinner, another glass of Old Forester, and reruns of The Big Bang Theory. Since his wife discovered an out-of-town affair with a very hot, very kinky waitress, which was frowned upon by the Bureau as well, Barry had fought his edgier urges and clung tightly to this schedule. He loved his wife. She was a fascinating person with a PhD in Comparative Literature who taught at the university level. But in bed, she was a dud. Certainly not as daring, or edgy, as Barry wished. For him, sex should be adventurous, a bit wicked. His wife was an exceptional mother and a loving wife. But she was neither nasty nor adventuresome. Barry had tried everything to loosen her up before they went to bed, but no matter how drunk, stoned, or turned-on, once he got her in the bedroom, it was consistently the same thing. And the only thing he loathed more than boring sex was some local cop pretending to be more than they were.

Being a regular, the bourbon was set down in front of him as soon as he picked a seat. Two quick sips, Barry's shoulders dropped, relaxing. This was just what he needed.

As he did every night, Barry glanced down the bar, first left, then right. When his eyes landed on her, Izzy matched his gaze, cocking her head and raising her glass, announcing she was alone. And interested. Barry turned away, staring straight ahead, causing Izzy to smile. He was struggling against his basest urge as if it were a knot that was tightening around his heart, and she could see it. Taking another gulp of his bourbon, he remained focused straight ahead until he couldn't stop himself. His eyes shifted sideways towards Izzy before his head turned. And when it did, Izzy was still staring in his direction, a breezy smile still on her lips. She raised her glass in his direction.

He raised his back.

Taking a shallow breath, Barry rationalized that a conversation with a sexy woman wasn't wrong. And his wife would never know he was tempted. 'Just talk,' that's what he kept repeating to himself as the bourbon began permeating his brain. Friendly conversation. A little playful banter. Something to take back to the hotel room and whack-off remembering. Not one piece of it a sin.

Standing, he steadied himself before he carried his glass down the bar and parked himself two seats over from Izzy, which let her know he was interested but 'just in conversation', he justified his stroll down the bar and his choice in seats. It was a respectable distance and far less obvious than plopping himself onto the seat next to her. Barry was smarter than that. And as he kept telling himself, 'It's not like I'm taking her up to my room.' Ordering another bourbon, he glanced over at Izzy again.

"Drinking the good stuff?" Izzy said to Barry without ever looking at him.

"My reward," he answered.

"We all need rewards," Izzy chuckled, nearly choking on the coyness in her voice.

Barry raised his glass. Smartly, Izzy held her beer bottle in his direction, making him lean towards her to tap them off each other.

"A wedding ring," Izzy said, finally looking right at Barry.

"Yeah," he responded, "but we're just sitting in a bar, two seats apart, aren't we?"

Izzy nodded. "And you don't even know if I like boys," she added with a grin, wanting to see how he responded.

Feeling safe but now really intrigued, Barry slipped from his chair onto the chair next to Izzy. Right where she wanted him.

****

Hugging Clara as she left, Deanna watched her drive off the block. Ava had gone home about an hour before, after making a great meal for Deanna's kids. They preferred Ava's cooking to Deanna's, which pleased Ava since Cassie hated most meals her mother prepared. As Clara's Impala drove off the block, Deanna noticed the town car at the end of the street. She stayed at the door as the car slowly drove down to the end of the cul-de-sac and stopped in front of her house. Martin stepped out of the back.

Deanna froze. Martin equaled bad news. Martin arriving unannounced equaled bad news plus an entire ration of shit she was not ready for. "What are you doing here?" Deanna quickly asked.

"Aren't you going to invite me into your new home?" Martin answered.

Wishing she really had a choice, Deanna stepped back from the front door. She said nothing to Martin but he took the gesture as an invitation, just as Deanna took his question as a demand. And she was in no position to deny the man who owned her home, entrance to his property.

****

Izzy guided Barry to the bed. The powder she slipped into his bourbon when he used the bathroom had really knocked him on his ass. He fell back, laughing, continually mumbling, "Fuuuuuccccckkkkk..."

Unhooking his belt and unzipping his pants, she slithered them down his legs. 'Black briefs,' she thought, 'of course.' Even stoned, having Izzy undress him aroused Barry. His legs were muscular like a runner's. As she worked his underwear off his torso, Barry grabbed at Izzy. She batted away his hands, but he kept groping her, still laughing until she had him completely nude on the bed. Izzy had never been with a man this incapacitated. Quickly, she undressed and climbed on top of Barry. Barry's hands instinctively grabbed hold of her waist. Using her free hand, she snapped pictures of the two of them with her phone. Moving around his body, positioning him as she wished and taking photos, turned Izzy on. He was a gorgeous guy, even better out of his clothes. And the drugs didn't seem to affect his arousal. "I want you," Barry muttered, his hands continuing to grope Izzy, pawing her like he was a seven-year-old finger painting, his eyes were closed.

"You're high," Izzy answered.

"No...no...nope. I want you, baby, I want you, I want you, I want you," Barry responded.

Smiling at his insistence, Izzy reached back and grabbed his manhood. He moaned deeply, which made her giggle as she stroked him. She enjoyed being in charge. It was part of the attraction to having sex with Kevin. Though this was different. And while this wasn't her plan, here Izzy was. Every fiber of her being told her what she was doing was wrong, not that that bothered her particularly, but what it gave her was power over this man. And that was intoxicating. She threw her hips over him and slid him inside her. After shooting a couple more pics, she switched her phone to video and set it up on the nightstand, framing them as best she could but making sure Barry was the star of the show.

She rode him hard, Barry growling like a bear as she did. He came, his face squishing up as if he just lifted the back of a car and then collapsed into the pillows surrounding him. Laughing harder as she crawled off him, Izzy shook her head. "What the hell...?" she continued to chuckle as she picked up her phone and padded off into the bathroom and shut the door. Once dressed, she peeked out, finding Barry asleep. On the way out, she went through his wallet and took the forty dollars he had folded neatly inside. She stopped and looked at the photo of his wife and kids, vague remorse rising inside her like the tide. Kids. Always change everything, which is why at this moment, Izzy was glad she never had one.

****

Examining the first finished gown, his hand caressing the material, checking the strength of seams and the hem, Martin shook his head in disbelief. "This is gorgeous," he declared. "You and your new friend did this in a couple days?"

Deanna nodded. "Once we get in the groove, we move pretty fast. Especially now that Clara is here."

"So, your friend is now part of this?"

"She's not really my friend. I mean she is now, but that's not how this started with her. But yes, she's invaluable. And she should be compensated for her work, just like the rest of us," Deanna responded, proud of herself for being so clear with Martin.

Martin's eyes clung to her, causing Deanna to grow uncomfortable standing this close to him. Finally, she tittered self-consciously. "What?" Deanna implored, hating that he was staring at her without talking.

"You're remarkable," Martin complimented. "This really is your operation. The rest of them, honestly, are expendable."

"We came into this together, we will leave together," Deanna replied defensively, finding it awkward that she was being singled out, even though she knew what he was saying was the truth.

"Absolutely. I just want you to know that I am aware. And that you looked quite beautiful at dinner," continued Martin.

Seeing Ford coming down the stairs, Deanna moved to him protectively and held him to her. "Thank you," she responded to Martin.

Martin smiled at Ford. "Do you like your new house?"

"I have my own room!" Ford crowed.

"That's wonderful!" Martin exclaimed. "I never had my own room as a child. Shared with my two brothers. Never did like it."

"It's great," Ford said, smiling. "Mom, can I get a fruit roll?"

"Go ahead," Deanna responded.

As Ford dashed for the kitchen, Martin smiled at Deanna once again. "The new house seems to agree with your children," Martin said.

"Yes. Thank you," Deanna answered, still uncomfortable with Martin in her home.

"I'm going to be in St. Louis for another couple days. I would like you to have dinner with me tomorrow night," Martin said, almost as if it was a given.

"Are you going to play us all again and ask us not to tell the others?" quizzed Deanna, only half-joking.

"No. I've learned my lesson, I will not do that again. I'm only asking you and if you wish to tell your partners, I'm leaving that to your discretion."

Then it hit Deanna, it was going to be *just them*. 'That's worse,' she thought, trying to remain calm, burying a gasp by pretending to clear her throat as she asked, "You want to take me to dinner?"

"Yes," he almost purred, a devious smile returning to Martin's lips. "Are you afraid of me?" he questioned Deanna with amusement.

Her head swam at the question. There was no suitable answer to this, and he knew it. Deanna felt he enjoyed trapping her. Though she wasn't sure if it was to prove he was smarter than she was or if it had to do with not wanting to be turned down. As Ford padded back through the room, eating his fruit roll on his way back to the stairs leading up, he said, "Go, Mom. You're always saying you need to get out of the house more."

Deanna watched her son bounce up the stairs before she turned back to Martin with an apologetic smile, still unsure of what to say.

"Out of the mouths of babes," he remarked. "I'll take his endorsement as a yes."

Because he knew, and Deanna knew, that she could not say no.

DINNER IS SERVED

Regretting accepting Martin's invitation almost immediately, Deanna was furious with herself for not finding some way out of it. And worse, she couldn't share her frustration with the other women. Deanna knew they'd be wary, Ava and Candy already expressing their uselessness in the new operation. Deanna didn't want to deal with their suspicion and misgivings, waiting in her home until she returned to find out what was said, each more scared than the other, knowing they wouldn't believe her anyway. It was completely reasonable to assume the worst now. Knowing whatever she said, no matter how reasonable it sounded, it would not quell their alarm. Being the only one who knew how to sew the designs, and having brought on Clara to assist, Deanna knew the others silently and not so silently recognized that Deanna was now the total focus of this hybrid enterprise. When they were working for themselves, they each had a part to play in the operation. Now, their participation was spotty, more on-call than on-deck. Announcing that Martin wanted to dine with her alone would only explode any tension that was already simmering beneath every smile they shared.

Deanna missed the window of time when the other women had actual assignments in the crimes they were committing, and Candy was the center. She was the one who would walk into a store with Ava and buy a few items for Deanna to copy. Ava was learning that part of the business and as they were making a little more money with each replica, Deanna figured it wouldn't be long before Ava would learn the ropes and be buying the items herself and allowing Candy to focus on the resale. Izzy, being a tattoo artist, had a great eye for detail, would help with color, material and accessories, running errands and being the muscle of the group when necessary. Hell, Izzy blew some guy's head off.

But now they no longer needed the muscle, so Izzy was off proving her value to Martin by taking on private projects. Candy no longer had to buy items, return the copies, or set up the re-sale of what they had copied, leaving her with little to do but cheerlead and occasional errands. And Ava had even less to do, relegated to cooking meals. Deanna and Clara were accomplishing the lion's share of the actual work, and she knew the menial tasks bored the others. And that boredom led to fear and mistrust. While the life they found themselves thrust into had quickly become comfortable, especially considering the circumstances they were each living in prior, Deanna knew it would not be long before all of this would erupt into a mess.

The doorbell ringing snapped Deanna out of her thoughts. Clara. They had to get busy this morning, since Deanna needed time this afternoon to get ready for her 'dinner date'. But she didn't see Clara's car in her driveway. It was a delivery van. Opening the door, the deliveryman smiled as he handed Deanna a large box. Not accustomed to tipping a delivery person, Deanna didn't figure it out until he was back in his van pulling out of her driveway. She quickly grabbed a few dollars from her purse, not even sure if that was the proper amount, and chased him down the block to hand it to him. Having enough money to tip anyone was new to Deanna.

Back in her home, she slid the lid off the box, reaching in and pulling a sparkly dress that unfurled as she held it up. Simple design, beautiful, she held the charcoal-hue cocktail dress against her body, then realizing it fell just above her knee, which is where she liked her dresses cut.

The straps were thin, almost delicate. Recognizing that this color would look spectacular on her made Deanna both giddy and uncomfortable. How would Martin know this? Is his eye that good? Inside there was a card that read: A car will pick you up at six. Looking forward to dinner. Regards, Martin.

Quickly, she laid the dress back in the box and placed the lid back on. 'Now he's dressing me?' she thought. Deanna sat on the sofa and tried to catch her breath. She couldn't fathom what angle he was playing. Was this to keep her off-balance and compliant? To make her feel less-than? As if without him, she had nothing. Or was this simply a gift, something he felt she would love and feel great in. Was he simply trying to make her smile? She'd given him no reason to actually like her. What was it? As she pondered what the reasons were for this attention, what kept popping into Deanna's mind was the cost. If there was one thing Deanna knew from being a marginalized female, it was that there was always, always, a cost.

****

Candy held Curtis' hand tightly. She knew he had to feel a sense of creepiness attending Ramona's memorial with her. Even though Ramona's house was already on the market, her daughters opted to hold the memorial in Ramona's home, since the funeral and burial were family only. Circling through the catered event, white-gloved servers carrying food and drink on trays through the crowded living room, Candy nodded at women she knew, many whose husbands opted not to attend. The women's eyes held on Curtis. Some because he was black, others because he was so handsome, all taking him in as surreptitiously as possible. He stood out. Not only because he was the only black person in the room without a tray in his hand, but also because of the way he carried himself, the way his tailored suit fit him perfectly, giving him an aura of not only power but a masculine glamor. Candy noticed the over-the-shoulder glances that would last long after they passed. Hell, if these women couldn't gossip at Ramona's funeral, where could they? And Candy was perfectly fine with it. She never minded a little jealous shade thrown her way. Made her feel good.

"You okay?" Candy asked, leaning into Curtis.

"Ghosts," was all Curtis whispered.

"Trust me," Candy responded, "Ramona's isn't the only one in this house. There are bunches of secrets that died with Ramona. Look around," she continued, stopping to take in the crowd in the expansive living room. "Not a single person here really liked Ramona. They feared her. Needed her. Wanted to be her. Whatever. But she didn't have any real friends. Even the women who started off as her friend...they eventually tired of Ramona's haughtiness and just took advantage of whatever they could rip from her bony hands, all the while smiling at her, and Ramona smiling back. I think Ramona screwed up every friendship she ever had. Most of the women in this room...they're only here to make sure she's really, truly dead."

"You're trying to make me feel better?" Curtis asked.

Her arm slipped around his waist, holding on even tighter to him. "You've taken care of me, Curtis. Now's my little chance to take care of you."

Turning to her, he kissed Candy. "I appreciate that. I love you. But we have to talk."

Candy froze, her eyes locking on Curtis'. Realizing how his last sentence was perceived, he shook his head. "Not about us. About Martin. And the situation we're in."

Candy let out the breath she was holding. But his clarification didn't make her feel any better. Because it was bigger and badder than any problem she and Curtis had.

****

Kevin climbed out of his underwear and into a jockstrap and cup, adjusting himself before pulling on his baseball pants. Having lingered in the hallway to talk to a new junior who transferred to the school a few weeks ago, Kevin was late for practice. He wiggled his foot into his cleats, laced them tight, and raced out of the locker room, still yanking on his shirt over his head. He didn't need Coach Cunello barking at him. The season was almost over and with a half dozen colleges looking at Kevin seriously; he wanted to keep things mellow and on track. Even his grades were on an uptick since moving to the new house. He kept telling his mother it was "the vibe" but truth was he and Theresa McGee had made up and she was 'assisting' with his work again.

"You're late for practice," Cassie said as Kevin exited the building past where she'd been waiting. "What were you doing? Getting a blowjob from the new girl?"

"What do you want?" quizzed Kevin, picking up his pace.

"I know who your sister is fucking," Cassie responded, hoping bluntness would stop Kevin.

"Tell me later," Kevin said as Cassie kept stride with him.

"I think you'll want to know now," she continued as they neared the practice field.

"Why would I want to know now?"

Cassie smirked as she caught sight of Coach Cunello working with Danny Washturn, one of the team's pitchers.

"He's coaching her in sex like he's coaching you in base-ball," Cassie said nonchalantly, almost with a shrug.

Kevin stopped in his tracks, turning to face Cassie who was smiling with a cool gotcha confidence. "Now that I have your attention..." she said calmly. "No bullshit, that freak is fucking your little sister."

Kevin turned towards Vince, his head filling with panic-fog. He wasn't sure what he was supposed to be feeling, or if what Cassie had just announced was even true. Part of him wanted to rush his coach, knock him down and start wailing punches. The other wanted to run the other way, to find a way to wipe Cassie's words out of his head. But all Kevin could manage to do was shake his head and mutter, "What the fuck...no way, no way, no way..."

****

"Well, what the hell did you do for Martin?" Ava insisted as she walked into Izzy's room, attempting to pick up the mess.

"We gotta get a maid or something," Izzy sighed, wondering how the place fell into such disarray this quickly. She moved in a few weeks ago and it looked like months' worth of mess. "My old place never looked like this."

"Whose are these?" Ava asked, holding up a pair of men's underwear she found jammed down into the side of an armchair in Izzy's room. "And when are you fucking men in the house. I'm here all the time!"

Izzy winced, shaking her head. They were Kevin's. Not that Izzy was going to tell her sister that. Instead, she snapped them from her hand and fired her a 'mind your own business' look. Kevin must have left them the other night when he came in through the back door when Ava took Cassie out for dinner and ran out when the headlights bounced into the driveway and down to the garage.

"I gotta put cameras in this house," Ava added.

"Knock yourself out."

"Jesus, Iz, there's a lot you're not telling me anymore. Used to tell me all your shit. What's going on? We living too close now?" Ava asked.

"We are," Izzy chided. "We were better miles apart."

Just then, Cassie stormed in.

"What the fuck?" Izzy barked. "You're like your mother."

"I live here too, your bedroom door is open. What am I supposed to do, knock? I need to tell you something because I just talked to Kevin, and I don't think he really believed me and it pisses me off," Cassie ranted.

"What happened between you two now?" Ava asked.

"It's not him," Cassie answered, calming herself. "It's his sister."

"Tracee?" Izzy quizzed.

"She's...she's having sex!"

Ava and Izzy shared a 'whatever' look, both wondering why Cassie would even care, before turning back to Cassie, who was eagerly waiting to announce the rest of her news.

"With Kevin's baseball coach!" Cassie finished.

Any amusement that Ava had knowing Deanna would shit herself when she found out her fifteen-year-old daughter was getting under some guy, vanished immediately once she knew who it was. Izzy's shoulders tensed, her jaw clenched.

"That piece of shit. Are you sure?" Izzy asked, her words spitting out.

"Very sure," Cassie said, the only one of the three now even close to calm. Which is just how Cassie wanted it.

As Cassie was relaying what she witnessed between Coach Cunello and Tracee, Tracee was assisting her mother as Deanna finished dressing. Tracee couldn't believe her mother could look so beautiful. Even Ford stood near the door, marveling that the woman in the dress was the same woman who made him a grilled cheese earlier. He had never taken in his mother as a man views a woman. She was his mom. Usually in a battered t-shirt and jeans. Jeans bought from a second-hand store. But before him was this woman. Her hair was wavy and pulled back. She had on lipstick, but that wasn't the reason her face looked so different. Ford had never really seen his mother with makeup on. Mascara, eyeshadow, blush...he didn't even know what they were, but he knew his mother was beautiful.

"You look awesome, Mom," Tracee exclaimed as Deanna checked herself in the mirror.

"Yeah, Mom...you look different. But pretty," Ford added.

Deanna turned and smiled at him. His eyes were wide with awe, which elated Deanna. Ford seeing his mother as a woman was rare, and she enjoyed that he recognized when she made an effort. When he heard a car pulling into the driveway, Ford ran from the doorway to the front window. "Mom! There's a really cool car here!" he called.

One more glance into the mirror before she grabbed her small handbag, something she wished matched her outfit. Tossing in her house keys, she clipped out of the room and towards the front door, her high heels clicking off the wood floor in the hallway.

"I won't be late," she announced to Tracee and Ford.

As Deanna carefully traversed the front steps and the walkway, the driver exited the car and opened the passenger door for her. As she climbed in and the door shut, Ava and Izzy exited their home, followed by Cassie. Their plan to fill Deanna in went belly-up as they watched the town car drive down the block.

"Where's she going?" Ava asked, not necessarily to Izzy or Cassie, more to herself. "In that car..."

"Never said anything to me," responded Izzy.

Turning, Ava, Izzy and Cassie saw Tracee standing at the front door of the house. Seeing them glaring at her, Tracee's demeanor soured. She glowered right back before walking back inside and shoved the front door shut.

"Bitch," Tracee uttered.

****

Throughout dinner, the conversation between Deanna and Martin stayed polite and cursory. Martin wanted to know the progress of the new gowns. Deanna filled him in. Deanna shared tidbits about her kids. Martin nodded. Martin complimented her on how beautiful the dress looked on her. Deanna thanked him. She told him she loved his suit. Martin smiled. Martin's eyes seldom left her, even to look at the menu. He liked what he saw, silently complimenting himself on the selection that he made. Realizing he was prouder of his choice than he was at Deanna's beauty, he smirked as he imagined Dr. Frankenstein had when the monster got off the table. But credit where credit was due, the dress he selected for Deanna fit perfectly. The first time he laid eyes on her, he knew with a little effort and some subtle guidance, that she could be beautiful. But he also surmised that there was little reason for that effort because Deanna wouldn't comply. But he was wrong. And what Martin wasn't prepared for was just how alluring she was when she put some effort into it. Martin always weirdly enjoyed Deanna's company. But now he wanted her in another way.

Deanna just wanted dinner over. She was miserable sitting across the table from him. Martin didn't seem the type to do anything casually, and this expensive dinner where there was too much plate with too little food, as far as she was concerned, proved her point. She knew Martin brought her here for a reason. And she wished he would just get to it, she wanted to go home and make a bowl of pasta with a little butter.

"Can I ask why you invited me to dinner? I feel like there's something you're not saying or asking," Deanna finally asked, wanting this evening to wind to a conclusion.

His eyes still on her, Martin smiled. "Can't a man just want to have dinner with a beautiful woman?" Martin countered.

"For most men, I would say yeah, probably. And thank you for the compliment. But I feel like I'm here for more than that," Deanna answered.

Martin shifted uncomfortably, which Deanna noticed. Martin felt a weird self-consciousness, surprising himself. He wished she trusted him, at least slightly more than she did. Martin firmly believed he'd proved his loyalty. The women were still alive. He bought them homes, paid them for their labor. Deanna's mistrust needled him. "You've been the woman who has put in the most work. I am not telling you something you don't know. Without you, there would be no operation. No money for your friends. Without you...they would not have crawled out of the situations they were in. And I'm quite happy with your work. And what I see for the future. This is my way of rewarding you," Martin stated.

"You could have sent a card. Or cash. Cash is always good," Deanna mused, a tiny smile wiping onto her lips.

Martin chuckled. "You don't like my company?" he asked directly.

"Honestly? I'm never sure what 'your company' means. You've had us under your thumb since this all began. You might be very frank with me but how would I know? I don't know you. Not really. I only know what you've done. To me. My family. My friends. And after all of that, you seem to believe that I should trust you. But I can't. You scare me."

"You are surprisingly honest," Martin responded. "I respect that, Deanna. Very few people are with me."

"Why do you think that is?"

Again, Martin chuckled. "I feel you're about to tell me."

"I don't know if I can. But I can try if you really want me to. I just don't know if I should."

"Why?"

Deanna smiled sadly. "I told you. You scare me."

"Granted," Martin smirked. "I'm not everyone's cup of tea. Now I'm going to be very honest with you. I'm not worried about how most people perceive me. But I want you to like me, to trust me. I want you to see me differently."

"Why?" Deanna wanted to know, completely honestly.

"Because I want more from you, Deanna. You're beautiful, talented, two things I don't think you see in yourself, which for someone like me only makes you more attractive. You're different from the women I know."

"Well, I don't know about the other women you know, but I would bet that most of them are rich and successful, I mean the ones that are your friends."

"Many are. But I don't want them like I want you."

Deanna drew in a deep breath, unable to breathe it out. Of all the things Martin could say to her, this one felt like a gut punch. Many women would be flattered. But for

Deanna, it only frightened her more. Her better sense told her to stand up and run out of the restaurant, but like a teen in a slasher movie, she was frozen, feeling as if she would soon be lying in a pool of her own blood.

LOTS OF PAIN, FORGET THE GAIN

The text came as Martin was talking. Deanna slipped her phone from her purse and looked at it, hoping it wasn't from one of her kids, but wishing for a reason to escape this dinner. It was from Ava. 'We need to talk,' was all it read.

All Deanna could think was, 'we certainly do.'

"Everything okay?" Martin asked.

Deanna knew it was her chance to slide out of this uncomfortable evening. "Just Ford...he doesn't like when I'm not in the house when he goes to bed," Deanna said, trying not to look as if she was lying.

"Well, we can get on our way," Martin said, taking his napkin out of his lap and setting it on the table.

"I think I've probably ruined your night anyway," Deanna responded, standing quickly before he changed his mind.

"Not at all, not at all," he said with a smile. A smile that only beamed with confidence and not of chagrin, which disappointed Deanna.

She was never so happy to get into a car to go home. Martin did try to coax her into coming back to his hotel room for a cocktail, but Deanna declined gently. While she did find Martin stylishly attractive, remembering the word 'jaunty' from a fashion magazine, she could not shake the fear that rumbled around inside her. She would never get over that this man gave the order to kill her son. She might work for him now. But not by choice. Nothing with Martin Collique was by choice. Everything was thrust upon her and her friends as a mechanism to stay alive.

"I'll see you very soon," Martin said as he held the car door for Deanna. "And please, think about what I'm asking."

"Did you ask me something?" Deanna answered, unsure, knowing she simply should have agreed and made her exit.

Martin smiled. "Maybe not directly. But I would like to go out with you again, Deanna. To know you better. On a different level. At least enough to calm this trepidation you have about me. I'm not who you think I am. At least I don't think I am. And if you knew me better, I think you would agree."

Looking up at him from inside the town car, Deanna nodded. She just wanted to leave. Now. This moment. So, she nodded and uttered, "Okay," just to get away, angry at herself the moment she did it, knowing she opened the door for another uncomfortable evening which would mirror this one. And that he would try and wear her down, hoping that with enough time, she would view him differently. Deanna accepted that there was no good answer. There was no good exit strategy. That Martin probably got what he wanted most of the time.

As the car pulled away from the curb, Deanna leaned back in the seat, slipping her phone out of her purse. She punched in Ava's number.

"Where've you been?" Ava answered.

"I'm heading home. What's so urgent?" asked Deanna.

"We'll talk when you get home. Where'd you go tonight?" Ava wanted to know.

"Like you said, we'll talk when I get home."

****

Ava and Izzy were sitting on their front porch when the town car pulled around the circle and stopped in front of

Deanna's home, the driver holding the door and letting her out.

Seeing them, Deanna waved, saying, "Two of you? This isn't good."

As she walked into her home, she left the door open for Ava and Izzy. As they followed her in, Ava finally got an eyeful of Deanna's new dress. "Wow. Shit. When did you get that?"

"That's what I want to talk to you about. Martin sent it to me."

Izzy nearly choked. "Collique?"

"He invited me to dinner. Sent a car."

"And bought you a very expensive dress. I guess he didn't like your clothes," Ava half-joked.

"I guess he knows I don't have anything fancy. At least not fancy enough for the places he eats. I'm still not sure what this dinner was about."

Izzy glanced at her sister and then back to Deanna. "What did he talk about?" she asked.

"Me. Said he wants me to like him more. Wanted to take me out again. It was weird," Deanna answered, her honesty completely naked.

"He hit on you?" Ava quizzed, astounded.

Deanna nodded and shrugged at the same time. "Yeah...I guess. It was so, like, crazy. He complimented me, said he'd like to get to know me better...well, for me to get to know him better. Like he already knew me, and I didn't know him. But I couldn't help but feel I was being punked or something," Deanna continued as she moved into the kitchen, Ava and Izzy following. Deanna opened a cabinet and pulled out a box of bowtie pasta and then moved to another cabinet and pulled out a bottle of wine. "I didn't drink much through dinner. I wanted to keep my wits about me. But I need one now. Anyone else?"

Both Izzy and Ava grabbed glasses, they were all in on this conversation...and knew a drink would be necessary for the one they needed to have with Deanna. With the bomb they were about to drop, a glass of wine couldn't hurt.

After she splashed the wine into three glasses, Deanna sat at her new kitchen table. "I thought this was going to be a business meeting. I want to bitch at him about the time frame he wants these gowns. We never got to talk about it. It was all pleasantries and then bam, he tells me he wants to have some sort of romance. At least I think that's what he was saying and I was like 'what'?! I barely know him and what I know scares the shit out of me."

"He's not a bad-looking man," Izzy offered.

"He tried to kill my son. He murdered Santos in front of us," Deanna reminded them.

Ava reacted sharply but didn't utter a response. As intrigued by this as she was, she wanted to move on from this topic and clue Deanna in on what was happening with her daughter.

"This is crazy," Deanna said, taking a gulp of the wine as she got up to look at the water she had put in a pot, wishing it would boil so she could make the pasta she was craving. "Now, what do you need to tell me. And please tell me it's not crazier than what's already happened, or I'll be up all night, drinking the rest of the wine and eating bowtie pasta in butter."

Ava grabbed the wine bottle and moved over to the stove, setting it on the counter in front of Deanna. Any remnant of a smile that Deanna held on to her lips quickly vanished.

"Kevin?" Deanna asked uncomfortably.

Izzy shook her head.

"Ford?" Deanna asked, surprised.

Again, Izzy shook her head. "It's about Tracee," Izzy said, as Deanna dumped the bowtie pasta into the pot of boiling water and then moved back over to sit at the table.

"Shit. What?"

Ava slid back into the seat across the table from Deanna.

"She's sexually active," Ava responded, hating herself for the way she presented it, even though the news obviously surprised Deanna. "Look, Deanna, she's been having sex with a guy. And that's not really the problem, I mean, you probably think so, but she's fifteen, right? Lots of girls have sex at fifteen."

"That wasn't what I was thinking," Deanna answered. "I didn't even know she was seeing a boy."

"That's just it," Ava huffed out, knowing how hard this was going to be for Deanna, because it was hard to say. "She's not seeing a boy."

"A girl?" Deanna responded sharply, even more surprised.

"She's hooking up with Kevin's baseball coach," Izzy stated, ripping off the Band-Aid.

Eyeing Izzy as if she spoke in a foreign language, Deanna couldn't register the information that the sisters just shared. Tracee. Sex. With Coach Cunello. No. No, that couldn't be possible. Not Tracee. Not that man.

"Are you saying he raped her?" Deanna breathlessly questioned.

"Technically, yeah. I mean, it's rape because she's underage, isn't it?" Ava said. "But it seems that Tracee thinks they're like, involved. Involved-involved, like this wasn't a one-time thing. It's been going on. I don't know how long. But for a time, I guess," Ava continued, stumbling through her words. "Anyway, you need to talk to her. And know we're here for you."

"What we need is to break this motherfucker in half," Izzy snapped.

Deanna fell completely silent. She had no idea how to respond to this. This day had already consumed every fiber of her patience prior to this news. Hell, the previous night still had her mind agog when all of this came down. Ava and Izzy wanted to reach across the table and take Deanna's hand, something physical to keep her grounded. They could see she was becoming lost in her jumbled, overwhelming thoughts. Just then, the water in the pot boiled over and Ava jumped up, turning down the heat and stirring the pasta. "I know this is a lot, girl. Especially after Martin. But you had to know. I know you need to talk to her. Get her side of things. But we are here for you," Ava softly said, as Deanna continued to stare off across the room.

Finally nodding, Deanna stood. "Okay. Thanks," was all she said before walking out of her own kitchen, leaving Ava and Izzy there.

The sisters traded 'what the fuck?' looks. Ava turned the pasta off, leaving the pasta floating, and signaled Izzy to go. She knew they had to let Deanna think and decide what course of action she wanted to follow. This news blindsided her and it was going to be a long night in the Brayton house.

****

Walking up to her daughter's closed door, Deanna put her hands on the door, partially to hold herself up, partially to feel the vibe, unsure if she should just enter, knock and enter, or just turn around and wait until morning. She had no clue what she would say to Tracee. And while Deanna seldom planned for a conversation, this seemed like a talk that she had to have something prepared or she would completely lose her shit. When her hand knocked on the door before her mind was ready, Deanna didn't wait for Tracee to answer before she pushed open the door. Tracee was on her bed, AirPods in, doing homework.

"Mom?" Tracee responded, sitting up. "Something the matter?"

"You. And Kevin's coach," was all Deanna could force out.

Tracee sat up more sharply. Her face frozen with anger, knowing where this information originated. "Let me guess. Cassie told her mom and her mom told you?" Tracee answered.

"So, it is true?"

"It's not what you think. Because I know what you think. Vince and I—"

"Vince?"

"That's his name, Mom. He's taken care of me. He understands me, I don't want to say he loves me, but he cares about me and my feelings matter to him. He's a good man. I didn't go seeking this out and I know he didn't. It just happened."

Deanna's body fell against the door jamb. This was her daughter spewing this nonsense. Her gifted, wise beyond her years, daughter. And worse, she was spewing these words calmly with a tone of intelligence that boiled Deanna's blood. What the hell?! "No. No!" Deanna barked. "He doesn't care about you! Or he wouldn't have done this to you! No man in his right mind, as much as they all think about it, would be involved with a fifteen-year-old girl! Much less a girl who attends the high school he teaches at!"

"God, Mom! Kevin fucks every girl he sees. He's been doing it since before he turned fifteen! You've never said a word to him about what he does!"

"I have too!" Deanna fired back.

"But me," Tracee yelled, "I finally meet someone that I have feelings for, someone that has feelings for me, and it's wrong?"

"He's a fucking teacher, Tracee! Twenty years older than you!" Deanna screamed back. "And yes, it's wrong! And I'm going to put his ass in prison!"

That got Tracee off her bed, standing, squaring off with her mother. "No, you're not! I...I love him—"

"Love him?! Are you kidding me?! No, you don't. You don't know what that is! What it feels like! And he doesn't love you! He's using you. He took something from you! He's a creep! I will kill him. And if I can't, I'll fucking have Martin kill him! You are not to go near that man again! Do you understand me?!"

"Mom—"

"No!" Deanna snapped, her voice growing shriller and more urgent as she rushed at her daughter, her finger in Tracee's face. "You stay away from him!"

Tears flooded Tracee's eyes. "You don't understand..." she sobbed.

"I understand! I understand he's in his thirties and you are fifteen! I understand he's in a position of authority at your school and he abused that! He is a sick man! What he did to you...that you can't even understand..."

Deanna flung her arms around her sobbing daughter, yanking Tracee to her. "He's got your head all twisted, Tracee. You may think you love him or have feelings and that this is a good thing, and he's a good man, but he's not. And this is horrible. One day, you'll get that. He did something that no adult man should do. I should fucking kill him for it!"

"Mom, stop! No! Don't do anything! Please! Don't tell the school. He'll lose his job."

"He should have thought of that before he messed with my daughter!"

"This was me, Mom! I wanted this! I want him! Why can't you get that? I don't regret this. What do you want for me, to have my first time be with some pimple-faced loser in my class? Because those are the boys that like me. That or guys who want to get their hand down my bra! Vince is different. I like him because he's a man. Please, please understand that! I want to be with him."

"He doesn't really want to be with you, Tracee," Deanna said, now crying as well. "He wanted to have sex with a young woman and guys like him know how to lure girls to them. To get what they want. But they don't want anything else. This is a conquest. A win. And he will move on. And Tracee, you aren't even on the pill."

"We were careful," Tracee pleaded.

As tears fell down her cheeks, ruining her mascara, Deanna raised her hands, half giving up, half to make Tracee shut up, Tracee's words crushing Deanna's spirit. How could the smartest person Deanna knew be so god-damn stupid!? She raised Tracee better than this. That was a given for Deanna. Did their sudden economic change allow Tracee to step out? Was it not having her father?

Was it her older brother's promiscuity what opened this door? Deanna's rage grew, blaming being so busy with the counterfeiting and Martin and all that bullshit, that she didn't keep an eye on her daughter. "Goddamn it!" Deanna cried. "This wouldn't have happened if we were living on the streets."

Tracee had no answer for that.

"This is how girls end up pregnant, Tracee! Do you want to be raising a baby for the rest of your high school days? It will keep you from going to college, and you're smart, you need to go to college! God, Tracee, only stupid girls have sex without protection!" Deanna ranted.

"Mom—"

"No. No! This is over. And believe me, I'm going to deal with Coach Cunello."

"I love him, Mom!"

"Will you stop saying that!?! You don't love him!" Deanna screamed at her daughter, bringing Ford and Kevin to the door of Tracee's room. "We're done talking about it! You're done! This bullshit is over!"

Deanna stormed out of Tracee's room, leaving Tracee sobbing. Deanna stopped in front of Kevin, glaring at him, her rage bare.

"What did I do?" Kevin asked.

"Your baseball coach is a dead man for messing with my daughter," she announced to him before stomping down the hallway.

Kevin's entire body tingled. Even after Cassie told him, he didn't want to believe it. But it must be true. His little sister and his coach. "I can't believe you'd fuck him! My coach! Is this to get back at me? I mean what the fuck!? Coach Cunello!?"

Tracee seethed through her tears. "Shut the fuck up, Kevin." She took a few steps towards him, pushing him out of her room and slamming the door. Tracee rushed back to her bed and buried herself in her pillows, sobbing so hard, her body shook.

****

No one spoke at breakfast. Deanna could barely look at Tracee, who she now saw differently, nor could she look at Kevin, who she oddly felt shared some of the blame for this. Not more than herself, but still he was guilty by proximity and action. Being a single mother was never easy. But icing that moldy cake with poverty only made it more difficult. Failing your children, and that is how Deanna felt about herself now, pierced her soul. Deanna had never really been proud of herself, or found something she could crow about, not until recently. Finally being able to say she lifted her kids out of poverty, something she never thought she'd be able to say much less do, gave her a sense of self she'd never had before. Deanna felt it gave her worth. But finding out Tracee was being sexually abused by Kevin's baseball coach, threw her deep into the well of unworthiness she had just crawled out of.

Once her kids left for school, Ford being last out the door, Deanna phoned Candy, Ava, and Izzy. She needed them there. This morning. She already knew that Clara was coming. She needed her posse.

Candy was the last one to arrive. And it was obvious to Izzy that it was because Candy had morning sex with Curtis. After explaining to Candy and Clara what Ava and Izzy already knew, Izzy was the first one to speak up. "Look, we are sorry we dumped this shit on you last night, but now that you've had some time, and probably a hard talk with Tracee, what do you want to do?"

"Cut off his balls," Deanna answered without hesitation.

"Are you serious, sugar?" Candy quizzed.

"I am," Deanna responded. "That's what I want. I want him de-balled, or whatever it's called."

"Neuter," Ava tossed into the conversation.

"Fine. Neuter. That works," Deanna responded.

"I grew up on a farm. I know how to castrate bulls, sheep, pigs," Clara piped up. "A man ain't no different."

"We have a professional in our midst," Izzy joked.

"Sugar," Candy stood up. "I'd be happy to talk to Curtis. Have him take care of this. I'm sure you could also talk to Martin as well. He didn't have much of a problem taking care of Santos."

"I don't want Martin to know about this. Not because I don't want him to know but because I want Coach Cunello to know this is me. I just need all of you to back me up. This is my little girl. If she gets pregnant...I do not want her stuck in the world I'm in. Present actions aside, she's too damn smart. She's got a future ahead of her."

"We got your back, girl," Ava stated. "You know that."

"Abso-fucking-lutely," Izzy seconded.

"Marcus has an arsenal. It's all in my house. You are welcome to come over and take a look. I'm sure I got what you need," Clara added.

"We need to teach this son-of-a-bitch not to fuck with another young girl again," Izzy said, standing in solidarity with Deanna, at this moment, unaware of her own hypocrisy.

"Mess with one of us, you mess with us all," Candy added.

Overwhelmed by their support, Deanna felt like she was going to cry. "I want to teach this man that you don't do this to people's daughters. At least not mine."

THE DAMAGE IS DONE

As he was driving out of the FBI office building's garage downtown, Barry's phone dinged. He'd programmed his phone for messages from various people. Work had a different sound than a message from his wife. This was from a number he didn't know, which immediately made him curious how they got his number. Turning onto Market Street, he picked up the phone to look. The caller simply read PRIVATE. Punching up the message, Barry couldn't make out what the photo was. He continued glancing at it as he drove, but he sensed he needed to stop and get a good look at this. Pulling into a parking space on the side of the street, he picked his phone up and glared. That's when he deciphered exactly what he was staring at. It was the woman from the bar. Even unable to see her face, Barry knew. She was nude. And on top of him.

He was nude as well, his hands on her hips and he appeared to be smiling, even though his eyes were closed. There was no doubt about what was going on. But even though he racked his brain, he couldn't remember the woman being in his room, much less naked and on top of him.

His phone dinged and dinged again, over and over. Each one was another photo of Barry having sex with this woman. A woman whose name he couldn't even remember. His breathing shallowed. His head swam. "Fuck!" he screamed. 'What are they going to do with these?!' he wondered, all too aware of what the answer to that was. This was blackmail. But why? What could this woman possibly want?

He had no answers but one thing he did know is he was totally screwed. Both professionally and personally. How the hell could he let this happen again? Barry laid his head against the steering wheel, grinding his teeth as he tried to settle himself, trying to force himself to think objectively, trying to formulate some plan that didn't include him losing his wife and his job.

****

Baseball bats. There were a lot of them in the house because of Kevin. And Deanna wanted to swing one at Coach Cunello's balls. She wanted to hear him scream in pain. With each hour that passed, Deanna thought she would calm down, her head would clear, and she would think of some way to make him pay for his sins other than physically hurting him. But that didn't happen. Each passing hour only made Deanna more irate. Both at Coach Cunello and her daughter, the smart one in the family. How could Tracee be this naive, this careless? Even Kevin wasn't this dumb, at least when it came to sex. And sadly, and secretly, with Kevin she came to expect his sexual irresponsibility. But not Tracee. Not at fifteen.

Deanna had every intention of hurting Vince. And she knew the other women were with her. Navigating her daughter's feelings both before and after would be a complete mess, but Deanna didn't care. This would be dealt with. Today.

What Deanna didn't know was that Kevin felt the same way. He didn't sleep all night either. All he could think about was beating the shit out of his coach, the man he looked up to, who was a huge part of Kevin's success on the field. Kevin left the house before anyone else got up. He didn't want to see his sister. Didn't want to see his mom. The only person Kevin wanted to see was Coach Cunello. How could this even happen? His sister hated sports. How would these two people even come into contact with each other? They had no connection other than him. And Kevin kept the pieces of his life separate. Kevin couldn't wrap his head around what this grown man, who could nail pretty much any woman he wanted, could see in his little sister? Nothing about this made any sense. And Kevin kept wishing it weren't the truth. There had to be something he didn't know, that Coach Cunello could explain that would make all this bullshit make sense.

Sitting in the locker room alone, the only sound Kevin heard was the echo of the showers dripping through the cavernous space. One of the track coaches wandered through the locker rooms, giving Kevin a nod. He'd had a class with just about every coach at the school. There was an unspoken understanding that every athlete at the school would take the coaches' classes. Classes they were guaranteed to pass without a lot of effort. Then, quickly moving through the locker room, Vince strode right past Kevin without noticing it was him and out of the locker room. Kevin stood and stormed towards the door Vince had just exited.

"What the fuck?" Vince heard from behind him.

Turning, Kevin was down the hallway. Vince shook his head, not understanding. "You got a problem, Kevin? What's going on?" Vince asked.

"My sister has the problem. And it's you," sneered Kevin. "How the fuck could you do this to me? What's the matter with you? Fucking my sister?!?!"

Panicked, Vince stomped right at him, his arms waving frantically. "Keep your goddamn voice down!"   Getting right in Kevin's face, Vince seethed. "Whatever your sister said, she's lying, she's off, she's got this fixation on me. I've been nice about it, because of you. I don't want to cause a problem for you, moving forward with colleges."

Locking eyes with Vince, Kevin's body stiffened. "My sister didn't tell me."

"I know who told you. She misread a situation. And she wouldn't listen when I tried to explain. You know she's crazy. Look at what she did to you, telling you she was pregnant! You can't possibly believe her, Kevin. Seriously. How dumb are you?"

Without warning, Kevin pivoted on his right foot and came around with his fist. His knuckles hit Vince's jaw, sending him staggering back into the wall. Vince pushed himself upright, ready to retaliate. Stopping himself before he escalated the situation, Vince shook off the pain, his head now pounding as his eyes narrowed at Kevin. Vince wasn't sure he could take this big kid, and he didn't want to add humiliation to the laundry list of shit he was already feeling.

"Are you trying to get yourself expelled?" snarled Vince.

"Sick fuck. You belong in prison," Kevin said, turning and walking away, his fury only building.

"Don't believe what they're telling you. They're lying!" Vince barked, standing frozen in the hallway. Always believing he was a step ahead, he now realized he was a few steps behind and if he didn't get in front of this somehow, Kevin would be correct, Vince would end up behind bars. Slinging his bag over his shoulder, Vince shoved past Kevin and raced back through the locker room, disappearing out the doors on the other side which led towards the ballfields and parking lot.

****

When Tracee discovered Vince wasn't at school that day, her anxiety became almost too much for her to handle. She didn't know what had happened earlier and that he raced home and called in sick from the car on his way home, before anyone but Kevin encountered him. Tracee needed to warn him. She had an inkling of what her mother was planning, especially with those crazy bitches next door chattering in her ear. Tracee wasn't sure if her mother could actually go through with something violent, but considering what came down months before left a dead police officer in their living room, Tracee knew better than to put anything past her mother and her friends. There was already blood on their hands. And Tracee was well-aware that she didn't even know the half of it. If Vince ended up disappearing or dead, Tracee wasn't sure what she would do.

Her mother and four other women were already waiting for Vince. At his home. When Deanna realized Kevin wasn't at home when she woke up after her own terrible night's sleep, she suspected that Kevin had gone to school early, to confront his coach. Which meant Vince knew that a shitstorm was about to rain down. Deanna had never found Vince a very bright guy. Self-possessed, yes, but not exactly smart, and even worse, not a wise man. So, she gathered her forces, had Candy find his address, and the five of them waited.

Pulling into his driveway, Vince spotted the car and the pick-up truck across the street from his small home. Vince recognized the torn bumper sticker on the small pickup. He'd seen it before. It took a moment, but he remembered, the night he watched a small group of people break into Goliath Printing and steal something. Stepping from his car, he saw the door open on the truck and a woman step out. His eyes went to his house. He needed to get in there. But when he saw a figure inside moving past the window, he turned to get back in his car, to relative safety. But he was met with a gun to the face and Izzy's smile. "Where the fuck you think you're going?" she asked softly.

Stumbling back, Izzy grabbed him by his crotch and forced him back against his car, the barrel of the gun pressing against his nose. "Get in the house before I break off your dick, rapist," she growled at him. Shoving Vince towards his house, she kept the barrel of the gun pressed into his back. Izzy had never seen Vince before. She'd heard plenty from Kevin but had never actually laid eyes on him. Sizing him up quickly, she knew he would be the kind of guy she would go for. Joe Poluka good looks, big, muscled without being gnarly. Now it all made sense to her. A man this good-looking paying attention to a teenage girl with low self-esteem. A warm smile, a little banter, and the girl melts. This made Izzy hate him more. This idiot could have pretty much his pick of women, and he's bumping uglies with high school girls he can control. She smiled to herself as she thought about fucking him once before she shoved that gun between his thighs and pulled the trigger.

Vince considered running, but being shot in the back would at best leave him paralyzed. As he got to the door, it opened. Ava was already inside, scowling. He shoved around her into his home. Deanna and Candy had parked themselves on his sofa. Clara shut the door and stood in front of it.

"What the fuck is this? You women are all going to prison for this, you know that, right?" Vince stammered.

Izzy smacked him in the back of the head with the butt of the gun, causing Vince to stumble further into his living room before he crumpled against the wall, catching himself as he slid to the floor. His hand patted the back of his head, checking for blood. Deanna stood up and moved directly in front of him, rage locked in her eyes. She put her foot on his chest and kicked him back until he was leaning back against the sofa. Her foot went to his chest again, staying there.

"With what you've done to my daughter...I am not sure if I want you dead or in prison. You know my family. You mean something to my son, and yet you do this to my daughter!?" Deanna barked. "How many other girls have you done this to?"

"The police are on their way," Vince bluffed.

Laughing, his words caused Ava to stand up too and move behind Deanna. "You do need your ass beaten. You wouldn't dare bring the police into this. That'd be like asking them to beat the fuck out of you before they put your rapist ass in prison and then let the inmates go to town on you."

Aware that he only had one card to play to keep himself alive and all his body parts intact, Vince held a defiant look as he said, "I can tell them all about how you were at the Goliath Warehouse the night before that guy was murdered there. I saw you stealing things that night. I could put all of you in a world of hurt!" Vince laughed.

Izzy and Ava shared a harsh look. Candy stepped up near them. "What are you talking about?" Candy asked.

"That truck out there. I watched you steal from the warehouse, put it in the back of that truck and race out of there. I'm already fucked. And I'm taking you with me."

Clara laughed. He had nothing on her, but more, she couldn't believe how stupid people were playing their ace card too early. Usually men. Usually men like this ass-clown, trying to weasel his way out of getting his ass kicked.

Candy shrugged, assuring her friends that they still had the upper hand. She stepped up and side-eyed Izzy and Ava. "Another reason this guy can't live," Candy said re-morseless.

Stepping past her sister and Deanna, Izzy pushed the gun barrel against Vince's head. He tried throwing his arms up to protect himself, but Izzy knocked them away with the gun. "You're going to make this go off, big boy, and that would do some real damage to that pretty face of yours. You don't know what life is like not being pretty. But you're about to."

"We can make a deal!" he begged.

Fed up, Deanna stepped right up and kicked Vince in the balls. "There's your deal!"

As Vince curled into a ball, Deanna then kicked him in the face, his head jacking back, blood spraying from his nose. Deanna kicked him again. And again. And again. Vince tried to protect himself as best he could, but she caught the side of his head and his face again, opening a cut just above his eye. Stomping on his chest and stomach as hard as she could, Deanna took pleasure in Vince's pain. Ava and Clara finally pulled Deanna back. She was shaking, closing her eyes tightly, fighting back tears. Candy flung her arms around her friend and held her, allowing Deanna to sob into her shoulder. Shaking her head at Vince, who sat up slowly, unable to take a deep breath. He knew Deanna had broken a couple of his ribs.

"Bitches," he mumbled.

"I'll ask again! Why is this guy still alive?" Candy asked, glaring at Vince, feeling a power she rarely expresses. "You aren't the first man we've had to kill, or the first one we've beaten the shit out of. Practice makes perfect. And when we kill you, the police will never find you."

"I got video of you leaving the warehouse. It's in the cloud. I sent it to friends," Vince maneuvered.

"So what?" Izzy responded, slapping him in the head. "I thought you'd put up more of a fight. But I guess you can only manipulate little girls. Women are out of your league." She settled the barrel of the gun against the back of his head as she sat down on his sofa, looking up at the other women. "We have a lot of other shit to do today. Let me just do this."

"I know where we can leave his body. Won't nobody find it," Clara added.

"They're going to know it's you!" Vince groaned, pointing at Deanna. "Or at least you. You'll be going to prison. Three kids, no mom. You kill me, they will pin this right on you."

"We could bury him alive," Clara remarked. "I'm telling you, I know a place they will never find his body. Once the police find out he's been raping underage girls, they will figure he ran. To Mexico. Or somewhere where he can continue fucking underage girls. Jesus man, you should run for President."

"Let's load him in the trunk of the car," Izzy said.

Vince grimaced, knowing if they get him in the trunk of any car, he's not coming out of this alive. Or at minimum, with his balls. "Your daughter loves me, Mrs. Brayton. She will tell. Tracee is her own person. She pursued me! I may be a weak man, but your daughter is the one who came on to me."

"Oh my God! Mister! I'd shut up if I were you," Candy snapped, swinging at Vince.

Vince's phone rang. Ava dug through Vince's pocket, pulling it out. Seeing who was calling, she flashed it to the other women. It was the school.

"They know I came in this morning and left," Vince reminded them.

"Kevin found you, didn't he? That's how you got that bruise on your jaw. I figured it was to find you," Deanna sniffed.

"Your whole family's fucked up! But Kevin knows what I've done for him to help him get into college. He doesn't want to ruin that," stated Vince, desperate to stay alive.

"Duct tape," Izzy remarked. "Anybody think to bring any?"

None of the women spoke up, Izzy sighed while Vince laughed. "Terrific planning. Professional," he chuckled again, causing Izzy to crack him in the head again with the gun which shut him up.

"Baseball tape. I'm sure there's plenty in this house. Find it, let's tape him all up, especially his mouth," Deanna said, waving the women to different parts of the house. "Izzy, stay here. Keep the gun on him. If you have to shoot him, we'll understand." Deanna then squatted down and got right in Vince's face. "You think I'm crazy...", she said, before pointing at Izzy, "meet my friend who owns that truck. She's got no reason not to kill you. And I got no reason not to let her."

****

"He didn't come in today?" Tracee asked her friend, Shia, when Tracee found out that Vince wasn't in his class, and a sub had filled in.

"I heard some people saw him this morning, but he left real fast. Some kind of emergency," Shia said.

Tracee stayed quiet as she heard a couple other students chatter about what the emergency might be. "Probably a venereal disease," one of the students laughed. Kevin had told no one about punching Vince, and as far as Kevin knew, no one saw him do it. Tracee debated whether to find Kevin and ask if he knew anything, but she suspected after what her brother had found out about she and Vince, he wouldn't tell her anything even if he knew anything. Following Shia and the other students who had moved on to another topic as they turned right down another hallway, Tracee turned left towards a set of double doors. She'd never been to Vince's home, but she knew it wouldn't be hard to find out where he lived.

****

His wrists and ankles bound, the women had also wrapped his arms to his body tightly so he couldn't use his arms to put pressure on the baseball tape they used to bind him up. Ava had also wrapped tape around his head so it completely covered his mouth a few times over. They didn't need him screaming or calling for help. Deanna didn't even want to hear him breathing. Pulling Deanna's car along the side of Vince's house, Clara and Izzy carried him out of the house and hoisted Vince into the trunk. Deanna slammed it shut quickly.

"Where we going, Clara?" Deanna asked.

"Kinloch," she answered. "Got an uncle that still lives there if you can believe that. Behind him is nothing but vacant houses, most half-standing. We can borrow shovels from him, bury this asshole behind any one of them. Nobody will see us. Nobody will look. And nobody will find him."

Hearing this, Vince protested through the tape, his muffled screams and kicking against the trunk door reverberated off the wall of his house. "Shut up," Deanna said, pounding on the back of the trunk, "or we can end this here!" Clara climbed in the passenger side, Deanna in the driver's side as the other three women squeezed into the back. As Deanna started the car and threw it in reverse to pull down Vince's driveway, Tracee appeared at the end of the driveway. Deanna and her daughter locked eyes in the rearview mirror.

"What the hell?" Deanna said, more to herself than anyone else, as she threw the car in park and stepped out facing her daughter. "What are you doing here, Tracee? Why aren't you in school?" Deanna barked at her daughter.

"Where is he?" Tracee calmly asked.

"He raped you. You may not understand this now, but he's a predator," Deanna responded as the other women stepped from the car as well and Tracee realized this was a team effort.

"Mom, please. He's the best man I know. He's been so good to me," pleaded Tracee. "Where is he? You didn't do anything bad to him?"

Deanna remained silent, her eyes glancing at her friends, but everyone stayed silent.

"Mom! What did you do with him?!?!"

"I'm not letting this man do this to another girl. And he will. He will use you and he will move on to another victim. He shouldn't be working at a school. He shouldn't be around teenage girls at all!" Deanna snapped.

"He's not using me," Tracee answered back. "Why can't any of you get that?! I know what's going on, I'm not stupid. I chose him. I chose to have sex with him. He may think he chose me, but he didn't. Mom, I'm smarter than him. And I knew what I was doing. How he made me feel. What I wanted. I wanted him to be my first."

"Then he should have said no! He's a teacher, he should know better and be smarter! He's the goddamn adult, Tracee!"

Tracee sighed. "He's a baseball coach, Mom! Like Kevin will be. Are you ever going to say that about him?"

As Ava and Candy side-eyed Deanna, waiting for a response, Deanna blinked a few times as it registered that her daughter was, in truth, a step ahead. If Deanna were thinking clearly, not acting out of emotion and fury, she would realize that her daughter planned exactly what happened between her and Vince. Tracee wasn't some dumb high school girl falling for an older man's charms. And while she might not be experienced, Tracee didn't react out of emotion, like her mother. Her steps were deliberate. Which made it impossible for Deanna to say anything to Tracee that would get her to change her mind. And while the women staring at Tracee from the other end of the driveway believed Tracee's myopia prevented her from seeing the truth about this man, what he did, what he should have done, and that she was blinded from the real-world realities of his actions, Tracee simply knew better. Vince's actions were criminal, but it was Tracee that acted as the puppeteer to get him to do exactly what she wanted once she realized he was interested.

"Criminals pay for crimes," Deanna announced to her daughter.

"Really, Mom?" Tracee answered, her eyes going to the women on either side of the car. "Are any of you paying for yours? Seems you've all been rewarded."

"We didn't rape anyone," Deanna answered.

Tracee took a few steps forward, her eyes narrowing at her mother and her friends. "No rape. I seduced him. My choice. Like you all make your stupid choices. Your stupid, illegal choices. Now, where is he? I don't want him hurt."

No one moved.

"Where the fuck is he, Mom?!?!?" Tracee screamed.

Izzy walked around to the driver's side of Deanna's car and popped the trunk. She moved to the back and grabbed Vince's legs and threw them out of the trunk and muscled him into a standing position, still bound and gagged. "You're not as smart as I thought you were, girl," Izzy growled towards Tracee.

"That's okay. I never thought any of you were very smart," Tracee responded as she moved to Vince to figure out how to get the tape off him. Figuring out the tape around his head, she pulled it off, taking some of his hair with it as he winced in pain.

"They're crazy! Thank you, Tracee. Thank you," yammered Vince.

"Shut up, Vince," Tracee said, closing her eyes tightly for a second and waving him quiet before looking at all the bruises and cuts on his head and face, blood running down one side.

"How bad are you hurt?" Tracee asked him.

"I think your mother broke my nose, and my ribs," Vince said, as Tracee worked on the binding around his wrists.

"You got mugged. Or you have drug debts. Whatever story, that's how you got hurt," Tracee answered, before turning to her mother. "Mom, you need to tell Kevin to keep his mouth shut. I don't want this all over school. And Kevin's got a big mouth." Tracee then turned to Ava. "Same things go for Cassie. She's got the biggest mouth of anybody." Once she got Vince's hands free, Tracee took in the other women for a moment, surprised they all weren't jumping her shit about this anymore than they had. "I know what you're doing. And why you're all living a lot better than you were a few months ago. I know about the dead guy you put in the river. And I know you're all still in a lot of trouble. So, my suggestion to all of you is, all this stuff with Vince and me...leave it alone, let me deal with it, it's none of your business. You got enough to worry about. I'll worry about me. Mrs. Corbin, please tell Cassie to stay out of my business with Mr. Cunello. After what she did to Kevin, pretending to be pregnant... extorting money from him to get an abortion..." Tracee eyed Ava, realizing she didn't know this story, which caused Tracee to smile. "Yeah, ask her about it. She tells everyone her whole life story at school and it gets around because all her friends have big mouths too. That could get her expelled or in trouble with the law. So, what I'm saying is you all clean up your own lives, or don't. Whatever. But don't try to rescue me. I don't need it. And Vince and I don't need your judgement. I didn't ask any of you for help."

For the first time, the realization smacked Vince in the face even harder than it had Deanna. It wasn't he who had been playing Tracee, she really, truly, was the one who had manipulated him. His knees went weak and with his legs still bound, he toppled over onto the concrete driveway. Tracee raced to him, assisting him in getting his legs un-wrapped, so he could stand up, Tracee not knowing it was her revelation that caused him to crumple.

Furious at her daughter's insistence that she stay out of her life when Deanna believed that Tracee needed her the most, Deanna stepped over Vince and got back in her car. "Clara, I'm going to take you home. We aren't working today," Deanna said.

Clara eyed Tracee for a moment longer as Tracee helped Vince to his feet. "If you were my kid, I'd whip your ass so hard you wouldn't sit down for a week. You're still a girl, not as grown up as you think you are. You got a momma that gives a shit. You need to listen," Clara said before she slipped into the passenger seat again as Deanna looked at her other three friends. There was a rim of tears in Deanna's eyes.

"Thank you. I know who has my back," Deanna said to them before starting the car.

She threw it in gear and glided the car down the driveway a few feet until she was face to face with Vince. "I'm going to cut off your dick," Deanna said softly before her eyes moved over to her daughter, who stared at her mother through the windshield. Neither woman blinked. Deanna put her foot on the gas and spun her car onto his front lawn and pulled around, bouncing the car into the street and driving off.

Without another word to Tracee, Ava, Izzy, and Candy walked past she and Vince and down to where Izzy's truck was parked in the street. Tracee watched as they drove off in the same direction as her mother.

"Thank you," Vince huffed as he sat down on the step leading up to the back door.

Tracee's eyes drifted down to him, rubbing his wrists. She'd never viewed him as a vulnerable man, but broken and bloody, he certainly was. Not the man whose name she decorated in the back of her notebooks. Who was the most beautiful person she'd ever seen. She couldn't grasp why, but right now she felt nothing but disgust for him.

"You want to come in?" Vince asked.

"I'm going back to school," Tracee huffed. "It's best we stay away from each other for a while."

No other student who Vince had been involved with had ever broken it off with him. He was always the one who sent them packing, ready to seek out someone new.

"Get yourself to the hospital," Tracee said, before she walked back down his driveway, leaving Vince sitting outside his house. And while she wasn't ready for what they had to end, wanting to have sex with him again, at least a few more times, her fantasy had become tainted, the gold patina of how she viewed Vince had now blemished, the gold only a coating. Tracee accepted that with the secret out, she would not get from this relationship what she needed, which was sexual guidance that would lead her towards feeling more secure as a woman. She didn't want that from a boy, she wanted it from a man who knew his way around a woman's body. But Tracee now accepted she had made a mistake. That the man she picked, while very handsome, was too immature and would never view her more than a sexual conquest. It's not like she wanted a "relationship" with him, but she foolishly believed Vince would be more adult than the average high school athlete. And now she recognized he wasn't. High school, maybe college, were the best years of his life. Playing semi-pro baseball, or whatever level short of the majors that he achieved, only made him feel less worthy. Tracee knew in her heart that she was destined for more. It would be hard because she wasn't good at a game, like her brother or even Vince, but she would eventually outshine them both. It was better to walk away, set her sights elsewhere. Let Vince heal, allow things to die down some and if she wanted him back, Tracee believed that she could manipulate this man again without much of a problem.

Sure of that, Tracee smiled all the way back to school.

****

Izzy ordered a large pepperoni pizza from Imo's. Ava wasn't a fan of St. Louis pizza, but Izzy loved it. She loved provel cheese; fuck Jimmy Kimmel and any of the other naysayers. But two bites into her third piece, Izzy felt her stomach knot up. Racing into her bathroom, she got sick. 'What the hell?' she thought. Izzy had eaten little all day and though it had been a hell of a day, she didn't think the tension of dealing with Vince was something she couldn't handle. Not after everything she'd been through over the last six months of her life. But something caused this gurgling in her belly and when she opened the pizza box again, another wave of nausea wafted over her, and she bolted back into her bathroom. This time she only made it to the sink.

And that's when it hit her. Izzy looked at herself in the mirror. Dread filled her eyes.

Jumping in her truck without a word to her sister, Izzy sped to the Walgreens on Kingshighway. She had to know. She needed to be sure it wasn't what her cynical nature was whispering in her ear. Pacing down the aisle, Izzy found the pregnancy kits. She bought three different brands. Her first thought was to pee on them in the bathroom in the back of the store, where she'd have a certain privacy, but stepping in, she knew she just couldn't do that here. She took them home, the boxes spread out on the seat next to her in her truck. At least there she could find out the truth in the privacy of her own bathroom. And then dispose of the evidence.

Peeing on the three sticks, simultaneously, Izzy felt like she was holding her breath. "It can't be," she kept repeating to herself. Izzy had fucked around since she was a teenager and never had a pregnancy scare. Ever. She wondered if she was even capable of having children but had never mentioned it to her gynecologist. What was the point? Kevin and she seldom used a condom. The only time they used one religiously was when she discovered he was banging other girls and she demanded it, knowing he hated pausing passion to slide one on. The few times she screwed other men, some wore a condom, some didn't, depending on how drunk they were. She knew it was stupid when they didn't, and it wasn't about getting pregnant, rather, it was about diseases. But Izzy loved getting caught up in a moment and just going for it. Thankfully, she had never contracted a disease and she'd never gotten pregnant.

Taking a deep breath, she picked up the first test and looked. Then the second. Then the third. It was unanimous. "Holy fucking shit," Izzy muttered, stunned, "fuck, fuck, fuck!"

ALL SEEING, ALL KNOWING

All the other women could see that finishing this batch of gowns for Martin took a substantial toll on Deanna. Even with Clara assisting, nearly as able and quick as Deanna now, and Ava and Candy taking care of everything else Deanna needed, the situation with Tracee had eaten at Deanna's soul. The gowns were perfect, and the remnants were enough for Deanna and Clara to create something of their own to pick up a few more dollars, but Deanna couldn't sleep. With Tracee not talking to her, Deanna felt as if she had lost her best friend. She felt she had slipped down the rabbit hole, with Kevin talking to her more than Tracee, especially when Kevin found out through Cassie, of course, that their mothers and friends beat the shit out of Vince. Kevin told his mother that Vince hadn't been at school for over a week, claiming he'd been in a car accident and was mending. "Easy way to explain the cuts, bruises, and broken nose," Kevin confided. But Vince was expected back at school the following week. Tracee said nothing about him. But she wasn't saying much of anything to Deanna. Izzy promised Deanna she would monitor Tracee, make sure she wasn't visiting Vince at his home. And if she was, Izzy would knock on the door and open another can of whoop-ass on Vince. As far as she was concerned, he knew too much anyway, and Izzy felt they would have to deal with him eventually. Izzy wanted that to happen sooner rather than later. Because later could be when she was nine months pregnant and forty pounds heavier.

Deanna wanted these gowns out of her house and to spend a full day in bed, hoping to stop all the noise in her head. While Tracee was her present dark-cloud preoccupation, Deanna still had two other kids to worry about. And running underneath it all, there was that Martin-thing. If there was any silver lining to her daughter being seduced by a teacher at her school, it was that she shoved Martin's proposal out of the front seat and into the back. If she had her way, it would be in the rearview mirror lying on the side of a desert road. As Candy boxed up the gowns to ship them to Martin, Deanna hugged each of the women she worked with. She needed the hug more than they did. And it meant that at least for a few days to a week, her home wouldn't be Grand Central.

"When we startin' on our own thing?" Clara asked when she had Deanna to herself.

"Next Monday good? I need a few days..."

Clara nodded, touching Deanna supportively. Clara could survive when their money came in from these gowns. The cash that they would make off of a dress they created was gravy. But more than the money, Clara enjoyed hanging out with Deanna. Despite Deanna's family drama, which didn't hold a candle to her own, it gave Clara a break from her own family, and Deanna was probably the nicest white person she'd ever met. Clara didn't hold half the affinity for the other three women, but Deanna made her laugh and treated her as an equal. She considered Deanna her friend, and while she'd never asked her, she sensed that Deanna felt the same toward her. A few days apart from all of them would make a reunion all warm and fuzzy.

****

As Kevin dressed, Izzy admired his torso. His muscled arms, his high ass, his back broad and taut. She reminisced about how gorgeous she was at eighteen. Tits were high with just enough bounce, ass wagged instead of waved, legs tawny and long. Women raced into their beauty around fifteen, far sooner than most guys their age. Being ogled and desired by men was passé by the time they were in their twenties. By their mid-twenties, they absolutely knew how to handle men, some women were just better at it than others. And some men were better to women than others. Izzy found most young guys gangly and gawky, unaware or uncaring of their looks unless they were the butt of jokes or had gained enough wisdom or self-obsession. Most teenage boys focused on their dicks rather than themselves until they were in their twenties and getting laid with some regularity. Some guys, like Kevin, were completely blind to how physically beautiful they appeared. Kevin mistook his athletic prowess and cockiness for the reason girls desired him. Two things that Izzy couldn't care less about. And while Kevin often behaved like an arrogant teenage prick, master of his tiny world, Izzy was willing to overlook his immaturity when his body was on top of hers. And while they were usually only together when they were alone, she had noticed when they were out, usually with his mother and Ava, how women, usually older, watched him, with a hint of desire flickering in their eyes. It made her smile because she had him. It may not be the best sex she ever had, but it was the most consistently good sex. Kevin was going to make his future wife – and if Izzy knew him as well as she thought she did – his sidepiece, both very happy women.

She then wondered how he would take to the news that he could possibly be a father?

Izzy had no intention of telling anyone she was pregnant. Not until she took care of it. She didn't need a baby. In fact, it was probably the very last thing in her life she could handle. While she was living better, thanks to Martin, and even living with her sister and niece, this house had plenty of room and was far nicer than any place she had ever lived. There was plenty of room for a baby. But motherhood? No. That was extremely low on Izzy's agenda, nor did she believe she would be any good at it. Ava would end up taking over, and the child would be reared by the village at the end of the cul-de-sac. And Izzy would have to pretend that it was a miracle baby, having no idea who the father could be. She knew Kevin would never say anything. Or more aptly, would try not to. But she couldn't be sure he was smart enough to keep his mouth shut or that his giant ego wouldn't come into play and he'd want to announce that he was the father of Izzy's baby, making her the female version of his baseball coach. She had climbed on top of that Fed as well. But only once. His little swimmers had to be as knocked out of it as he was. Isn't that how it worked? Couldn't be him.

She couldn't even remember his name. God, that's all she needed, she mused, shaking her head, her face scrunching up as if she'd tasted something rancid. Getting pregnant by a Federal Agent she drugged and took photos of. Photos her boss used to extort his silence. 'No, no, it's Kevin's,' she thought, debating which choice would be worse for her since neither was very good.

As Kevin turned and gave Izzy a smile, pulling his t-shirt back on over his head, Izzy tried to smile but couldn't. That Fed couldn't be the man who knocked her up. He couldn't be.

"You okay?" Kevin asked.

Izzy nodded a little too enthusiastically. "Sure. Yeah. Great."

****

There was Izzy, mounted on top of Barry. Riding him like Annie Oakley. Staring at it, Barry couldn't remember this event happening. Much less this woman's name. He knew what had occurred. She slipped him something, got him into bed, and fucked him. But what did she, or whoever sent her, want? The most obvious objective was to force him to stop investigating what he was looking into. He hadn't found much of anything of any interest. Yet. But apparently someone wanted to make sure he didn't by heading him off at the pass with a little sexual blackmail.

Which also meant they knew he'd been in trouble before because of it. Barry surmised that whatever was going on was bigger than he assumed when he was handed this assignment. These photos, while a huge megillah for him, a vex that would destroy his fragile marriage and cost him his career, intrigued him just as much. Why would someone go this far?

Whatever the reason, Barry knew one thing. He had to find this woman. If she wasn't the one behind the blackmail, she knew who it was. It was the first step in making all of this go away. Because Barry wasn't going down without a brutal, ugly fight. There was too much at stake for him. Whatever it took, he had no choice but to do it.

"It's her life or mine," he said aloud, so he could hear it. And for him, that wasn't a contest.

****

"We should get out of here for a few days," Curtis suggested to Candy. "Go to Florida for a few days. If that's too far, we could just head to Augusta or Hermann. Drink some local wine and be alone."

Candy's eyes narrowed, confused by Curtis's statement. "We can't leave now. There's too much going on."

"What? What's going on for us?" Curtis quizzed. "Candy, if you were gone for a few days, what wouldn't go on? I can tell you that if I was out of the picture, everything would continue on its merry way. Martin's got you all doing what he wants. You don't need me to protect you. I'm sure Martin has that covered."

Candy moved over and sat next to him. "Is that what this is about? You feeling like you don't have any place in...whatever this is we're doing? You're still making money."

"He could cut me out at any time."

"He could cut any of us out at any time. Except maybe Deanna. And he hit on her," Candy told Curtis.

"He hit on her?" he asked, disbelief in his voice. "How does that work?"

Candy laughed. "I guess like it works for most people. Except, according to Deanna, he just sort of told her."

Curtis slipped his arm around Candy, pulling her to him. "How does she feel about it?"

"Creeped out. I could see Ava going for something like that. Ava rolls. Deanna, not so much. I think it scares her. He scares her."

Tucking Candy under his arm, Curtis kissed her. The kiss lingered. He slid his body over hers, straddling her, his lips maneuvering over hers and down her neck. "I think it's time."

Smiling, Candy asked, "Time for what?"

"Time I move in with you, full time," he answered, looking down at her, placing her hand on his crotch.

"What about your daughter?"

"Erika is going to have to get over it. She needs to be with me, but I tell her where that is. I want to be with you. Living here...she's just going to have to deal with it."

Candy unbuttoned his black jeans, gripping the zipper and pulling it down. Curtis smiled. "I think there is something I can do for all of you women."

Slipping her hand into his briefs, she wrapped her hand around him, causing him to groan. "What's that?"

"Make sure you're safe from Martin. All he really needs right now is Deanna. The rest of you could disappear," he said, shimmying out of his jeans until he was nude. Candy held onto his manhood, as he leaned over and kissed her, saying, "I'll make his sorry ass disappear before any of us do."

****

Expecting their money the day prior, Deanna wondered if Martin didn't like the copies and was withholding payment. If that were the case, she wasn't sure how to handle it. If she called him, asking what was going on, Deanna feared he would construe her interest in getting paid as interested in him. She wondered if that was his plan. Have her chase after him. Have her grovel for their money. To need him.

"Ava," Deanna said into her phone, "he never wired the money. It's supposed to be here today, this morning!"

"You're calling me?" Ava asked with a chuckle, not at the missing money, but that Deanna calling her to do something. "I thought you two were thick as thieves, holding hands between classes, saving seats for each other on the bus?"

"I'd tell you to kiss my ass, but I won't," Deanna replied. "But know I am thinking it."

Ava laughed heartily. There was little she enjoyed more than busting someone's chops, and Deanna was always an easy mark.

"What do we do?" Deanna then questioned.

"You want me call the motherfucker, and I hope I'm not using that word literally..." Ava answered, smiling. But hearing Deanna simply breathe, saying nothing, Ava sighed and added, "Tell you what, if he doesn't have the money in our hands by the end of today, I'll call him. I got his number too...in more ways than one."

"Thank you. Because you're right, I don't want to talk to him if I don't have to," Deanna stated.

"Who does? But he owes us the money," Ava said in all seriousness before a smirk washed onto her lips. "You know, maybe you should give him a little rub and tug and he'd cough it up quicker."

Ava waited for a rebuttal from Deanna, but she said nothing.

"Girl, I'm making a joke," Ava said.

"I know," Deanna responded, sighing. "But my fear is that's what he wants."

It was Ava's turn not to speak.

"You there?" Deanna asked.

"Yeah, yeah," Ava answered. "I just got no good comeback for that."

****

Tracee walked by Vince's classroom. Unable to help herself, she peeked in. Forcing a smile, she nodded at Mrs. Van Truby, who was subbing. As she turned to go, Cassie was standing across the hallway. Squaring off with her, Tracee glared. "I bet he doesn't come back," Cassie announced, the students passing, unsure what the hell she was talking about.

"Thanks to you and your big, fat mouth," Tracee called back.

Stepping across the hallway towards her, Cassie added in a flat voice, "It's rape, Tracee."

"You don't know anything about it. About us. What happened. How it happened. You don't know anything,"

Tracee let the words slither out between her clenched teeth, "but that never stops people like you from flapping your gums."

"I know a lot about this. A lot," Cassie said, shaking her head. "I've let guys play me most of my life. You don't end up like me without that happening. One day, you'll get that this fucker played you. He took your virginity because that's what assholes like this do. They play girls like us, tell us what we want to hear, make us feel like women, like we're wanted, they stick their dicks in us for their pleasure, not ours, and then sooner rather than later, they bail. Vince'll bail. If he hasn't already, scared because other people know what he did and it could put that asshole in prison. Believe me, don't believe me, I don't care. But it's the truth. You were played. And instead of defending him and acting like you love him, you should hate him. You should want to rip off his balls. One day you will."

Tracee stepped forward, her nose less than an inch from Cassie's. "Will I? Well, it's not today. Go fuck yourself." Tracee slammed into Cassie with her shoulder and pushed past, leaving Cassie there. Cassie turned and watched Tracee disappear around the corner, heading to her next class.

"Stupid girl," muttered Cassie, any understanding washed out with Tracee's 'go fuck yourself,' willing to let Tracee suffer her own fate.

****

Deanna was busy helping Ford in the kitchen with his science project when the doorbell rang. She knew it wasn't any of the women. They'd gotten used to knocking quickly and entering. Hating science, Ford raced for the front door before Deanna could stop him. She heard the door open and knew the voice immediately, "Hello, you must be Ford. I'm Martin. Is your mother available?" A chill went up Deanna's spine. This she didn't want to deal with. And having him in her home made her miss her shitty upstairs apartment.

Coming into the living room, Deanna forced a smile, thinking to herself, 'You better come bearing cash.'

"What are you doing in St. Louis?" Deanna actually said, a smile plastered on her face.

"You know I have other business in the area. And while I am here, I want to check on my various business associates. But that's not for you to worry about. I just wanted to come by and tell you personally how perfect those last gowns were," he said, reaching into the pocket of his jacket, handing her checks sealed in envelopes. "There's one in there for your new employee as well. She's been very beneficial to you."

"Yes. I told you, Clara is a godsend. Didn't have to teach her anything. She's amazing, and she's worth it," Deanna said, tapping the envelopes against the palm of her free hand.

"So," Martin said, "would you do me the honor of joining me for dinner again tonight?"

"Honor?" Deanna questioned, raising a brow. "You make it sound like I'm something special."

Martin stepped around Deanna further into her home, making Deanna even uncomfortable. "I don't think you realize how special you are."

"Mom, you are special," Ford said, peeking around the corner from the kitchen, a chocolate Yoo-hoo in his hand.

Deanna chuckled as Martin nodded in Ford's direction. "Smart boy," Martin said. "Listen to your son. He knows things," Martin half-joked. "Again, are you free for dinner?"

"Honestly, I'm tired. Getting these gowns out at the pace we're putting them together is killing me. And I'm going through some things here. Family stuff. It's difficult."

"Your daughter?" Martin pondered.

Stunned, Deanna reacted harshly. She should have suspected he would know. She wondered when they moved into the house if there were recording devices peppered along each of the floors and basement. But Martin probably assumes that knowing everything that's going on with the women is simply business.

"Would you like me to take care of it?" Martin asked matter-of-factly.

"No!" Deanna reacted sharply. "We...we are dealing with it. I'm dealing with it."

"Curtis can deal with it. That's why he's on the payroll. You ladies shouldn't be handling these kinds of things."

"I'm Tracee's mother. I am exactly who should be handling this kind of thing," Deanna insisted. "You stay out of it. Please."

But Deanna knew Martin well enough now that she recognized a few of his 'tells.' And she could see by the way he cocked his head to the side as she talked, so as not to look directly at her, that Martin had already made up his mind. He would prod Curtis into hurting Vince. But Deanna believed there were many ways to kill a chicken other than ringing its neck, and she had witnessed Martin's form of punishment firsthand. He wouldn't ring Vince's neck, he would bulldoze him into the ground. Deanna decided to hold back on telling Martin that Vince knew that Izzy, Ava, and Candy stole the sewing machines from the warehouse. That would certainly put an even bigger target on Vince's back. Not that Deanna would mind if he were six feet under. But she envisioned that it would be her committing that sin.

"Please, let me…us, handle it. If we need Curtis, I can ask him." Deanna told Martin.

"Deanna, this business venture of ours can be even more successful. But I can't have problems. And when they pop up, I need them to disappear. Quickly. With little attention. I hope you understand. Now, are you free for dinner?"

Ford peeked around the corner from the kitchen again, which Deanna noticed. His eyes hung on his mother as his head nodded furiously. He liked this man. "Go, Mom, go."

Seeing her attention was off to her right, Martin turned, seeing Ford nodding. "Listen to your son. He knows things," Martin stated, a rare, warm and genuine smile lodged on his lips.

"Dinner, tonight. Sure," she caved.

****

Before he left to change, Martin walked over to Ava and Izzy's home and rang the bell. As he did, he saw Kevin dart from the back of the house, carrying his shoes, across to his mother's home just before Izzy answered the door.

Martin held out a check. Izzy took it and looked at it, impressed. "Deanna has the other checks, this is a little something extra to say thank you," Martin commented. "He's been contacted. With a few of the photos."

Izzy slid the check from the envelope. Five figures. She nodded with satisfaction. "Hopefully, he will take the hint," Izzy said, wanting this conversation to end so she could run to the bank and put the check in.

"That should buy a lot of baby clothes," Martin said, causing Izzy to step back with surprise. "Who's the father? Is it the Federal Agent we are dealing with? Or the boy next door?"

Izzy opened her mouth, not to respond but out of surprise. She stammered for a moment but said nothing, her lips tightening as she glared at Martin.

"I know everything that goes on in these houses," Martin stated, his direct glare drilling right back at Izzy. "Everything. So, what are you going to do about it?"

"Since you know everything, you tell me," Izzy fired right back, unable to mask just how pissed off she was.

"You really want my opinion?" Martin asked.

"Thanks for the check," Izzy responded before she slowly closed the door, leaving Martin on the other side of it. She leaned against the wall, allowing her face to screw up, unsure if she wanted to scream or just cry.

RECKONING AMONGST FRIENDS

I zzy was on the phone calling her sister as soon as Martin walked down the driveway and slipped into the back of the waiting town car. Because the check she held fluttered, Izzy noted her hands were shaking. She couldn't give Martin an answer to his question. She didn't know who the father was. She had suspicions, yes, but it would take a DNA test to figure it out and Izzy was in no rush to know. But that wasn't her biggest concern. Her larger fear was the fact that Martin knew. Which meant, as Deanna had suspected, the houses were bugged. Maybe cameras. Maybe someone digging through their trash. As she looked at the new phone in her hand, Izzy recalled that Martin had bought each of them new iPhones as well, causing Izzy to immediately disconnect the call she was making to her sister. She had to talk to Ava and the others, but now it meant getting together outside the house, no phones, someplace Martin's big ears couldn't hear, and his big eyes couldn't see. Did he have someone following them? It would be easy to monitor them, all of them situated on the end of this cul-de-sac. Izzy grasped that Martin didn't select these homes because they were suited to the women, he chose them to keep them in a herd, close together, vulnerable. She wanted to get a sledgehammer and take it to all the interior walls, rip out the wiring, search for bugs and cameras, find out how the fuck he knew she was pregnant, since Izzy hadn't discussed it with even her sister. It enraged Izzy that the only way Martin could know was that he listened to her and Kevin having sex, and the discussion they had afterwards. Worse, that he could now leverage that information against her. And even worse than that, Martin knowing she was pregnant, no matter what she chose, complicated her already complicated life even more. Now, the man who held the purse strings also held an anvil over her head. There was no expectation of privacy, no more secrets. Izzy couldn't remember ever being this terrified.

Neither could Deanna. She was dressing to go out with this man again. A man she was sure she didn't like, a man who scared her. Why her? Because she was the center of the group? She couldn't grasp what he saw in her other than that. She wasn't his intellectual equal, Deanna knew that. Nor was she on the same wavelength socially. And did he really care to hear her talk about basting stitches or a whipstitch? She couldn't figure it out. The only thing she did know was that Martin did not like taking no for an answer.

And worst of all, he was not without a certain slithering charm.

****

As she knocked on the door, Tracee thought about bolting. Admittedly, she hadn't thought out this moment as well as she should have. Not seeing him at school, she just wanted to know if Vince was okay. She hadn't talked to him after she left his house the day of his beating and wanted to know he was still in one piece and if he went to the hospital to get checked out. Vince being dead was a possibility after she left him battered and bruised in the driveway of his home. Getting no answer, her heart sank. She tried to peer through the windows, but his thick curtains prevented her from seeing in. As she turned to walk off the front porch and see if she could see anything through a back window, she heard the front door creak open. A relieved Tracee turned with a smile as Vince leaned against the doorway as if it were the only way he could actually hold himself up.

"Are you okay?" she asked hesitantly.

With slow deliberation, Vince answered, "I've been better." He opened the door wider. Vince was shirtless, his ribs wrapped. Two black eyes, bruises on his face, neck, arms, and upper body. "Do I look like I was in a car accident?" Vince quizzed with a weak smile.

Feeling oddly guilty, Tracee nodded remorsefully. At this moment, she was not the mistress of her universe who told him, that it would be better if they didn't see each other for a while. She felt something for him, though she couldn't distinguish between affection and pity.

"I'm sorry. My Mom and her friends...they are—"

"Criminals?"

Her shoulders tensing, Tracee stepped back. She didn't know if she found him attractive or revolting, wondering if there was a space in between those two. "My mom is not—"

Again, Vince cut her off. "She and her friends stole something from a warehouse. I was a witness. Recognized the truck her friend was driving. They are criminals. And they stand in judgment of me. Of you."

"I just came to make sure you're all right. Did you go to the hospital?"

Vince forced a smile. "You really think that would have been a great idea? I had a nurse friend wrap me up. I'll heal."

Tracee shifted her weight from foot to foot. "Well, I look forward to you getting back to work. And you know, back on the ballfield."

"Is your brother going to come after me with a bat?" Vince questioned, his tone making light but he really wanted to know what he was still in store for.

All Tracee could do was shrug. "I don't control him. You're lucky baseball season is almost over. I just want you to know I've been thinking about you and I'm glad you're okay and I want to say...I don't regret anything we did. I don't think it was rape. I wanted to do it. With you."

Smart enough to know the less said the better when the word 'rape' was launched into the middle of the conversation, Vince nodded back. "I'm just sorry about how it ended."

It was Tracee's turn to nod, still not exactly sure now how she felt about this thing with Vince actually coming to an end. As she turned to go again, Vince played the only card he held and opened the door wider, asking, "You want to come in?"

Of course, she did. More than she had the better sense to glance around to see if they were being watched. Which they were. Vince had no idea just how big of a problem Tracee had become for him, not because of her mother and her friends, but other people who wanted Tracee safe, because they wanted Deanna focused.

Vince was a problem. Problems get solved.

****

Deanna figured the candlelight had to look more attractive than she did in broad daylight. She didn't like getting ready at the last minute and eating in a nice restaurant where everyone's eyes drifted to the people at the neighboring tables, she felt an obligation to look as good as she could. And even though she was in full make-up, buying better cosmetics than she used to, she found herself uncomfortable being the object of Martin's gaze. She still couldn't figure out why Martin had taken a cotton to her over someone like Ava, who was far chattier and out-there than Deanna. But Martin kept reaching across the table, taking Deanna's hand. She found it odd that his fingers would roll around her ring finger as if he were feeling for a ring that wasn't there.

"When all your children are gone, will you stay in St. Louis?" Martin asked.

Deanna never gave that a minute of thought. She shrugged.

"You've never thought about it?" he quizzed.

"I haven't," Deanna shrugged again. "Where would I go?"

"You ever wanted to live anywhere else?"

"Sure. Lots of places. Some days anywhere else," Deanna chuckled.

"You need to see Italy. France. I'd love to show them to you."

Sitting back in her chair, she pulled her hand away from his. Her eyes stayed on Martin, wishing her wine glass weren't full because she wanted nothing more than to chug the whole thing, and she wasn't sure she could get it all down. These statements coming from his mouth made her terribly ill at ease. He had to be able to see that, the nervous smile, the eyes darting, the tension in her shoulders that were only covered by spaghetti straps. After a quick sip from her wine glass, she made herself believe she was fortified to ask, "Why me? We don't have a thing in common. I mean besides the clothes, so I guess that's something, but not something you can build a relationship on. I'm just not sure what these dinners are about. Do you think we're going to be...a couple?"

"Is that a foreign concept?"

Stymied into silence again, Deanna's eyes widened. She was too frightened by this answer to say a word as her head fogged up like a windshield before a thunderstorm.

Martin smiled, with what to Deanna appeared to be delight, before he asked, "Does that idea scare you?"

Steadying herself, and as if by reflex, Deanna took another sip from her wine glass. "You never answered me. Why me?" Deanna managed to get out before her mouth got dry again.

"I think you're beautiful. You probably don't know it because you haven't had anyone to tell you. At least in a long while. But you are. And I admire your work ethic. I admire how you've raised three kids on almost nothing and then when you were presented with an opportunity, you seized it. That's attractive to me," Martin responded. "And now that I have your attention and for total transparency, I intend to take you to bed."

Feeling as if she was being scorched by the sun, Deanna said nothing, unable to even put a simple sentence together. Her fingers wrapped around her wine glass and she almost splashed it on herself before she got the rim to her lips and swallowed a mouthful. She couldn't think of a comeback to that. She knew she needed to say something, and fast, but nothing congealed in her brain.

Finally, she blurted out. "You...you're very sure of yourself."

"I don't think that should be a surprise to you," Martin countered.

"What if I say no?"

"You already have. And have I stopped pursuing you?"

Deanna had to admit that Martin was correct. She had never met a man this forward, and she'd been around plenty of drunks in bars, especially when she was younger. This was aggressive, which she found terribly off-putting and yet she had to admit to herself was also weirdly, strangely, begrudgingly flattering.

Martin suddenly stood. Deanna felt even smaller as he peered down at her. He was long and angular to begin with, and this only accentuated those attributes. He extended his hand towards her. Before she could stop herself, Deanna reached her hand out to his. As he took it, feeling his tapered fingers wrap around it, she wanted to pull her hand back, but something wouldn't let her. Her desire to know what this would be, and how she could use it to free herself, free her family and friends. Was sleeping with Martin the bullet she would have to take?

And she wanted to know if he was good in bed.

They didn't speak the entire way back to his hotel. But once they got into the room and he kissed her deeply, Deanna surrendered to it, her lips accepting the kiss as his hands trailed the course of her body from her shoulder to her waist. As much as she knew she would hate herself afterwards, Deanna needed to know what this was.

****

Candy counted out the money she made from Deanna and Clara's latest creation concocted from the leftover material of the last set of gowns. She found a buyer quickly, but the woman, Alicia Cordy, the wife of a lawyer who advertised on bus benches across the city, didn't want to pay what Candy was asking. It wasn't until Candy corralled another buyer who wanted the gown that Alicia begrudgingly agreed to buck up what Candy had asked initially. Competition upped the price. "You snooze, you lose," Candy told Alicia. And Candy was smart enough to have Curtis in tow when they dropped the gown off and collected the fee. In cash. Something Candy insisted upon, knowing that Alicia had access to a free lawyer at her disposal. Collecting on a bounced check could take years. Candy wasn't having that. And she wouldn't be offering Alicia any more gowns from the "hottest designers on the St. Louis scene," as Candy sold Deanna and Clara. Alicia eyed Curtis warily as he stood the entire time he was in her home. Candy made herself comfortable on the sofa and counted out the cash Alicia handed her in piles, making sure it was all there. "Thank you. Enjoy the gown. I'm sure it will look beautiful on you," Candy said in such a way that it vaguely sounded like a threat.

Curtis took a handful of mints from a bowl on the foyer table as they walked out, giving Alicia a sneering smile.

Once outside, Candy chuckled. "Are you going to eat those?" she asked.

"Hell no," Curtis laughed in return as he threw them into the bushes before they climbed into his BMW. "Sometimes things are just for effect."

Once in the car, Curtis leaned over and kissed Candy, his lips holding hers. Candy was feeling it, wanting to stick it to Alicia for the pain in the ass negotiation that she had to haggle through until Candy had secured another buyer. Right there in front of Alicia's home, Candy climbed on top of Curtis, undid his pants and worked them down as he arched his hips to assist her. She pulled her panties aside and allowed him to slip inside her. Having sex in front of Alicia's home seemed like the apt period at the end of the deal. She knew Alicia was staring out a window somewhere in her big U-City house. Candy was all for giving her a show, especially suspecting that Alicia and her husband rarely had sex. At least with each other.

As she was counting out the money and dividing it, Candy's doorbell rang. Usually Curtis answered the door, but he ran an errand, leaving Candy to check who was there using their camera doorbell system that Martin had installed on each of the homes. Seeing Izzy at the door with Ava, Candy slid the cash into a kitchen drawer before answering the door.

Ava waved Candy out onto the porch.

"You know where Deanna is?" Izzy said softly after Candy shut her front door behind her.

"No," Candy answered, seeing the concern on their faces.

"Tomorrow, ten o'clock, the four of us are going for a walk in Tower Grove Park," Ava stated. "Leave your cell phone at home."

Hearing the less-than-subtle anxiety in Ava's voice, Candy eyed her oddly. But as Candy opened her mouth to question what all the unspoken drama was about, Ava shook her head, stopping her. "We'll talk tomorrow. Don't say anything to Curtis about this. Not yet," Ava stated.

Candy nodded as the two sisters backed away, turning to walk down the steps from her front porch. Candy couldn't imagine what the hell this clandestine meeting could be about. Did they find out about her selling the new dresses for Deanna and Clara and were pissed off they weren't cut in on it? Did they know something about Martin and were afraid to share it, believing Candy would tell Curtis right away? Watching the two sisters walking side-by-side, talking closely as they returned to their home, made Candy nervous. Considering everything they had been through up to this point, this furtive behavior made Candy believe this had to be really, really bad.

****

Being driven home from the Ritz-Carlton, where Martin stayed when he was in St. Louis, Deanna leaned her head back and stared up through the moon roof, confusion and exhilaration battling for control of her face. She could not deny the sex was amazing. Martin was easily the most skilled lover she had ever been with. And it was clear to Deanna that he wanted to impress her with that skill. The guys that Deanna had sex with in the past, especially her ex-husband, were often athletic but coarse and fumbling. Not that the men didn't get the job done, but there was little finesse and often less connection. Martin made sure that he and Deanna were in sync, often face to face, his eyes peering into hers. He made sure she came. Multiple times. And that Deanna knew that this was only the first layer of pleasure he could bring to her. Yet, Deanna couldn't help but feel a strange dissatisfaction. Maybe knowing that, like so much with Martin, even sex was a show of power, a performance for control. She was so different than this man. As much as he had a good life, and as much as Martin seemed to possess, Deanna couldn't help but feel that he did it all for others to see. It felt needy. They were just so different from each other, Deanna could not figure why he wanted to impress her so much. While she was the core of this counterfeiting operation, it had to be small potatoes for him. It changed her life, not his. She remembered a Bible verse, somewhere in the Old Testament, where it talked about a man and a woman being equally yoked. They weren't. And while Deanna and her kids could get used to a life that Martin could give them, she knew what he did to make a large piece of his fortune. And she wasn't prepared to live off blood money.

Using her kids as an excuse, Deanna was relieved to make her escape after sex. She wished that somehow, she could reconcile the pleasure she had with her lack of desire for this man. And even though Martin was good-looking, and surprisingly even better looking out of his clothes, there was still a sharp, nagging fear. A fear that if she ever disappointed him, he would kill her.

And that fear meant she didn't sleep well. Not only was her mind racing after her evening with Martin, the overly pleasant message that Ava left about taking a walk through Tower Grove Park at ten the next morning also bothered her. When the hell was Ava ever this cheery? And why wouldn't Ava walk a house over to talk to her? After she got the kids off to school, Kevin having overslept, and was nasty about getting up and getting out of the house, Deanna found her leggings, something she rarely wore, and a sweatshirt. If they were walking for exercise, she wanted to at least look like she'd done it before. Deanna waited until she saw Izzy and Ava leave the cul-de-sac, Ava in her new SUV and Izzy in her truck. Candy kissed Curtis on the porch and bounced down the steps to his BMW and drove off. Deanna then got in her car and drove towards the park alone.

As Izzy saw Deanna pull into a parking space parallel to the park, she walked back to Deanna's car and opened her car door. "Leave your phone," Izzy said softly, only making Deanna more nervous.

"What if one of my kids calls from school?" Deanna countered, causing Izzy to raise her finger to her lips to silence Deanna, motioning her to stop talking and leave the phone. Sliding her phone under the seat, Deanna got out of her car, concern on her face. She faced her three friends, unsure.

Joining them, they walked away from their vehicles towards one of the pavilions that dotted the park. "I'm assuming we're not going for a walk," Deanna piped up, as Ava sat on top of one of the picnic tables in the pavilion.

"Are you fucking kidding me? I only walk through a mall or to the refrigerator," Ava replied.

"Then what's this about?" Deanna asked.

"I was just about to ask the same thing," Candy added.

Izzy faced Candy and Deanna. "Martin's bugged our homes. He knows everything that goes on inside."

Deanna froze as Candy barked out, "What?!" indignation filling her voice as it raised an octave.

"He hears everything we do. I wouldn't doubt there are cameras hidden inside as well," Izzy stated.

"You're sure about this?" Deanna asked, furious but tamping down her emotions.

"He all but admitted it," Izzy responded.

"That fucker," Candy seethed, realizing Martin had been listening to everything Curtis and she talked about, as well as them having sex. "With what we've talked about together, and I'm sure separately, it's a wonder he hasn't had us all killed."

Deanna knew it was true and now made the previous night even more baffling.

"Now we got to figure out what we're going to do about it," Ava offered.

"I'll tell you what I'm going to do, I'm going to tell Curtis, and we're going to meet with Martin and drill him a new asshole," Candy growled.

Laughing, Ava grabbed Candy by the shoulder. "Who is this killer bitch and what did you do with my old friend Candy? Getting fucked every night has done wonders for your attitude and your complexion."

"Seriously," Izzy butted in with a chuckle. "We have to come up with a game plan. This is bullshit. He knows too much and can use it against us, keep us doing whatever he wants. We will never get out of this. And since I'm now standing around most of the time, he doesn't have much of a need for me."

"Or me," Ava added.

"We're living in nice houses," Deanna said, wishing she hadn't.

"Yeah, where the walls have ears. And probably eyes. He bought us those cell phones. Do any of you think he's not monitoring our calls? Everything we search on the Internet? Every website we visit? That doesn't scare you?" Izzy questioned.

"Does me," Candy inserted. "And Izzy's right. He doesn't really need me, or Izzy, or Ava. Only you, Deanna. You and Clara are the ones copying the gowns. All we're doing is minor stuff, running errands and cooking meals. It sucks. Even Curtis hates it. Now that Martin's in the picture, Curtis doesn't feel he needs to protect us."

"He does more than ever," Ava added. "From Martin."

Now Deanna wanted to run. What had this man heard in her home? She slept with him. He now had that to lord over her as well. This was all too much. Now she was pissed off at herself that she hadn't trusted her instincts about this man. Everything he did felt like a chess game where she was maneuvered for an advantage. Did he pick her because she was the least savvy? The one he believed he could manipulate the easiest? "I would be happy to go back to doing what we were doing before he came into our lives," Deanna said, causing all the women to turn to her. "It would mean giving up the houses and all the other stuff. But with Clara, we could copy more pieces. We wouldn't be living like we're living now, but we'd be free. We'd control what we do. You all would be a bigger part of this again. We could step up our game."

"I'd actually love that. But it doesn't answer the bigger questions," Ava huffed, causing all eyes to turn to her. "Martin isn't going to just let us go. What do we do about him?"

There was silence. And it lingered, like the aroma of burning leaves in the fall.

"We all know the answer to that," Deanna responded darkly, her words coming out slowly, as if she were just making this decision. A decision that when vocalized, surprised all the other women. Once she had all their undivided attention, she nodded at them, adding, "We have to do it to him before he does it to us."

OH BABY, BABY, BABY

Deanna didn't sleep that night. She tossed and turned, wrestling with the sheets, hot, then cold, then clammy. When she dozed off, Deanna dreamt that she was forced to sew a dress she thought was ugly. Not that she considered all the gowns she'd copied beautiful. Some she felt were clunky, some she felt exposed way too much, some she found flouncy. But she never felt one was flat out ugly, but the one in her dream was. The shade of yellow looked more like baby shit, and the dress wasn't symmetrical, which Deanna complained to no one, since there was no one else in her dream, that the gown would make you look like you had one leg shorter than the other. And she woke herself as she yelled out, "I'm not doing this!", sitting up, realizing all the drama was in her head. And now, awake, she was exhausted.

Luckily, Martin wasn't one of those men who called the day after. He wasn't much of a caller anyway, more of a 'drop-by-er'. And as the day progressed, the few cars she heard circling through the cul-de-sac didn't stop, relieving her of the burden of Martin stopping in, though she suspected he was still in St. Louis "on business." After the unnerving conversation with her friends the morning before, Deanna didn't want to see him. All day she said little inside the house, worried he was listening. Or someone was. If Martin appeared, she knew she couldn't hide what she was feeling. Her fear would permeate, and Martin was too astute and watchful not to notice. The last thing Deanna wanted to do was give away what they knew and what they were planning to plan, since they didn't really have a plan. Regardless, Deanna did have a result in mind for the plan that wasn't, and it was Martin dead.

Ava also slept very little that night, as well. Their lives should have gotten easier when they started this endeavor. Wasn't that the point? And for a brief, shining moment, their lives were better. Or at least getting there. They were making money, it was fun, Ava fancied herself a desperado – a real-life Robin Hood, stealing from the rich to give to the poor. The poor being her and her friends. The women had buried hatchets from past wrongs and were digging themselves out of poverty. Ava believed they could have grown their little operation into something truly lucrative, if left to their own devices. And then all the shit with Santos blew up, got ugly, and next came a dead cop, and then Martin, who was more intimidating than Santos and Marcus put together. As she sat on her back steps, staring out at the backyard, which was mowed by a service, something else Martin must be paying for since she hadn't seen a bill, Ava sipped her coffee and muttered to herself about their plight. There had to be a way out of this. But she couldn't think of a single one that didn't include her pulling a trigger.

Candy sat in Curtis's BMW to relay what Izzy believed. She couldn't tell him in the house and had to wait until the next morning when he was going to go to the gym, to jump into the passenger seat of his car to have this conversation. Having worked in security at banks, Curtis suspected this himself, and had been checking the walls to see if he could see any place where microphones could be hidden. But he had come up empty. And while he wouldn't put anything past Martin. His dealing with him had been different than the women's. Curtis knew that what they had going with Martin was small potatoes compared to the other illegal operations Martin Collique had his hands in. Why would these women counterfeiting a few gowns be so important to him he would bug their homes? It just seemed far too inconsequential to Curtis, and the only thing he could rationalize was that Martin was an odd man who was obsessed with control. That alone would be enough for Martin to want to know everything that was happening inside their homes. And it infuriated Curtis to imagine Martin sitting in some big, comfy chair with a glass of scotch, listening to him and Candy having sex.

"We're living in a gilded cage," Candy bemoaned. "And this cage isn't even all that gilded, I mean come on, it's not like he moved us to Ladue or Clayton! But that son-of-a-bitch has been listening to us. What we say! What we do! He knows all our secrets."

Curtis remained stoic, taking deep breaths, keeping his head and not responding out of emotion, even though all he was feeling was pure emotion. Raw. Cold. Bitter. Having Candy upset and scared was something Curtis needed to handle. Focusing his mind, he had to weigh what the assets of working for Martin were, and what would happen if they were back freelancing, knocking off clothes they copied out of the stores. What would life be if they crushed Martin and left all of this behind? He recognized that leaving would mean losing their homes and taking a step back in lifestyle. To a degree it wouldn't matter since moving onto this street still felt like a vacation more than anything permanent. But Curtis had given up his "day job" to handle any problems the women had in their operation. He promised Candy. And Martin now certainly seemed like a problem. Something that Curtis would have to eliminate. Turning to Candy again, he asked, "Did you all talk about what you want to do about it?"

"We did," Candy said. "We want him gone from our lives."

****

Izzy was on top of Kevin as he held her hips and drove himself into her. He loved looking up at her as she came. Her mouth open, her eyes closed as she growled out breath after breath. It always brought him to climax. It was also the first time he noticed her tummy pooched just slightly. Something he never noticed before. Instinctively, his hand slipped up and ran over the slim bump. Reacting sharply, Izzy slid off him, pushing his hand away from her abdomen. Immediately furious with herself for her overt behavior, she hoped Kevin was as oblivious and self-involved as she thought he was. She turned and gave him a pitiful smile. "Sorry. I'm a little self-conscious. Gained a little weight."

"We're not fucking enough," Kevin responded.

Izzy kept her back to Kevin, reaching for the thin robe that lay on the chair near the bed, wanting to hide her body. She was sure that he never thought about pregnancy, believing she was on the pill. They'd been hooking up for over a year, and nothing had ever happened. It wouldn't even occur to him that she could get pregnant. And she was in no hurry to tell him.

"You don't gotta be self-conscious around me. You're hot," Kevin stated. "Got a better body than most high school girls."

"Yeah," Izzy huffed. "You're a kid. An athlete. Your body is ridiculous. And being a guy, you'll hold on to it for decades. Not like women. We don't get that lucky. We peak before we even know what the hell to do with our bodies and then watch as we drop, bloat and wrinkle. Guys just don't have that problem. Not like women. Our bodies are meant to do one goddamn thing."

Izzy stood, the robe sliding over her shoulders before she tied it tightly. Kevin watched her walk across the room to a pack of cigarettes on her dresser. The only time Izzy smoked was after sex. She wasn't sure if it was because she felt the need or because she'd seen it in a movie and thought it was cool. Picking up the pack, she paused, punting it across the top of the dresser with her finger as her face screwed up bitterly. This was a habit that had to stop now that she was pregnant, and unsure what she was going to do about it. Seeing the pursed look on her face, Kevin sat up. He kicked off the sheets until his naked body was sprawled on top of her bed, so she could see him as he pressed his penis down to his thigh, wishing it would go flaccid. But he was already amped to go again. Usually, he and Izzy would take a brief rest, and he would initiate the next round. But she had already climbed out of bed and had the robe tied around her, giving the signal that the fun for the day was over.

"You know you're hot, right?" Kevin asked, hoping to lure Izzy back into bed.

Wishing she had that cigarette between her lips she announced, "I fucked someone else."

Not sure how to respond, Kevin squirmed, unconsciously pulling a sheet over himself to hide his erection. "I figured that. I mean, I don't think I'm the only guy you hook up with. It's not like we're exclusive or anything? Right?"

"You poke every high school bitch with a decent set of tits," Izzy responded with iciness etching into her voice. "I do what I do."

"Okay. Cool. As long as you're cool, I'm cool," Kevin responded, expecting as much. He really liked Izzy. Loved that she was older, experienced, had a wild streak. Her body was rocking and she had an attitude. Most high school girls might lean into the bitchiness, but they didn't know their way around a guy's body. So, the sex with Izzy was stellar. But Kevin's feelings went a little deeper. He would never call it love, he wouldn't let himself go there with any woman. Not yet. He had plans that didn't keep him tied to St. Louis. And while Kevin was mostly oblivious to other people's feelings, he knew if he fell in love it would end in disaster. Besides, he didn't know if he was even capable of that emotion for a woman yet, other than his mother. And that was different. Kevin would always tell girls he bedded that he couldn't really commit to them, he was still "working on himself." But truth was, he didn't even know what that meant either.

"Drugged this guy and took advantage of him," Izzy admitted, angry, but feeling compelled to tell someone, and believing Kevin was the most innocuous and wouldn't question her too deeply.

"You did not," he laughed, thinking she was fucking with him.

"I did," Izzy said, laughing at herself. "It was stupid."

Kevin eyed her carefully, knowing a few of Izzy's tells. He believed she was telling him the honest-to-God truth. "Why?" he wanted to know.

Staring at Kevin for a moment as she fought herself to keep from retrieving that pack of cigarettes, Izzy wondered what it would be like to be such a good-looking guy. Kevin was beautiful. Body like a statue and a handsome face. He was a show-er and a grow-er. She wanted to crawl on top of him again and put him inside her, feel the girth as he slid in and let him hit that spot that made her forget everything. What would it be like to be a guy and be that beautiful?

"If I told you, you'd think I was fucking crazy. And I guess I was," Izzy admitted, her eyes searching his angled face, even more beautiful in the shadowy bedroom, for some compassion rather than simple interest. But Kevin wasn't mature enough to understand what a woman needed. At least not Izzy. Not at this moment.

"You do it for fun? To see if you could? For money? What?"

"To keep all of us out of trouble," Izzy said, again glad she was telling someone. "I fucked a Federal Agent. He's onto what your mom and all of us are doing. Martin, he's blackmailing the guy to keep him from coming after us."

Kevin gasped, recognizing it was the truth. "No way," he said, believing her but not sure to what extent.

Nodding, Izzy shrugged. "It was fucking stupid. I shouldn't have done it. Why the fuck should I be the one who ruins someone's marriage? I think he has kids and shit. If I had thought about it for even a second, I wouldn't have done it. I didn't need to fuck him. I could have just made it look like it happened, but I didn't even do that.

I actually put the fucker inside me. Idiotic. I think I liked having this guy under my control, you know?"

"You like having me under your control," answered Kevin with an honesty that caused Izzy to shiver.

"You're young. It's fun," Izzy admitted. "Kevin, you're going to have women throwing their pussies in your face all your life. You already do but you're still such a boy. You got no idea just how good looking you are. But do yourself a favor, find something other than baseball that you are good at. Because baseball, that shit's not going to last. It'll get you into college, but while you're there, find something that you want to study, something that's yours. You're smarter than you give yourself credit for."

"Okay..." Kevin responded, for the moment wondering if Izzy was going to die or something by the way she was expelling life-advice.

"You know we beat the shit out of your baseball coach," Izzy then said, turning the conversation.

"They said he was in a car accident," Kevin said.

"He looks like it. Your mom is a tough bitch when she wants to be."

"He deserved it. Fucker. Plowing my sister. What a fucking creep," answered Kevin.

"Am I a fucking creep? Our age difference isn't any more or less than theirs," stated Izzy sadly.

"I wasn't a virgin when we started."

"So, it's your sister's virginity that makes her thing different?"

"I don't know..." Kevin uttered, musing. "I guess so. He seduced her. At least that's how it looks. I know Tracee thinks she was the one who initiated it...getting what she wanted, but guys, they know how to get all over shit like that. I know Coach Cunello has fucked other girls at school. At least that's what some have told me. And I believe them."

"What, while they're sucking on your dick?" Izzy snarked.

"Usually somewhere around that time," Kevin spoke again with honesty.

Izzy again took in Kevin's beauty. He looked sad, like he wanted to have a genuine conversation and she kept trying to tear it to shreds, to make him feel bad about what they had going on, about his sexual appetite. But Izzy knew Kevin wasn't wise enough to recognize that, not yet anyway. He just felt bad because her nastiness hurt his feelings. Maybe he would never understand it past that level. Izzy sort of knew that Kevin might never take the time to analyze anything in his life. People born under a lucky star rarely have to.

Tears filled Izzy's eyes. Kevin slid off the bed and moved to her. Placing a hand on her shoulder, hoping she wouldn't bite it off or bat it away, he slowly slipped it around her and pulled her to him.

"I'm fucking pregnant," Izzy whispered through a sob.

Having déjà vu of the moment Cassie told him she was pregnant, Kevin's body tensed. But Izzy was different. She wasn't using this as a weapon.

"I don't know if it's yours, Kevin," she continued. "Might not be. Could be this guy I drugged. I don't know and I don't know what I'm going to do about it. Don't tell anyone."

"I won't."

Izzy shifted her body towards him, looking into Kevin's blue eyes. She could see the glimmer of understanding. Leaning up to his ear, she took a moment to let out another sob before she whispered to him, "I'm pregnant, and Martin Collique knows it. He knows about us. We need to kill him before he tells your mother or anyone else."

Pulling back, it was Kevin's turn to peer into Izzy's eyes. And what he saw sent a tremor through his body. Tears aside, she had the dark, blank look of a stone-cold killer.

TWISTING IN THE WIND

Clara still hung her wash on a line. Even living close to highway 70 and under a flight pattern for Lambert Field, when the planes came in from the east, she believed her laundry was fresher hanging it outside rather than shoving it into a dryer with one of those smelly sheets. She could breathe a little easier now that the SLPD had officially classified Marcus' death an accident. She was now entitled to his pension. Clara would never tell the women she was working with this news, she wanted to keep her position with them. And if they believed she still needed the money, which she did, just not as much, they were less likely to toss her aside if money got tight.

She wanted to sew the gowns and make even more by creating something new with Deanna that they could sell and pick up even more. While her older kids didn't go to college, Clara could now put something away, and being a police widow, she figured there had to be money when it was their turn. And she would demand that they go. Hell, someone was going to have to make enough money to take care of her in her old age.

Nice cars pulling down Clara's block were not an uncommon sight. People in Clara's 'hood often drove a car that cost not much less than their home. If they owned their home at all. It was all about what you drove. But a town car? That was rare. And when it stopped in front of her house, it really threw her. She didn't know anyone who sat in the back of a car while an employee drove them around. Though, she'd heard of one person.

Martin stepped from the back of the car and stood in the street, staring at Clara's home. She watched through the front window, folding her laundry on the dining table, as Martin, who she had never met, wandered around in front of her home. Clara carried a stack of t-shirts to her son's room before moving to the hutch in her small dining room, opening a drawer and pulling out one of Marcus' many handguns.

"Can I help you?" Clara asked from her porch, making sure the revolver was displayed in her hands.

Martin stood a little bit taller when he spied the gun. "Are you Clara? The Clara I've heard so much about and have never had the pleasure of meeting?"

"You're Martin Collique…"

Martin smiled warmly. Clara could tell it wasn't genuine, and after what she'd heard about him, he wasn't capable of being genuine. Maybe he didn't know how much she knew about him from the other women. But he had to know they talked.

"May I come in?" Martin asked.

Clara took a moment, eyeing him with distrust and detachment. She wasn't sure she wanted this guy in her house. He would know too much about her, and if nothing else, the layout. If she had an alarm system, which she didn't. A dog, which she didn't.

"We can talk here on the porch. I've been inside all day, it feels good out here. Come on up and sit," she said, signaling to the two old wood chairs on the covered porch.

Martin opened the gate and stepped onto the property, listening for a dog to come in charging. He walked sharply up the steps to the porch. Clara nodded to one of the chairs as she sat in the other. Martin wanted to wipe it off but didn't want to be rude, so he decided to chance his three-hundred-dollar slacks and sat down.

"Deanna tells me you're indispensable," Martin stated, again with a disingenuous smile.

"She and I work well together. She knows what she's doing. So do I," Clara responded, not sure how much she should tell this man, but certainly wanting to make herself appear as important to the process as possible.

"I'm sorry the other women aren't as much help," Martin continued.

"They help...they just don't have the same talent with a needle and thread. They're learning. And they help with other things that would take a lot of our time. This operation you got going, it needs all of us," Clara answered, adding, "it just needs me and Deanna most because we know our way around a sewing machine."

Martin smiled again. This time it came off as patronizing to Clara, as if he knew she was building herself up and was somehow proud of her effort, which only pissed off Clara. "Let me ask you something..." Martin said, leaning over towards her as if to make this conspiratorial. "If any of the women leave, are you willing to step in?"

"I already have stepped in," Clara responded.

"Yes. But I mean, if one of them were to opt out, would you be willing to move over to a home near them?"

Her initial reaction was to scream, "Hell yes!" but Clara felt the ominousness of his statement cover her like a heavy sweater. Knowing that Santos worked for this guy and disappeared after her husband's death, she felt he was cloaking the word 'murder' or some derivative, talking around what he was planning on doing. And while Clara didn't feel she owed the other women in the group much of anything, she didn't want to be the one holding a secret. Most especially one that had had blood dripping from it.

"Yeah, of course, I'd like to be living over on that street where the other women are. Better schools. Safer than here," Clara answered. "But like I said, we need all of us. Everybody's doing something."

"And I appreciate that," Martin replied before standing, looking down at Clara, which only made her realize how tall and angular he was. Like a store mannequin come to life, his clothes hung on him perfectly as well. "I won't take up your day. I just wanted you to know you're appreciated. Your contributions are not without notice. And I'm not upset that you and Deanna are using the leftover material to make your own gowns and sell them."

This froze Clara. Though she did everything possible to hide that from Martin, allowing her eyes to stay locked with his, believing what he said wasn't a blessing but a threat, she simply nodded slowly and said, "I appreciate that. Helps me around here with things, you know."

Martin returned her nod before he stepped off her porch and walked back to the waiting town car. Since the driver never turned off the engine, it disappeared quickly down the block. Clara stood. 'Fuck him,' she thought, picking up the revolver. She knew if he came for her, or if anyone did, she would put a bullet in them no problem. Marcus had beat a lot of the fight out of her, but he was dead and buried. She had spit on his grave after all the policemen had left. For the first time in a long time, she didn't feel burdened by life, and this tall, skinny white man wasn't about to steal her joy.

WHAT IN THE FRESH HELL NOW

"Nothing so far, sir," Barry lied, speaking into his phone as he jogged on the treadmill in the hotel gym, working up a sweat. "I have a few more persons of interest I need to talk to. I will get the information we need. There will be arrests."

Hanging up, Barry ran harder until he felt his heart pounding in his chest, he believed he was moments from giving himself a heart attack. He liked to take himself to the point where the pain was so acute fear surged through his body. Slowing, he could feel the blood rushing through his veins until his pulse slowed to a more tolerable level. He stepped off the treadmill in the hotel gym and picked up his phone again, calling his wife to relay that everything was good, he was making progress on the case, and he hoped to be home next week. After asking her to kiss the kids for him, Barry hung up. He was used to lying to his wife, Melissa, to the point where it became perfunctory. He did it more than he told the truth. Barry had started it even before they married. Barry was a sex addict. That affliction started in junior high school when he considered himself a serial masturbator. His needs only grew from there. But he got so good at lying about it, when he took the polygraph as part of his FBI background check, he passed when asked about addictions and sex. He'd only been caught cheating once by Melissa. Everything else that fed his desirous predilection had gone undetected. The Bureau had caught wind of his behavior, very little got by them, even in agents' personal lives, and his itch was antithetical to their image. Granted, the image was a relic from yesteryear, but still, it was enough for him to be dressed down and demoted. Demoted to these shit cases in St. Louis.

But considering how many times Barry cheated, the times he picked up a hooker or met a woman in a bar, and the number of girls he banged who were of questionable age, Barry believed he lived under a lucky star. He hadn't caught a disease, his wife believed it only happened once, and he could pass a polygraph for the Bureau. 'If they only knew the truth,' he thought, as he toweled the sweat off his body, the memories of his sexual conquests making him horny again. Barry was pissed at himself. Everything made him horny. Secretly, Barry went to therapy for his sexual addiction, but all talking about being horny did for Barry was make him hornier. He believed he had it under control, he hadn't picked up a woman in over half a year when Izzy roofied him and got him back up to his hotel room for some illicit and damaging photos, leaving Barry with a real problem. And he was pissed. Barry didn't know how to bury this, and having these photos on his phone were a ticking time bomb that would not just ruin his career but destroy every aspect of his life. And Barry accepted that to bury this completely, he would have to bury someone the bitch who had left him little choice.

As he showered, stroking the soapy water over his penis, he got hard as he imagined putting her in the earth and covering her with dirt, shovelful by shovelful. He worked too hard to get this far to let this conniving bitch take him down. He just hoped that lucky star he believed shone on him continued glimmering long enough for him to kill Isabel Ruiz and get away with it.

****

Except for Clara, all the other women made themselves comfortable on Deanna's new living room furniture as she made the call. There were eight more big boxes also in the living room containing gowns and fabric, which made

Deanna wish Clara was there for support. Curtis stood back against the wall closest to the front door, his arms crossed over his chest. His mind meandering through ways to take out Martin, from beating him to death to a more Russian method of poisoning or the equally Kremlin-like method of having your victim fall from a tall building. But he knew it wouldn't be that easy. This would be even more complicated than wrestling Clara's husband to the floor of Deanna's old apartment before they were able to kill him. Martin wouldn't go easy, and he would be ready. Curtis assumed he was always ready. And if they failed, they were all dead. Curtis got into this because he fell in love with Candy and wanted to protect her. He'd already taken the lives of two people and had to bargain for the lives of the four women. Blowing out a deep breath as Deanna put the phone to her ear, he steadied himself. Maybe in the long run it would get easier but, in the days ahead, he accepted it was going to be brutal. How brutal, he didn't know. He just wanted all of them to come out alive and free from the urban jail cells they were now living in.

"Martin, it's Deanna. Hi. Yes," Deanna chipped lightly, her eyes shifting, putting the call on speaker.

"Did you just put this call on speaker?" Martin asked.

"Yes...I'm cleaning as we talk," lied Deanna.

"Take me off speaker, please..."

Knowing she had no choice, Deanna did as he asked. But it pissed her off even more that he again was controlling everything. "Umm, I got your shipment today and the due dates. We can't do all this. It's too much work on the schedule you gave me...us," she said, doing her best to keep her anger out of her voice.

As Deanna listened to Martin's response, Ava itched to grab the phone from Deanna's hand. Deanna was always so goddamn nice. Ava wanted to growl into the phone that Martin was a pervert, they knew he bugged their homes, and they were done working for him. If he came after them, they would take his ass down. Consequences be damned. And while she knew that wouldn't happen, it didn't stop Ava from wanting it. Just as with Santos, priority one for all of them had to be staying above ground and breathing. They'd have to deal with Martin, who had resources and people, very different from how they handled the Santos situation. 'Which I completely fucked up,' Ava thought. She was the one who pushed to let him go free when she should have never let the son-of-a-bitch leave her house alive. But her heart got in the way. This time, she swore to herself, that wouldn't happen.

"We will do our best, Martin, but what you're expecting is unreasonable," Deanna continued, but stopped speaking as Martin responded. Her eyes rolling, she then nodded as she added, "I said we will do our best. Now, onto something else, when are you coming back to St. Louis?"

Deanna caught Izzy's eye as Deanna listened to Martin. Deanna could tell that Izzy had something else on her mind. She didn't know how she knew that, but something was clearly rolling around Izzy's head, and it had nothing to do with the conversation with Martin. Izzy was the toughest of the original four women, and Deanna always felt safer when she was around. She needed Izzy's total attention on this hot mess and what they were planning. What could possibly be more important than that? "Yes, yes, I'm here, I'm listening..." Deanna said, drawn back to Martin and the phone call but kept her eyes on Izzy.

And Izzy felt Deanna's gaze. 'Women are funny,' Izzy thought. 'They know shit. Even when you don't want them to know it.' She had to come clean about this pregnancy with her sister and her friends. Especially since Martin knew. She certainly didn't want him telling the other women, making each promise not to say anything, which had been his style. But she still didn't know what she wanted to do, or who the father was. The variables were still a fucking mess, too messy to allow Izzy the ability to focus. She still didn't feel pregnant. Nor had she come to grips with this growing peanut inside her being an actual baby. For Izzy, she felt as if she was living in a foreign country and everyone knew the language but hers. She could grasp what they were saying, maybe the importance by their tone and inflection, but none of it made much sense. She knew once she announced this pregnancy all shit would break loose. Especially since she couldn't name the baby daddy. She would never ruin Kevin's life – or hers - by naming him as a possible father. And if she claimed it was the Fed's baby, that would open up another can of worms. But at least that was the least horrible of the two choices. But they only had sex once, and Izzy figured they'd never have to find out how this occurred, other than it was at Martin's request she seduce the Fed. Izzy accepted that one she announced this it would be an emotional clusterfuck, and she didn't know if she wanted to keep this baby, terminate, or have it and give it up, something she knew her sister would fight her on to the death.

"Okay. I understand. Yes. Yes. You too," Deanna said into the phone. "Okay. Bye." Hanging up, she took a deep, dramatic breath.

"Well?" Candy jumped in quickly.

Deanna put her fingers to her lips and pointed outside. They all quickly filed out of the house into the yard between her home and Candy's, realizing that the grass needed to be mowed. "He said he doesn't know when he's coming back to St. Louis. He has a lot of travel to do for deals he's making. But he needs the clothes as quickly as possible. Kept reminding me there's a lot of money in it for us," Deanna relayed. "Bottom line, he agreed to come to St. Louis again when all the clothes were finished and give us our money in person."

"What are you all doing out here?" Clara asked as she walked up from the street, startling each of them.

"We'll explain," Candy assured Clara, waving her over. "We just got a big order."

"In a short amount of time," Ava added.

Clara's eyes narrowed. "What's going on?"

"Houses are bugged. He's listening to us," Izzy stated.

Clara's eyes widened, but she was hardly surprised. And it made moving onto this street a lot less of a grand gesture, and more a horrifying warning that she suspected it really was. "The guy we're working for? One that bought these homes for you all?" she asked, not willing to give away that Martin had paid her a visit.

Deanna nodded.

"Everything we've been saying?" Clara continued.

Deanna nodded again.

"Fuck," Clara said, elongating the vowel.

"Yeah," Ava laughed, "that's what we're all feeling."

"I mean, I don't want to lose my livelihood, but damn. That's like being in prison," Clara added.

"With better appliances," Candy added, giving everyone a chuckle.

"We know what we got to do," Curtis inserted strongly. "We've agreed. The bad news is, we have to wait. Good news, we have time to plan."

"There's something you all need to know," Deanna sighed, knowing she had to tell the truth because they all needed to know. And that she felt it was their ace card. "I had sex with him."

"Martin?!?!?!" Ava shrieked loudly.

Deanna nodded.

"Girl!" Ava howled, high-fiving her. "I knew he liked you, but I didn't know you were into him."

"I'm not. I regret it," Deanna answered before adding, "but...he actually said when we're finished copying all the clothes, he'd come in and give us our money, and he wanted to see me again."

Curtis smiled as if he were reading Deanna's mind. "You willing to do this?" Curtis asked Deanna.

The women all looked at each other. It took a moment for what Curtis was asking Deanna to sink in and make sense to all of them. Once Deanna knew that everyone got the point, she nodded.

"Am I missing something?" Candy quizzed.

"Deanna's the bait," Curtis stated. "If she's capable of luring Martin back here because he's interested, it keeps us in the driver's seat. And it gives us the time frame to plan and execute our move."

Izzy waved her hand in the air, breaking the tension of the moment. Everyone's eyes turned towards her making her incapable of turning back. "Fuck...well, Deanna was brave enough to say what she said, it's my turn."

"You're not sleeping with him too?" her sister asked, causing the others to laugh.

"Fuck no. Not him...Jesus, that's all we need is that motherfucker chasing after all of us," Izzy waved off Ava's question. "You all know he asked me to do something for him. There's a Federal Agent who is, I don't know, sniffing around what we're doing, or the warehouse with the sewing machines...something...something that could lead to him. And this Agent is here in St. Louis. A guy named Barry Wimmer. Martin asked me to help out with him."

"Help out? How?" Ava's eyes bored into her sister.

Shrugging, Izzy threw up her hands in confession. "I drugged him and fucked him," she admitted, regretting telling them the moment all the words escaped her mouth.

"What the holy hell?!?!" Ava snapped. "Martin made you sleep with this guy?"

"He didn't make me...it was just...once I got him in bed and naked, he was really hot...and I thought, I don't know what I thought...I guess 'why not', you know?"

Ava froze up like a statue, furious. Candy grabbed even tighter to Curtis. Deanna's mouth moved but she couldn't form a single word, all of which made Clara howl with laughter.

Clara then high-fived Izzy. "Girl, you kill me!"

"You may take that back, Clara," Izzy said. "Because it gets worse...I did something really, really fucking stupid..."

"Oh God," Ava huffed, bracing herself.

"I filmed it. With my phone. And Martin is using it to blackmail him into silence."

Even Curtis was surprised by this news. "What the fuck!?" he barked. "Why didn't that motherfucker Collique come to me? You shouldn't be doing that! We could have gotten another woman."

Izzy shook her head. "He thought I could do it...and I did. Only I overdid it. I didn't need to really do it to get the pictures. I don't know what was going through my head..."

"Fucking Martin. He pisses me off!" Curtis continued. "He's going around us all! Playing each one of us for his advantage."

Candy took Curtis' hand and squeezed it, trying to calm him down. Her eyes pleaded with him to not blow this up any bigger. They were all in on the plan. Whatever that plan amounted to. Candy knew that Curtis being this irate would shake the women's confidence in anything they decided upon.

"It gets worse...," Izzy continued, shifting the attention back to herself.

No one said a word. Considering what Izzy had shared, whatever this bomb was it was going to scorch the earth.

"I'm pregnant," Izzy said flatly, shocking them all.

No one spoke for what seemed like an eternity. For Izzy it felt like no one was breathing.

"You got to be fucking kidding me! You're carrying some Federal Agent's goddamn baby!" Ava nearly yelled. "Oh, all the shit we've been through in the last year, and that's been a mountain of crazy, this takes the cake!"

Izzy shrugged. She was aware this was the result of her massive idiocy. And she was aware there were two ways all of this could go.

"Does this Fed know you're pregnant?" Ava then asked.

"No, I don't think so. But Martin does."

It was Curtis' turn to laugh out loud, causing Candy to slap him on the shoulder. "Look, ladies, this is something we can use to keep the Fed in line if the pictures don't work. No matter what you decide to do, Izzy."

"I don't know what I want to do…"

"Fair enough," Curtis continued. "But our priority is getting Martin's ass back to St. Louis and ending all this shit."

"Well, the faster we get these clothes done, the faster we get Martin here," Deanna stated, looking at her friends. "You all are going to learn what Clara and I do. Because you're going to start sewing. After Martin gives us the money for this next set of gowns, then we take care of him. And after that we figure out our next move from there. Am I right, Curtis?"

"Dead on," Curtis answered.

"Then let's go to work," Ava said with absolute certainty.

PUNCH LIKE A GIRL

Deanna spent the next four days teaching Izzy, Ava, and Candy the work she would need from them on the sewing machines. They'd been watching her for months, assisting every so often, so they caught on quicker than either Deanna or Clara expected. But Clara still hovered over their shoulders, keeping a watchful eye. She could not afford to lose this operation because of their sloppy work. And any mistake would take twice as long to fix, if it could be fixed at all. And with the mountainous workload sitting in what should be Deanna's dining room, they couldn't afford to lose a lot of time either. Not with the turnaround that Martin demanded for these gowns. The women were very careful while inside Deanna's home not to badmouth Martin or mention anything associated with the plans they were devising. Using an audio jammer he bought at Walmart, Curtis scanned Deanna's house, as he had done with Candy's, jamming the feed which prevented Martin or whoever was receiving the feed from listening in. But even then, the women, skittish as they had learned to be, waited for a break and would take their discussions outside to the cul-de-sac.

Daily, Clara returned home, elated to be back in her own home, away from the gilded mayhem the other women were living in. While her home was cramped, messy, always filled with some sort of teenage or child drama, she was away from the tension of her "new job." And while she felt part of everything, an equal partner, maybe more than equal, considering her visit from Martin, but still separate. She wasn't living in the nice house on the cul-de-sac, but those women resided in a fishbowl. A fishbowl with microphones in the walls. On top of it, the women knew way too much about each other. Making their secrets, which she knew they had, hard to keep. Clara didn't want her secrets to be known by anyone. Hers were hers. Having an abusive husband, you cultivate those skills. For most of her marriage, she plotted her husband's death. Marcus was a violent bully. When he hit Clara, she knew it. And she knew the St. Louis Police Department knew it. Everyone in his family knew it. Pretty much everyone he ever met knew it. Yet, no one did anything about it. Fear was the primary reason. Marcus had a gift of homing in on anyone's weakness and being a large, powerful man with a vicious streak, anyone who crossed him accepted that the confrontation could turn physical. And they would lose. Clara knew that better than anyone. So, she learned to keep things in, keep it secret, and retaliate with subterfuge.

Twice, she almost killed Marcus in his sleep. And twice, she regretted not finishing the deed. She got to where she rationalized she deserved the beatings Marcus gave her for not killing him when she had the chance. But she had kids. She did not want to go to jail. She did not want them to be parentless, or worse, left with their father if she failed at killing him. Marcus, being a police officer, guaranteed that she would end up in prison for life if she killed him. And being a black woman would guarantee it. No matter the jury, they would convict her for those two reasons alone. And if Marcus survived the attempt, he would turn his rage on their kids and there would be no one to stop it. It was the only thing that kept her from slitting his throat while he slept off a night of whiskey, fearing that he would somehow survive.

But now, with Marcus dead and buried, and her burgeoning new career and friendship with Deanna, Clara felt her life had finally started, opening her to something brand new: purpose. Marcus's life insurance through the police department would give her a nice pad, money that would help her and the kids escape the 'hood, where Marcus preferred to live. But she had never had anything, other than the kids, that was her own. But counterfeiting clothes and designing other dresses with Deanna gave Clara her first actual sense of self. A sense of worth. And though she would never say it out loud, Martin's visit also boosted her self-esteem. She was valuable. Clara wasn't about to give that up without a fight. And if the other women believed this man had caged them - even though she knew they didn't know what the hell that actually meant, their view much vaguer than her own - then they were correct, that son-of-a-bitch had to go. Marcus left her enough of an arsenal to help with that. But she didn't want to erase Martin until he made sure the other women knew just how important she was, more valuable than most of them, and part of whatever came next.

****

When Kevin found out his mother knew about Izzy being pregnant, the ramifications that eluded him when Izzy told him broke through Kevin's self-involvement and he felt his heart clench in his chest. Even though his mother and her friends believed Izzy was pregnant by the FBI agent, Kevin grasped that the baby she was carrying could very well be his own. And Kevin couldn't tell a soul. If

Izzy opted to keep the baby, it would change the course of his life. And not in a good way. But strangely, Kevin was even more bent about Izzy carrying another man's baby, while she was still having sex with him. He didn't tell her when he should have, and Kevin grappled with his proprietary feelings when it came to Izzy. It's not like they were a couple, she could have sex with whoever she wished, so could he. And Kevin did. But now, with Izzy pregnant, and the intense possibility that the baby could be his, Kevin wrestled with the obligation to man-up and take responsibility. To ask her for a paternity test. He could figure out why he felt that way, but he did. He loved Izzy. In his own way. And he was sure she loved him right back. Kevin surmised that was why Izzy pinned the pregnancy on the Fed. To protect him from having his future turned upside down by fatherhood.

But when he saw Izzy the next night hanging out on her front porch with Ava, Ava waving a glass of red wine in the air as she talked, while Izzy sipped from a bottle of water, he couldn't help but focus on the slight pooch that appeared under her tank top. He couldn't let go that this child inside her was probably his. Even if she had a one-night stand, he'd been with her dozens of times in the last six months. Even since moving into these houses, he and Izzy hooked up whenever Ava and Cassie were gone for an afternoon or a night. The fact Izzy had announced to 'the sewing circle' – as Kevin started calling his mother and her group – that the father was this Fed, had Kevin battling his fury. She could have warned him that she was going to tell her group, so that his jaw wasn't lying on the floor when his mother casually passed along the news, and how furious they all were that Martin coaxed Izzy into doing this exploitive subterfuge.

As he headed to his car, he also wondered why Izzy hadn't gotten an abortion immediately. Why tell anyone? Why wait? Granted, she had time, but Kevin couldn't imagine that Izzy really wanted this baby if it was from an illicit and illegal one-nighter. His mind then shifted to images of having sex with a pregnant Izzy. Even if she was carrying his kid, the idea of her stretched belly creeped him out. Could he poke it with his dick? If they continued to have sex, would it mess with the kid's genes or chromosomes? Would Izzy stop wanting to have sex at some point? Kevin wasn't turned on by any of these thoughts, and the idea of having intercourse with a baby involved irked him. Especially if it wasn't his kid.

As he unlocked his car, he heard Ava holler hello to him. Kevin turned and waved, calling, "Hey Mrs. Corbin, hey Izzy." He stopped, his eyes boring in on Izzy. "Hey, my mom told me you're pregnant," Kevin called to her, keeping his tone casual, as Candy came out of the house next door, walking over to Ava and Izzy's front porch with a bottle of wine.

"Yeah," was all Izzy said.

Kevin nodded, baffled. "Congratulations..." he said, forcing a smile. "You getting married?" he then asked.

Recognizing the game Kevin was playing, Izzy simply smiled back and answered, "No. The father doesn't want to be involved."

"Oh wow," Kevin launched back. "What a dick. When I have a kid, I'm going to be involved. Maybe because my own father split on us. I don't want to be like him."

"I think that's admirable, Kevin," Ava said. "Sometimes you learn who not to be from your parents."

"Yeah," Kevin responded, moving to his car. "You all have a good night. And congratulations again, Izzy."

The women all waved as Kevin got in his car and backed out of the driveway. Kevin's eyes stayed with Izzy, hoping she could see him glaring right at her. But he could see that she almost immediately turned away and began talking with her sister and Candy. "Fuck her," Kevin said to himself as he turned up his radio. Kevin knew he had an outlet for his sexual appetite, and he would start playing the field at the high school again. At the end of the school year, there were a few new girls he had noticed who he could work his 'baseball magic' on. Kevin was sure he could bed one or two, maybe shake Izzy from his thoughts. And loins.

****

Sitting in her room, Tracee fought with herself about whether she should pick up the phone and check on Vince, to see how he was healing. It had been a few days since she did, and she was hoping that he would get a message to her. But he had not. She heard he was coming back to school the following Monday, but she felt it would be awkward to stop into his classroom. These last couple weeks since her mother and friends kicked Vince's ass – and if she hadn't shown up, probably killed him – Tracee spent a lot of time in her new bedroom, mulling her "relationship" with Coach Cunnello. And a lot of time, pleasuring herself to the memories of Vince going down on her, where Tracee truly felt in control and his skills caused an ecstasy she wouldn't have believed existed in real life, and she had read enough romance novels to believe they had to be true.

She slid her phone off the nightstand and pulled up her secret contact for Vince. But just as she was about to press CALL, Ford pushed open her bedroom door.

"You want to come outside and play?" he asked.

"Play?" Tracee quizzed right back as if the word were foreign.

"There's no kids on this street. The guys in the old neighborhood were butts but at least there was always someone to play with."

"Well, you wanted your own room," Tracee said, hoping her brother would look on the bright side.

"You're a butt too," Ford snarked as he walked out of her room, slamming the door.

Tracee felt her little brother was right. She was a butt. Her life had returned to the boring, lonely, and empty. Until her secret affair had been uncovered, Tracee felt she had blossomed, found something that made her feel adult, unique, special. Now here she was again, lying on her bed in her room, not in control, not with a man, not a woman nor a girl, not anything, doing nothing but pining for her life to go back to the way it was, and knowing that was never going to happen.

Which pissed her off. What if her mother was wrong? What if they were all wrong? What if Vince really, truly had feelings for her that extended past the carnal? Yeah, she was young and it was 'legally' wrong, but in some states, she and Vince could legally have sex. 'Missouri was seventeen, for no apparent reason other than the state was run by a bunch of farmers and religious zealots, all who had secret porn addictions,' she thought. And if her mother was going to call the police, she would have. But she wouldn't because she and the other women beat the crap out of Vince as penance for his sins, and she didn't need him telling anyone about it, most definitely not the police.

What made it worse for Tracee, was Tracee knew that once Vince was back roaming the hallways of the high school, she would be history and he would set his sights on a new girl. He would avoid her, hoping that it never became known how he really got so banged up. That could cost him everything and put him in jail. At minimum, he would have to move away. And Tracee would be left with just horny, gangly high school guys. All who would whisper about her fucking Coach Cunnello. 'I can't survive two more years of that,' she thought to herself. Not because she cared what they would think, she didn't, but because she didn't regret what had happened and didn't believe she had done anything wrong. Even her mother had skirted away from talking to her about it, other than to say, "That's never going to happen again!" more as a demand rather than a conversation. And her older brother simply side-eyed her with a grimace every time they passed. She felt Kevin was vain enough to think that all of this happened because of him, and more accurately, to him, that he was the real victim in all of this. Not because he cared so much about what happened to her, but because his coach disrespected him by fucking his little sister.

"Fuck them all," Tracee said aloud. She wanted what she wanted. And picking up her phone again and pressing Vince's number, she was going to get it.

****

After midnight, Kevin pulled around the circle to park his car out front of the house. He liked being able to see his car from the front window. They may have moved up in the world but they were still in South St. Louis and car theft was still a thing. As he shifted into park and turned off the car, his passenger door opened swiftly and Izzy slipped into the car, slamming the door.

"What the fuck?" Kevin asked.

"What was that shit?" Izzy volleyed back.

"What?"

"About this baby I'm carrying. What was that shit in front of my sister? You didn't have to say anything. Could have just waved and got in your car and left."

Kevin's eyes locked on Izzy's lips as she spoke. He couldn't look her in the eyes. "Tell me the truth. Is it mine?"

"No."

Kevin expected that answer but hoped that whatever was the truth would come out in how Izzy said it rather than her answer. But it didn't. He was still in the dark.

"How do you know?" He asked.

"We've been fucking for over a year. You don't like using protection, and I'm not great with it either. Have I gotten pregnant in all that time? So, what would make you think that now that I banged this other guy, that this, whatever's inside me, is yours? I would suggest you should go to the doctor and see if your sperm has any little swimmers. There is probably something wrong with you."

Kevin knew she was trying to get into his head and turn this around on him. And that incensed him even more. Izzy understood Kevin, knew exactly how to play him. And over the course of time they were hooking up, she had become adept at getting exactly the outcome she wanted from him. Especially physically, but she had also learned to manipulate him on a psychological level, usually only for her physical pleasure but she sensed that she could influence him in every other way as well.

"Are you keeping this kid?"

"I...I still haven't made up my mind," Izzy answered.

"What's so hard to figure out?" Kevin asked. "If you didn't want it, you would have already got this taken care of."

"I don't know what I want."

"Well, I know what I want. I want a test. To see if it's mine," Kevin responded.

Izzy's face hardened. "I told you, this isn't yours. This is the Federal Agent's. And it was a mistake. Not...this baby, but getting pregnant. I shouldn't have been a fool. I shouldn't have been in his hotel room, period. But I was. And now..." Izzy's voice trailed off as she glanced away. But her eyes turned back to Kevin with an icy stare. "Just know it's not yours," she finished.

Kevin held his gaze on her lips, not wanting to look into Izzy's eyes. "I don't know that. Because we're still fucking. Or were. But it could be mine, and I gotta know. I went through this shit with your niece. I am not going through it again."

"I'm not asking you to pay anything to do anything, so get over yourself. It's not yours," Izzy stated flatly one more time, flinging open the passenger door of the car and disappearing after slamming it shut.

Kevin sat in his car, his hands still wrapped tightly around the steering wheel. This was his baby. Izzy's defiant attitude announced it. While no one had said it to him, he suspected that Izzy having sex with some Federal Agent had something to do with the cagey, feline looking guy who was visiting his mother, Martin Collique. And while Kevin basked in the financial boon of whatever the hell his mother was doing with those dresses she was making, he was also keenly aware that his mother was on edge or exhausted almost all of the time since she started working with those sewing machines. And that too had to do with Martin Collique. And that this magilla his mother and Izzy were caught in with their other friends now controlled all their lives. More aptly, this Martin Collique person controlled their lives.

But Kevin believed he had a remedy for a few of his problems. Vince Cunnello. Kevin fantasized that he and Vince could make Martin Collique go away, and with the same bullet baseball bat or knife, that his baseball coach could wheedle his way back into the good graces of the 'Sewing Circle', despite what Vince had done to his sister. While his mother would see it differently, Kevin took Tracee at her word. That she was okay with what went down with Vince, that she executed the seduction and Vince was her victim, not the other way around. Kevin still found his coach a creeper for having sex with his younger sister, certainly not correlating it with what he had going on with Izzy for the last year and a half, starting when he was sixteen. After Tracee told Kevin implicitly how she lured Vince in, Kevin couldn't help but give her props. He would never say it out loud but Kevin felt his sister was always the smartest person in the room, and even though what Vince did was wrong, Tracee's active participation controlled the direction and speed that things went down.

Vince was the dupe. It may not have been that way with the other girls Vince was rumored to have seduced, but Tracee told a different story. And Kevin knew her well enough to know that she was smarter than him, and smarter than Vince.

Stepping out of his car, Kevin tingled. He had a plan to bring some normalcy back into his home and his life. And it energized him, provided him with an aura of power. And that gave him a hard-on. Crossing the lawns from his home over to Ava and Izzy's, Kevin moved around the side where Izzy's bedroom window was on the second floor. The light was on. He pulled out his phone and pressed her number.

"Yeah..." Izzy answered.

"You were shitty to me."

"So...?"

"I'm outside. Come down and open your door."

"My fucking sister and your former girlfriend are home."

Kevin smiled. "So?"

Izzy said nothing but Kevin could hear her breathing intensify.

"Fuck...if you won't let me in, come outside."

"For what?"

"I got something in my car for you," Kevin answered, still feeling powerful.

"I bet you do," Izzy responded, and then again, Kevin heard her breathing grow more rapid.

He remained silent, breathing right back until she said, "You're lucky…"

"How's that?"

"Being pregnant has only made me hornier."

"Come down to the car while we can still both fit in it," he laughed.

Izzy hung up. Kevin wasn't sure if he had overstepped, that maybe she hung up pissed off at his last comment. He moved back to the front of the house and waited. There was no movement through the front room which he could see through the thin curtains. 'Fuck,' he thought, angry at himself for making the joke, even when he knew it would piss Izzy off. Kevin turned and stalked back towards his home when he heard in a whisper, "Where you going?"

Turning, Izzy was coming around from the back of the house, still in the shadows.

"Put the seats down," Kevin replied.

He pivoted and headed for his car, opening the passenger side. "Get in. We're not fucking here."

Izzy didn't bother replying as she moved from the shadows into the passenger seat, Kevin shutting the door before he dashed to the driver's side and got in. He pulled down the block to a connecting street, where they were still building new homes. Pulling into an open garage of a nearly-finished home, he turned off the ignition. In the darkness, he ran his hand to the back of Izzy's neck and pulled her in for a hard kiss, their tongues meeting. With his other hand he grabbed the lever and let his seat back push back so Izzy could climb on top of him.

After they both came, Izzy crawled off Kevin and slipped back into the passenger seat, propping it back so she could lay down as well while Kevin stepped out of the car to stretch and pull up his shorts. In the shadows, he could see his reflection in the car window. The shadows made him look even more muscular than he was, which pleased him.

As he looked at the light and dark shadings of his torso, Kevin wondered how women in college would receive him. Would it be like high school where he had his pick, or would the co-eds quickly tire of his self-involved bullshit, leaving only the easiest, most damaged, or those who found it a badge of honor to bed an athlete for sex? Kevin never doubted his hotness. He knew he was. Which remained a problem for him since puberty. As Miguel Ortega, the catcher on Kevin's baseball team, who was the only guy on the squad that got laid more than Kevin, said to him after listening to Kevin brag about banging a cheerleader from an opposing school, "You don't deserve a girlfriend, payaso, just get yourself an eight-foot mirror. You're in love with yourself." Kevin laughed the statement off, never letting Miguel know how much that hurt his feelings. Or that he never forgot it. When Kevin looked at himself in the mirror, he saw the best of both his parents. His body lean and muscled like his father, the blue eyes from his mom. While he didn't hear it much growing up, Kevin still believed he was special, that he was born with some great magic whirling inside him. Magic he didn't understand how to harness but still felt its power oozing through his veins. Kevin believed there would always be a girl, hot and beautiful, who would deem him the prize in their relationship.

But when Izzy looked over at Kevin staring blankly in the darkness, she shook her head, knowing exactly what was ping-ponging in his head. "Hey, lover boy, take me home. I need to get some sleep," she called out.

That's when it hit him that woman would never be Izzy. That while they had a chemical connection, a history, it was defined by sex and nothing else. She didn't find him the prize in the relationship and never would. He was just a hot, perpetually horny teenager that could please her physically but offered nothing else. She would eventually find another hot man closer to her age and put him on a leash.

They drove back to the front of their homes in silence, the aroma of sex lingering in the car. As Izzy got out, she looked back in at Kevin. "I need to be honest with you," Izzy said. "I think I'm going to keep this baby."

Their eyes locked in on each other. Kevin's grew sad, Izzy's hopeful.

"I pretty much figured," was all Kevin said before asking why.

"I didn't want it at first. But the more I think about it, the more I feel that I might never find anyone who is a good father. So, what am I waiting for?"

"If that guy's the father, you going to tell him? Have him in the picture?"

Izzy shrugged, squinting as if she'd bit into rotten fruit. "I don't even know him. And no, I don't want him in the picture. He's married. Got a family. I'm really not up for ruining his life, you know. I want a baby, not some asshole telling me how it should be raised or fighting me for custody."

Kevin remained silent for a moment, then finally the first time all night, he locked eyes with Izzy. "I'm going to ask one more time, is it mine?"

Even though he'd blasted her with the question in the past, this time it jolted Izzy. Maybe it was the genuineness in his voice coupled with the beleaguered look on his face that jarred Izzy, like stepping outside from an air-conditioned building into the middle of a St. Louis August.

"Truth. I...I'm not one-hundred percent sure. But I don't think so."

Kevin sat up taller. "Not sure or no?"

"Even if it is and I keep the baby, your name will never be brought into it. I promise."

"What if I want to be the dad? You know, if I am."

"Do you," Izzy pointedly asked, "want to be the dad?"

Kevin couldn't answer, but he felt self-conscious enough to pull his shirt back on over his head, his eyes darting back and forth as all the ramifications of being a parent this young were finally coalescing into a reality for him. Could he live his life not knowing for sure? Could he tell his mother if it was? Could Izzy tell her sister and her niece? What if the baby looked just like him, wouldn't people know? What would all this mean? What kind of father would an irresponsible teen be?

"I'm...I'm not sure," Kevin finally blurted out, "But I want to know. I don't think I could spend my life just not knowing and always suspecting."

Izzy nodded, simply saying, "Okay," though already in her mind she was manufacturing ways to prevent him from ever finding out if this baby is, in fact, his.

****

Being a Federal Agent had its perks. One was that you understood weaponry and had a basic knowledge of several ways of killing someone. And while Barry didn't know St. Louis as well as he would like, disposing of a body could not be that hard, considering the reputation of certain parts of the city. He spent days daydreaming about making Isabel Ruiz disappear. And while he knew she was working for a much larger enemy he couldn't get to, at least not yet, he knew she could wipe out everything Barry had worked for like a tsunami could take out a seaside village. His wife would not give him a third chance. The Bureau would cut him loose as well. His first indiscretion hurt his career. This one would certainly be fatal.

And he wasn't about to let that happen. He had kids, and as bad as it was that he saw them so little, what was worse was rebuilding the trust with Melissa. She was a staunch Catholic, and his indiscretion wounded her deeply. Any other woman would have filed for divorce, but for Melissa, that was an absolute last resort. Barry loved her. Not because he was sexually attracted to her, certainly not as much as he was attracted to the other women he slept with on the side. But she completed the image. An image that Barry was more in love with than Melissa. For Barry, marriage was complicated and messy. Certainly more complicated than casual sex. And for Melissa, after having the kids, which she felt she was raising single handedly, having sex with Barry was a chore. Not as bad as vacuuming the house, but more than washing the dishes. Barry liked the sport of sex. Various positions. Games. Trying new things. Melissa wanted to get on her back, kiss him for a few minutes and let him slip inside her. She faked orgasms. It got the uncomfortableness over faster. Usually when she feigned an orgasm, he would grunt in her ear, arch his back and come. And it would be over. Once he was off of her, Melissa slid out of bed, padded to the bathroom, shut the door, turned on the warm water and found the douche. After Melissa discovered he was cheating, not that she didn't suspect it for years, sex with Barry now made her feel dirty, and she had lost what little desire she had for him. Even his muscular body and blue eyes couldn't get her into the mood with Barry. She felt he was sick. And now, to make sure her children had their father, she endured her husband's predilections and played pretend to save the marriage.

But Barry knew Melissa had lost the morsels of carnal interest she once had in him. It was a chore to get her to even go through the motions. An infrequent chore, like cleaning the garage. But Melissa didn't need sex. Barry did. If he didn't have a job he loved, and to a lesser degree, his two kids, he would walk away from Melissa. But he loved his job and he could not walk away from his two young children. They deserved a father in the home even if he isn't home full time. But there was no way he could wrestle his urges. He needed sex. There was no way on earth or in heaven that Melissa's lack of desire was going to dictate him being celibate. Figuring it would be easier to ask for forgiveness than permission, he rationalized that it would be better for all involved for Barry to find the partners he needed to ebb his desire, especially when he was out of town. He wouldn't rub Melissa's nose in it, he would find women who were looking for nothing more than a roll in the sheets. But as much as Melissa didn't want to have sex with her husband, she didn't want him straying either. And when she found out, she made sure the Bureau found out. As the pressure built, eroding his marriage, Barry put his "balls on ice," going to therapy, making Melissa promises he wasn't sure he could keep, and being the good soldier at work, taking this crappy assignments, all to atone for his sins.

Sins he was destined to commit again. It wasn't like that itch was going away. It only became more dominate the longer he abstained, metastasized. Barry knew his addiction was terminal.

Worse, he now had these photos that he had to deal with. Someone had used his predilections against him and that both engulfed and enraged Barry. Sexual blackmail. He'd worked a few of those cases in his past, and he always wondered how someone let themselves get foisted into that position. Clothes had to come off. Bodies had to touch. Most likely fluids were traded. Now he knew. Staring at the photos on his phone, Barry felt this was karma was attempting to snub him out like the butt of a cigarette and that just wasn't going to work for Barry. He had to get Izzy to meet. He had the ability to convince witnesses to testify. In this case, he needed to convince her it was in her best interest to keep her mouth shut. If he could get her alone, Barry was sure he was within the margin of error that he could get her to agree.

And if things fell outside the margin of error, he was ready to let the rest play out with a cold finality so he could cling to the job he always wanted and a marriage in name only that he regretted.

****

As she was about to leave her house to walk over to Deanna's, Izzy's phone buzzed. It was a text from Barry Wimmer. It read: *I need to talk to you. Whatever you need. Whenever you're available. Can we please meet?*

Ava had strolled into the living room and saw her sister through the picture window, standing on her front porch, reading her phone.

Opening the front door, Ava smiled, asking, "Everything okay?"

Izzy glanced up and nodded, holding up her phone. "Baby daddy. Wants to meet," she said. "Collique will be happy."

"Wait! What?! No. You're not going to meet this guy?" Ava stated more than questioned.

"Why wouldn't I?" Izzy answered. "Somewhere public. Time we tell him what we need from him." Leaning towards her sister, Izzy's eyes caught her sister's. Speaking softly so not to be recorded, Izzy whispered, "Think about it...who better to get rid of Martin Collique than the agent that's after him?" Izzy's eyebrows raised and a sliver of smile washed onto her lips. "We could have him do what we need and we're in the clear."

Backing away from Izzy, Ava's eyes lit up. She allowed a wicked smile spread across her face, "I like the way you think. But still, you're not going alone. I'll be there."

"No," Izzy stated with flat assurance as they walked over to Deanna's door. "I can handle him and I don't want to spook him any more than I am planning right now."

"Oh, I'm sure you are," Ava stated. "But I don't trust anyone anymore. Most especially some super cop that got his ass put in this position."

On Deanna's front porch, Izzy returned Barry's text.

Tomorrow. Noon. West County Mall Food Court. Public enough for you?

"Perfect. I'm still going," Ava shrugged, undeterred. "Someone needs to watch your back."

Izzy stopped herself from knocking on Deanna's front door. "Ava," she sighed. "Stay out of it. I'll be fine. I don't need you there. It's the goddamn mall. What's he going to do?"

Ava didn't bother knocking on Deanna's front door, instead simply opening it and waving her sister in. Ava pulled out her phone as she crossed through Deanna's living room, heading for the kitchen.

"Coffee made?" she called to Deanna.

"Candy is making a fresh pot," Deanna answered.

Finding Candy in the kitchen pouring coffee into a filter, Ava stepped close, speaking softly into Candy's ear, "Call Curtis. I want him at the West County Mall Food Court tomorrow. Noon. Izzy is meeting the Fed who knocked her up. She thinks she's reeling him to our side, but I got a bad feeling. I think Curtis needs to be there."

Candy nodded, also speaking quietly. "He'll be there. We can't count on anybody else."

Ava glanced up as Clara, who had already been busy at one of the sewing machines, was explaining something to Izzy, speaking quietly in Izzy's ear. Ava held her gaze on her sister. She had protected Izzy all her life, allowing Izzy to believe her own bullshit about how tough she was. But more often than not, it was Ava who stepped in, sometimes overtly but usually behind the scenes and took care of any problems.

That had to stop. Izzy had to understand the ramifications of her actions. More to the point for Ava, Izzy's own stupid reactions that always made things worse. She was pregnant now and had killed a man point blank. They had survived a few horrors. But Izzy has a penchant for taking a bad situation and making things worse. Ava vowed right then that this child her sister was having wouldn't bear the brunt of their mother's idiotic choices. She may not have done all that well raising her sister, but she would make sure that baby wouldn't suffer the same fate.

THERE'S MAGIC IN THE MAYHEM

Vince heard the knock at his front door. He was downstairs in his home gym, trying to work out as best he could. Limping over to grab his phone off a bench, he punched his doorbell camera to see who it was. He had cameras hooked up at the doors the week after the beating. He saw Kevin standing at his front door, bouncing from foot to foot. Vince put the phone up to his mouth and said, "What do you want?"

Kevin looked down at the doorbell realizing it was like the one they had on their new house, which he used as an excuse to stiff the DoorDash guy by announcing through the intercom, "Just leave it at the door."

"Hey Coach, it's Kevin Brayton."

"I can see that. I'll be back at school next week, we can talk then."

"I don't want to talk there," Kevin answered.

Vince caught sight of his body in the full-length mirror on the wall of his basement weight room. The bruising on his body was fading. But he still had one very black eye, and his legs were still a mess. He'd gained some weight since he'd been laid up as well, which on any other guy his age would look normal, but Vince was too body conscious to consider it anything but another hurdle. And now working out, especially in his basement rather than the gym, was a chore. Even though he spent a small fortune on the equipment he had, Vince didn't much like working out down in the basement. He liked having people around when he lifted, people checking him out. Especially women, but the men too. A little envy made him feel good. Here he had no one but the broken-down guy in the mirror. Lifting his phone back towards his mouth, he sighed, "Hang on..."

****

Deanna was exhausted. She'd worked around the clock, trying to finish the massive load of copies that Martin dumped on them. There were five sewing machines buzzing in her living room. Deanna had taught Candy the detail work, Ava was working on buttons and Izzy, who had a pretty good eye for detail, was working on the hems and sleeves. Clara oversaw everything, while she and

Deanna were planning out what they were going to do with the leftover material.

At the other women's bequest, each day Deanna found a reason to phone Martin, to give an update on progress and wheedle out the date of his return. They hadn't discussed the details of how they were going to make Martin "disappear." Not knowing the date gave them enough of an excuse for the women to push off making a concrete plan about the how and where of Martin's demise. On the daily calls, Deanna would complain to Martin about the due dates for this recent load of gowns, then coo how much she missed him and couldn't wait to see him again.

But Martin had to know by now that the bugs he had placed in the walls of the homes were jammed. Deanna wondered if Martin suspected something. And when her calls went to voice mail the next two days, without a call returned, she was sure of it.

"How the hell could he, sugar? We don't even know what we're planning," Candy shrugged.

"Still... him not calling me back for two days is weird. Not to toot my own horn, but he was pursuing me. Now he won't call me back. And he's got to know he can't hear us anymore."

"We don't know what he knows. He could just be busy, Deanna. I mean, we don't really know what he does when he's not here. Or what other illegal things he's got his hands in," Candy huffed.

"I just got a bad feeling," Deanna concluded.

Candy touched her arm. "We're good, honey, we're good," she reassured Deanna. "And we will be ready."

Deanna forced a compliant smile, but she didn't believe that for a hot second.

****

"You want me to do what?!" Vince bellowed, half-laughing, half-agog, as he eyed Kevin who sat in a chair with his forearms on his thighs, leaning towards Vince as if they were in a dugout having a conversation about a game.

"Yeah, yeah, yeah, I know it sounds insane. But it would get my mom and her friends off your ass for what you did to my sister," Kevin insisted.

"Kill a guy?! Are you fucking serious?!"

Kevin sat up tall and shrugged. He was. "It'll keep them from killing you. Or sending you to prison," Kevin responded.

"Don't forget, I know what they did. I watched them steal something from a warehouse."

"Blah, blah, blah. Really, Coach...come on, man, you can't prove that. And what would you tell the police you were doing back there in the middle of the night? You willing to answer those kinds of questions? Even if it's true, you're going to look like you're coming up with bullshit and hope it sticks, and people are going to want to know why and then guess, you're the new pedo in cell block six. I just want to help, man. Seriously. You know Tracee isn't shy about telling people you had sex. She was fifteen, you're a grown-ass man, you're still up shit's creek without a paddle. And some guy's going to be up your shit's creek in the showers of that prison in Bonne Terre."

Vince huffed out a breath, knowing full well that Kevin was accurate. Vince's ass would be behind bars. And even if Tracee's protests gave him cover from prison, Vince would lose his job and never get hired in a high school again.

"Who is this guy?"

"He's the guy who tried to kill me out on the baseball field. Almost killed us both."

While a little retribution for that terrifying day that left one of his players injured, Vince would gladly beat someone with a metal pipe. But still, all of this didn't add up in his head. "If you know that for a fact, why haven't you gone to the police?"

"He's got something on my mother and the other women. He's running their lives. Moved us all into a nice house, but my mom like works for him now."

"Something illegal?"

"Yeah, making copies of really nice dresses and shit," Kevin nodded. "And we need him gone."

After taking another deep breath, Vince's eyes narrowed at Kevin. "I don't like being pushed into a corner."

"Should have thought of that before you fucked my sister."

"That's between me and Tracee. Not you."

"Well, you got caught. Now it's between a whole fucking bunch of people. Any one of them can take you down. Me included. And just so you're edified, people at school know you've fucked other girls at the high school. They talk, Coach. All the time. I can't believe no one's complained, but sooner or later the administration is going to hear it, if they haven't already, and they're just trying to make sure they have enough girls coming forward to bury you. You don't hide it well and the girls you fuck all yap like Pomeranians. It's kinda stupid on your part. But I'm offering you a chance to get some cover. At least long enough for you to knock the shit off your cleats before you step into another pile. If not, then what happens to you next happens, Coach. I can't and won't help you."

The men sat in silence for what seemed like a long time. Kevin then shrugged. Vince shrugged back. Kevin stood. He didn't know what else to say to Vince that could or would convince him. Walking to the front door, only the heaviness of Kevin's steps made a sound. He exited through the front door. As Vince slowly pulled himself up from the sofa, the front door swung open and Kevin stuck his head in.

"FYI, Fuck with me on the ballfield, or mess with me getting a scholarship, and I'll be the one fucking you up. Before turning you in for banging my sister. Know that."

As he slid out of the doorway, pulling it shut, Kevin heard Vince say, "Let me know who this guy is and when and how this is going to come down. But you better keep all these fucking women and whoever else off my ass."

Kevin turned back, pushing the door open so Vince could see him. Kevin nodded and then pulled the door shut behind him as he left. Walking down Vince's front walk, the lightness in Kevin's step returned. 'That was actually easier than I thought it'd be,' he mused as he bounced down the front walkway to his car. As he got in his car and started it, a realization crystallized for Kevin. Adulting is hard, especially if this is an indication. But Kevin also found this shit exhilarating. All this illegal stuff...if college doesn't work out, he has something to fall back on. Crime.

****

Izzy hadn't been in a mall since she was a teenager. Walking through the doors, she was hoping to feel seventeen again, but all she felt was annoyed. In the middle of a weekday, it was all grown women, only a few younger people, and not many of either. The food court where she was meeting Agent Wimmer was more crowded, with people opting for an inexpensive lunch. She wondered if Wimmer would even know what she looked like since she roofied him and he was in a stupor for most of the evening when they were in bed. She would have to find him in the crowd.

And it wasn't hard. He looked like a Federal Agent coming into the dining area of the food court. He wasn't in a suit jacket and tie, like more than a handful of other men ordering lunch, but he still looked like he worked for the government, with creased slacks and a pressed button-down shirt, and the haircut. Always the haircut. She let him glance around, walking through the tables. It was obvious to Izzy that he didn't recognize her. After he continued through the tables, she raised her hand. Barry turned towards her. He wasn't exactly scowling, but he didn't look happy to see her either as he strode towards her, his body almost rigid, trying to appear taller and more imposing than he was.

And neither saw Curtis lurking near the Panda Express, where he had a clear view of Izzy and now Agent Wimmer.

Curtis sized him up, trying to estimate what would happen in a physical fight. The man was tall, but Curtis had a few pounds on him. Aware that law enforcement of that caliber has been trained to fight, trained with a gun, and that Barry Wimmer probably had some military training behind him as well, Curtis figured he would have to hit him out of nowhere. It would have to be a surprise. And Curtis didn't want to tangle in the middle of a food court, with mall security and God knows how many people were carrying. But he was glad he was here, keeping an eye on Izzy. She was pregnant, which Curtis knew would be a surprise to the Federal Agent, who, according to Candy, only knew he was being blackmailed with a sex tape. The pregnancy might completely flip him out, and Curtis couldn't tell if Wimmer had a gun on his belt or strapped to his ankle.

Slipping into the chair across the table from Izzy, Wimmer placed his hands on the tabletop and locked his fingers. It kept him calmer, knowing that if this grew increasingly tense, he would be making fists, and his intention wasn't to tip off Izzy that he had the potential to be violent.

"Why are you blackmailing me?" Barry asked.

"I'm not the one blackmailing you. Actually, I need your help with the one who is."

"Did just asking ever cross your mind?"

"It's not something you're going to like doing."

"What is your name?"

"You know my name," Izzy snarled, sharply, having no time for this.

"I do. And I'm assuming you know my name, since you text me. And you know I'm married and have a family. And you know what I do for a living."

Izzy didn't answer, her expression showed she knew much more than she was saying.

"I don't remember having sex with you. And I'm still not sure how you roofied me."

"You opened that door," Izzy responded.

"That wasn't a crime. What you did was," Barry stated.

"Yeah, yeah, yeah..." Izzy waved her hand at him, not needing a lecture.

Barry went silent, his hands squeezing together tightly. Undoubtedly, he had. He allowed himself to be set up. And it pissed him off even more.

"So, what is it you need me to do?"

Izzy glanced to her right as a couple of women sat down at the table near them. Her eyes then returned to Barry's face, locking on his blue eyes. "We are trapped in something with a very bad guy. The bad guy who made me roofie you. Who will use the pictures of you and me to get you to back off whatever you're investigating here in St. Louis."

"Who is the 'we'?"

"Not important, but there is a 'we', and every one of them has the videos too," Izzy said, shaking her head. "The guy's the important thing."

"Give me his information."

Izzy smiled. "Slow your roll, Agent Wimmer," she replied. "How do I know you'll do what we need? That you won't go after us, or someone else will?"

Barry's head dropped until he was looking at Izzy almost through his eyelids. It was exactly what he expected. "I make this guy disappear, which I assume is what you want. Then what prevents you from still blackmailing me for something else?"

Izzy never considered that. She shrugged. "I guess not a thing, really. Other than I know you have a wife and kids. And I don't want to hurt them. Not my intention at all."

Barry shifted uncomfortably. "That sounds really nice but I need something more tangible than your word. Don't forget, I take out this guy...that just leaves you."

"No, it leaves a 'we'. Don't forget that."

The way Barry's eyes narrowed at her sent cold tingles though Izzy's body. She figured he used that stare to intimidate people, and it was quite effective. This guy could be scary. Just how scary she didn't know. But she knew this conversation was over. There was nothing more to say, at least face to face. This guy scared Izzy, and that took some doing. Ava was right, she shouldn't have met him. Not here, not anywhere. Izzy bolted upright, standing.

"I'll be in touch," she said.

But as she turns to bolt, Barry hand snapped around her wrist, holding her. Her head tilted towards his hand and then back up, looking into his eyes. She didn't see Curtis moving in her direction.

"Let me go, you son of a bitch," Izzy growled softly.

Quickly assessing his moves, Barry knew this wasn't the place or time. He released her, his hand returning to the table. It was then that Izzy saw Curtis moving up behind Barry. She fired Curtis a cool look that told him to stay back.

"I'm keeping the video," Izzy stated. "You have the power of the law behind you, I have this tape that says you won't come for us, once you eliminate this man from our lives. I won't use it. I won't have any reason to. But if you come after us ever...it's still there."

"You're leaving me little choice but to eliminate you as well," Barry uttered softly, directly at Izzy.

"And kill the mother of your unborn child?" Izzy answered, a mockingly breezy smile crossing her lips.

This startled Barry visibly. He coughed out a breath and sat back in his chair, his eyes never leaving her. He was ready for pretty much anything coming into this face-to-face, but not this. His head swam through pudding, his wife's fury and the FBI dismissal calcifying in his brain. He was fucked. This couldn't be. It just couldn't.

"You're lying," Barry said.

"I wish to fuck I was. It would make my life a lot easier. But know, this baby is mine. I won't bother you with it…it will never know you are the father. If I get what I'm asking for. And then you make sure if you ever see my name in a report, or other agents looking into anything I'm doing, that it goes away. I want to be untouchable."

"None of us are untouchable."

"You certainly aren't. But you have to make that happen for me. I don't want you or anyone like you, sniffing around me or anybody I'm working with. That happens, I got no problem publicizing the whole dirty truth."

Barry said nothing, his hands gripping each side of the small table.

"You know what I need. What I expect. I get it, you and I will never see each other," Izzy said as she backed a few steps away. "We'll talk soon. I'll give you a name and when he will be in St. Louis again. It'll be a short window of time. So be ready."

Then quickly Izzy spun around and darted through the tables, getting a head start away from Barry if he chose to chase her down here. Curtis instantly followed in her direction, tailing her. But Barry didn't move. He knew better than to go after her in such a public place. Even the parking lot here was easily viewed. He let her go, opting to sit in thick silence, the echoey food court seeming to engulf him in other people's conversation and strange noises. Curtis passed right next to him and kept after Izzy.

Outside, Izzy moved across the roadway into the parking lot, hiding behind a car as she watched the door from the mall. Barry didn't exit, but Curtis did, glancing side to side. She should be miffed that Curtis was there but she knew that was at Candy's insistence, and Izzy was relieved to see him, knowing if things had gone south, she would have been grateful for able-bodied back-up.

As Curtis jogged across the roadway into the parking lot, Izzy stepped out, giving him a slight wave. He quickly moved next to her.

"Where's your truck?" he asked.

Izzy pointed and Curtis took her arm, striding quickly in that direction. Curtis glanced back over his shoulder, making sure they weren't followed.

"What did he say?"

"He didn't. I said I'd be in contact. He threatened me, and I told him about the baby."

Curtis' eyes widened. "Shit...that was a big give. And it puts you in danger."

Shaking her head, Izzy responded, "No. He's a family guy. I think that might have kept him from following me out here and killing me. I am not sure he would take out a pregnant woman. Especially a woman pregnant with his kid."

"Maybe a pregnant woman who wasn't now using that pregnancy to blackmail him on top of the blackmail you're already using. Speaking as a man, a child with another woman will ruin your life more than a sex tape. And that gives him more reason to want you eliminated, Izzy."

"Just felt like the smart thing to do."

"Time will tell. I just hope you didn't kick the bull in the balls. Right now, get out of here, get home. Let's see what he does next and what he does when you contact him."

Izzy climbed in her truck and backed out of the spot, leaving Curtis there. Curtis watched her go, making sure no one was following. As he walked back to where he parked his car, he saw Barry exit the mall, talking on his phone. Barry walked right towards Curtis, still talking. Curtis froze for a moment, but continued to move to-wards Barry, holding his breath, ready for anything. But

Barry walked right past Curtis, still talking on the phone. As Barry did, Curtis looked into his eyes. There was fear in Barry's blank stare. And a dangerous man is even more unpredictable when they are forced to work out of fear.

Now Curtis was terrified as well.

****

Vince limped out onto the field. It was his first full day back and his legs were still bothering him. He couldn't wait to run again and work out with heavy weights. Vince had started to piddle around the school gym again but wasn't back at full strength. Every place those women hit him, his body still ached. Vince felt his body had suffered through the last few weeks of inactivity and healing. Getting fatter. More out of shape. And he hated it. Vince knew they would never ask him to join Mensa. His looks were the asset. And these women had almost destroyed them.

"Welcome back, Coach," Vince heard from behind him. Turning, Kevin was strolling out onto the field. "Seem to be healing up good from that car accident," Kevin added with a snarky grin. "Don't forget our deal."

Vince said nothing as Kevin walked past like he owned the world.

But Vince had been hustling long before Kevin was a snotnose in diapers. Allowing Kevin to believe he was running the show gave Vince cover and would come back to bite Kevin in the ass. Vince simply had to wait. But Vince despised anybody lording anything over him, which was only exacerbated by Kevin being a teenager. And Kevin still needed him. Colleges were circling and Vince could quietly ignore or squash their interest. Kevin's sister came onto him. What occurred was mutual. At least in Vince's assessment. Right or wrong, it was consensual. He'd paid for it. There was no way Vince was going to let Kevin Brayton continue any sort of reign of terror in his life. And he certainly would not kill for this kid. He knew he was more willing to kill Kevin. Vince stared at Kevin, throwing a ball back and forth with another player. Vince believed if it came to that, that's exactly what he would do.

****

As they worked, side-by-side at the sewing machines, each woman having to tell their 'worst lay' story, laughing as they shared their most embarrassing sex story, Izzy's phone buzzed. She reached into her jeans and pulled out her phone. But as she looked at the caller, Izzy's face tightened, her thumb moving over to open a text.

"What?" Ava asked.

Izzy flashed the phone in her direction. It read: 'I want to be involved in the baby's life. I'm telling my wife everything. We need to talk again.'

"That from the Fed?" Ava asked.

Izzy nodded.

"You believe him? I mean that he wants to be involved in the baby's life?"

"Fuck no," Izzy responded. "He's scared. I think he just wants to get me alone again. But even if he's serious, I don't want him to have anything to do with this baby."

Besides the fact that Izzy knew her baby might not be Barry Wimmer's, she didn't need nor want an FBI agent becoming part of her life, even if it was on the other side of a plexiglass partition.

"What are you going to tell him?" her sister quizzed.

Izzy quickly punched something into the phone. She showed her sister before she sent it: DON'T WANT YOU INVOLVED. GO BACK TO YOUR LIFE. I'LL GET HOLD OF YOU WHEN WE NEED YOU.

Ava nodded in agreement and Izzy sent it, neither of their expressions changing.

Ava knew, or, more aptly, she suspected, there was more to this than her sister was telling. She always knew, ever since they were children. Izzy couldn't lie when she was younger. She couldn't be bothered with it. No matter what, Izzy opted to tell the truth. She'd take her punishment and move on with her life. As she got to her teen years, when Ava was more a mother than a sister to her, Izzy found lying to Ava kept Ava from being disappointed in the wildness Izzy craved as if it were part of her DNA. Regardless, Ava had been too close to her sister. And Izzy wasn't practiced enough at lying that Ava wouldn't know. And she knew now. Something else was going on with Izzy and this baby.

****

Izzy's response infuriated Barry but he had to bury his feelings quickly because he was about to meet with Stacy Lipton and give her a weekly update on the case. If he didn't dislike her before, Barry had come to really abhor these weekly catch-ups with Stacy. She cared too much and he couldn't afford her digging too deep and finding something that would lead to someone who could blow up his world. Even if he didn't have so much to lose, Barry was exhausted by her being up his ass with daily emails and half-dozen texts, with more questions than answers, which Barry assumed was Stacy's attempt at making a name for herself within the police department, aiming for a promotion and a bump in pay. Any cop in that state of mind was always a nightmare for the Feds. And with some blackmailing bitch who could be his baby-mama telling Barry to back off until she needs him, both of these women were digging under his skin.

Seeing her coming down the hallway towards him, Barry opted for the alpha-douche move and spoke as he passed her, "Got nothing new for you, you got anything for me?"

Stacy stopped in her tracks and watched him keep walking. "Nothing?" she called after him, almost daring him not to stop.

Barry craned his head and fired her an icy look, his pace picking up slightly, the exit in sight.

"This is bullshit," Stacy snapped in his direction, even louder.

Barry wanted to stop, to turn on her and release all this vitriol he felt towards her, towards Izzy, towards himself. But he knew that would never get that genie back into the bottle. And he wasn't about to give her that, he might as well just give her his badge. She was already suspicious about his lack of progress. And he'd rather her think he was inept and uncaring than subversive and volatile.

"Why are you dragging your feet?" Stacy asked as they made it to the door.

"I'm not dragging my feet. I'm just not making much headway. And neither are you. Which makes me think your department doesn't really care about this case, or they don't care about you," Barry answered, pushing through the door.

Stacy followed. As she stepped out into the humid air, gray clouds hanging overhead, Barry searched for his car, not remembering where he parked in the crowded lot.

"I'm a one-man band," Barry said to Stacy who was standing behind him.

"You haven't bothered to utilize the department. Or me," Stacy countered.

Again, Barry's over-the-shoulder, frigid glare gave Stacy the answer, just not the one she wanted.

"Well, I made progress. I have a lead into the clothing counterfeiting ring that was or is running in South St. Louis, manufacturing fake sportswear," Stacy said.

Barry gulped but still said nothing as he beeped his car to find it. "What did you find?" he asked, walking in the sound's direction.

"Considering you got nothing to share," Stacy shrugged, "I have no obligation to share any information with you, Agent. I'm not an idiot. And I resent you continuing to treat me like one. Whatever your hiccup is in this investigation, and there is something, I'm moving forward. And in the end, if it embarrasses you, so be it. Don't say I did not warn you."

As she spun on her toes and disappeared back into the building, Barry continued to his Bureau-issued sedan. Climbing in, he took a hard breath and punched the dashboard over and over. Women were ruining his life. He would not live with the sword of Damocles hanging over his head, ready at any time to slice off his balls. Shaking his head to clear away his panic, one thought solidified for Barry. Getting rid of his biggest problem, the woman carrying the baby, would allow him to placate his lesser problem, the bitch trying to make a name in the police department, and get back to the job, as well as keep his family intact. It was that simple.

Something had to be done about Isabel Ruiz. And as he turned over the engine of the car, Barry vowed to himself, one way or another, and either one would be nasty and violent, he was going to take her out as quickly as he could.

****

Tracee came in as the other women were leaving. She said nothing to them. She hadn't said a word to any of them but her mother since they attacked Vince. Ava tried to greet her, but Tracee brushed past and headed to her room.

"She doesn't get it," Candy offered with a shrug.

"She doesn't have to. We do. And we took care of it, which is why she's pissed," Ava responded as they bounced down the steps to the walkway, and both cut across the grass to their houses.

Deanna had nothing ready for dinner. Ford was turning into an eating machine, and Kevin could devour what would be a meal for all of them. She would have to run out and pick up the go-to, chicken or burgers. Popeyes or Sonic. She'd been doing that a lot since this large load of work came in and Deanna required the other women to learn at least enough sewing skills to assist. Now none of them had the time to be parked in her kitchen, making meals for her family.

"I'm going to pick up some dinner," Deanna said through the shut door of Tracee's room. She heard nothing back.

Instead of the usual fast food, Deanna drove out of the neighborhood and over to the Schnucks Market on Loughborough. Whoever was frying the chicken over there knew what they were doing. While it was still seasoned lightly, it had flavor. And it was a lot cheaper than what she could get at Popeyes. Besides, she needed milk for the morning and a couple of boxes of frozen waffles. Better to make one stop than two.

Parking in the shade on the east side of the building, Deanna stepped from her car, locking it. She didn't see the other car swing behind her car until she felt hands on her shoulder. She couldn't get to the mace in her purse as she fought, trying to turn. But a hood covered her head, terrifying her. She fought harder, screaming as she felt her feet leaving the ground, realizing whoever had her had picked her up. She felt her body hit the back seat; strangely aware it was leather. She tried to push her purse off her shoulder but couldn't get untangled. The car door shut quickly, and Deanna could hear the car pull through the lot and onto a street, unsure if she should pull off the hood and see who was behind the wheel, or if that would hasten her death.

****

Izzy sat at the bar, nursing what she wanted to call her gin and tonic, sans gin. The thing she hated most about being pregnant was not drinking. Even more than not smoking. And it wasn't like she wasn't tempted. But Ava agreed to join her at the Tower Pub to keep her on the straight and narrow. But Ava was late, per usual. And the one thing about tonic, it always made Izzy have to pee.

Signaling Mikey, the bartender, not to take her tonic and to make sure he saved both seats at the bar for her and Ava, Izzy scooted off to the bathroom just as Ava walked in. As her eyes adjusted to the light, she saw her sister slip around the corner towards the bathroom. Smirking, Ava followed. Women's bathrooms were a great place to screw with people, and Ava felt like fucking with Izzy. As she slipped into the bathroom, the first thing Ava saw was the gun. In Barry's hand.

"Ava!" Izzy called, just as Barry swung around with his fist and caught Ava in the chin, sending her flopping back to the floor, unconscious. As Izzy gasped and opened her mouth to scream, Barry grabbed her roughly and shoved the barrel of the gun under her chin.

"Shut the fuck up or you and your sister will die in this bathroom," Barry demanded as he pushed her out the bathroom door.

Shoving her towards the back exit, the alarm went off as he pushed her through the door. His car was right there, the driver's door open. Izzy wanted to jam her hands on the side of car and fight, but she knew Barry would kill her there. If she wanted to keep her baby alive, she had to stay alive. 'Whatever it takes, whatever it takes,' echoed through her head as Barry manhandled her inside and slammed the door.

Jumping in behind her and shoving Izzy over to the passenger seat, Barry was out of the rear lot in less than ten seconds.

Izzy just kept repeating in her head, 'Whatever it takes...'

BADASSERY

Deanna wobbled as she was set on her feet and the black hood was pulled off her head. It took a moment for her eyes to adjust, making it hard for her to believe what she was looking at. Martin. Standing directly in front of her with the men who grabbed her.

"Thank you, gentlemen..." Martin said, dismissing them.

Deanna immediately recognized the airplane hangar where Santos was killed. She was standing in almost the same spot. She caught her breath, rage burning in her eyes. "What the hell is the matter with you?" Deanna nearly screamed as she glared at Martin, a slippery smile on his lips. "Why did you do that?!?!"

"You need to be more aware," he told her.

"Of what?!"

"We're in a dangerous business," Martin reminded her.

"We?" Deanna snapped back, "I'm sewing clothes. I'm not sure what you do exactly." Deanna took another deep breath, still shaking. "Don't ever do that to me again. God-damn it! You're insane! Take me back to my car."

"I needed to talk to you. Alone. Away from the others," Martin stated.

"Then ask me to dinner, ask me out for coffee, don't fucking kidnap me!" Deanna barked.

If she didn't think Martin was demented before, Deanna certainly had proof now. She could see on his face that having her kidnapped in a parking lot and brought to him was not something odd or over the top for him. He felt Deanna had overreacted. She realized that Martin only saw the world through his own lens, a prism of narcissism, for his self-involved amusement. It outweighed everything else about him. And that made him dangerous. He would always come first, his self-preservation was paramount, and he would step on the skulls of anyone who got between him and what he wanted.

"Why did you all disarm the recording devices in the houses?"

"Are you seriously asking me that, Martin?" Deanna couldn't help but let her incredulousness at his question cause her voice to squeak. "You were listening to us without our consent!"

"I own those houses!" Martin reminded Deanna, in no uncertain terms. "They were not a gift. You are employees and living in housing I provide. I have a right to know what goes on in them."

"No, you don't! Now take me back to my car," Deanna demanded. "We've been working our asses off trying to get those gowns you overloaded us with. And now I realize that was on purpose too. What was it, a punishment?"

"I needed the gowns. I have buyers," Martin countered as he reached over and took Deanna's hand.

Deanna pulled her hand back. The yin and yang of his behavior exhausted her as much as frightened her. She wasn't sure what he knew about their plans, but she was sure that his petulant selfishness was too much for her to even play pretend any longer. He'd crossed the line.

"When you spend most of your life trying to figure out where the next meal for your family is coming from, everything you say and do means exactly what you think it does. There's no time for nonsense," Deanna said. "This seesaw of crazy that we're going through is over. We'll get the gowns done, but you need to give us more time, and don't ever pull this shit again on me, or any of us! We love the houses, but we've all lived worse, so we can go back to that again. You need to stop!"

Martin blinked but said nothing, amazed by Deanna's rage. There was a piece of him which was excited by it. Her standing up to him, enticed him, making him want her more. Martin wanted to tell her that, to rush off some place where they could be alone. If he could, he would march her aboard his plane and have sex right now. But he couldn't, and he was sure if he tried she would completely lose her mind.

"Drop me back at my car!" Deanna demanded, wishing that plans to make Martin disappear had been finalized because if she could, she'd do it right here.

"I can't. My flight leaves in a very short time."

"So what was the point of kidnapping me? For what reason would you do something that insane?"

"To see you. All week you called me, wanting to see me."

"Not like this! Jesus, Mary and Joseph! Who does that to someone, much less someone they say they care about?"

Martin's brow knitted together as if the question perplexed. His awkward silence only made his weirdness more apparent to Deanna. She realized that he could kidnap her, terrify her, and still want to romance her. But in the next breath, he was all about the business, chastising her for cutting off his access to what was happening in the houses. For regular human beings, all those strands would be separate, often never crossing. But for Martin they were braided together into something only he recognized. He could threaten her but still want to make love to her. He could joke with her but terrorize her the next moment, as if juggling the moments was normal. It was all adrenaline and caffeine, and no days at the beach.

"Well, I have to be in New York tonight. And then I'm heading out of the country again," Martin announced.

Deanna's head was spinning. This was all crazy to her, but she also knew she needed to get a date upon his return, so the women could plan, so she quickly asked when he would be back.

"One month. That's four weeks. Exactly. Get the gowns in, and I'll have another four gowns, four copies each, for you. Can you have those gowns finished by then?" Martin wanted to know.

"I...I don't know. I can't answer that until I see the intricacy of each gown," she answered. "But I will see you in a month...you promise? Without a kidnapping or anything ridiculous!"

Martin looked at the time on his phone and then his eyes returned to Deanna, nodding before doing the same thing to his driver. He moved to Deanna, taking her by the shoulders, kissing her deeply, as if he was a character in some 40s movie. Again, the whiplash she felt made her woozy, not the kiss.

"We will talk," Martin said to her before moving to the waiting jet and climbing in. She watched as the engines revved and the jet rolled out onto the tarmac, preparing to take off. In a moment, the plane was in the air, leaving Deanna with the men who had taken her, wiping Martin's kiss from her lips.

She looked at the men, a scowl crossing her face. "Get me back to my car!" she snapped, before suddenly shaking her head. "No, forget it, I'll call an Uber."

And with that, she turned and moved away from the men, pulling out her phone.

Sitting in the back seat of the Uber, Deanna mulled the reality that those men grabbing her could have gone another way. If she had fought, if someone had seen her taken, if the police had been notified, all of this would be different, and maybe, just maybe, she could have had Martin hauled off to jail. And then with Curtis' connections, maybe, just maybe, had him murdered in jail. It made her smile slightly. 'A girl can dream,' she thought. But she wasn't living a dream. Yet this shit, these people, dead and alive, they were very, very real. Made her miss the days when the worst thing that happened at the dry cleaners was Leo glancing down her blouse.

****

"Where are we going?" Izzy asked, the barrel of Barry's gun pressing against her rib cage.

"Did you think you're going to ruin my life and I'd sit back and allow it to happen? I'm not letting you blackmail me into killing someone for you. And I'm not letting you fuck up my career or my family," Barry responded, his eyes locked on the road, a glimmer of amusement on his face.

Izzy thought about jumping. Letting him try to get off a shot as she opened the door and threw herself into the street. If it were just her, she would. But there was something inside of her now, and she feared she would traumatize the tiny fetus or she would lose it altogether. Izzy was only sure of one thing. There was no way she was letting Barry kill her. Or this child.

"God, you're a dumbshit," Izzy fired back. "My friends know you're the father of this baby. You kill me, kill your baby, you think your life is shit now? Think how the guys in prison will take to a Fed sitting on death row for murdering his unborn child. Jesus...what a stupid, man-thing, to believe that you can get rid of me and this baby and return to your life like nothing happened. Cheating on your wife is one thing, but murdering your kid?"

"Shut up," Barry snapped.

But Izzy felt like she was winning, and she wasn't about to hand him back the power. "And don't forget I got proof. I got the video of us and I told you, I'm not the only one who has it. I die, you're so fucked you won't know how to get un-fucked..."

Barry ground the barrel of the gun hard into Izzy's side, which was Barry's less-than-subtle way of saying "shut up" without repeating himself again. But Izzy still felt empowered, and when she mentioned the baby, Barry's reaction told her that her threat was working. He was a fucking federal agent, for God's sake, he knew that he wouldn't get away with this fumbling, simple plan. Barry was working out of emotion and she wasn't going down without a fight. Izzy sensed that Barry didn't have it in him to kill her. This was an attempt to scare her into silence. A display to prove to Izzy just how easy it was to get to her. And ultimately when she had her child, to the child as well. She had to play this right because she didn't want to scare him into pulling the trigger, but she wanted to mess with head, to infuriate him enough to make a mistake that played in her favor.

"Do yourself a big fucking favor, pull over and let me out," Izzy demanded. "That gun goes off, your sorry ass is gonna be strapped to a table as they poison you to death in front of your children. If they'll even claim you after killing a pregnant woman. I mean, your wife would go back to her maiden name, she'd change the kids' name too. Wimmer, that's your last name, right? They couldn't go anywhere without someone asking if they were related to the Fed who murdered the woman and her baby. That's the legacy you'd leave your family. How fucking stupid are you?"

Barry said nothing. As he pulled up behind a few cars at a stoplight, Izzy felt this was her chance. The longer she was in this car with this guy, the more unhinged he would become. The sweat on his brow told her that much. Izzy unsnapped her seat belt.

"What the fuck are you doing?" Barry screamed.

"Getting out," Izzy responded in a low, steady voice, her eyes lasered in on his.

"Don't even try!" he barked, the gun coming up in her face as he reached over and tried to strap her back in.

Izzy pushed the gun out of her face, aiming the barrel towards the windshield as she slapped his other hand away from the seatbelt, causing him to tussle with her. "What the fuck!?" she growled, "I'm getting out of this car!" And she wrenched the belt away from her body and popped the lock on the door.

When he grabbed for her, Izzy's free hand came around with a closed-fisted punch. She clocked him across the bridge of his nose, blood gushing, and got her boot up high enough to kick him in the side, her hand coming down on the gun, knocking it just as he fired. Into his own thigh. Barry screamed as blood ringed the bullet hole and expanded out, soaking through his slacks.

Recognizing she was now sitting next to an unpre-dictable wounded animal, Izzy threw the door open, falling out of the car into the street. Barry grabbed her leg, the gun coming up again, but Izzy kicked free and rolled under the door, kicking it shut, the door catching his hand. The gun clattered to the pavement as she scooched herself back, away from his car. As she did, a few men in surrounding vehicles stepped from their trucks and cars to help.

"He tried to kill me!" Izzy yelled at the men as she got to her feet. "I'm pregnant! He wants the baby dead!"

As four men moved towards Barry's car just as the light changed. Barry pulled his service weapon – not the gun he planned on shooting Izzy with which was untraceable and now lying in the street, something he bought from a guy he met at a gun show in St. Charles days prior. He wasn't about to let ballistics match a bullet to his service weapon. As the cars ahead pulled through the light, Barry gunned the car forward, nearly hitting two of the men, and powered through the intersection, whipping around another car and racing south on Grand, quickly turning on a smaller side street to disappear from sight.

Two men assisted Izzy onto the sidewalk as she watched Barry's car disappear. She thanked them, then moved over surreptitiously and picked the gun up from under a parked car, where it skittered after Barry dropped it. Smiling at the men, she said, "I think I might need this if he comes

back." She then crossed to the opposite sidewalk and started walking in the opposite direction so no one could follow her, leaving the men wondering if this was just a lover's
quarrel that got out of control.

She called Ava as she paid for a bottle of water from a
Quik Trip, the gun tucked behind her, under her shirt.
"Hey, it's me, I need a ride," she stated, still out of breath,
knowing this was not over with this enraged Fed with the
bullet in his leg. At least now Izzy grasped how far he was
willing to take things to protect himself.

"No, I'm not alright," answering the obvious question
Ava asked as Izzy moved to a corner of the store where she
was alone, adding, "The Fed tried to kill me..."

****

The word spread quickly among the women that Izzy
had been grabbed by Barry, his whereabouts unknown,
and that Deanna had been grabbed by Martin, who was on
a plane to New York. Curtis had had enough. Bad enough
he felt sidelined by Martin, having little to do now that the
women were copying gowns, and seemingly didn't need
his muscle or negotiating skills. Since bargaining for their
lives with Martin and helping set up the new arrangement, Curtis was left standing around, with "his thumb
up his ass," he would tell Candy. And knowing the women
were done with Martin's intrusion in their lives, Curtis

didn't want them dealing with Martin on their own. For many reasons, he wanted to get his hands on him. Curtis needed to be the one who put an end to the overlord he had shackled the women to earlier in the year. Curtis felt responsible for the mess they were locked in, and even more responsible for getting them out. He loved Candy and wanted her safe. And that meant ending this bullshit. Though he had no idea what Martin's network consisted of, if Martin was the top of that food chain or somewhere in the middle and there was a bigger, badder enemy still in the shadows. They would have to be ready for whatever fallout came with eliminating Martin, because that's just what he intended to do. With his daughter living with him and Candy, Curtis couldn't take the chance that Martin would do something to her. He intended to rein every-thing in, reboot and restart their lives post-Martin. Once he had his daughter and Candy safe, he could step up for all the women and help them rebuild their original business and help it grow so they never have to go back to their former lives.

But more than Martin, the trouble that Izzy had found herself in with Agent Wimmer, agitated Curtis and he was going to deal with that first. After the frantic call from Candy that Agent Wimmer went through with his threat and kidnapped Izzy, intending to kill her, Curtis' head throbbed with fury. Her escaping kept the storm off the coast, but Curtis knew the next time it blew in it would be catastrophic. Curtis had to find the Agent before Wimmer cornered Izzy again. Curtis had kept silent when he found out she had gotten pregnant doing bullshit dirty work for Martin. Martin got his way, giving him leverage to keep the Feds from getting close to him, but may just get her killed. None of this was really about the clothes they were copying, it was about clawing their way above the poverty line. Curtis believed that the profit from these gowns was probably nothing more than pocket money for Martin. Which meant this had to be about something else for him. Deanna? Maybe, but Curtis felt she was nothing more than a challenge, the woman in this port. He was sure Martin had other women in other cities. Curtis had one goal, free all of them from Martin's web. What came after would be their decision, not his.

Once she had Izzy home, Ava called Curtis to tell him Izzy was safe and relay the information that Izzy had told her. While he listened, Curtis loaded two guns. With Wimmer shot in the leg, Curtis knew the Agent would have to be in a hospital somewhere in this city. Probably for a few days. Digging in a box under the medicine cabinet, Curtis found a bag he was looking for. Inside were half a dozen syringes. He took two of them and put the rest back in the bag. Loading up both syringes with ammonia, Curtis knew if he could slip his way into Barry's room while he was either drugged up or asleep, which he knew would be difficult but not impossible, he could inject the poison right into his drip and walk out. It was faster and more efficient than putting a pillow over his face and wrestling to keep it there until Wimmer stopped fighting.

Curtis called all the hospitals within a twenty-five-mile radius of where Izzy said she jumped from Barry's car, until he found out that Barry arrived in the ER at the Barnes-Jewish in Creve Coeur. And was in surgery. The hospital was comparatively new, and the ER was small and not over-staffed. If it felt like the right fit for Barry to remain as under the radar as possible and still get the help he needed. Curtis was sure it was a better place to kill a man and go undetected.

To keep from complicating his plan with too many opinions, Curtis only shared it with Candy. He didn't want the other women's voices in his head. Especially as he was exterminating Barry. If he could get rid of Izzy's problem without any detours or other problems leaking in, this wouldn't become a 'thing', and he wanted this taken care of before word drifted back to Martin and he sent a well-armed posse after the Fed, leaving the women in the middle. Climbing into his Beemer, Curtis put one gun under the seat and the other in the glove box. As he did, the passenger door opened. Kevin looked in at him, cold seriousness on his face.

"I'm going with you," Kevin stated flatly, slipping into the seat without Curtis's permission.

"What the fuck, kid?" Curtis barked.

"I was in the house. Brought over the gown that Clara and my mom made for Candy to sell. I heard what you told her. This son-of-a-bitch tried to hurt Izzy? I'm going with you," Kevin continued.

"This is no time to deal with your fucking crush or whatever this is."

"I don't have a crush on Izzy. And I'm going."

Curtis opened his mouth to order Kevin out of the car but then it hit him. He didn't know why he hadn't sniffed it out before. "Holy shit, you're right, this isn't a crush. You're fucking her," Curtis said, turning to Kevin to watch his reaction.

And Kevin reacted exactly as Curtis expected. The kid had balls, but he wasn't very smart.

"Is this baby she's carrying yours?" Curtis quizzed.

Kevin's face scrunched up for a moment, then he relaxed. "I don't know. Could be. She says it's this FBI guy's but..."

Curtis nodded. "Kid, your dick is going to get you into a lot of trouble."

"You can't say nothing. Especially to my mom or any of the Sewing Circle," Kevin warned.

Laughing, Curtis shrugged. "Not my monkey, not my circus. But I am going to take care of this prick. Today."

"And I'm going too. Because if that baby is mine, he tried to kill it," Kevin added. "I don't give a shit who he is or what he does for a living."

"What about him trying to kill Izzy?"

"That pisses me off too. But Izzy knows how to take care of herself. I don't think this guy knows who he's messing with," Kevin stated.

"Let him die not knowing," Curtis responded, pulling away from the houses.

PROBLEM SOLVER

Curtis stopped at the Dollar Store. "Fifty balloons. Make sure some say 'Get Well'," he ordered Kevin, sending him inside with a wad of cash. Kevin walked inside the store in the strip mall not far off of Jefferson and I-44. Fifteen minutes later, Kevin wrestled out two handfuls of balloons, which took ten minutes to stuff into the backseat and trunk of Curtis's Beemer. As they continued to the hospital, Curtis explained to Kevin that once inside, to keep the balloons in front of him, obscuring his face. He handed Kevin a pair of opaque plastic gloves and told him to put them on before he grabbed the balloon strings.

"What will I tell the lady at the counter?" Kevin asked.

"That you're allergic to mylar. No fingerprints," Curtis answered.

Once inside the hospital, balloons bouncing in the air, Curtis stayed behind the balloons as they traipsed down a hallway, surveying the locations of the security cameras, and checking for an unlocked office door e as Kevin continued to quiz him about the plan.

Finding an unlocked door, Curtis slipped in, telling Kevin to stand outside. He was sick of the kid yammering. Using an internal hospital computer, Curtis searched for which room Barry Wimmer occupied post-surgery on his leg.

Stepping back into the hallway, Curtis uttered, "They have him in a regular room, not ICU. That's good for us."

"How is that good?" Kevin quizzed.

"Too many nurses and doctors in ICU, and you have to pass the nurse's station to get to a room. Right now, this hospital is short-staffed, which helps us," Curtis added. "Unless the Feds have him under guard, which is unlikely. He may not have even told them yet and if he did, I am sure he didn't tell them what actually happened."

"If he told the truth, he'd be off to prison," Kevin shot back.

"He should be in prison," Curtis responded, but then, thinking, shrugged. "But so should we."

"You need to tell me how we are going to do this?" Kevin questioned as they moved to the stairwell with the cloud of balloons that made everyone they passed smile, no one bothering to look at the men holding onto them.

But Curtis didn't answer as they waited for the elevator to open. Once it did and they were the only two people to step in, the doors closing, Kevin's head smashed against the wall, his body pinned there by Curtis who was just as large as Kevin, and right now twice as pissed off. "We aren't doing this. I am," Curtis growled in a low voice, right into Kevin's face. "You are going to do what I tell you, when I tell you. Nothing more. But the actual deed, you are not involved. I'm not having you live with this for the rest of your life. Let me. You are not a killer. Don't ever turn into one."

Curtis let go of Kevin, who was stunned and humiliated by Curtis's sudden physicality. Neither said anything as they arrived on the ninth floor and quickly moved off in the direction of the room, Kevin asking no questions. As they passed Wimmer's room, Curtis gave Kevin a nod, letting him know it was the room. But they said nothing. They were wrong about one thing. There was a cop at the door. And worse, Stacy Lipton was inside the room, talking to Wimmer.

Slipping down the hallway, Curtis slid into an empty hospital room, followed by Kevin.

"Fuck," Curtis uttered. "He's already reported the shooting. They have to do an investigation, even if he told them it was accidentally self-inflicted."

"So, what do we do?"

Curtis thought only a second before he said, "Give me your clothes."

"What?"

"Your clothes, take them off," Curtis ordered, snapping his fingers at Kevin.

Surprised but compliant, Kevin obliged, shimmying out of his jeans and yanking his t-shirt over his head, Curtis ripped the sheet off the hospital bed and shredded it into a few swaths.

"Underdrawers too," Curtis said.

With a roll of his eyes, Kevin pulled off his underwear. Curtis glanced at Kevin's muscled, tight torso, and immediately missed his own youth as he took Kevin's underwear and stuffed them in the pocket of Kevin's jeans before tying the jeans around Kevin's neck like a cape. "You're not shy about your body, are you?" Curtis mused aloud, more as a statement than a question.

"Dude, seriously? Nobody likes me for my brains," Kevin answered.

"Apparently not," Curtis responded before taking a strip of sheet and wrapping one around Kevin's head like a bandana, hiding his hair. He then tied Kevin's t-shirt around his face like a bandit mask.

"As I am carrying the balloons down the hallway, I need you to dash out there and run, yell, laugh, wag your dick at people, I need you to draw as much attention to yourself as possible. Run past Wimmer's room. I'm hoping the cop comes after you," Curtis told him, pointing in the direction he needed Kevin to run. "I will slide into Wimmer's room and inject this shit into his IV. If not..." Curtis continued, pulling out his gun with a silencer on the end from under his shirt.

"Haul your ass into the stairwell at the end of the hallway, take it down to the parking garage. Remember where I parked my car?"

Kevin nodded as Curtis handed him the keys. "Get in and lie down in the backseat, get dressed and wait."

"This isn't much of a plan," Kevin offered.

"I wasn't planning on you joining me. Or for the cops to be notified already. But you're here, so make yourself useful."

"What if this rag falls off my face?" Kevin asked.

Curtis gave Kevin's body the once over. "With that body and your Johnson flopping around, nobody's going to be looking at your face, but the cameras will. So, make sure it doesn't. I don't need anyone to see your face. Run fast, make a scene, and then get the fuck to the stairwell."

Again, Kevin nodded.

"Ready?"

With a shrug, Kevin moved to the door of the room and peeked out.

"Go!" Curtis barked.

Kevin dashed out of the room into the hallway. His first instinct was to cover his penis with his hands but then he realized that was a big sell for this job. Instead of running, he slowed to a saunter, then a strut, his body flexing with each step, making sure his penis slapped against his thighs as he did. Kevin laughed out loud and babbled as he made his way down the hallway. Two women were the first to see him, one laughing, the other screaming as she giggled. The further down the hallway Kevin pranced, the more people caught sight of the naked man, causing doctors and nurses to rush from the rooms, mobile patients joining them, all enjoying the show.

Curtis waited until Kevin was almost to room 419 before yanking the balloons out in front of him and starting down the hallway in that direction. No one gave a glance at the fifty balloons held by some man who was clothed while Kevin's naked ass was bouncing down the hallway in front of him.

The police officer outside Agent Wimmer's room stood back and let the babbling, screaming, naked man bounce past. That wasn't his job. Stacy quit talking mid-sentence as she and Barry heard the commotion in the hallway. Stacy stepped out into the hallway, just as Kevin strutted past, her eyes landing on the tattoo of a baseball on his hip. Kevin stopped and swiveled his hips, his penis snapping back and forth from thigh to thigh with a thwacking sound right in front of her and the uniformed cop. He then took off running, as Stacy and the police officer shared a look.

"Fuck..." Stacy mumbled as she and the uniformed cop went after Kevin, chasing him down the hallway and into the stairwell.

As they did, Curtis slipped into Barry's room right behind her, the balloons in front of his face. Barry was on the bed, his bandaged leg elevated. He was trying to see what was going on, which made Curtis's hope of injecting poison into Barry's IV all but shot to hell.

"Who are those for?" Barry asked, referring to the balloons, unable to see Curtis's face. "They can't be for me."

Curtis reached behind him, his hand gripping the handle of the gun. "They aren't..." he uttered, adding, "...this is."

In a sweeping motion, the barrel of the gun swung directly at Barry. Being versed in weaponry, Barry knew automatically what was happening. He tried to flip his body off the mattress and onto the floor on the other side of the bed. Two bullets caught him in the back as he went off the bed. His scream of fear instantly changed to bellows of pain.

Being an athlete, there was no way some older county police officer, who devoured too many fast-food meals and spent too many nights at the bar, was going to catch Kevin. Stacy would have a chance, but when Kevin barreled through the stairwell doors, she stopped, letting the uniformed cop continue chasing. Kevin leapt down four steps at a time. The cop had a gun, but there was nothing he could shoot at if he couldn't get close enough. Kevin laughed at him as he descended the stairs, getting further and further away from the cop who finally gave up the chase.

Curtis let go of the balloons and paced over calmly, shooting Barry twice more as Barry tried to crawl to the window. As his bloodied body slumped to the floor in a heap, Curtis turned and walked back through the room, grabbing the balloons. Just as he got to the door, Stacy stepped back in. It took her a second to realize Barry wasn't in his bed as she was being rushed by someone behind a cloud of balloons. She tried to knock them out of her face until she caught sight of Barry's bloodied, lifeless body on the floor between the bed and the windows. Reaching for her gun, Curtis pulled his up. Instead of pointing the barrel at Stacy, he aimed directly at the oxygen tank near the bed. Firing, Curtis clipped off the top of the tank. The thin, green tank flew around the room, like a swatted wasp, causing Stacy to dive to the floor. But as Curtis tried to rush through the balloons to get to the door, the tank hit him in the face, knocking him back with such force, he tumbled back against the room's window. The window shattered behind, causing him to lose his balance. Blood splattered across the sharded glass as Curtis' body sailed out the ninth-floor window, a few of the balloon strings still in his hand.

Kevin was tugging on his pants in the parking garage as Curtis' body hit the ground just outside the structure. For a moment, he wasn't sure what had happened. As he wrestled his t-shirt over his torso, he walked in that direction as people descended towards the scene from every direction. Seeing Curtis's body contorted and broken, people screaming, medical people rushing outside to the scene, Kevin backed away. Blood filling his ears, his head pounding, Kevin couldn't make out anything anyone was saying. He found his shoes and put them on. Then Kevin used the piece of cloth that he had tied around his face to wipe down Curtis's car for fingerprints.

As he walked out onto Olive Boulevard, Kevin noticed the balloons overhead, buffeted by the breeze, sailing higher into the blue, as if they were taking Curtis' soul to heaven but couldn't find it. Kevin knew there was such a thing as a metaphor and guessed this must be one. But he wasn't entirely sure what a metaphor was, as he pulled out his cellphone and dialed.

"Hey, I know this is weird me calling you, but I need a ride..."

****

"What are you doing over here?" Cassie asked as Kevin got in her car in the Walgreens lot across the street from the hospital.

"A bunch of shit just came down," Kevin answered, his voice shaky as he pointed ahead. Glancing across Olive Boulevard at the scene of Curtis' death, Kevin yelped, "Drive, drive..."

Cassie drove on, heading down Olive back towards Highway 270. She could barely pay attention to the traffic, her eyes darting back to Kevin over and over as he stared forward blankly.

"You gonna tell me what happened?" she asked.

"Curtis...Candy's boyfriend, he's dead."

Cassie almost stopped in the middle of the lane. She blinked, hoping Kevin would say more than that, but he was trapped in his own thoughts. "You were with him? Where?"

"Oh fuck…" Kevin said. "It's crazy. I was with him. He went to take out that Fed who knocked up your aunt."

"What?!"

Kevin finally turned to look at Cassie as they moved over into the right lane to turn down the ramp onto 270. "You didn't know who knocked her up?"

"No…" Cassie said between harsh breaths. "She wouldn't talk about who the father was."

"Well, supposedly it was this G-man. Martin Collique, the guy who our moms are working for, he asked her to get some dirt on this Fed. And, and…well she banged him and got herself pregnant. They were going to use it against him, to make sure, I don't know, that they and Martin never got in trouble. This guy's married and got a family, so he was scared, and he kidnapped Izzy and wanted to kill her."

"What?!" Cassie barked.

"Relax, she got away. But G-man shot himself in the leg. Curtis found out what hospital he was in and came here to take him out."

"Take him out?! Jesus, Kevin, you say that as if you're talking about a movie or something. You mean kill him. For real."

"Yeah. Kill him."

"Well, what the fuck are you doing here?" she asked.

"I don't know...I was mad. Izzy's my friend..." he admitted, causing Cassie to turn and give him a hard look as she drove. "I went with Curtis to run diversion, so he could get into the guy's hospital room. And next thing I know, Curtis' body lands on the concrete outside the parking structure. It was insane! Dead, Cassie, he is fucking dead!"

Saying nothing more, Cassie sped up as she got into the middle lane of the highway. "Does Candy know?"

Kevin's head shook back and forth. "I dunno, can't think how she would yet," he said, and then added, "They're all fucking crazy. All of 'em. My mom, your mom, they're working for some psycho. Fuck...FUCK!"

"What should we do?" Cassie asked, having never seen Kevin this distraught.

Again, his head shook. "Tell them. And then somebody's gotta deal with Martin Collique. And now it might be me. He needs to be taken out before this all blows up even more, or we're all going to die. But all this shit...it leads back to him."

Neither of them spoke the rest of the way back to the cul-de-sac.

****

Nervous and hiding his shaky emotions, Kevin stepped out of Cassie's Nissan, which her mother had bought her when they moved into the new house. Cassie joined him, taking his hand. They had to get all the women together, make sure they had hold of Candy before they passed along the news of Curtis' death. They separated, Cassie going into her home, and Kevin going into his. They would talk to their moms, let Ava and Deanna then tell Candy. As he walked in, Kevin flipped on the flat screen to the local news, which was covering what happened at the hospital earlier. It was then that he knew Curtis completed what he came to do before he died. Kevin had little feeling about the dead Federal Agent, simply mumbling the word, "Good," as he watched the story, the hospital he left less than an hour ago in the background of the shot.

"Mom!" Kevin bellowed, his voice echoing through the house. He heard his mother's footsteps as she came into the den.

"What are you screaming about?" she asked as she came into the room.

Kevin went directly to her and wrapped his arms around his mother, burying his face in her shoulder.

"What's going on?" she whispered to him, her body tense with fear.

Kevin kept hold of his mother as he spoke. "Curtis is dead."

Stepping back to look right at her son, Deanna sucked in a gasping breath. She held onto Kevin's arm to keep from stumbling back.

"I went with him to the hospital. He went there to kill that Fed."

"You went with him?!" Deanna gasped.

"Don't wig out. I went with him. I was outside, and I don't know what happened, but he fell out the window. The Fed-guy is dead too."

"No...no," uttered Deanna, her first thought being Candy.

"It's all over the news," Kevin said.

"What were you doing with him?" Deanna asked her son.

"I went along to help. I...I um, I ran naked down the hallway to distract everyone while he went into the hospital room."

Deanna took another step back. "You what?"

"Don't worry, I had my face covered. I was the distraction so Curtis could get into the G-man's hospital room. He was going to put some chemicals in the guy's IV. I don't know what happened. I was too busy running from the cops. I got away and next thing I know, Curtis is laying dead in the middle of the sidewalk."

The information making her swoon, Deanna waved her son back. "I have to gather the girls. Tell Candy. You stay here. Don't leave the house for any reason. There's a whole lot that's going to be messed up now. And I'm afraid that shit is going to come raining down."

Kevin only nodded.

"Keep your sister and your brother here. I don't want them leaving either."

Deanna moved for the back door but stopped herself and rushed back to Kevin, hugging him tightly, before she exited. 'The sins of the parents,' she thought to herself as she closed the back door behind her.

****

Deanna found Ava and Izzy together, tears in their eyes, Cassie relaying what Kevin had told her, the local news on their big screen as well. The fact that a Federal Agent was killed at Barnes-Jewish West and the murderer was dead from a fall was huge news in St. Louis and would easily make the national desk as well. All three women silently knew the FBI would flood into town. There was no doubt they would investigate the death in association with the case Agent Wimmer was working. If the authorities connected Curtis to them, all hell was about to break loose. And worse, their friend was home next door, oblivious that the man she loved was dead, and would be blamed for the death of a Federal Agent.

"Cassie, stay close to home. I told my kids to do the same," Deanna warned Cassie.

"Once Martin hears about this, his ass is going to be back in St. Louis," Ava said once Cassie was out of the room, knowing Martin would have to come to St. Louis to clean up this mess.

"Probably to kill all of us," Izzy added.

"It could send him into hiding. Leave us to fend for ourselves, which is what we need to be prepared for," Deanna countered, more dubious that Martin would put himself in the middle of this public shit show. "He's very good at taking care of himself first."

"We'll deal with it. Right now, we have to tell Candy about Curtis..." Izzy said, standing, feeling a sense of responsibility since Curtis went there to deal with Wimmer because of what he did to her. "This is going to fucking kill her."

Ava stood next to her sister and took Izzy's hand supportively. "Nothing is going to be easy from here on out. We have to be ready for anything. But if Collique shows up in town, this is all the more reason to take him out. Like now, today, as soon as he is here."

"Yeah," Deanna responded, taking Ava's other hand. "Before he does it to us."

REALITY FAILS

Ava knocked on Candy's door. Deanna stood with Izzy right behind her. When Candy opened the door, her smile wide as she peered at her friends with confusion. "Why didn't you all come in the back door? If Curtis and I are having sex, the door would be locked," Candy chuckled.

But Candy instantly saw the looks of horror on their faces. "What happened?" she quizzed quickly, bracing herself, though she didn't know for what or why. "You girls are scaring me," Candy admitted with a nervous chuckle that didn't break the tension.

Izzy reached out and grabbed Candy's hand as they all moved into Candy's home. Izzy took Candy over to her sofa, sitting next to her, her hand never letting go. Ava and Deanna traded glances, silently asking who would drop the bomb.

"Should Curtis be here for this?" Candy asked, hoping to gauge the problem they were here to share.

"That's what we want to talk to you about," Deanna stated, unable to look Candy in the eyes. "It's Curtis. He...he was...Jesus, there's no easy way to say this. He was killed."

Deanna's words simmered but didn't seem to come to a boil for Candy. The others waited for Candy to grasp the concreteness of what Deanna had just said. They watched her. Izzy had never noticed before that Candy almost always had a smile on her face. Even at the worst of times. But now, her smile wavered, starting at the edges.

"What? What happened...?" Candy asked, her lower lip quivering.

"He went to the hospital. To deal with the FBI agent. Something bad happened. He fell out the window. He's gone," Deanna said slowly, hoping this would get through to Candy.

Tears squeezed from Candy's eyes let the women know it did. Ava quickly sat on the other side of her and she and Izzy held Candy tightly. Deanna moved over and knelt in front of Candy, rubbing her legs. "I'm sorry, honey. We all are. You loved him," Deanna cooed sympathetically. "We all did. We are here for you. We are gonna take care of you."

Ava and Izzy tightened their grip on their friend as Candy's tears fell. Deanna could see Candy's sorrow hardening into rage. "We have to kill him," Candy said in a soft voice.

"What, honey?" Deanna asked.

"We have to kill him," Candy repeated, equally softly.

"Who?" quizzed Izzy.

Candy shook off Ava and Izzy, standing. Deanna fell back to the floor, looking up.

"Martin!" Candy screamed. "Martin! We have to kill him! I want him gone! This is his fault! All of the horrible things that happened lead back to that man! Goddamn it, we have to get him out of our lives before he kills all of us!"

And then the flood of heaving tears took over and Candy fell to her knees. Ava pushed herself up off the sofa quickly and grabbed Candy, engulfing her in an embrace. Izzy climbed to her feet and wrapped her arms around both of them as far as they would reach. Candy crumpled into them, sobbing. Deanna sat on the floor, listening to the painful sound of Candy's sorrow. She knew her friend was right. While their lives on the surface had changed for the better, every ounce of pain, every horrible thing they had done over the last year, led back to Martin Collique.

And in that second, Deanna accepted that Martin would be hers to deal with. She was closest to him. She didn't know what they were doing with each other, but she'd slept with him, she was important to him for reasons that Deanna still couldn't completely grasp. Deanna couldn't tell her friends what she had decided. This would be a solo plan. If she could take him out without anyone else involved, with as little notification or fanfare as possible. Something sudden. And deadly. That would unburden all of them and give Deanna a necessary sense of finality. As Deanna knelt on the floor, she put her arms around Candy from behind as Candy sobbed against Ava's chest.

As she soaked up Candy's pain, it solidified in Deanna what she knew she had to do. Martin would be back, and she would kill the son-of-a-bitch.

****

Hearing his mother on the phone, leaving a message for Martin Collique, demanding that he come to St. Louis because everything was about to blow up, the overly-lubricated gears in Kevin's mind twisted and turned. If she could get him here, and Kevin could find when, he could make sure that he and Vince were ready to "disappear Collique." Once that was over, and his mother and her friends were rid of whatever this guy was lording over them, Kevin assumed that life would be better, though he wasn't sure exactly how. He had to accept that their source of newfound wealth would vanish. And no one loved the pleasures of money more than Kevin. But Kevin also believed he would land on his feet. His mother did. 'Well, at least the ditches she ran into didn't kill her,' he mused. And as much as Kevin had fought with his mother, as much as he often resented most everything she did and what he felt she didn't do, deep down he was proud of her, and Kevin would always have his mother's back. He saw what she had sacrificed for the family, especially after their father walked out on them.

"What are you doing?" Tracee asked her older brother as she caught him listening to their mother's conversation demanding Martin come back to St. Louis now. Kevin signaled Tracee to stay silent as Deanna finished leaving a message for Martin. Leading his sister away from their mother's closed door.

"Curtis is dead," he told his shocked sister. "Shit's going to lead back to Mom."

"It's this dress business, isn't it?" Tracee responded.

Kevin answered with a nod.

"What's she going to do?" Tracee asked her brother, concern leaking into her voice.

Shaking his head, Kevin leaned towards his sister. "It's what I'm going to do. And that fucker who messed with you is going to help me."

"What? Who?" Tracee quizzed, unsure.

"My fucking baseball coach, your...whatever."

"Vince? How...how is he involved in this at all? I don't want him involved."

"You don't want him involved?" Kevin asked. "Little late for that. He's up to his ass in all of this now too. He owes us."

"Us?" Tracee fired back. "He doesn't owe you anything! He's helped you, he's talking to colleges for you. Despite all your efforts to cheat your way through high school and screw that up. How is he even any part of this mess?"

"I asked him."

"You're gross. And stupid. And now he knows even more about us than he should. God, you're so dumb, Kevin. You don't think past the end of your dick."

"What?! We can't live like this. Mom can't. Why do you care about the guy that raped you?"

"Shut up! You just sound more stupid every time you open your mouth. I am the one who initiated what happened between Vince and me. God, stay out of my life. I don't need you trying to right some perceived wrong. This will backfire on you. And him. Neither of you is smart enough to pull off something like this."

"You don't think I'm smart enough to take out the prick who is hurting Mom?" Kevin snapped.

"I assure you, you are not! You're just a dumb high school kid who has been riding on his looks and the fact that he can swing a baseball bat. Just because girls want to fuck you doesn't mean you're some badass, Kevin. It means you're an easy lay. That's all! Please. Stay out of it. And keep Vince out of it."

Tracee stalked away from him just as Deanna walked up the stairs to the second floor, the weight of what was happening locked in her eyes.

"You okay, Mom?" Kevin asked.

Deanna gave her son a smile, her hand going to his chin. "I will be, honey. Today has been a lot. Candy's going to need us now."

"What's going to happen to Curtis' daughter?" Tracee asked.

"I would assume her mother will take her," answered Deanna. "I don't want either of you getting any more involved with any of this. Understand? Let me take care of it," Deanna added, not waiting for a response from either of them as she walked past them and into her bedroom, shutting the door.

Kevin turned and stared at her closed bedroom door. He was the man of the house, and he was not letting his mother put herself in any more danger than she already had. Fuck it, he would take care of it. And positive he had Vince by the short hairs, Kevin was more than willing to let his coach go down for whatever happened to Martin. If Vince went down, it was only karma for his sins, and would prevent Vince from turning on him and talking shit about him to potential recruiters.

Coming out of her bedroom, Deanna eyed her two kids who were still standing in the hallway. Walking past, Deanna touched Tracee warmly, before heading downstairs. Tracee and Kevin could hear the front door open as Deanna yelled up, "I'll be back. Could one of you find something for Ford to eat for dinner? And for God's sake, keep him away from the TV."

Once Deanna was gone, Kevin locked eyes with his sister before bouncing down the stairs and also leaving through the front door without a word. Alone in the house, Tracee was overcome with a feeling that either her mother or brother would be dead soon. It chilled her. Her mother would try too hard, and her brother just wasn't smart enough. But Tracee knew she could. She was smart enough. And she wasn't in too deep. She could handle this situation with a subtlety that neither of them could manage. If anyone could pull this family out of the fire, it was her. It had to be.

Tracee would need details, but before either her mother or her brother did something that wrecked this family forever, she assured herself she could devise a plan that would save them both from themselves. And end whatever this swirling, gray mess was that smothered this entire end of this block. She had never contemplated taking someone's life before, and Tracee knew she would have to frame this some other way for her to actually do it. Not that she believed Martin Collique didn't deserve it. He did. And now she felt it was him or them. Tracee understood herself well enough to accept that she would pick her family over a guy who attempted to have her brother killed and was blackmailing her mother and the other women on the block to keep them doing his bidding.

Taking a knife from a drawer, she cut the sandwich she was making in half as she called, "Ford! Dinner!" her hand still around the hilt of the knife.

As he came running into the kitchen, she piled French fries onto his plate from the air fryer, and scooped sliced peaches out of a can, spraying some whipped cream on top.

As he bit into the sandwich, Ford scrunched up his face. "You could have warmed up the sandwich," he complained.

"You want it hot, you know how to work the microwave. I'm going to head over to the library for a little bit. Tell mom when she gets back. She's next door. And no TV."

"Video games?" Ford asked.

"Sure…" Tracee said as she quickly walked across the living room to the front door. Once she was gone, he grabbed up the plate and his glass and dashed up the stairs to his room. At the top of the stairs, Ford heard footsteps. Heavy. Like Kevin's. Turning at the top of the stairs and looking down, Ford couldn't see anyone.

"Kevin?" Ford called.

No one answered.

"Tracee?" he called again, but no one called back.

Quietly, Ford set his plate and glass down at the top of the stairs and padded down the stairs in his socks. He dashed back into the kitchen and grabbed the knife that Tracee put in the sink. As he tip-toed towards the front room, staying close to the wall, a man walked right by him, pacing into the kitchen quickly. The man spun around, searching the room for the voice. He didn't see Ford until Ford plunged the knife into the man's leg and ran.

The man barked out in pain, grabbing for Ford. Ford's hand grabbed the ornate, glass bowl his mother had recently bought from the coffee table and smacked the man in the hand with it, causing him to pull back as Ford bolted for the front door. Swinging it open, he took one fleeting step before he ran face-first into another man who stood at the door.

He shoved Ford back in and shut the door.

BEFORE THE FALL

Ford backed up as the man came at him. He knew all the safe places in the house, places these men would never find him. He'd scoped them out the day after they moved in. Just in case. And now, he just had to get to one.

Once he backed up far enough into the living room, he twisted around and bolted for the stairs. Caught flat-foot-ed, the man gave chase. But Ford had him by five steps and knew where he was going. He dashed down the hallway to his mom's room, dove under the bed and slid to the other side between the dresser and a chair, where he couldn't be seen. His hand reached up and grabbed a pair of scissors off Deanna's nightstand as he crouched down and waited.

Ford heard the commotion downstairs, recognizing his mother's voice. She'd come home. Hopefully, to save him. Ford could hear the walking back down the stairs and wriggled out from where he was hiding, scissors still in hand, and scampered to the top of the stairwell.

His mother was in an argument with the men. He quickly scampered down the stairs, scissors ready. "I don't give a good goddamn if Mr. Collique sent you! You do NOT enter my home without permission! Who the hell do you think you are?" Deanna screamed at the men. "Get out! Get out!!!"

Ford saw his mother dialing her cell phone quickly as he came into the living room and moved to her, the scissors still in his hand.

"Your goddamn kid stabbed me!" barked the man who Ford pierced with the scissors.

"What the hell are you doing, sending men into my house and terrorizing my family!?!" Deanna yelled into the phone, "First you kidnap me so we can meet and now this?! Seriously, what in the hell is the matter with you?!"

"And I'll stab you again! You heard my mom, get out!" Ford demanded, waving the scissors at the men.

"I didn't ask for people to come into my damn house! I asked for you to get here! We have a problem. A big problem. I don't need men to protect me! I need you here to deal with this mess. A mess that will lead back to us! Damn it, Martin, get back to St. Louis! And have the money you owe us for the gowns!" Deanna continued before she hung up, turning back to the two men and screaming. "I said get out of my house!"

The men backed up towards the door, blood dripping from one man's leg wound, and they disappeared out the door. Deanna rushed to the door, slamming it and locking it quickly.

"You all right?" she breathlessly asked her youngest son. Ford nodded.

Deanna reached down and took the scissors from him. "You're brave," she said, pulling her son to her, holding him tightly. "God, if anything ever happened to you..."

Ford wrapped his arms around his mother. He believed nothing would happen to him as long as he had his mom. And he wasn't about to let anything happen to her.

****

Candy stumbled through her home aimlessly. The reality of Curtis being gone, of the police inevitably showing up and asking questions, of her life being turned upside down again by the death of the man she loved, ached inside of her. She'd found the number for Erika's mother and called her, relaying the news. Curtis's ex-wife told Candy she would pick up Erika from school and break the news to Erika and that her daughter would stay with her. "Just let me know the funeral arrangements," Erika's mother said with a deep brittleness locked in her voice. "I'll make sure Erika is there."

A funeral. Candy wasn't in any shape to plan an event like that, certainly not for Curtis. She feared that when the truth of why Curtis killed Barry Wimmer was uncovered, and that she and Curtis were cohabitating, she would be bombarded by the press and the police. As would Izzy, if they wormed deep enough and found out that the man Curtis killed was the father of her baby. But more than the impending maelstrom, the present anguish of losing Curtis this abruptly was not something Candy thought she could survive. He had filled her world with love and passion. He lifted her up, protected her. Made her feel more of a woman than she ever had in her life. And he was gone, leaving her in this house alone. Candy loved being with him, in bed, out at dinner, with her friends, anywhere. In the short time they were together, he gifted her with a fullness she had never experienced.

Asking her friends to go so she could lie down, Candy hugged the long pillow on her bed. Candy sobbed into the pillow, heaving deeply. As she rolled over and saw Curtis' clothes she had just washed folded and lying on a chair, she realized all his things didn't belong to her. The furniture he brought from his home, and the artwork he loved, she was not entitled to anything other than the memories and the mess. Even the few things she still had at his place would be off-limits to her now. At least with Earl, she could deal with the aftermath of his death. Candy had to come to grips with the fact that Curtis would simply be erased from her life.

Pulling herself off the bed, she moved to his closet in the master bedroom where his clothes hung neatly, color-coordinated from light to dark. Her hand moved across the material as if he was wearing them. She pulled out her favorite of his jackets and smelled it. The aroma of his favorite cologne lingered in the suede. She crossed to his dresser, which he and Candy picked out at an antique store, so they wouldn't be sharing the same one, and opened drawer after drawer, her hand running over his clothes. He favored soft cottons and light wools. They felt like him when Candy rested her face on his chest.

As her hand moved over everything in the bottom drawer, she felt something hard underneath. She gently pulled the clothes from the drawer and found the small arsenal that Curtis had in the house. Four handguns and a disassembled high-powered rifle with a scope. Candy didn't know guns very well, even after Earl made her get her license to conceal carry. She checked to see if each of them was loaded. They were. Feeling as if Curtis was giving her a sign at this moment, she knew what he wanted her to do. What she wanted to do. As she held up the Glock automatic, Candy dropped the magazine inside and then racked the slide a few times to see if there was a bullet in the chamber. Picking up the magazine, she slammed it back up into the gun and racked the slide again. She would be ready. She had to be. For whatever was to come.

****

Izzy's guilt kept her up that night. She took this thing with Barry too far before giving any of it serious thought. And if she hadn't slipped him inside her when he was sloppily incoherent, none of this would have happened. Why did she feel she owed this to Martin, fearing he could cut her and her sister out of 'the Sewing Circle,' or worse? Curtis' death ramped up the probability that everything would blow up in their faces or that Martin would have to eliminate all of them to protect himself.

But gnawing deeper into Izzy's soul was the real possibility that the baby she was carrying wasn't even Barry Wimmer's. It was Kevin's. That somehow, after all this time of not getting pregnant with him, of seldom using protection, there was a bullet in the chamber on this round of Russian roulette. If she had admitted to the possibility that Kevin could be the father of this baby, admitted the truth and all the repercussions that would come with that, maybe this thing with Barry wouldn't have escalated the way it did. Curtis wouldn't have felt obliged to get involved. They had the picture of her on top of Agent

Wimmer. That's all they needed to blackmail him. And if Izzy hadn't announced to him she was pregnant, to get him off her back, again taking it a step too far, none of this would have come down the way it did. But Izzy couldn't stop herself. She was to blame. "How the fuck am I ever going to be a mother?" she said aloud for only herself to hear. 'This kid is so screwed,' she didn't say out loud, but it rang in her head clearly.

The results of her brazen, thoughtless actions were coming to fruition. The consequences of being a terrible mother from the onset would haunt her for the rest of her life.

****

Ava's back windows faced east. Of all the houses on the end of the cul-de-sac, hers caught the morning sun the best. Though there were mornings when she felt the sun warmed up the house too fast, she had never lived in a home that filled with sunlight the way this one did. And she loved it. But sitting out back and sipping coffee, Ava accepted that all this sunshine was an illusion. And she was about to step back into the dark.

"What are you doing out here, Mom?" Cassie asked from the back door.

"Just...sitting."

"Thinking about Curtis?"

Ava took a moment before nodding. She then looked at her daughter with a tired seriousness in her eyes and said, "Things are going to get a bad. I think it's best you be prepared."

"Prepared for what?"

"I am not sure. But whatever happens from here, just expect it to be bad," responded Ava. "Worse than any of the shit we've already been through."

"Okay," Cassie answered uneasily, her mind flipping through the litany of 'worse' that could occur. "Should I pack a bag? Will this mean we have to like, disappear?"

Ava sipped her coffee. It had already cooled off and she didn't feel like getting up and shoving it into the microwave for thirty seconds. "Maybe," she said to her daughter. "But my guess, it will mean we will move out of here. Just be prepared for anything."

Cassie's eyes widened, and she opened her mouth to quiz her mother more, but she stopped herself. She knew her mother didn't have the answers she was looking for. Her mother was simply waiting for the next shoe to drop. Whether it be whatever Curtis did, or whatever her mother and her friends were involved in at the end of this cul-de-sac, Cassie expected it to blow their world apart. Cassie knew her mother was involved with some sketchy people. But unlike her mother's penchant for bad boyfriends, these people were deadly. Cassie silently understood that even Kevin almost being shot on the ballfield was somehow tied into all this bullshit. That her mother did it to give her a better place to live. Turning and looking back into the kitchen, she shook her head. "Well, it was nice while it lasted," she said.

Ava chuckled. "Yeah. I guess it was," she said, before thinking, 'At least the house was...' But where they would be living a year from now, hell, six days from now, was a complete mystery.

****

Martin flew into St. Louis commercial, which he abhorred. He hated airports. Lines. Most people. But he couldn't get a pilot for this last-minute excursion to St. Louis to quell the problems the women foresaw with the death of Curtis and the Federal Agent. He had a briefcase filled with cash that he paid off an airline employee to slip through security. He wasn't about to check in over two-hundred grand and have them throw it into the belly of the airplane.

While he waited for his flight, he called Deanna. She was shrill with worry. Martin did his best to calm her down, telling her to inform the other women he was taking them all to dinner that night. To "celebrate Curtis's life." He wanted them all there. With Curtis gone, Martin felt the women were more apt to 'behave like women.' Curtis kept a lid on things for him and dealt with whatever he needed in St. Louis. Though he had no idea Curtis planned on killing him, next, Martin assumed that it was Curtis' influence that kept the women working and the creation of the gowns on track. The operation, while not a huge money maker for Martin, was making enough of a profit to justify the buying of the homes and the cut he was giving the women. And all of this was running smoothly with little attention, until the stupid Federal Agent that he sent Izzy to blackmail suddenly lost his mind and shot off like a loose cannon. Now the entire situation would have to be pulled back if not turned inside out altogether. And he wasn't sure what that would mean for each of the women. And their families. The attention Curtis' death and the murder of Agent Wimmer would cast a harsh light on all of this. And Martin could not afford that. He couldn't wait for the dust to settle. This dust had turned into a complete sandstorm. Its effect would be persuasive and destructive. He hadn't decided how he would handle it, but it would be just as persuasive. And Martin accepted, if need be, just as deadly.

If there was any positive to this for Martin, he would get to see Deanna. He recognized what he had done to her, the whole kidnapping thing, was a step too far. He had to make amends, reconstruct himself back into a human being in her eyes. Right now, he knew she viewed him as some sort of monster.

His fascination with her astounded even him. She was not some international beauty, nor worldly in any respect. Her aspirations were as small. She was happy having moved her family one rung up the economic ladder. But he was transfixed, as if she was his potential Eliza Doolittle, someone he could reshape and transform into a woman he could introduce around the world to his associates. Martin loved the idea of having a moll, and a remade Deanna would be perfect in that role.

As the flight attendant poured vodka over a small glass of ice, he recalled making love to her. Maybe it was working-class background, but she was grittier and more physical than most of the women he bedded. It made him feel younger, nastier than he actually was. And he wanted to be with her again. Once he calmed the waters for himself, whatever that would entail, he would then make a decision about Deanna. Of course, she was expendable as the others if that was necessary, but Martin knew he would strangely miss his walk on the wild side with her. While he expected her to deliver the gowns on the dates he specified, which might sometimes seem overwhelming, he rewarded her with special attention, letting her know she was unique to him, someone he would take care of. And if she let him, take care of her family as well. Her loyalty to him had to outweigh her allegiance to her friends. They weren't paying her bills.

And Martin felt he already had Clara lined up as a replacement for any one of them. If not all of them. Downing the last of his vodka, he accepted that if he deemed Deanna a liability, even as dearly as he held her, he would protect himself and his enterprise first. He tipped the glass hard, letting the last of the vodka burn as it shimmied down his throat. Martin then let his eyes slowly close. He needed the rest. Because either way the events of the evening turned, he knew tonight would be exhausting.

AFTERMATH

The entire time he was in the back of the town car, Martin was making calls. As he pulled onto the cul-de-sac, he had had an enormous bouquet sent to Candy with a sympathy card. He made reservations at Tony's, had evening dresses sent to each of the women so they would be appropriately dressed, and conversed with a 'security detail' he arranged for in St. Louis. Just in case. He also made calls about moving his entire operation out of the St. Louis area to Oklahoma City. All the trafficking and counterfeiting would be done there, rather than St. Louis, ending his arrangement with the women. Including their kicking them out of the houses. One of Martin's lawyers explained that the women wouldn't go to the police because they would have to implicate themselves. And the Feds would have a hard time extraditing Martin because he moved around too often. "As long as you don't turn this into something uglier than it already is," his lawyer told Martin. "The closest they can get to you is the woman who was dating the man that murdered the Federal Agent. And I just can't imagine any of these women will want to do time for turning you in. Deed them the houses, don't deed them the houses, that's up to you, just don't do anything that will draw any attention to yourself. Right now, no one has connected all the pieces. Now is not the time to draw them a map."

Tonight, Martin had to determine if any of the women had the intention of pointing the authorities in his direction. If Martin garnered any inkling of that from any of the women, he'd have no choice but to have them all suffer the same fate. These weren't just loose ends he'd have to tie up, they were the threads that held the operation together. When one snapped, they all would unravel, and all have to go in the trash.

****

The dress was gorgeous. Candy held it up and stared at herself in the mirror. She knew that Curtis would love this on her. But what she couldn't figure out was how the hell Martin knew what she would look good in, much less what size she wore. Granted, he had been listening to everything in their homes until Curtis interrupted that, so it wouldn't be much of a stretch to believe that he had placed cameras in various locations around the house as well. And if he thought a goddamn dress and a meal would make things all right now that Curtis was gone, he was crazier than she already believed Martin was. Beautiful dress, creepy guy. The guy who caused all of this. Candy's eyes drifted to the gun on the dresser. It was going with her tonight. Martin would never think that one of them would shoot him, least of all not her, but she knew she'd have all her girls with her and if they had gotten skilled at anything other than counterfeiting clothes, it was getting rid of bodies. Especially someone who Candy felt no one would really miss.

****

The last thing Ava wanted to do that night was go to some fancy dinner with fucking Martin. She still had a bruise on her cheek from where Barry Wimmer punched her, and she would have to cover that with makeup. And while the meal itself sounded great, she didn't want to have to sit at a table with Martin and smile at his bullshit bon mots, or whatever the hell he called what he thought was supposed to be funny or witty or whatever the hell it was supposed to be that she found stupid. And she didn't want him to be able to reach over and touch her, as he enjoyed doing. The only exception to that being if he was falling dead into her arms. That image at least gave her a smile. But having no idea what concrete plans the other women were making, Ava wanted to be ready if this turned into a shitstorm, most especially if she sensed he was going to take them all out. With Izzy being pregnant and Curtis gone, Ava felt it was now her place to deal with this big, fat problem. And there was no way she wasn't going to be ready.

"Fuck this dress," Ava said, tossing the expensive tog that Martin selected for her onto her bed in a ball. She wanted to wear something with pockets. Deep pockets preferably. But relenting, she picked it up again and placed it against her body and turned towards the mirror, realizing she might as well wear it. She'd probably never get another chance. 'Unless it's his funeral,' she thought, which made her smile again. Besides, if there was any chance that whatever she wore would get covered in blood, it might as well be the dress she didn't want to wear anyway.

****

Izzy received a text that a car was being sent to take them to dinner. Which meant she couldn't hide the Glock under the seat of her truck as she had planned. The dress he had sent was tight, and her belly was expanding. She'd have to figure out some other way of smuggling the gun in with her. 'Even if I have to shove this gun up my hooch with the baby, I am bringing this thing,' Izzy thought to herself, moving to the window to look out at the cul-de-sac. If she could get him alone, even for a few minutes, she could do the deed. Somehow, she would have to. But she wasn't getting into that limo without a weapon. He had too many reasons now to get rid of all of them. Too many reasons to make sure they didn't talk when that inevitable knock on the door came and it was the police or the Feds there to question them.

****

Clara was told to be over on the cul-de-sac by six-thirty. The call came directly from Martin. She agreed, unsure if the other women knew she was coming along. Martin had sent a dress for her as well. It was more beautiful and more expensive than anything she'd ever owned. And while the dress was nice, what Clara really needed was to be paid what she was owed. Paid what she felt she was worth. Since Marcus's death and the runaround from the SLPD over his death benefits, even the money she was awarded, finances were still tight. This payout wouldn't last forever. She still needed the money she made off the gowns.

Clara was well aware that the other women wanted Martin out of the picture. But she couldn't see how this business would work without him. He was necessary to unload the gowns they duplicated. They didn't have those clients. They were simply the hired help. And she wasn't sure if their old business, which sounded small, and more hand-to-mouth would provide them with an income to survive. Clara might be okay once the final determination about Marcus' death is settled and she gets a monthly check and a big payout. But how would the other women make it financially, especially if they are thrown out of the free housing they are living in? She wasn't sure that any of them had thought this through. But now with Izzy being kidnapped and Curtis' death, there's no way they were in any emotional state to recognize the mistakes they were making.

With Curtis dead, Clara knew the women felt exposed. That the police would connect the pieces and be knocking on their doors with questions. Especially Candy. And if the police implicated any of them, all of this would come crashing down. And some of it on top of Clara, who was still at loggerheads with the SLMPD over Marcus' death benefits. And she also knew that Martin would do anything to keep himself from being cornered into a vulnerable position that could blow up his life and his livelihood. Yet, Clara wasn't sure if eliminating Martin was good for her or bad. And no one had asked. She was still on the outside looking in. The other four women were caught up in their own dramas, battling their own fears. Climbing out of poverty hadn't exactly made any of their lives easier.

Pulling her car around to the back of her house, Clara popped the trunk. Dressed in the clingy dress Martin had sent, she loaded a small arsenal into the trunk and threw a blanket over the weapons. Not exactly sure why she felt she would need a choice of guns for the evening but Clara did. She sensed that whatever was going to come down that night. And it was going to be messy. Better to be prepared.

And as she caught her reflection in the window of the car, she smiled. She certainly was 'dressed to kill'.

****

Seeing the limo parked in front of his house on the cul-de-sac as he pulled onto the street, Kevin pulled to the side of the road near the entrance and parked. He knew who was in his house. Taking a few deep breaths, he grabbed his phone and called Vince.

"Coach, it's game time," he said into the phone, "so saddle up, I'm coming to get you."

Disconnecting the call, Vince plopped down onto his sofa. 'This is fucking crazy,' he thought, trying to reassemble the bad choices he made that led to this moment, and what was about to go down. He wanted to believe this was about Kevin wanting to protect his mother, but Vince sensed it was deeper than that for Kevin. Well, as deep as Kevin Brayton could mine, which was shallow at best. Did Kevin feel he was now the guardian of whatever this operation his mother had going? Did the kid feel obligated to step into the shoes of the guy who had been killed taking out the Federal Agent? Whatever it was, Vince accepted that it was completely misguided. How could it not be if Kevin Brayton was calling the shots? But Kevin had him over a barrel. If he didn't assist Kevin with the folly, that kid would certainly ruin him. Something that he felt Kevin seemed hellbent on doing, regardless. As he stood up and took a deep breath, it solidified for Vince exactly what he needed to do. If he was forced to take a life, he was going to take two. He'd helped Kevin Brayton, with all Kevin's manic, big swinging-dick energy, to focus on baseball and get better. Good enough that colleges were interested. He'd both coached him and parented him, transforming Kevin into a ballplayer that scouts paid attention to. And in return, the ungrateful, cocky, asshole was now trying to make him complicit in a murder.

And that's where Vince would draw the line. Fuck Kevin. Kevin's undoing would be Kevin's fault. And Vince just needed to make sure this shitstorm fell on his protégé, not him. If he couldn't outsmart Kevin Brayton, Vince felt he deserved a stint in prison.

Arriving at Vince's door, Kevin pounded on it with his fist until Vince answered, glaring.

"You ready?" Kevin asked out of breath, as if he had run over to Vince's house.

"What's your plan, Capone?" Vince fired back, matching Kevin's urgency with his own laconic indifference.

"Who? Never mind. Look, we get back onto my street. It's a cul-de-sac. One way in, one way out. And we wait. My Mom is going to dinner with this guy. He's taking them in a limo, which means they will come back by limo. After the women get out, we race up to the car and just blast the motherfucker. He's trapped in the car. Where's he going to go? Then we run. On foot. I'll leave my car a few blocks over. We can be there in minutes," Kevin explained, adding, "He's a bad guy. There are probably a bunch of people who want to kill him. Police aren't even going to put us on their list."

"You know how dumb you sound? Won't your mother and her friends know you?"

"Masks, dude. We wear masks and baggy clothes, so they can't see our bodies. Come on, Coach, you had to give this some thought," Kevin responded. "Besides, we are doing this for my mom and her friends. You think they'd turn us in? Did they turn you in for fucking my sister? No. At least not yet. But this will help get you off their shit list. Let's just get this done. We do it right, nobody will know it's us except me and you."

"You talk like you've murdered someone before?" Vince pointed at Kevin.

The serious glower on his face brightened. "Nope. This is the first and last time," Kevin smiled as if he'd won the argument.

"I'm not even sure I can do this. Which could make expecting something from me I'm not sure I can accomplish very, very dangerous for you."

"Then your ass is going to be in prison for statutory rape," Kevin fired back.

"Not if you're dead, Kevin. And since you're not as savvy as you think, or as smart as you want everyone to believe, you fucking this up and getting killed yourself is a very real possibility. You're no criminal mastermind. You're just a dumb jock who is a step up from having someone wipe your ass. Look at me, kid...you're me in fifteen years."

"I'm going to amount to more than you. Already do now. And I won't have to fuck underage girls to make myself feel better," counters Kevin.

"Who are you fucking now?" Vince snarked, eyes narrowing.

Unprepared for the question, Kevin went silent. Vince nodded.

"Underage girls, right?" Vince laughed. "You're me..."

"Shut up," Kevin snapped as he stalked toward the door. We do this tonight. We're going to test your killer instincts, Coach."

Vince's eyes narrowed as he followed Kevin to the door. "You got no idea what you're dealing with, kid. Hope you come out alive."

Scowling, Kevin answered, "I hope you do. But as far as doing this...you got no choice, so shut the fuck up and let's ride."

****

As Martin's hand slid up her thigh, Deanna did everything she could to keep from freezing up. His lips slithered along her neck, causing her to reach up and put her hand in his hair. She wished she could yank him to the floor and drive a nail file through his neck, but she feigned enjoyment. She had to. This wasn't the place. Not in her house. Been there, done that, with Marcus.

"Should I call the girls, tell them we are about ready?" she asked Martin in an effort to escape his grip.

"We have time. Reservation isn't until seven," he responded, trying to sidle up his body against hers again, but Deanna slipped past and into the bathroom.

"I want to look good tonight," she exclaimed as an excuse.

Martin watched her fuss with her hair and makeup from the entrance to the bathroom. Deanna forced a smile.

"Don't watch. Go downstairs or something," she offered.

"You don't know how beautiful you are," Martin responded. "That's one of the reasons I find you so attractive..."

His words couldn't help but melt some of the ice that shielded her heart. But she could not let him get to her. Not now, she couldn't regret, she couldn't collapse. Steeling herself was the only way forward to what had to happen.

"Thank you," she said with embarrassment and too much self-judgment for her own liking.

Martin snickered, shaking his head as he disappeared from the door. But as soon as she heard him pattering down the stairs, Deanna sighed with relief. Quickly, she moved out of the bathroom and retrieved the gun she'd bought from Clara a few weeks earlier. The .35 was small enough to slip into a handbag.

This ended tonight.

****

As Deanna descended the stairs into her living room, Martin perched on the sofa, drink in hand. Sitting in a chair across the room, Tracee pressed her hands between her knees as she spoke with Martin. Having Martin worm his way deeper into her family made Deanna uncomfortable. Tracee had already proven to Deanna how vulnerable she was. Regardless of what Tracee said, or felt for that matter, she was seduced and raped. A victim. Deanna hated that she didn't go to the police instead of dealing with Vince herself. She should have let the law handle him. He would be in jail awaiting a sentence that would send him to prison. Tracee might see what really happened instead of believing she was in control. But Vince was back at work. And Deanna felt guilty about that, knowing the beating she and the women gave him would eventually wear off, and he would return to seducing high school girls until his looks and charm fade enough that they simply laugh at his attempts to get them into bed.

"What are you two talking about?" Deanna questioned as she came into the room.

"Mr. Collique asked me about what I wanted to study in college."

"College...?" Deanna asked.

"He said he'd help us out, you know, paying for it. So, I can pick where I want to go," Tracee added before asking, "You want something to drink, Mom?"

"Drink?" Deanna countered, surprised.

"She made me a bourbon and soda. Pretty good too," Martin said with a smile.

"See, Mom. I'm not a kid anymore. I can pour you a drink," Tracee said, smiling, as she walked into the kitchen. "I'll get you a glass of wine."

After she poured her mother a splash of wine and handed it to her, Tracee smiled oddly. Deanna shivered. She didn't know why, but she quickly swallowed the wine and settled the glass on a side table. Suddenly nervous, Deanna watched Tracee as she sat back down in the chair and stared at Martin.

"I'll call the girls, I think Clara is over at Candy's, helping her," Deanna said, her voice strained. "I'll check to see if they're ready."

"Remind them the limo is already out front. They can pour themselves a drink since I'm already one ahead. We'll be out in a minute," Martin stated, standing and moving to Tracee. He extended his hand. "It was wonderful talking to you. I enjoy hearing a young person's perspective on things, especially a young woman. We will discuss your college plans again and how I can help you reach them," he said, handing her back the glass she handed him with the bourbon.

"Thank you. That's very generous," Tracee responded with a smile, a joking lilt in her voice as she carried the glass towards the kitchen, moving past her mother, kissing her on the cheek as Deanna was making quick calls to the other women.

"Have a good night, Mom," Tracee whispered to her mother before she moved to the front window and peered out. Tracee saw the other women exit their homes, each one in a beautiful dress. Clara walked out of Candy's house, her dress hugging her curves, and Clara knew it, so there was a sashay in her step, her arm around Candy's shoulder. Tracee noted that all the women carried bags. On a night where not one of them was paying for the meal. And at the end of the block near the entrance to the cul-de-sac, her brother's car pulled up, idling. Wincing, she could see there was a second person in the passenger seat.

After giving Ford a kiss and telling him not to leave the house, Deanna walked out the front door with Martin as she said to Tracee, "We won't be late." Deanna made sure she locked the door behind her. Tracee glanced back at the clock on the kitchen wall, her eyes narrowing, as her finger tapped the glass of the front window. Watching her mother and Martin join the other women, they all shared cursory hugs, except with Candy who each of the women held for a moment, whispering in Candy's ear.

Sitting next to Kevin, Vince eyed the women and the single man with them outside the limo down the block.

He didn't want to wait all night for them to get home from dinner. If there was ever a moment to do this, it was now.

"Fuck this, pull on that mask, let's do this now," Vince stated, his voice flat and indifferent.

"Now?" Kevin responded.

"You're the big motherfucking killer! Come on big man, you want to kill this guy, he's right there! We drive down, we pop him and we take off. It's over. I want this over! I want it over now!" Vince bellowed.

Kevin pulled down his mask and settled the gun onto his lap. Vince did the same. Kevin drove slowly towards the limo down the middle of the street, so there was no way for the limo to get by, just in case.

Tracee saw her brother's car slowly roll down the block towards the limo. Seeing the women in the beautiful dresses he gifted them, Martin was distracted, smiling, clasping his hands in front of him. "You all look beautiful!" he called to them, causing each of them but Candy to strike a pose, amused. Martin and Deanna moved to the other women, everyone hugging. The limo driver stepped out and opened the back door. As the women hugged Deanna, each one whispered something in her ear, Candy and she locking eyes. Something that didn't go unnoticed by Martin.

"Ladies," he said, standing amid them. "I want you to know, you all will be taken care of. I'm sorry things have gotten out of hand. And Candy, please know how terribly sorry I am about Curtis. I'm broken-hearted. And I intend to make it right. I will handle all the funeral expenses. It's all being taken care of. Including whatever investigation will occur."

As Candy nodded without responding, the passenger door of Kevin's car flew open, and a masked person stepped out. Even with the mask and baggy clothes, Tracee recognized Vince and her brother as he stepped from the driver's side also in a Halloween mask. They both held revolvers. As they came towards the limo, the women saw them first, because Martin had his back to them. The women stepped back, all knowing one of the men was Kevin.

Caught by surprise as he turned, Martin stepped back, pushing through the women, trying to put them between himself and the gunmen. The driver of the limo quickly pulled out his own revolver and raised it. As he did, all five women pulled out their own weapons. Everyone but Martin was armed. Four guns were pointed at Martin, three at the limo driver, whom had no idea at who he should most fear.

"Put your gun on the ground!" Izzy demanded, taking a step towards the limo driver.

As he did what she commanded, Martin's face screwed up harshly. "What are you doing?!" he exclaimed. "None of you have any idea what you're doing? Do you all think I'm the problem?! That I'm the enemy?! You will find that there is someone far bigger, far deadlier, far more willing to eliminate all of you! I'm the person standing in between them and you! How stupid can you all be?"

As Martin's words sank into each of the women, each glanced side-to-side, wondering if it were true. If it were real. If this pit they had dug would only get deeper. Izzy could feel her finger tighten around the trigger of her handgun. 'How the fuck could this get worse?' she thought, terrified.

Tracee unlocked the front door and stepped outside, rushing towards the scene in the cul-de-sac. Deanna measured Martin's threat, that he was just the rung above them, that there were dangerous people lording over him as she recognized that it was her son behind one of the masks. And by the slight limp and the broad shoulders, she wagered it was Vince underneath the other. As Martin continued to curse at all of them, the stand-off growing more tense by the moment, Tracee stepped past her mother into the center of the mayhem next to Martin, as if she was possessed to stop this insanity. Stepping up to Martin, she looked directly into his eyes. "I'm sorry. You don't run our lives," she said to him.

As he opened his mouth to respond, Martin's eyes bulged, and only a gasp of air emerged from his bluish lips. Martin's mouth closed suddenly, the corners turning down as his lips trembled. He coughed but couldn't control it. Coughing harder and harder, Martin's body convulsed from the trauma until blood spat from his lips, spraying onto the white hood of the limousine.

Tracee stepped back as Martin reached towards her, coughed up a wad of blood. His quivering body teetered as his legs gave out and he fell into the street. None of the women moved. The limo driver was frozen in place. Martin pulled his body into the fetal position, blood running from his mouth.

While coming to grips that her son had a gun in his hand and had intended to kill Martin, it crystallized for Deanna that her daughter had beaten Kevin, and all of them to it.

Turning to Tracee, Deanna grabbed her by the shoulders. Deanna's eyes widened in horror as she anxiously asked, "What did you do?"

Tracee blinked, her eyes holding on her mother. "I told you, I'm not a child," she answered through her tightening lips. "I did what was necessary for this family. For all of you."

Clawing at his throat, Martin continued to try and speak but all that happened was more blood continued splattering into the street, covering Martin's lips as he reached up for the women to help him. But when his hands went in someone's direction, they stepped back from him. His eyes pleaded for his life as blood now drained from his mouth, forming a blackish puddle around his head.

When the limo driver took a step towards Martin to aid him, the barrel of everyone else's gun swung in his direction. The limo driver froze and Vince moved up behind him and wrenched his gun from the limo driver's hand. "Leave. Now. Don't say a fucking word, and you will stay alive," Vince said to him as he put the gun to the limo driver's head and reached into the driver's back pocket, pulling out his wallet. Flipping it open, he eyed the driver's license. "You understand me, Phillip Nacern, 2993 Drakeston Rd., Fenton," Vince added aloud, making sure everyone heard it. "We know who you are, so you say anything, you will die."

"I can't leave him," the driver countered.

"Yeah, you can," Tracee stated. She held out her hand to her mother and her friends, "Cash," she called to them.

They each opened their bags and handed her what they had, which she in turn shoved at the limo driver.

"What you're going to do is drive to the restaurant and drop off this man here," Tracee continued, grabbing hold of Vince, pulling off his mask and locking eyes with him. "You're going to get out of the limo and move towards the door of the restaurant, then stop, pretend you're taking a call outside, talk into your phone, call your dumbshit partner in crime, whatever, I don't care...but as you're talking walk away," Tracee ordered. "If there's security, that's what they'll catch on their camera. When they question you, Phillip Nacern of Fenton, there is film of you doing just what you were hired to do. Make sure you drive away right after dropping him off and try and forget this ever happened. Everything here will get taken care of."

"That's smart," Ava piped in.

"You sound surprised," Tracee responded with a drop of disdain in her voice, to let Ava know she took it as an insult.

"We'll take care of him," Candy added, glancing down at Martin on the sidewalk.

"Go, get the hell out of here," Deanna told the driver.

Vince moved to the back of the limo and slid in. The driver got into the front and the limo as Kevin got into his car, allowing the limo to back up and disappear down the block. As the limo drove off the cul-de-sac, Kevin pulled around the women and into the driveway of his mother's home.

As he stepped out, Deanna glanced between her two oldest children, her head shaking. "What am I raising?" she asked almost to herself, her voice filled with surprise, but there was a hint of pride as well.

"Kids that are resourceful," Tracee responded solidly. "If we weren't, you'd all probably be dead by the end of the night. And hasn't there been enough of that?!"

Ava reached over and put her arm around Tracee's shoulder. Deanna turned and looked down at Martin, who took his last breath, his rigid, tensed body slumping to the concrete, dead. The vitriol in her eyes mixed with a sadness. Deanna blinked twice, put her shoulders back and asked, "What now?"

"Kevin, pick this bastard up and put him in the back of my truck," Izzy ordered. "Let me get out of this dress and we have to get rid of him."

Clara moved to her car and opened the trunk, taking out a pair of sweatpants and a t-shirt, "I'll go with you. I know where we can dump him."

As Kevin grabbed Martin under the arms, Candy stopped him. "Hold on!" she ordered.

Kevin backed away from the body, allowing Candy to step closer, kicking Martin over and over. "You motherfucker! You piece of shit! You ruined my life! I hate you! I hate you! I hate you!" Every syllable was accompanied by a kick. After she was out of breath, Deanna grabbed hold of her and let Candy sob into her shoulder, leading her away from the body.

Kevin then hoisted Martin's long, thin body up so he could carry him to Izzy's truck parked in the driveway. He'd never touched a dead body before, much less carried one. Izzy turned to Tracee. "Thank you. Something tells me you're right. We wouldn't be alive in the morning if he stayed alive."

Deanna took a deep breath and then spoke to the other women. "Get out of those dresses and put on something comfortable, it's going to be a long night. Clara, you can change in my house. Well, if it's still mine...who knows. We have to figure out what happens from here. If he was telling the truth, there's going to be people searching for him. And we don't know who they are, or if they know about us. And if they do, what they intend to do to us."

The women nodded in agreement, each peeling off towards their homes as Ava took over as Candy's shoulder to cry on. Deanna grabbed Clara by the arm. Clara went with Deanna into her house as the others walked to theirs as well. Tracee moved over to her brother as he covered Martin's body with a tarp, holding it down with bricks.

Kevin glanced at his sister. "You're a freakin' psychopath," Kevin said, almost laughing.

"I didn't know if anyone else would have the balls," Tracee replied.

"I did. Seems everybody did. You just beat us all to it. He had to go," Kevin stated.

Tracee nodded. "We have to wash this blood off the street."

Deanna watched her two kids from her bedroom window. Kevin waited by the truck for Izzy as Tracee pulled the hose down from the house and washed the blood off the street, the crimson turning to a pale rose as it mixed with the water and slithered its way to the sewer atop the newish concrete.

What had she turned these kids into? Survivors? Monsters? What had she become? And even scarier, what came next? All Deanna knew was that whatever storm was out there on the horizon, it was going to take aim at them. They weren't free. Not as long as they were living on the cul-de-sac. But she wasn't going back. She had to fight. For the life she had. For her children. For all of it.

"Tracee," she called from the upstairs window, causing her daughter to look up. "Make sure you do the driveway, too."

Tracee nodded.

As Deanna's eyes went to Kevin, he waved, letting her know things were going to work out. At least in the short term.

"Mom, can I go out and ride my bike in the circle?" Ford asked from behind her.

Deanna turned seeing her youngest, his eyes wide and a slight, innocent smile on his lips, completely oblivious to what had just happened. She immediately prayed that God would save her youngest child from the burdens that Deanna felt she had mounted on the backs of her two oldest. She grabbed Ford into her arms and hugged him tightly.

"Mom!" he protested, not sure why she was squeezing him so hard.

Releasing Ford, she kissed his head. "Go ahead. But stay on the cul-de-sac. There's bad people..." Deanna warned.

"Where?" Ford quizzed.

Deanna opened her mouth to speak, but she stopped herself. Hugging her son again, Deanna took a deep breath and answered, "Everywhere."

Ford rushed outside to ride his electric bike around the circle, splashing through the puddles of water left over after Tracee washed down the driveway and street. Deanna's words played in a loop in Ford's head. There were bad people everywhere. Outside. Inside. Everywhere. Ford believed his mother was the smartest person he knew. That she knew everything and that's what he trusted.

But what Deanna didn't know was that a plane was flying directly overhead, heading for Lambert Field where it would land. In seat A2 was a very bad person. And this very bad person only knew one name. Deanna's.

The person's last name was Collique. Mrs. Martin Collique. Sophia, to her friends, business partners, and the other women in the world of couture. And Sophia had a bone to pick with the commoner she believed was fucking her husband. Worse, a woman her husband was falling in love with.

And Sophia intended to end that. Permanently.

THE END

THANK YOUS AND SALUTATIONS

I first want to thank my family, Joe, Isaiah and Emmanuel, for their love and support. And my extended family, the Born Bad/Married Bads, who are a constant source of inspiration and laughter. They are my biggest fans, be it a book or a movie. I love them all. Family first, family always.

Also to my friends who support me in whatever endeavor I'm involved in. I am grateful for all of your love and cheer you bring me. Friends are family by a different mama. And to my writer friends, thank you for your guidance and wisdom. I wouldn't know a tenth of what I know about this business if it weren't for you. The support and cheerleading that comes with these writer groups, The

Authors Conference and Writers on the Storm, my two go-tos for anything and everything related to writing and selling books, thank you so much. Master Classes every day.

I dedicate this book to all the women in my life. Their strength and resilience are palatable forces. I've been blessed to have strong women in my life, and they always offer me motivation and guidance. Thank you. You may find a piece of yourselves in these characters. Because they are molded from the women I am blessed to know.

If you want to know more about me and my writing – my books, my movie projects, you can check me out at www.bartvbaker.com or find me on Instagram at thefirstbartbaker. Or on TikTok @firstbartbaker.

Thank you, readers, for taking these journeys with me. I hope you're entertained. I hope you laugh and cry with my characters, and at the end of a book or film that I've written, you feel like you've been an emotional voyage. One that's satisfying and thought-provoking. But thank you for your support. It's why I write.

Be blessed – Bart